DATE DUE

GAYLORD			PRINTED IN U.S.A.

Books by
Gary E. Parker
FROM BETHANY HOUSE PUBLISHERS

The Ephesus Fragment

Rumors of Peace

BLUE RIDGE LEGACY

Highland Hopes

Highland Mercies

Highland Grace

A Novel By

GARY E. PARKER

HIGHLAND GRACE

3 | BLUE RIDGE LEGACY

BETHANYHOUSE

MINNEAPOLIS, MINNESOTA

Published by Bethany House Publishers
11400 Hampshire Avenue South
Bloomington, Minnesota 55438
www.bethanyhouse.com

Bethany House Publishers is a Division of
Baker Book House Company, Grand Rapids, Michigan.

Printed in the United States of America

Library of Congress Cataloging-in-Publication Data

Parker, Gary E.
   Highland grace / by Gary E. Parker.
      p. cm. — (Blue Ridge legacy ; 3)
   ISBN 0-7642-2454-9 (pbk.)
   1. Women—North Carolina—Fiction. 2. Blue Ridge Mountains—Fiction.
3. North Carolina—Fiction. 4. Rural families—Fiction. 5. Mountain life—
Fiction. 6. Land tenure—Fiction. 7. Aged women—Fiction. I. Title.
II. Series: Parker, Gary E. Blue Ridge legacy ; v 3.
   PS3566.A6784 H535   2003
   813'.54—dc21
                                             2003001419

As I conclude this series of three books about the fictitious life of Granny Abby, I want to dedicate it to my own granny, a woman named Nettie Ruth. Although she's deceased now, my grandmother served as an early influence in my life, teaching me about a personal faith in a living God. Somehow, Granny, I think you know of my gratitude to you.

Acknowledgments

On completing this third and last book of the BLUE RIDGE LEGACY series, I remind the reader that the story of Abigail Faith Porter and her family is fiction. But it is based in the reality of a group of people who were my ancestors.

A number of books helped to bring this reality home to me in what I believe and hope are historically correct ways: *Our Southern Highlanders* by Horace Kephart; *The Land of Saddlebags* by James Watt Raine; *A History of Buncombe County, North Carolina* by F. A. Sondley; *Appalachia Inside Out: Culture and Custom,* edited by Robert Higgs, Ambrose Manning, and Jim Miller; *The Man Who Moved a Mountain* by Richard C. Davids; *Mountain Voices: A Legacy of the Blue Ridge and Great Smokies* by Warren Moore; and *Asheville, a Pictorial History* by Mitzi Tessier. These were the key resources that helped me know the history of the people of western North Carolina. Others, such as *National Geographic Eyewitness to the 20th Century*; *The Century* by Peter Jennings; *A People's History of the United States* by Howard Zinn; and *Hard Times* by Studs Terkel all grounded me in the basic facts of the twentieth century. I am grateful for the kinds of study these authors have accomplished. Their work makes my story come alive with truth. Any historical mistakes in this story are mine.

As always, my thanks to editors David Horton and Luke Hinrichs.

Finally, I want to express my gratitude as a memorial to a man now deceased, Dr. Bill Leverett, formerly of Furman University. While I was there as a history major under his tutelage, he taught me how to see history in a grand scheme. He taught me how to take small facts and see the bigger story. It was this education from the late Dr. Leverett that enabled me to write a story such as the Blue Ridge Legacy.

GARY E. PARKER, a Ph.D. graduate of Baylor University in Christian theology, now serves as senior pastor at the First Baptist Church of Decatur, Georgia. Gary, his wife, Melody, and their two daughters, Andrea and Ashley, make their home in north Atlanta.

PROLOGUE

A heart monitor beeped. The woman lying on the bed inhaled slowly, her gray hair fanning out around her head. A clog of wires ran from under her gown near her chest to the monitor. The monitor showed her pulse rate at ninety. Her copper eyes were cloudy but still open.

Perched on the bed beside her, I lightly squeezed her hand. A heart attack had brought her to the hospital three days earlier, and she had returned to consciousness just a few hours ago. She opened her mouth to speak, but I held up a finger and shook my head. She needed to save her strength.

"What . . . day . . . is. . . ?" she asked, her voice scratchy.

"Don't worry about that," I said. "You're doing fine."

She pulled up a little. I eased her back down. A scowl rolled over her forehead. "Don't try to quiet me," she whispered.

I tried to look stern but failed. Abigail Waterbury Holston, my great-grandmother, had never taken well to someone bossing her. Never had, and now, a few days past her one-hundredth birthday, she obviously didn't plan to start.

"It's Thursday," I said.

"I been here a couple days, then."

"Yes."

Granny Abby considered the matter for a minute. "I'm a hundred years now."

"Seems so."

She lay back on the pillows. The sun from the window to the right lit up her well-lined face. A long time ago that face had looked a lot like mine. I had pictures of her from her wedding day to prove it. High cheekbones, angular chin, pert nose. I wondered how I would look at one hundred, not that I expected to live that long.

Granny Abby turned toward the window, where the sun was streaming in, and stared out.

"Everybody came for your birthday," I said. "Stayed over the weekend. Most had to go home on Monday. But Rose is here. Steve and Jim too. Rose took the night shift last night; I got the day shift."

Granny Abby smiled when I mentioned her daughter and sons. "I got fine kids," she said. "Although they aren't kids anymore."

I smiled at the notion of Rose, Steve, and Jim as kids. Steve and Jim had long since received their AARP cards and started qualifying for senior citizen discounts. Rose would turn fifty-five in a few months.

"What's the thought from the doctors?" she asked.

I dropped my eyes.

"Hey," she said. "Don't go hiding glum tidings from me. I'm old but I am not ignorant."

I chuckled, then turned serious and faced her again. "The doctors say we take it one day at a time."

"Not going out on any limbs, are they?"

I smiled. Granny Abby had always lived one day at a time. In a sense, nothing had changed.

She licked her lips and closed her eyes. I felt heat rising from her hand. The sun warmed my face. I wondered what would happen now. With a camcorder and several notebooks in hand, I had traveled to Blue Springs, North Carolina, a week ago to capture Granny Abby's life story. At first I had pretended I wanted it for my family's sake. But in my heart I knew better. I wanted the story for myself, for Lisa Abigail, a thirty-one-year-old with no husband, no children, no job, and no joy. Somehow I had decided that Granny Abby's past might help me find my future, might help me to come to grips with who I was and who I could be.

I patted her hand, stood and walked to the window. A bank of puffy April clouds rolled over the sun and dulled the color in the room. I wiped my face with my hands. Although Granny Abby had already told me most of the first half of her life's journey, we had a long way to go. Up to 1975 or so, anyway. After that, I could remember most of what had happened. But that left 1945 to 1975 to cover, when my kinfolk gathered together on Blue Springs Mountain in an effort to re-claim the family land, a thousand acres in the upper highlands of North Carolina. But now, with Granny Abby's fragile condition, I didn't see how I could ever hear the rest of her story.

The clouds bunched up heavier around the sun. A gust of wind danced the branches of a cluster of oak trees that shaded the side of the hospital. A spring thunderstorm looked to be near at hand. I recalled quickly the history Granny Abby had already revealed to me. Her birth in 1900, her mama's death at her birth, Abby's struggle to find some connection to her pa, the loss of the family land through a wager by her late brother Laban, and her brother Daniel's desperate attempts to buy it back.

What hard years she'd lived. How had she managed to keep such a peaceful heart? Such strength of character?

I knew what she'd say. "God gave me strength," she would declare. "Not any of my doing."

Laban had died during World War I, her pa the year the Depression started, her middle brother, Luke, a few years later, her first husband not long after that. Daniel had collapsed in those awful years, took up drinking and almost lost everything.

Though scarred and bruised, Abby had survived, her courage a wonder that made others shake their heads and look up to heaven as if to see if some of that strength might fall on them. I knew how they felt, how just standing in Granny's presence seemed to pour steel into the spine. When Granny Abby walked into a room, everybody else took heart.

I turned back to her, my hands shoved into the pockets of my khakis. Inwardly I chided myself for my selfishness. Here she was in the hospital, and I wanted her to nurture me. I gritted my teeth and decided to give up on my project. So what if Granny Abby didn't finish the story she had started telling? She had bigger concerns right now.

Back at her bed, I reached for her hands again. She opened her eyes, pointed to a chair by the bed. "Sit," she ordered. "We got talking left to do."

I shook my head. "Not now," I said. "You got to save your strength."

Granny Abby pointed at the chair again. "Don't go fighting me on this. I want to do it, say out all that happened."

"You've said enough for now," I argued, truly wanting to protect her. "We can pick up the tale in a few days, once they let you go home."

Her eyes cleared, and she stared at me like she wanted to climb out of bed and shake me by the shoulders until I did what she said. I shrunk back half a step. Her face burned with a determination that only a woman who has survived a hundred years of hard mountain living can summon, the kind I knew I didn't have.

"You asked me to tell you the story," she said, her voice gaining strength from the fire in her bones. "I already got a lot of it said. So I plan to finish; don't cotton to starting something and then leaving it undone."

"But the doctors said—"

"Don't care about the doctors. If I'd listened to them, I would've died a long time ago."

She pointed at the chair one more time. "Unless you want me to get a switch to you, you best go on and take a seat. I don't know how many more days the Lord plans to give me, so I need to talk now."

Not knowing what else to do, I eased into the chair and smoothed down my navy blue blouse.

"You bring a notebook?" Granny Abby asked.

I picked my purse off the floor, lifted out a black leather notebook and held it up. "No camera this time, though," I said.

"Good. Don't need a camera showing what I look like right now, something everybody will stare at after I'm six feet under."

"You'll outlive us all."

She waved a hand at me. "Don't go blowing smoke at an old woman," she said. "I'm too smart to fall for that sort of thing."

I pulled a pen from my purse and opened the notebook.

"You got it up to the time of the Mingling," she said.

I nodded. In a ceremony as ancient as the hills in which she grew up, Granny Abby and Daisy Clack had marked the end of the feud between their families by exchanging their babies for the first three years of their lives. While unimaginable to me, Granny Abby believed God had called her to do it to make sure that nobody from either family took up a gun or knife against anybody else. To do so meant the forfeiture of the child.

"Did the Mingling hold?" I asked. "After they put Ben Clack in jail?"

"Well . . . that didn't quite work out like we all hoped."

"He break out or something?"

"Stay patient, child. I'll tell you the story in due time."

"What about that Gant fellow who had bought the family land? Was he the son of the man Daniel knew from the war?"

"You plan to let me tell this or not?"

I perched on my chair and told myself to calm down. "Okay," I said. "You talk and I'll write."

"That'll work," she said. "Now remember, people told me some of this later. I didn't see all of it firsthand."

I nodded. Granny Abby opened her eyes. Thunder rumbled outside. She stared past me to the rain-heavy clouds.

"You'd think that once a family gets the wolf away from the door that a lot of the worst temptations would pass," she began, her voice soft. "But events show that's not always true. A full belly seems to bring on as much trouble as an empty one does."

"Things got better for our folks after World War II, didn't they?" I ventured.

Granny Abby smiled but only for a moment. "For a spell," she said. "For a spell. But having a few dollars brings no guarantee of happiness. None at all."

I wrote fast as Granny Abby told me the story.

SECTION I

August 1945–July 1946

CHAPTER
ONE

Her fingers busy with a needle and torn brown shirt, Abby Waterbury Holston sat in a rocking chair by an open window in her front parlor in Blue Springs, North Carolina. The August sun hung low, and Abby knew she'd have to turn on a lamp soon if she wanted to finish repairing the shirt she held. A colorful array of pansies and petunias pushed up from the ground around the front porch of the house. A puff of breeze eased through the window every now and again, occasionally pushing out and into the room the lacy white curtains Abby had made. She shifted the shirt in her lap and stitched the tear on the front pocket. Her husband, Thaddeus, sat across from her, his eyes busy with the newspaper he'd bought at the general store. A man of average height, Thaddeus had thinning gray hair, a square chin, and a body now headed a touch toward heaviness. Every now and again he glanced up and commented to Abby how glad he was that the war in the Pacific had shut down.

Abby sipped water from a glass and reminded herself again of the way the good Lord had blessed her. Not that she hadn't stared down a few big bears in her day—heaven knew she had. A first marriage that had turned sour, a baby lost in childbirth, her first husband killed at another man's hand, a child now that, well, she didn't want to think of Rose Francis right now, the baby born to her and Thaddeus less than a year ago. It hurt too much to do that.

Her fingers moved faster with the needle, and she forced herself to focus on Thaddeus. Think of happy things, blessings and not sufferings.

Thaddeus was such a good man. She'd known him most of her life. Had loved him before she knew it, before she married Stephen Waterbury. But sometimes it takes some living to know what a body wants. Least it had for Abby.

She closed her eyes and thanked sweet Jesus for her husband. He taught school, like she did. Of course, he had a college degree, while she had never quite finished hers. But that didn't matter. They both loved reading—the way a body could learn from books, could go anywhere in the pages of a story. They spent a lot of their free time talking about their reading, this writer or that one. Thaddeus liked adventure stories by men like Jules Verne and Robert Louis Stevenson. Abby preferred tales like *Little Women* and *David Copperfield*.

She opened her eyes and studied Thaddeus. He wore plain brown pants and a white shirt. His face held a low brow and deep eyes. After Stephen died, she and Thaddeus had found each other again. Better said, she'd gone looking for him and they'd ended up marrying. Now they could live the rest of their lives together, helping each other through the ups and the downs of it all. They would have both of course; every marriage did. Like now with Rose Francis, her precious baby. Abby accidentally stuck her finger with her needle.

"Ouch!"

"You need some light?" asked Thaddeus.

"Reckon that would help."

He stood and switched on a lamp, then sat again.

Abby marveled as she always did when the light turned on so easily. She and Elsa—her pa's first wife and the woman she loved most in the world—had gotten the electrical run to their house less than five years ago. Most of the folks on the mountain still didn't have it.

"You want the paper when I'm done?"

"I already saw it this morning," she said.

Thaddeus pointed to the front page. "The air boys dropping that atom bomb has put a stop to all the fighting."

"Thank the Lord," said Abby. She thought of her son Jim recently returned from the war. Although blinded for a while by a war injury in the head, his vision had completely returned in the last year.

"No way Steve will have to go and fight now," said Thaddeus.

"It's a blessing," she said.

"Not to Steve."

Abby considered her second son, two years younger than Jim and of less height and weight. He'd wanted to join the Army since he turned seventeen, but the slowdown in the war and poor eyesight had kept him out. He groused a lot about missing the chance to go fight, making Abby worry about him. Sometimes a man of less stature ended up trying to prove himself in ways he shouldn't. Living in Jim's shadow all his life hadn't been easy for Steve. Abby knew the two boys loved each other. Even so, Steve tended to see a lot of things as a competition. When he and Jim had played as boys—shooting pellet guns at tree stumps, tossing horseshoes, running races—Steve always made it a contest. Sadly for him, he almost always lost. But he never quit trying. Abby had to give him that.

Thaddeus picked up a water glass from a side table and sipped from it.

"I feel some bad for those folks in Japan," said Abby. "Lots of children in those cities that got bombed."

Thaddeus folded the paper. "Me too," he said. "But if we had been forced to go in there, thousands of our boys would have died. I reckon these bombs were the lesser of the evils."

"Lot of mamas already lost too many sons," she said. "Them and us."

She thought again of Steve, who worked at a farm equipment

store out on the road near Piney Grove. When Jim went to war, Steve told her he'd take care of her until his time came. She smiled as she remembered how helpful Steve had been in the last few years. He gave her money almost every week from his job, kept plenty of wood in the box by the fireplace, helped in the planting, hoeing and picking from her garden.

"Reckon all the boys will come home now," said Thaddeus. "Maybe they'll find Ed in a prisoner camp."

Abby bent lower to see where to point her needle. "Hope so. Would relieve a lot of hurt in Daniel and Deidre."

"They've been through enough."

Abby considered her brother Daniel. After years of heartache and backsliding from the Lord, a change had come over him in the last couple of weeks, no doubt about it. But he still had a son—a gunner on a B-29—missing in the Pacific and believed that the enemy had killed his boy. With no way to know for sure, Abby had urged him to wait and see. But Daniel didn't do well with waiting.

She finished the shirt, folded it in her lap and reached out for Thaddeus's hand. He smiled, laid down his paper and drew her fingers to his lips. "You sure do look fine," he said. "Best-looking woman on the mountain."

Abby tapped his cheek in a mock slap. "You ought not lie to your wife. I'm forty-five and look every year of it. Gray streaking in my hair, getting rounder on the hips. And I got lines on my face, around my eyes. No spring chicken anymore."

He stood and pulled her from her rocker. "You're as pretty as the day I met you," he said. "Least to me you are."

Abby settled into his arms. "You're going blind, then. Blind or losing your mind, one of the two."

For several seconds they stood that way. The breeze from the window played on her neck. Abby snuggled against Thaddeus, drawing from his strength. She felt her eyes well up. She needed him more now than ever, now that Rose Francis—

Something crashed through the window and splattered glass on the wood floor. Abby jumped back, her eyes wide. "What!"

Thaddeus hurried to the window and looked out. Abby searched the floor to see what had broken the window. She spotted a rock the size of a cantaloupe in the center of the room.

"Don't see anything," said Thaddeus, turning back to her.

Abby picked up the rock, saw a piece of paper tied to it.

Steve ran in from the back of the house. "What's that?" he asked, pointing at the rock.

"Don't know," said Abby. She pulled the paper off the rock and moved to the lamp so she could see better. "Somebody wrote on it," she said. She handed Thaddeus the stone and studied the handwriting on the paper. Her face turned pale as she read the words. She thought of baby Sam and rushed to the small room just down the hall from where she and Thaddeus slept. Hurrying in, she saw the baby was still asleep, and she breathed a sigh of relief. Thaddeus and Steve ran in behind her. She quickly turned and put a finger to her lips, and they all left the room.

Back in the parlor, she sagged into her rocker and reread the note. Finished, she handed it to Thaddeus. He eased onto the fireplace hearth and read the note. Steve took a seat in a rocker.

Abby faced the broken window. Weariness suddenly took over, and she wondered how much more she could take. So many years and now this. A whip of wind puffed the curtains out. Abby breathed raggedly. The sun dropped completely out of sight as shadows swept across the room.

"I thought we were done with him," said Abby, her voice hanging between anger and fear. "Thought the law would keep him in jail."

"Don't rush to conclusions," said Thaddeus. "You don't know that it was Ben Clack."

"Who else?" argued Abby. "He's out on bail. He's the only one who didn't go along with the Mingling. You know it's him as well as I do."

"Let me see that," said Steve, pointing to the note.

Thaddeus handed it over and shook his head. "I reckon a man like Ben Clack don't quit too easy," he said. "No matter who stands against him."

"You reckon the law will call his trial up anytime soon?"

"No way to know. We don't have a regular judge, have to wait for the district folks to get it on the docket."

"This is pure meanness," said Steve, the note in his lap.

Abby nodded and remembered the night less than a month ago that Clack had shot Thaddeus. Thankfully the wound hadn't proved serious and her husband had recovered, leaving only a red scar on his side to show he'd once been wounded.

"He may not serve long even after the trial," Thaddeus said. "He claims he shot me by accident and that his brother Topper did all the shooting back in '37 at the Lolleyville jail."

Abby almost laughed. Ben Clack lied easier than a skunk put off a bad scent. Everybody knew it, but somehow he kept getting away with it. Who knew what a judge and jury would decide if and when he ever faced a trial?

"The man has nine lives," Steve said. "Especially when it comes to the law."

Thaddeus stood and moved to Abby's side. "He'll eventually come to a bad end," he said. "You know that. If the law fails to get him, somebody else will. A man that mean can't survive forever."

"Ben Clack is overdue," Steve said. "Maybe somebody ought to take care of him if the law won't."

Abby shook her head. "You know that's not right. No matter what he does, it's not our place to seek vengeance."

Steve sighed, and she could see he didn't agree with her.

Thaddeus reached for the note and read it again. "Sounds like he plans to make trouble as long as he can."

"The Mingling comes with its own code," said Abby. "You'd think even a bushwhacker like Clack would respect it."

"I don't believe Clack respects anything. Not man or beast, not God or law. He runs by his own code, and it's as low-down as anybody I've ever heard tell of and nobody can change it."

Abby thought again of Sam, sleeping so peacefully. A ten-month-old boy born to William and Daisy Clack. Given into her care for three years in the ancient ceremony of the Mingling.

Tears pushed to her eyes as she thought of her own baby, Rose Francis, born to her in her forty-fourth year, born from the lifelong love she shared with Thaddeus. William and Daisy now cared for Rose Francis. She missed her child every day, felt a hole in her heart the size of a washtub. Sometimes, in the weeks that had passed since the Mingling, she cried herself to sleep, wondering in her dreams how she could ever have gone through with such a thing.

She remembered the Mingling. At midnight at Jesus Holiness Church. All the kin of the Clacks and Porters close enough to come—except Ben of course—gathered there for the ceremony, Preacher Tuttle speaking it out for all to hear.

"Now is the hour for peace to come," Tuttle had said, repeating the ancient words always offered. "Time for bad blood to end. Time for the laying down of guns and knives. Time for men to stop fighting and seeking revenge on other men."

The crowd held its breath. The kerosene lights in the church house flickered.

"Time for families to come into union with each other."

Abby had shivered that night; shivered because she couldn't believe she was making such a sacrifice, that she was giving up her baby in hopes that two families that had warred against each other for over half a century might move beyond their hatred. She knew, though, it was the only way. The good Lord had called her to do it; she believed that with all her heart. How else could she go through with it—give her child to the Clacks and take a Clack child to her own bosom? Each child became a hostage to the other family so that if anyone of one clan took up anger toward the other, they would forfeit the child to their enemy. Only a sure sense of God's leadership had given her the strength to go ahead with such a thing.

Tuttle had called the two women to bring their babies to the altar at the front of the church. They faced him. He waved over the congregation. "Are all those gathered here in agreement that the time has come?"

"We here are all in agreement," said the people.

Tuttle looked down at Abby, then at Daisy. "Unwrap the babies," he said.

The moment had come. Abby took the blanket off Rose Francis and laid it over her shoulder. Daisy did the same. Now Rose Francis and Sam were completely naked, covered only by their mothers' arms as they held them to their chests.

"Is this your natural-born child?" Tuttle asked Abby.

"This is my natural-born child," she said.

Tuttle asked Daisy the same question. "This is my natural-born child," she said.

"It is time," Tuttle said.

Holding Rose Francis with her left hand, Abby reached for the buttons on her dress with her right. It took a few seconds but then she had finished. She covered her bare shoulder with her blanket.

Tuttle looked at the crowd. "They come bare before us and God. To share in the Mingling."

"Bare before us and God," repeated the crowd. "To share in the Mingling."

"From child to family, the mercy is offered," Tuttle said. "Mercy to forgive and forget, mercy to leave the dead in the ground so the living might find peace."

The people nodded reverently.

"Child of Porter shall be child of Clack," said Tuttle. "And child of Clack shall be child of Porter. By the mercy of God. Amen."

The Mingling took place. Abby exchanged her child for little Sam and nursed him at her bosom. Daisy did the same with Rose Francis. By doing so they signified that all people came from the same origins, that all deserved life and love. Together they had agreed the Mingling would last for three years, plenty of time for all to come to peace with one another. If anyone broke the peace, his or her family forfeited their family's baby.

Abby sighed, still amazed that she'd done it. She thought of Jesus. If God could give Jesus up to death, she could sacrifice her child for three years.

She took the note from Thaddeus, folded it and put it in her apron pocket. She'd done all she could. But now, the window shattered, the note delivered, she didn't know if the Mingling would hold. What if Ben Clack made good on his threat? What would happen? Although the law had firmed up a lot since the old days when the feud first started and no longer allowed much knife- or gunplay, Ben Clack had shown more than once that he didn't care about the law. What if he took out after Thaddeus? Or her again, like he had so many years ago? She had defended herself back then.

Would she need to do that again? But how? She was forty-five, a mature Jesus woman. She couldn't allow herself to get mixed up in a fracas with Ben Clack.

Abby walked to Thaddeus. He turned from the window, his eyes grave.

"I wonder if Clack threw a rock through Daisy's window," Abby said.

"Maybe not yet," he said, picking the rock off the hearth. "Just heaved this one less than an hour ago."

"He'd have to drive fast to reach them by now," Steve said, "with them up on the mountain and all."

"What about Jim and Rebecca?" asked Thaddeus. "Their baby, Porter?"

"You reckon he'd go after them too?" asked Abby.

"Better not," said Steve. "Jim will handle him for sure if he messes with Porter. I'll help him."

Abby studied the matter. Her older boy, Jim, fresh back from the war, had married Rebecca Stowe, a nurse he met in Italy during his recovery from his battle injuries. Only after he'd fallen in love with her did he find out that her ma had birthed her out of wedlock and that her pa was Ben Clack's dead brother, Topper. At first he had wondered if he could marry her. But then he realized he couldn't live without her. If their families wouldn't accept them, they'd just move away from the highlands.

To their pleasure, though, everyone except Ben had eventually agreed to their marriage. The baby, Porter, had arrived within a year of their nuptials, one of only two children ever born from a mix of a Clack and a Porter.

Abby's heart ached as she realized that, yes, Ben Clack might go after Porter. Fact is, he almost surely would.

"Why won't Ben just accept the Mingling?" she asked Thaddeus. "Can't he see that the feuding ways have passed? That law has come to the highlands, won't tolerate his meanness anymore?"

Thaddeus took Abby in his arms. "A man like Clack pays no attention to all that. Never has."

Abby snuggled close to Thaddeus and thought again of Sam, with his wide brown eyes, as innocent as a pup. Curly black hair topped his head. He had slender fingers for such a young child. He liked to reach for her nose when she held him. Abby's heart warmed. The boy hardly ever cried. Caring for him had come easy. He loved it when she rocked him on the front porch, and he always started cooing when she did. His cooing, a sound made when he rounded his lips into a tiny circle and blew bubbles from them, sounded sweet as music, and she wondered if maybe someday he might become a singer like Luke had been.

She wondered if Daisy felt toward Rose Francis the way she did toward Sam. Would she care for her with the same love? Teach her at least some of the same values?

Even though Daisy didn't attend services, the two of them had agreed that most weekends they would exchange the babies before church at Jesus Holiness Church on Sunday. That did two things: made sure that Rose Francis grew up with the chance to learn about Jesus, and it provided both the babies at least some connection to their rightful families. That way, when the time arrived for them to go back to their true homes, they would at least know the people from their real families. Occasionally they exchanged the babies for the whole weekend so they could have a little extra time together.

"I'll not let Ben Clack bring hurt to Sam," Abby said.

"I expect you won't," said Thaddeus. "Seems Ben will know that too. You've handled him in the past, can do so again if the need arises."

"I'll go to the store and call Daisy and William," Steve said, standing. "Make sure they take warning to care for Rose Francis."

Thaddeus stepped back from Abby. "I'll go to the sheriff's office and see Sol," he said. "The law needs to see to this."

"They will keep her safe, won't they?" Abby's voice pleaded for assurance.

"They got as much to lose as us," Thaddeus said. "Anything happens to Rose Francis and they forfeit their boy. They'll provide for her; you can trust that."

Abby moved back to her rocker. "I'll keep watch here."

As Steve and Thaddeus headed to the door, Abby had a chilling thought. What if Clack had thrown the rock but not gone anywhere? What if he waited now around the corner for her husband and son to leave? Would he come back then, come to steal Sam and cause her to lose Rose Francis forever?

She moved to the door and caught Thaddeus and Steve on the porch. "Your pistol in working order?" she asked Thaddeus.

Thaddeus grunted. "I've not used that weapon in a long time. School teachers don't do much shooting."

"Where is it?" she asked.

"Closet in the bedroom."

"I might take it out and give it some oiling," she said. "Just in case."

Thaddeus grinned briefly. "You are a fierce woman. Can't take the mountain out of you."

"I'll protect my own," said Abby. "Ben Clack better know that."

"Don't say crazy things, Ma," said Steve. "If there's any shooting to do, I'll take care of it."

Abby smiled at her son. He wanted so much to become a man.

"You both are talking nonsense," Thaddeus said. "Neither one of you are going to take a pistol to anybody."

"Go on," said Abby. "I'm okay."

Steve kissed her on the forehead and walked off, Thaddeus beside him. Abby headed back inside the house and checked on Sam. He opened his eyes and cooed at her, then grabbed his toes and played with them. Abby rubbed her fingers through his thick hair.

"You're a sweet boy," she said. "Not like the Clacks I've known." Sam cooed again. "You rest awhile longer now."

Sam stuck a foot toward her face. She gently pinched his toe.

"I'll protect you," she said.

He smiled as if he had no doubt she would.

Leaving the crib, Abby moved to the small closet in her bedroom. She saw the pistol lying in an old shoebox on the floor. Her hands trembled as she reached for it. She hesitated, her soul in turmoil. Did the Lord want her to do this? Would He approve of such a thing?

She thought of Sam, then of Rose Francis. The Lord would surely want her to protect those babies.

She lifted the pistol and stepped out. The weapon felt heavy but not so much that she couldn't handle it. Any highlander woman worth her salt knew how to clean, load and shoot a pistol.

Abby ran her finger over the barrel. Dust brushed off. The pistol needed a good cleaning. Grabbing a rag from the closet, she moved back to the living room and over to the fireplace. She sat the weapon and rag on the floor and picked up the wadded note Thaddeus had left on the mantel.

Her hands shaky again, she flattened out the note. The handwriting squiggled in all directions. Words were misspelled. Smudge stains soiled the wrinkled paper. But she had no problem understanding the message.

I am not dun. You and me got business left, jus between us, nobody else. Don't matter about my famlee, yours either. I will see you in Hell. Sweet Jesus knows I am true about this.

No signature, though she knew without question that it was Ben Clack who had scratched out the note.

She thought of going to her half brother, Sol, the county sheriff, with the note. But with no signature, she knew Sol probably couldn't do anything about it. Hopefully the district judge would call Clack's case to trial soon, and they could get him behind bars before he could do anything.

She wadded up the paper and crushed it in a fist. Then she fell to her knees and raised her hands toward heaven.

"I'm afraid," she prayed. "Afraid of what this man will do."

The curtains on the window billowed out as the wind stirred. "I don't want to deal with him with violence. I know that is not your way."

The wind whipped the curtains and they popped. "But I need to say this now, no reason to add lying to what I might need to do."

The wind blew steady now, the curtains standing out almost as if in a salute like a flag.

"I will shoot Ben Clack if he comes for this baby. If he comes for this baby or if he does anything to harm my own."

The wind seemed to keen now, a shrill sound as it whipped through and around the house.

Abby continued to pray, her arms outstretched, her heart sad but determined. She didn't want to shoot Ben Clack. But a highlander woman would not let a man do harm to her child so long as she had breath in her body. If Ben Clack tried to hurt Sam or Rose Francis and she had to shoot him, then the Lord would just have to understand.

CHAPTER
TWO

A light mist fell from a steel gray sky. Daniel Porter climbed out of his six-year-old truck and kicked the mud off his boots. A floppy black hat sat on his head. Shoving his hands into the pockets of his overalls, he hunched his shoulders against the wet air and hurried to the front porch of a white wood building just across the street. Somebody had recently painted the single-storied structure. A logging truck was parked next to it.

On the porch he paused, pulled off his hat and brushed a hand through his hair, then his beard. Streaks of gray colored both, and the hands, while still strong, had in recent years begun to gnarl up some at the finger joints from arthritis. On cold days his shoulders hurt.

Clearing his throat, he knocked on the door. Nobody answered. Daniel knocked again. Still no response. He stepped to the right and looked inside. He knew he had the right place. Over the last three weeks, he had asked enough questions to assure himself of that.

A man named Billy Gant now owned his family's land. Gant hailed from Raleigh. Had come home from the war about six months ago, a scar from his left ear down to where his shirt covered his neck, a sure sign that he hadn't run from any fighting. Folks who talked to Daniel about him said he carried himself well, not too high and mighty but not fearful either. He and a crew of five other men had rented this building where Daniel now stood and taken up operations here. He had hired seven other men and set them to laboring in the woods cutting down the trees.

Daniel started to knock again, but then the door opened and a redheaded, round-faced man stood before him, his flannel shirt green and clean, his boots spotless, his denim pants fresh and rolled up at the ankles with a single roll. Daniel recognized him immediately as the man he had seen three weeks ago on the bald, that day he almost . . .

Daniel pushed the memory from his head and shifted his feet.

"Yeah," said Gant. "What can I do for you?"

Daniel stuck out his hand. "I'm Daniel Porter. You got a minute I can take up a matter with you?"

Gant glanced at a watch. It looked new. He pushed his hands through his hair. "I reckon I can spare a minute."

"Much obliged," said Daniel.

Gant led him inside. Daniel glanced quickly over the room. A round table, five chairs around it. A calendar decorated with a truck advertisement tacked on the back wall. A telephone hanging by the calendar. A quiet radio sitting in the corner. A coffeepot on the floor, three cups beside it. A stack of papers by the cups.

"Still moving in some," said Gant, noticing Daniel's inspection. "A lot yet to do."

"You staying awhile?"

Gant scowled, and Daniel realized he had broken a cardinal rule by asking such a direct question so fast. Inwardly he fussed at himself.

"Sit," said Gant, pointing to the chairs.

Daniel took a seat.

Gant sat across from him, looked again at his watch.

"You got somewhere to go?" asked Daniel.

"Yeah," said Gant. "I'm not out here in the back of nowhere on a vacation."

Daniel raised his eyebrows. Gant didn't seem too friendly. But what did he expect? A tea party? A busy man didn't like interruptions; nothing wrong with that.

"You looking for work?" asked Gant.

Daniel shrugged. "Not why I came."

Gant studied him, and Daniel suddenly wanted to leave. What right did he have to come here? Even if his hunch was right? Even if he had met Gant's pa back in the Great War, that night that he . . .

Daniel cleared his throat. "Look," he started, "I ain't a man of a lot of gab. And I'm . . . well, I ain't sure why I've come here. But I knew a man named Gant once, back in nineteen and eighteen."

Gant sat up straighter but said nothing.

"I fought in a war," said Daniel, studying Gant to see how he'd react.

"I guess we all have," Gant said. "Did my time over in France. Normandy invasion, you know all that."

"You boys did good."

"A lot of men never made it back from those beaches."

"War is always that way."

The two fell quiet for a minute. Daniel thought of his brother Laban, buried over in France.

"They said my war would stop any more wars," said Daniel.

"Reckon we'll always have wars," said Gant. "Long as we got crazy men like Hitler."

"I reckon."

"My pa died in that war you fought, in nineteen and eighteen." Gant kept his expression blank. Daniel tried to read him but failed.

"How did it happen?"

"I don't know a lot. My ma never got many details. Of course I never knew him. He died over in France when I was just barely a sprout."

"You recall the name of the place your pa died?"

Gant studied him a second. "Why you want to know?"

Daniel sat his hat on the table. "I thought maybe I knew your pa, that's all."

Gant stood and moved to the coffeepot, poured a cup without offering any to Daniel, then walked back to the table. "So what if you did? That was a long time ago."

Daniel leaned back and tried to figure why Gant seemed so standoffish. "I ain't here to ask for anything," he said. "No reason to rile yourself."

Gant sipped his coffee, sat the cup on the table. "Look," he said, "my family isn't rich, but we do have more means than many. We own land, here and in Raleigh. Do logging mostly. We suffered like everybody else during the hard days, almost lost everything my folks had built." He paused, wiped his lips and then continued. "Lots of men showed up at our door in those days, more than a few who claimed to know my pa from the war. Ma did all she could for them, gave them money she really couldn't afford to give. They pretty much drained her dry. By the time I reached working age, she didn't have much left. It wouldn't have been so bad except for something I found out back in '39, right after I stepped in to run the business. Many of the men who begged off my ma never knew Pa at all. They just said they did. Had heard in the hobo camps that my ma had a soft heart for soldiers, would give away the coat off her back if you showed up with a sad story and told her you knew my pa." Gant cleared his throat.

"Folks with hunger in their belly don't always worry too much over the truth," said Daniel.

Gant shrugged. "I reckon not. But you got to agree, I got good reason to act suspicious when a stranger shows up on my porch to tell me he once knew my old man."

"Better put a hand over your dollars," agreed Daniel. "Figure that stranger wants to walk away with some of them."

Gant smiled slightly and Daniel saw him thaw a touch. "Don't take any offense," he said. "Just staying cautious."

Daniel held up a hand. "Sounds reasonable. No offense taken. I'm not even sure the man I knew was your pa. Just figured to see."

"You got a first name?"

"Sure, Oscar."

"I reckon you did know him. Least you got his name right. Where did you come up on him?"

Daniel studied his boots. The story held some sorrow for him. Would for Oscar Gant's son too. "On the field at the Marne River."

"My pa died near the Marne. Battle near Château-Thierry."

"I know," said Daniel. "I was the last man he ever saw."

Gant stood and walked to the window, faced Daniel again. "My ma told me about a man who stopped by our house on his way back from the war. Said he waited with my pa that night, waited until he . . ."

"I am that man," said Daniel.

Gant moved back to the table, sat down and laid his palms flat. "Tell me what happened," he said. "Ma would never say it all, said it hurt too much."

"She might have it right."

"I'm almost thirty years," said Gant. "Time I heard what happened."

Daniel nodded. "We jumped off before daylight, all of us runnin' straight at the Germans. Artillery boomin', machine guns barkin'. Took some heavy losses in those first few minutes." He paused, pulled his pipe out of his overalls and stuck it in his mouth. "I come up on your pa a few minutes after the start. He had lost an arm, below the elbow. Already lost a lot of blood. I tied it off best I could."

"He still able to speak?"

"Yeah. He asked me to take off his wedding ring, asked me to take it home to his wife. Said her name was Lydia, said she lived in Raleigh. Asked me to tell her he loved her."

Gant held up his right hand. "This ring?"

Daniel nodded. "Looks to be it. I gave him a drink of water. Then he passed. Peaceful-like."

Gant took a big breath. "He died well," he said.

"Chin set toward the enemy," said Daniel. "In a war, that's about as good as you can ask."

The two men fell quiet. Daniel stared at Gant's ring. Gant held it up. "You brought this to my ma when you came home."

"Soon as I landed."

"Ma always spoke highly of that."

"How's she doing, anyway?"

"Okay. She stays busy." Gant stood and walked to the window once more. "I always wanted to meet the last man who saw my pa. Every now and again I thought about looking for him. But I didn't know where to start."

Daniel suddenly felt unsure of what to say next. "I been right here," he finally said. "Strange that you turn up in my backyard. I saw you on the land below the bald, up near Blue Springs Mountain."

"Yeah, I've been in town awhile, getting things organized."

"You got a big crew. Planning on cutting the timber all out?"

Gant faced him again. "What does it matter to you?"

Daniel noted the suspicious tone again but decided he might as well lay things straight out. "My family once owned that land."

"It's good land," said Gant. "You sell it?"

"Nope. My older brother lost it in a bet a long time ago. We got moved out after that."

Gant looked puzzled. Daniel wanted to tell him more, wanted to tell him that he had spent his whole life trying to buy the land back, that right before the Depression he had put the money together to do it but then lost it when the bank failed. But no high-lander volunteered such tales, tales that would seem like he couldn't deal with his problems all by himself.

Gant went to his desk near the wall, perched on its edge. "My family bought it back in '36. Picked it up cheap, what with the Depression on and all."

"People with dollars could do that."

Gant looked at him as if watching a dog he didn't trust. Daniel didn't know what else to say so he decided he ought to go. Gant had come by his family's land in a proper way. No reason to take offense at that. He stood, put on his hat. "I know you got things to do," he said.

Gant checked his watch.

"Do good by that land," Daniel said. "My ma rests on it, my aunt too."

"You born there, I reckon."

Daniel nodded. "In the burned-out cabin close to Slick Rock Creek."

"That's a good spot for a cabin. Best spot on the property."

"I always thought so."

"Reckon you love that spot."

Daniel studied his boots. "Reckon I do," he finally said. "Made a promise to my pa a long time ago that I'd get it back someday."

"That's a hard promise to keep."

"Harder than puttin' a bib on a bear."

Gant chuckled and followed him out to the porch. Daniel headed to his truck. As he opened the door, he heard Gant yell. Daniel turned around. Gant bounded down the steps. "Look," he said. "Come back in for a minute. I got something you might could do for me."

Daniel eyed him curiously. "What you mean?"

Gant waved him back inside. "Come on in. Let's have us a talk about a few things."

Daniel squared his shoulders. Somehow he knew that Gant didn't want to talk about the weather. Yet, whatever he had to say, Daniel wanted to hear it.

CHAPTER
THREE

On a sunny Wednesday morning three days later, Jim Waterbury and his brother, Steve, met up with their uncle Sol and Thaddeus outside of the county sheriff's office and headed to Sol's county-issued sedan. Jim and Steve took the backseat. Sol adjusted his mirror and looked through it to the back.

"I still think I ought to do this by myself," he said. "Don't need all this company."

Jim shrugged. "Clack threw a rock through my window too," he said. "I don't plan on letting him get by with that without hearing from me. Either I go see him with you or I go by myself."

"I'm with Jim," said Steve. "Taking care of my ma."

"Leave it be, Sol," suggested Thaddeus. "We've already argued this more than enough."

Sol grunted. "Well, keep your mouth shut if we find Clack. This is law work. You got to stay out of it."

"What about Thaddeus?" asked Jim. "You agitate him like you're doing us?"

Sol grinned. "Thaddeus is a calmer man than you two. Don't expect him to go off half-cocked like you might do." He backed the sedan out of the driveway and headed out of Blue Springs.

"When did you ever see me anything but calm?" asked Steve.

Thaddeus grinned too and turned to the boys. "Your ma says you especially were always into everything."

"I got to agree with that," teased Jim. "Not much of anything calm about you."

Steve leaned back. "So you're ganging up on me," he said, accepting the ribbing.

"Got to," said Sol. "A stout young man like you, it takes all of us to keep you in your rightful spot. Keep you from getting too high and mighty on us."

Jim slapped him on the leg. Steve shook his head, but Jim could see he wasn't mad. Sol had picked on both of them for years.

Sol steered the car past the gas station, the last building on the outskirts of Blue Springs. Jim kept his eyes steady on the road, but his gut churned hard. Three days ago a note tied to a rock had crashed through the window of his house about a mile out of town. Even if unsigned, he knew the note's author. Ben Clack, no doubt. The note said, *Clacks and Porters don't mix. Better not sleep heavy.*

Sol turned the car onto a gravel road.

"You reckon we'll find Clack?" asked Thaddeus.

"Don't know," said Sol. "But we know where to look for him. A run-down four-room shack about three miles down this gravel road."

"You would think he'd have a fancier place," said Jim. "Didn't he make a bunch of money a long time ago, back when moonshining was a cash-paying business?"

"That's been shut down for years," said Sol. "The Clack fortune ain't what it used to be."

"Some say Ben stashed away a lot of money," said Steve. "Up in the far corners of the highlands. Like to get my hands on some of that."

"He might have," Sol said. "At one time they were the richest folks in the county."

"Never could tell it from the way they looked," said Thaddeus.

"Hardly ever shaved or bathed," added Sol. "Got bad teeth too."

Jim listened quietly. He knew a lot of the story. The Clacks and Porters had feuded for as long as anyone could remember. Sol, the son of Elsa Clack, Ben's sister, and Solomon Porter, Jim's grandpa, had long been hated by the Clacks. Two different times Sol had taken a Clack bullet. The last one had paralyzed him for a while, and some said he'd never walk again. Only an operation, hard work and prayer had made it such that he could recover, take back his old job. Sol had no love for Ben Clack. But he wouldn't go past what a proper lawman would do to make trouble for him. So long as the law left him out on bail and he had no full proof that his hand had written the notes that had crashed through Jim's and Abby's windows, he wouldn't straight out and arrest him.

Like everybody else in the Porter and Clack families, Sol knew that the feuding days had passed for all of them except Ben. If they could find a way to deal with him, peace could stand a full chance.

Sol headed the sedan up a final incline, then pulled off to the side and parked it. "Walk from here," he said. "About a hundred yards or so."

The men climbed out. Sol adjusted the holster on his hip. Jim stretched his back. "Hard to believe he still lives without any electrical," he said.

"Lots of folks up high like this still don't have it," said Thaddeus. "Some don't even want it."

"Some folks won't ever take to modern ways, I reckon," said Steve. "Foolish as that is."

Sol headed up a trail off the road. The others followed. It took about ten minutes to reach the top of the ridge where there sat a log cabin with a front porch and a couple of dogs resting in the shade under it. Sol motioned a halt. "Reckon we might go in quiet," he said. "If Clack hears us, he might go to shooting before talking."

The men nodded their understanding. Sol pulled out his pistol and led them through the undergrowth to the front porch. Once there, he motioned them to wait, then stepped softly onto the steps. The dogs turned to look at him but didn't bark. A few seconds later he moved to the door and knocked.

"Clack!" he yelled. "This is Sol Porter, sheriff. I got a word to say to you!"

Several seconds passed. Jim heard feet on the floor inside the cabin. Then the door opened and Ben Clack stood in the opening. A stale smell rolled out of the house. Jim studied Clack. Faded black brogans. Overalls rolled up at the ankles. A brown jacket with a torn left sleeve. Floppy hat low on his eyes. A crooked nose and spotty teeth.

"You a long way from home," said Clack, breaking the silence.

"And you been busy lately," said Sol.

"Who you got with you?" asked Clack, easing out to the porch. "Some extra help?"

"You know Thaddeus," said Sol. "And Steve and Jim Porter."

"You boys come to see me. How nice. I hope you understand why I don't ask you inside. I ain't much for hospitality."

Sol shifted his feet. "You know why I came," he said. "No reason to beat around the bush."

"I'm listenin'," said Clack.

"You threatening folks. Throwing rocks with mean notes through their windows."

"You got proof I did what you sayin'?"

"Nope, none to stand up in court."

"That's a bad thing for a lawman. Got to have proof to do anything."

"We all know it was you," said Steve. Jim threw up a hand to silence his brother. Steve scowled.

"Well, the young man speaks," said Clack. "Didn't figure any of the Porters to have the guts to say much."

"Leave him be," said Jim, stepping between his brother and Clack. "He's not involved in this."

"Got your brother taking up for you?" asked Clack, his eyes on Steve. "Big war hero fighting your battles?"

"I have fought much tougher men than you," said Jim, edging up a step toward Clack. Steve grabbed Jim's arm and started toward Clack, but Sol stepped between the three men and faced Jim and Steve. "I told you both to stay out of this," he said. "Not your place."

Not wanting to appear disrespectful, Jim eased back by Steve. He knew he'd made his brother mad, yet he didn't know how he could have avoided it.

"Listen to your uncle Sol like a couple of good boys," said Clack.

Jim ground his teeth but kept his silence. Clack faced Thaddeus, a crooked grin on his face. "You got a handsome woman for a wife," Clack said. "Pretty baby too from what I hear. A shame if anything happens to either of 'em."

Thaddeus clenched his fists. "I won't dignify your coarse ways with a reply," he said.

"I always had a hankerin' for your woman," said Clack. "Her and me goes back a long way, back to the time when she was a girl."

Jim felt the tension rise.

"You stay away from her!" growled Thaddeus. "My baby too."

"She's a strong woman," said Clack. "I admire that. Takes somebody like that to satisfy a man like me."

Jim took a step toward Clack, Steve right behind him. No man would talk about his ma that way! Thaddeus moved to Clack too. Clack's hand moved to his side. Jim saw the flash of something metal and realized Clack had reached into his overalls for a knife. Sol's hand moved to his holster.

"Hold it right there," said Sol. "No reason for this to get out of hand."

Clack dropped his hands, shoved them into his pockets. For a couple of seconds nobody moved. Then Clack said, "I'm telling you to leave my place. Unless you got some proof to arrest me for something, I got nothin' left to say. Time for you to move on."

Sol nodded. "Okay," he said. "Just take this as a warning. I'm keeping my eye on you. You make one mistake, do anything to harm either of these families, anything to their babies, and I will come down on you like a mountain cat. I won't wait for your trial to start. I will do you in right then and there. We clear on that?"

Clack grinned again, obviously not too concerned. "Ye're clear," he said. "Now, let me be clear on this." He eyed Sol dead straight. "I'm the only one left. The only Clack true to his blood.

All the rest have turned traitor on me, to their kin and all their history against the Porters. I will not do that. No matter about the Mingling, no matter about any trial that may or may not happen. I'm going to stay a Clack long as I live. If that means I butt heads with the law over and over again, I can live with that. Long as I draw breath, I will hate Porters. Anything else betrays my pa's memory."

"You're a lone wolf now," said Sol.

"I reckon I am."

Sol nodded. "Then we're both clear."

"We are," said Clack.

"I reckon we'll see each other again."

"It seems so," said Clack. "Until I'm dead, I'll fight this."

"I would prefer that we settle this another way," said Sol.

Clack studied his boots for a second. "You know we ain't got any other way. No choice in the matter."

"I'll uphold the law," said Sol. "You decide whether you'll break it or not."

"A man does what he has to do," said Ben.

Sol waved everybody off the porch, and the men headed down the incline.

Jim took a deep breath. "I hope the judge calls his trial soon."

Sol nodded. "We've done all we can. We warned him."

"And he warned us," added Thaddeus. "Now only the good Lord knows what will become of things."

Once back in the sedan, Jim glanced at Steve, who sat glaring out the window, and knew he'd done a wrong thing by stepping between him and Clack. "Hey," he said, "I'm sorry about that . . . back there."

Steve waved him off.

Jim sighed. Sometimes he just didn't understand his brother.

CHAPTER
FOUR

Abby's parlor stretched at the seams to hold the crowd that Daniel had asked her to invite to her house. Sol and his wife, Jewel. Elsa and her husband, Robert Tuttle—the preacher at Jesus Holiness Church and the man she had married in 1939, ten years after Abby's pa had died. Daniel, Deidre and their son Raymond. Daniel's oldest child, Marla, lived down in Greenville with her husband and couldn't make it, and of course nobody had heard anything about Ed. For all anyone knew, he was gone for good, shot down over the Japanese mainland.

When everybody added in with Abby and Thaddeus, the place swelled at the corners. In spite of her most recent troubles with Ben Clack, Abby smiled a lot as everybody arrived. It had been years since so many of her kin had gathered in one spot. She could lay a lot of cause for that at Daniel's feet. He had been the one going his own way for so long, a lost soul cut off from those who loved him most. But that had changed now, and Daniel was the one who had called them together.

Their mouths going faster than an auto going down a mountain without brakes, they all squeezed into her front parlor on the last Saturday in August on a day so clear it made your eyes hurt to look at the sky. It was warm too, hot enough to make you need to sit down every few minutes and take up a glass of lemonade so you could breathe good.

Abby kept her eyes on Daniel as everybody took a seat. He had stayed real quiet since he arrived an hour or so ago. Thaddeus kept asking him what he wanted to tell, but Daniel just grinned and held his peace. "I'll tell you when everybody is here," he told Thaddeus. "Just hold your water awhile longer and you'll find out."

Never one to let company come to a dirty house, Abby's place sparkled from the cleaning she had given it. The handmade curtains, freshly washed, hung sharply on the windows; the wood furniture in the kitchen and living room glistened with fresh oil she had rubbed into it; and every spider within a hundred yards had fled because she had brushed away the webs in every corner.

The house smelled good. "Like a bakery," Thaddeus had said as he inspected the four pies—two apple, one blackberry and one rhubarb—that she had set out on the kitchen table early that morning. "Too good for anybody in this family but me."

Abby had shooed him away, and he hugged her and left the kitchen. Daniel drove up with his family about nine in the morning, his body heavier than Abby had seen it in a long time. She smiled as he climbed out of his beat-up truck, touched his walking cane on the ground and stepped onto her porch. The weight looked good on Daniel, like he had gained some substance with it, some heavier grounding that he'd not had in a while.

"Come on in," she said, pushing back the screen door. "You looking fit."

Daniel kissed her cheek and followed Deidre inside. Abby led them to the kitchen table, poured them all a glass of water. Sitting, Daniel handed a glass to Deidre, then drank from his. Abby patted him on the back. Less than a month had passed since that day on the bald, the day Daniel had reached the bottom of the pit and climbed out, the day his life had changed so much for the better when he reconnected with the Lord. Since then he had stopped all his drinking. Plus, he and Deidre, who had moved back to their home up in the holler after her ma's death in Asheville, seemed to have fallen back in love with each other.

"You plan on telling me what's going on?" Abby asked him.

"Not till the rest get here."

"Not even for a biscuit?" she said, holding out a plate of fresh baked. "With apple butter?"

"You're temptin' me hard. But I will not yield. Reckon you'll just have to hold those biscuits, cruel woman that you are."

Abby shook her head and handed him the biscuits. "Don't let it be said I let a hungry man starve," she laughed. "Even if he is my brother."

Laughing, Daniel and Deidre each took a biscuit. An hour or so later, Sol finally arrived, Elsa and Preacher Tuttle right behind them. Now everyone had a seat. Abby's heart thumped heavily. She sipped from her water over and over. Thaddeus moved to a chair beside her and held her hand.

Daniel checked the clock on the mantel over the fireplace. Almost eleven.

Abby squeezed Thaddeus and he leaned closer. "I'll get Sam if he wakes," he said. Abby smiled at him.

Daniel rested his cane over his legs. Abby studied the cane her pa, Solomon, had given to Daniel as he lay dying. Carvings Solomon had cut years before decorated its length, images of the tablets that held the Ten Commandments, the Ark of the Covenant, Jesus on the cross, among others.

That cane had saved Daniel's life just a few short weeks ago. The Lord had used it to give Daniel a vision, one so simple and yet so miraculous. Even from the grave Solomon Porter still influenced his family.

Abby looked around the room. The elders of her kin were here, the men and women who had shaped her life, the people whose lives had carved her character into her soul as surely as Solomon had carved the figures into the cane Daniel held. Abby pondered the notion for a second. She couldn't separate who she was from the people who had walked with her all her years. Their words stayed in her mind.

She thought of her boys, Jim and Steve. Just as the people in this room had shaped her, so she had shaped her sons. For better or worse, her ways had cut lines into their lives. With their pa gone almost from the time they were born, she had shaped them more than most other mothers with their children. Sometimes that seemed a heavy load to carry.

Her hands in her lap, Abby pictured Rose Francis and her heart tugged. Rose lived with Daisy and William Clack. They would shape her life now, just as she would Sam's. Would Rose Francis turn out sweet? A woman of faith and trust in the good Lord? Had she made an awful mistake going through with the Mingling? At the time she had believed it to be God's will, but could she truly know His will?

Unable to answer, Abby pushed back the sadness. In her heart she knew the Mingling was the right way to go, the only way to ensure peace with the Clacks.

"I reckon you all want to know why I asked you here," said Daniel.

Abby clasped her hands and focused on Daniel.

Sol pointed his pipe at his half brother. "We got some curiosity about it," he said. "Takin' up a Saturday morning this way, you best have a good reason."

Daniel pushed his hair out of his eyes. Abby studied him. Fifty-three years old, he had lots of gray in his slicked-back hair, and his shoulders had rounded some from earlier years when they were square at the edges. His face wore the marks of some hard living too, lines crisscrossing under the eyes and down into the beard he had worn for as long as she could remember.

The clock clicked to eleven. Daniel stood, walked to the window and stared out for several seconds. Abby knew that something big was headed their way, something that might change them all for a long time to come. She felt shivery and nudged closer to Thaddeus.

Daniel faced them again, his cane clutched in his right hand. "You know I been through some tumblin' waters these last years," he said. "Times I thought my head might not come back up. I didn't always live right in those years. Backslid a far ways from the arms of the Lord."

Abby's heart ached. Her brother didn't need to apologize to them for anything. So long as he had confessed to the Lord, that was all that mattered.

Daniel talked on. "Thanks be to Jesus, though, the good Lord never gave up on me. He kept on after me, kept on hounding me." He rubbed his beard. "He seen me through all those rough spots. Losin' our land. Laban. Then Luke dyin'. Then losin' the land again. The times I couldn't find any labor to do to make a living. Ed gone missing."

Abby saw that the mention of Ed's name had slowed him some. He cleared his throat, then moved ahead.

"Well, you know all those troubles. No use passin' back by them." Everybody nodded. "I think I got some good news for a change. Maybe the waters have smoothed out some." He rolled the cane two or three times. "Fact is, maybe they have smoothed out a lot."

Abby smiled. She loved Daniel more than anybody on earth outside of her children and Thaddeus. And life had indeed dealt him some sorry cards. Nothing would make her happier than to see some good things come his way for a change. He deserved it, had labored harder than any man she knew, kept his shoulder to the wheel for years trying to do good by his family. But over and over again everything had turned sour on him, most of the time through no fault of his own. She didn't know why. Fact was, she sometimes wondered about it, why the Lord let such painful hurts come into Daniel's life. But she never found the answers to her questions.

"You hear news on Ed?" asked Sol, going to the logical thought.

Daniel's face darkened for a second, and Abby could see that Sol had missed it. Then what? Daniel stared out the window again.

"Who you waitin' on?" asked Preacher Tuttle.

Daniel waved him off but the grin reappeared on his face. "Hold on one more minute."

Abby heard a truck pulling up outside. Daniel moved to the door, opened it and stepped back. Less than a minute later, a man whom Abby had seen a few times around town but had never met walked in. He was wearing a green-and-black checked shirt, denim pants that had a crease, and brown boots. In his late twenties or so, he looked clean-faced and innocent, like a pup hound that had never been in a fight.

"This is Billy Gant," said Daniel. "He's from over to Raleigh. Some of you already met him."

The men all stood and shook Gant's hand. Abby poured him some water from the pitcher on the coffee table. He sipped the water. Daniel motioned him to a chair by the fireplace. After he sat down, Daniel stood by him, one hand in his pocket, one on the cane.

"I met Billy a couple of days after . . . after what happened with me up on the bald," he said. "I done told you all about that."

Abby nodded. The good Lord had reached out to Daniel on the bald. Daniel had told the story but only one time.

"Well, as I already said, I saw Billy that day, down in the valley on our old family land. Something about him seemed familiar to me. A couple of days later I drove over to talk to him. Knew I had to dig to the bottom of it all, find out what he was doing there, who his kin was."

Daniel turned to Gant and smiled. Abby saw hope in his face, something she figured Daniel had lost.

"I found out a whole lot more than I ever expected," said Daniel, his voice softer. "Gant owns our land now, ever bit of it, a thousand acres."

Abby squeezed Thaddeus harder. Her ancestors, good Scotch-Irish immigrants who had made their way to the highlands of North Carolina from Pennsylvania, had toiled hard to make a better life for their families. After several decades, they gradually scrabbled together a goodly sized piece of property in some of the most remote mountains of the Blue Ridge. This was the land her now-departed brother, Laban, had lost in the infamous bet with the Clack boys. For years Daniel had done everything possible to reclaim that land but had never met with any success. So what did it all mean, with his bringing Gant here like this?

"I found out I did know him," Daniel continued as if to answer her question. "Least, I met his pa over in France, back about the time I got shot."

The room fell real quiet. Daniel had fought in the first big war, the one in which Laban had died. For a long time Daniel carried a heavy guilt around with him, like he should have saved Laban from the bullet that killed him.

"Daniel here's the last man my pa ever spoke to," said Gant.

Abby remembered something now, and her breath caught. Something about Daniel back when he returned from France. He had made a stopover in Raleigh to take care of some business from the war, yet he never said anything about what he did there.

"His pa was already shot when I first laid eyes on him," said Daniel. "He knew he had taken a mortal wound."

Gant rubbed his face. "I never knew my pa," he said.

"He spoke his last words about his family," Daniel said. "His love for his wife."

Gant smiled, held up his right hand. "He asked Daniel to bring this to my ma," he explained. "His wedding ring. He did what my pa asked."

"Any man would have done it," said Daniel.

Gant shook his head. "Maybe. Maybe not. But you did and that's what counts. When I got old enough, my ma told me about Daniel, about the kind young man who visited our house just before the war ended, how that man gave her comfort by telling her that her husband had died nobly, that her husband spoke his love for her with his dying breath. I never forgot that tale from my ma."

Daniel stared at the floor. Abby knew he didn't like it when too much attention settled on him. He cleared his throat and spoke again. "Anyway, when I drove over to meet Billy, I already knew the name was the same. When I saw him up close, I knew without a doubt he was Oscar Gant's boy. It all came back to me, that morning in France."

Abby tried to figure what all this meant. Gant owned their land. Gant owed Daniel a debt of thanks. Daniel had a light in his eyes she hadn't seen in a long time. But still she felt uneasy, almost as if the good news Daniel carried had a hook in it, something to bait them to what looked good but maybe might not be.

Gant stood by Daniel in front of the fireplace. Daniel gripped his cane, and Abby saw his knuckles turn white.

"Ma gave me this ring when I got older," Gant said. "Told me to do as good by it as the husband who wore it, as the man who brought it to her after the war."

His eyes glistened. Abby wanted to cry with him. He obviously had a good heart beating in his chest.

"I want to do right by Daniel Porter."

Abby wiped her eyes. The air in the room felt like lightning about to crack in the sky.

"Daniel and I have had us a talk," Gant continued. "He told me how he tried to buy back the land, how Mr. Tillman almost got it back for him, just before the Depression. That's when we bought it, about halfway through those hard times." He glanced at Daniel, but he still had his head down.

"So I made an agreement with Daniel. I know he loves this land, wants to care for it."

Daniel looked up at him.

"I want the timber off it. But not stripped bare so the dirt washes away with the rain. Up in Raleigh, at the state college where I studied, they tell us to take only the timber that's full grown, the mature trees. Leave the rest for later, come back and cut it when it reaches prime. They tell us to replant some as we go so that we can cut another crop later."

Abby glanced at Thaddeus, who had his eyes fixed steady on Gant.

"I want to treat this land with respect. Do right by it." He stuck his hands in his pockets. "But I can't stay out here all the time. I got me a wife in Raleigh, two young children. I missed out on so much during my time in the war. I don't want to stay out here, away from them. So I need somebody who cares for this land as much as I do to handle my business for me." He faced Daniel again. "I have asked Daniel to work for me, oversee the timber cutting."

Abby smiled. Good for Daniel. He could at least labor on the land he loved. If he couldn't own it, that was the next best thing. He could see to it that nobody stripped the land like so many other lumber cutters had done elsewhere, could protect the mountain at the same time that the loggers took the timber off it.

Gant cleared his throat. "Daniel has agreed to the job. He will become foreman for my crew so I can go back to Raleigh."

Abby checked around the room. Everyone was nodding and smiling at Daniel.

Gant said, "I want Daniel to live on the land too. Stay close by it."

It made sense, thought Abby, to keep the foreman right on the property.

"For payment for his labor, I am going to give Daniel fifty acres of the land, where his family house once stood. Figure I owe him that much for taking care of my pa in those last minutes, coming back to my ma with his ring."

Abby almost jumped from her chair. She looked to Thaddeus. He seemed frozen in place. Everyone started talking, and Daniel rapped his cane on the floor to get everybody quiet again.

"Hold on just a second," Daniel said. "It ain't all told, not quite yet."

Abby couldn't imagine what other surprises Gant and Daniel might tell them. After all these years, her brother had at least part of his dream fulfilled. God surely had blessed him.

"I also plan to let him buy back as much of the land as he wants," Gant said. "At a price we set as fair at the time he buys it. I don't need the land itself, just the trees off it. As long as Daniel gives me the right to take timber from it in the way I have already said, he can purchase land as he gets money to do it."

Abby tried to catch her breath. Daniel could buy back the land! A miracle had come to pass! The Lord was good, no two ways about it.

The room turned quiet for a moment. Abby wondered how many acres Daniel would be able to buy. Not that much really, she guessed, what with wages still low and all. But this way he at least had the assurance the land could one day be his. Surely that should make him look forward again to getting up in the morning. For the rest of his life he could strive to get back the family land—a worthy goal.

Daniel rapped his cane again, this time as if to wake them up instead of to settle them down. He looked slowly around the room, caught the eye of everybody in it. "This is truly a blessed day," he said. "You know how much I have wanted this day to come. You got to know, though, that I am not wanting this just for myself. I want it for everybody here."

Abby folded her hands in her lap. Daniel made sense. It had been the family land, not just his. But they all lived somewhere else now. She and Thaddeus here in town. Elsa and Preacher Tuttle in the house owned by Jesus Holiness Church. Sol and Jewel a couple of miles out in a place her pa had built for them. Even Daniel had a good spot—a farm on about eleven acres that old Solomon had bought from their uncle Pierce back after he got burned out by the Clacks. Why would anybody want to move?

Daniel rubbed his beard. "The more dollars I can collect, the faster I can purchase more land," he said. "That stands to reason." He propped a foot on the fireplace hearth and laid down his cane. "I don't know whether any of you have any interest in this, but I want to open the chance to everybody. I want you to help in buyin' it back. Anybody who wants to can come in with me. We pool our dollars, whatever we can spare. We take that to Billy here and buy the land a whole lot quicker."

Abby glanced around, saw everybody studying Daniel. Except for her and Elsa, nobody else had ever lived on the land Gant now owned. Why would they want to spend their hard-earned dollars to buy it back? In some ways it was still real isolated. In spite of all the roads that had been built in the last few years, the cabin where she was born still sat in a spot over a mile from the nearest pavement.

Sol raised a hand. Daniel nodded his way. "You figuring we would all live up there someday?"

"Don't know about that," said Daniel. "Up to you as we buy up more land."

"Reckon sheriffing would be hard to do from up there," said Sol.

"Taking care of a church flock too," said Preacher Tuttle.

"I expect you're both correct," Daniel said. "The land might not be what you all want anymore."

"Dollars are better than in a long time," said Thaddeus. "But they're still not falling off the trees. Might take some real effort to come up with any spare ones to spend on this land that we don't know if we'll ever want to live on."

Abby thought about the school where she and Thaddeus taught. Getting out and back from up on the mountain every day would take some hard effort. Everybody fell silent again. Daniel's shoulders sagged some, and Abby knew that their response had taken some air from his lungs.

"I reckon we need to think some about this," she said. "Hitting us without warning and all, it's hard to figure right now what's best to do."

Daniel nodded. "I reckon you're right. Take some time, then. Don't need to do nothin' on the spur of the second. I just wanted to give you all the same chance Mr. Gant has brought to me."

"What about the boys?" Thaddeus asked, facing Abby. "You reckon they might want to pitch in on this?"

Abby turned to Daniel.

"I want everybody in the family to go in if they want," he answered. "My boy Raymond already said he wants to help. If Jim and Steve like the notion, I'll welcome them too. We can put a number of families on a thousand acres."

"I will talk to them," said Abby. She stood and moved to Daniel, put her hand on his shoulder. "I am not saying what we will or will not do," she said. "But either way, I am glad for you. This is what you've wanted for a long time."

Daniel smiled and she saw some sparkle in his face again. "It's what Pa always wanted," he said. "For our family to live on the land, up there by the mountain where he said he could see God's face."

"He did love those highlands, didn't he?"

"Next to us, he loved them the most."

Abby hugged Daniel.

"What do you want most?" he asked her.

Abby thought but only for a second. "What any woman wants. A loving husband, happy children—all of them in the circle of the Lord."

"You don't ask for much."

"Reckon not. Ben Clack out of my life, I'd take that too if the good Lord wants to give it."

Daniel chuckled and said, "That might be the hardest to get."

Abby smiled. For the moment, Ben Clack didn't seem so fearful.

"It is a blessed day," Daniel said.

Abby nodded. For a few seconds at least, it seemed that God had declared everything right with the world.

CHAPTER
FIVE

Daniel, Deidre and Raymond drove up to the clearing at the fork in Slick Rock Creek two days later, on a morning as clean and crisp as starched cotton. Walking cane in hand, Daniel parked his truck, took out a brown paper sack filled with three sandwiches and apples, and headed up the overgrown path that led to where his family's cabin had once stood. They didn't say much on the way up. Daniel kept his head high, his ears eager to hear the sounds he had listened to as a boy—sounds undisturbed by anything human. Birds chirped at them as they passed, and the gurgling of the creek went with them as they walked. The trail bent and twisted a number of times but gradually made its way to the top of a ridgeline and then back down toward the clearing where the creek ran through the valley.

When Daniel reached the hand-cut bridge that his pa had built way back before the century had turned, he squatted, laid his cane at his feet and dipped his hand in the creek. Cupping the water, he took it to his lips. The water tasted sweet. He breathed in like a man who hadn't had any air in days.

"Take a drink of this, boy," he said, flicking creek water at Raymond. "Nothin' ever taste this good, you can trust me on that."

Raymond knelt beside him, Deidre too. Both drank from the creek. Daniel studied them with pride. Raymond, seventeen now, had square shoulders, blond hair from his ma's side of the family, and a thick neck like a young bull. Diedre, although showing her middle age by some wrinkles around her mouth, still kept herself up, and her figure was as fetching as ever.

"It is good water," said Raymond. "I got to give you that."

Daniel grabbed a handful and flung it at his youngest. "Good don't do it fair," he said. "It's better than good."

Raymond splashed water back at him. Deidre dodged out of the way. Daniel playfully grabbed Raymond and pulled him off the ground. Yanking hard, he stepped into the creek, his brogans covered with water. Raymond struggled, but Daniel's grip hadn't lost much in spite of his fifty-three years. He rolled his boy to the left and tossed him into the creek. Raymond thrashed around in the water for several seconds before he caught his balance. Jumping up, he moved to Daniel, but his pa beat him to it. Daniel jumped headlong into the creek, his bearded face disappearing under the water like a duck going after a tadpole. As if through a tunnel, Daniel heard Deidre laughing at him.

"You have lost your mind!" she yelled. "Gone plumb loco on me."

Raymond jumped on his back then, and the two wrestled in the creek, each trying to drown the other. Daniel reveled in the play, his heart pounding with as much joy as a man could ever expect to feel, his heart lighter than in many a year. Water splashed everywhere. Deidre continued to holler, but Daniel didn't care. He opened his eyes under the water and looked up into the clear stream toward the sun. A golden ray of light filtered through the trees and struck the water right above his head. Raymond let go of him, and Daniel was enjoying the sun's warmth and the water's cool wetness when all of a sudden something took hold of him.

The stream rushed over him from head to toe and washed him as it moved. Daniel trembled but not from cold. The water felt like fingers scrubbing his skin, rubbing off the sins that had made him so dirty for so long. Hurts peeled away too, the scars from so many bad memories. True, he still had no word on his boy Ed, and he figured him dead. But war did that to men; it killed them off as surely as a hard winter killed off some of the deer that lived on the mountain. Nothing a body could do about it.

The water soothed his grief like a dipper of cold well water slaked a man's thirst. Daniel felt like the Holy Ghost had rolled through him and made him all fresh again. His lungs gasping, Daniel burst out of the stream. The water dripped off his beard. Raymond stood by, equally drenched. Deidre had moved to the creek bank. Her skirt was wet at the ankles.

"Never been a day like this one!" Daniel shouted, climbing up the bank.

"You are loony," Deidre declared.

"Come on," said Daniel, taking his cane in one hand and holding out the other to Deidre. "You need to see where I am going to build you a cabin."

Still shaking her head, Deidre took his hand and walked across the old bridge. Raymond followed. Daniel's brogans squished as he walked, but he didn't notice. His heart raced up another notch and he moved fast so that Deidre and Raymond fell a couple of steps behind. Less than a minute later, Daniel pushed through a laurel bush, turned to the right and stopped in a clearing. The sun beat down on his face. He took off his hat, pushed back his hair as if to spruce up some before going into church. His eyes felt watery. Raymond and Deidre stepped up alongside him.

"There," Daniel said, pointing to the near level stretch of ground about a stone's throw from where they stood. "Ma bore me right there."

"This is a special place," said Deidre.

"And Pa built that chimney," Daniel added, pointing to the only thing left standing after the day Clack and his boys burned the place down. "Before the turn of the century."

"Your folks did a lot of labor on this place," said Deidre.

Daniel stepped forward, his clothes already beginning to dry in the hot sun. "We had a shed over there," he said and pointed to his right. "A fence built around everything."

"The Clacks burned down everything," Raymond said as he walked around the site. "No sign of any shed or fence."

"The Clacks showed no love for us, I can tell you that."

"Your brother Laban lost the place to them in a bet." Raymond spoke as if to assure himself that it had actually happened the way the story had been told him.

Daniel nodded and said, "Laban didn't always choose right."

"He saved your life, though," said Raymond, again pulling from family lore. "Over in France."

"That he did," Daniel agreed. "I owe him."

They went to the chimney. Weeds sprouted out from its base in all directions, covering the ashy remains of the old cabin. Daniel kicked at the chimney. It felt solid still. He moved past the chimney, turned and faced Blue Springs Mountain. He pointed at the bald— a bare spot of rock where no trees grew.

"My pa got lost one time," he said. "He was ten, out coon hunting with his pa and brothers. In the middle of the hunt, he chased a dog on a false scent. The dog split off from the rest, and Pa found himself cut off from everybody. Rain started to fall so hard he couldn't hear any guns fired for him to follow out of his lostness.

"He found a cave in the rocks, hid there till morning. When the sun rose again, he remembered what his pa had told him to do if he ever found himself alone in the woods. He climbed to the top of the highest ridge he could find, hauled up into a tree and climbed to the top branch. From there he looked in every direction.

"He saw the bald off to the northwest, knew it hung over his home. 'If you ever get lost, find Blue Springs Mountain,' his pa had always said. 'It will show you the way home.'

"So Solomon set out. At the foot of the mountain he found his cabin. As he stepped into the yard, his pa stood on the porch and waved a hand.

" 'I told 'em you'd know how to get home,' said his pa."

"So old Solomon found his way by looking for the mountain," Deidre said.

"Always said he could see God's face there," said Daniel. He studied the bald. A wide rock face like a man's chin cropped out from its middle. Another rocky bump looked like a nose. Shadows covered the top like eyes, and another rocky edge gave it the appearance of a heavy human forehead. Daniel pulled his beard. The mountain seemed to come alive. "I am home," he said.

"Reckon you are," said Deidre.

Daniel scuffed his brogans on the ground and looked away from the mountain. "Got a lot of work to do here."

"We can do it," Raymond said.

Daniel turned to Deidre. "I don't expect you to live here for a while yet. You stay down in Asheville with your pa if you want. Me and Raymond will live up here, me laboring for Billy Gant in the day, Raymond working on the cabin. Only when we got a decent spot will we move you."

"I can stay half and half," she said. "Half in Asheville to help Pa, half at home until you get the place built."

Daniel stepped close and hugged her. "A man never had no better wife," he whispered. "You been through a lot with me. Building up our spot on Uncle Pierce's after Elsa gave it over to us, now this."

She kissed his cheek and stepped back. "Getting the electrical up here will take some doing," she said. "Might not get it for a long time."

"Running water either," said Raymond.

"We'll live like mountain folk again," said Daniel.

"You talk like that's a good thing," said Deidre.

"You know it is," he said. "Nothin' better."

Deidre surveyed the terrain. "It sure is a pretty spot," she said. "I can see why your folks picked it. I can put a garden over there." With Raymond trailing, she walked to the left of the chimney, and Daniel watched her go. He rubbed his beard and knew he needed to check one more thing.

"I'm goin' up there a ways," he said, pointing up the ridge behind the place. "Back in a few minutes."

Deidre nodded and Daniel stepped toward the ridge. His breath labored as the incline grew steeper. But it didn't take him long, and when he reached his destination he stopped, leaned on his walking stick, and sucked in a long draft of air. Sweat rolled off his face, and he wiped his hand across his brow. A pair of oaks stood on either side of him. A light breeze played in the branches. Daniel knelt and patted the earth. Three wood crosses stuck up from the ground. At least the Clacks had enough respect not to touch the graves. His ma, his aunt Francis and a brother he never knew lay under this soil.

Daniel again took off his hat. Memories flooded him. The morning of the day he and his family moved away. Sixteen at the time, he had come up to say good-bye to the ones in the ground. He had found his pa there.

"I am gone miss this place," Solomon had said. "It's a peaceful spot."

Daniel had heard shaking in his pa's voice and knew he wasn't just talking about the land. More than anything else, he would miss coming to the graves and talking to his dead wife, Rose.

Daniel had put a hand on his pa's shoulder.

"We got to stay strong today," Solomon said. "Strong for everybody."

Daniel nodded. Inside his head, though, he wanted to let his pa know that it was not a sin to show that a matter like this hurt deep, hurt like a knife wound stuck full in the back. But he had no words for such a thought and so he didn't say anything.

Solomon started back toward the house. Daniel hurried after him. He had to say something, couldn't let his pa just walk away from Ma's grave and never hope to see it again. Without thinking, he grabbed Solomon and spun him around.

"I . . . I . . ." Daniel sputtered.

"What you want to say?" asked Solomon.

"I will get our land back."

Solomon nodded, but Daniel could see he had no conviction in it.

"I mean it!" Daniel said again, his teeth clenched. "I will find a way to claim back what belongs to us, to you . . . to you and . . ." He pointed back at the grave. "To you and Ma and all of us."

Solomon laid a hand on his shoulder. "We will do okay," he said. "The Lord will not leave us."

"I will get back the land," Daniel said, quivering as he realized the vow he had just made. "As Jesus is my witness, Pa, I make you that promise."

Solomon pulled him close. For several long moments the two of them stood that way, Daniel's head on his pa's shoulder. "You will . . . come back to . . . to Ma's grave. . . ." sobbed Daniel. "As God is my witness. . . ."

A blue jay landed in the oak tree to Daniel's right, and its cry brought Daniel back to the present. He hadn't managed to keep all of that promise. His pa died without ever seeing his first wife's grave again. Yet Solomon had told him more than once that he never held him to that promise anyway and that Daniel shouldn't take it all so hard. But Daniel had, of course, and it had almost killed him.

Daniel moved to the head of the graves and rubbed his hands over each of the crosses. He thought of his pa, buried over on property that his brother Pierce had let him use when they got kicked off their place. "I am home, Pa," Daniel whispered. "Sorry it took me so long."

The blue jay called again. Daniel sat down by his ma's grave and rested the cane over his knees. Overhead the sun blinked through the oak's branches. He closed his eyes and said a prayer of thanksgiving, and a feeling of contentment he hadn't felt in a long time settled into his soul.

"I will lay down right here someday," he whispered. "On this land of my family."

CHAPTER
SIX

Abby and Thaddeus met with Jim, Rebecca and Steve the next Saturday. Abby had done some heavy thinking about the matter since then and had concluded that for her part, it made some sense. Even if she never moved up there, she still wanted to aid Daniel in whatever way she could. And, truth to tell it, the notion of re-claiming the land where her ma lay buried gave her a jolt of joy that warmed her bones. It would feel good to walk up to the oaks every now and again and say a prayer at her ma's marker.

Thaddeus had taken to the idea too. "We don't make much money," he had said only two days ago when they talked about it, "but what we make goes pretty far. If we can scratch up a few extra dollars every now and again, I see no reason not to pour it into buying that land. A man with property can always live off it if the need comes, keep his garden, fish the creeks. Property always pays off if you know what to do with it."

Pleased with his decision, Abby hugged him and said she agreed. So, they had decided they would do what they could to help Daniel buy up the land. Now she would see what Jim and Steve wanted to do.

The boys arrived at almost the same time, Jim and Rebecca in Jim's car and Steve on foot from where he had hitched a ride from his job. Abby looked them over as they stepped inside, Jim at twenty and Steve, eighteen. Jim had served in France during the war. Had met his wife, Rebecca, over there. Abby knew the story well, though not because Jim had told it. Like all true highland men, Jim kept his words tight. Rebecca, however, liked to tell how she and Jim had found each other.

Blinded by shrapnel, Jim ended up in the field hospital near Naples, Italy, where she was stationed as a nurse. Recognizing his name, she checked to see if he was in fact the man she knew from her childhood. When she found out he was, she made sure she got assigned to him.

"You've spent time in the highlands," Jim told her one morning as she led him out for a walk. "A body can't hide the mountains from their voice, no matter how much education they slap on it."

Rebecca Stowe laughed, admitted she hailed from North Carolina but revealed nothing more. He continued to question her about her upbringing and how she ended up in the Army.

"I've wanted to nurse since I was twelve," she said one day. "I lost a baby sister to the fever that spring, stood by helpless and watched her die. Figured that if I became a nurse, I might stop such a thing from happening to somebody else."

Jim asked more about her background, yet she offered little. Only that her mama's name was Elizabeth and she had a pa with a few rough edges.

As the days passed, Rebecca visited him every time she could, taking him on walks and reading to him from the Bible.

The days warmed and Jim grew stronger. His doctor told him that his vision should improve, maybe come back all the way, maybe not.

Near the end of April, Rebecca took him for a picnic. As she led him out of the hospital, she realized she had fallen in love. But did Jim have feelings for her?

"Sit," she said after they had walked awhile. "I put a blanket down and there's a tree for you to lean on."

Jim took his spot while Rebecca arranged things and sat down beside him. She handed him a sandwich and he ate. Then he faced her, his mouth set firm.

"I'm eighteen," he said. "Nineteen in June."

"A regular old man," said Rebecca.

"War can make you that in a hurry."

Silence then. Rebecca took his hand. "Jim," she started, "I need to tell you something."

"That makes two of us. You go first."

Her voice caught. He touched her face, and she guided his hand to her cheek. He fingered off the tears.

"Why are you crying?" he asked.

"I've . . . kept something from you," she said. "I shouldn't have done it but I did."

Jim pulled away. "I reckon you already got a husband."

Rebecca chuckled. "I wish it was that simple."

"Then what?"

"I don't know how to say it."

"Just say it straight out."

"Okay." She paused to gather herself. "I didn't see any need to tell you this at first. But . . . but now I have fallen in love with you."

"How is that bad?" he asked. "I feel the same way but didn't think I should tell you 'cause I can't see."

"You don't understand."

"Tell me what I don't understand."

She stood. "You know I've got the highlands in my blood."

"Sure," he said. "That's a good thing. Means I won't have to teach you how to make corn bread."

"I've known you for a long time," she said, not laughing at his remark. "I saw your name when you came in, asked to be assigned to you. Wanted the chance to see if what I'd always heard was true."

"So? We met somewhere; what about it?"

"You still don't understand, do you?" She knelt beside him.

"No, I don't understand."

"I grew up real close to Blue Springs. Saw you there in town from time to time."

"What are you tryin' to say?"

"I told you my name was Stowe," she said. "But there's one name I left off. Left it off because my pa never claimed me in any public way."

"Who's your pa? That's the head of the matter, I expect."

"My pa is Topper Clack."

Jim's face lost its color. Long seconds passed.

"Say something!" she pleaded.

"I got nothin' to say." Jim's fists balled up tight.

"I guess this means the end for us."

Jim hung his head. Rebecca Stowe put a hand on his knee. "My mama said your folks were the salt of the earth," she said. "Said everybody in the highlands knew they could trust the Porters. I never had any respectability, grew up without a pa. So when I saw your name, I just had to find out what kind of man you were. Then, I don't know, the more we talked, the more . . . well, I . . . I fell in love with you. I didn't mean to; it just happened."

"Clack never claimed you?" he said.

"Nope. He had a wife, remember? My mama loved him on the side."

"Not easy on you, I reckon."

She laughed but it had no joy in it. "A highland woman with a child but no husband lives a hard life. The child too. I got out of there soon as I could. Had an aunt in Raleigh. Mama sent me there, made Clack pay for it."

"How'd she manage that?"

"My mama is a looker. She told Clack she wouldn't see him anymore if he didn't provide money for my schooling in Raleigh. That's where I got my nurse training."

Jim slumped. "You know that your pa killed mine, don't you?"

"I'm aware of the squabbles between our families. I met your uncle Sol once. He came looking for my pa, a few months before I left Blue Springs for good."

"But you still wanted to take care of me?"

"Like I said, I've long admired your folks. When I saw it was you, it just seemed right, a connection from back home, you know?" Jim nodded. She continued, "I never knew my pa that well. He just showed up every now and again. Stayed a day or so, then disappeared again. Guess I'm far enough removed from the Clacks that I didn't hold it against you that your family hates them."

Jim gave a half smile. "Mighty nice of you," he said. "But that don't solve all the problems we got."

Rebecca laid a hand on his shoulder. "I'm sorry about your pa. But I had no part in that. I hope it won't keep us from each other, from what we might have together."

"My pa wasn't the finest of men either," Jim finally said, admitting something he had never voiced until now.

"Even so, he didn't deserve what he got," she said.

"That's not your fault." He paused, then said, "I fear what my mama will say about all this."

"Your mama is a good woman, I hear," Rebecca said. "Surely she won't shut me out just because I got Clack blood in me."

Silence came. When Jim spoke again, Rebecca knew he had made a decision.

"You as good-lookin' as you say your mama is?" he asked.

"Well, I don't look like a pig, I can say that."

He reached for her hand. "This won't be easy. I still can't see, you know."

"I know that."

"Some of my kin might not take well to you."

"That won't surprise me."

"You sure you want to try this?"

She kissed his hand. "As sure as anything in my whole life."

"Then I reckon I'm asking you to marry me."

"And I reckon I'm saying yes."

Jim's hands moved to her face, and he ran his fingers over her lips. "I reckon I want to kiss you."

"I reckon I want you to go on and do it."

"I haven't kissed many girls."

"I thought the Porter men weren't given to a lot of talk," she said.

"You wantin' me to shut up?"

"If that's what it takes for you to kiss me, then yes, that's what I'm wantin'."

"I love you," he said.

"And I love you."

He kissed her then and, for the moment at least, all her worries disappeared.

Abby came back to the present as she watched Rebecca sit down by Jim on the sofa, Steve on her other side. Abby didn't know much about Rebecca's family. Her ma lived in Raleigh and she had two brothers, one in Asheville who had managed to become a lawyer and another off in Knoxville. The one in Knoxville showed up to see her every once in a while, while the lawyer hardly ever came around. Rebecca didn't say much when Abby asked about him, just shook her head and sighed.

Abby focused on Jim again. Thankfully he had regained his eyesight. He and Rebecca seemed happier than about anybody she knew, outside of her and Thaddeus.

Abby offered lemonade to everybody. Steve didn't drink his, just held it in his lap. She put the lemonade pitcher back on the tray, set it on the coffee table. Something about Steve made her uneasy, yet she couldn't put her finger on it. She smoothed down her apron.

"I expect you know why I called you here," she said. "You've heard about what happened with your uncle Daniel." The boys nodded. "He has asked us if we want to join in with him in buyin' back the land. We pool our dollars, do it as a family. I'm here today to see what you two think of the notion."

Jim sipped his lemonade, turned to Rebecca. "Me and Rebecca have talked some about this already," he said. "Got a couple of questions."

"Ask them," said Abby.

Jim sat down his glass. "How will we split up the land? And when? Say I put in fifty dollars in a year. Will that deed come to me right off or will we buy it all and then divvy it up somewhere down the line?"

Abby shrugged. "I don't know answers to all that," she admitted. "Nobody yet figured it that close, I reckon."

Jim leaned forward and said, "I don't mean not to trust anybody, but making some of this clear might keep any hard feelings
from coming in the future. You know how it goes—you get a lot of
knives trying to cut one pie, somebody's finger is liable to get cut."

Abby arched her eyebrows. Her son had a good head on his
shoulders. Making things plain from the beginning made a lot of
sense. "I'm sure Daniel will work with us to keep matters clean,"
she said. "I'll see that he does."

"How do we decide who gets which parcels of the land?" Jim
continued. "Some pieces are better than others; you know that."

"You talking like a business man," said Thaddeus, his tone neu-
tral as to whether or not that was a good thing.

Jim glanced at Rebecca. "I reckon I am," he said. "I just want
to keep things straight. Something I learned in the Army. Keeps
confusion to a low ebb. Best for all of us."

Abby sipped her lemonade. "If we get these matters answered
for you, you plan to throw in on this?"

Jim looked at Rebecca again, took her hands and said, "I reckon
so. Least for a while. Let us all choose a spot we want to buy, then
we pitch in and buy it."

Satisfied with Jim, Abby turned to Steve. He still held his lemonade, the glass moist. "You've stayed mighty quiet," she said.
"What are you thinking?"

Steve dropped his eyes, and Abby knew he had something
heavy on his mind but didn't know how to speak it. She wanted to
go to him and pat him on the shoulder but knew she couldn't. He'd
grown into a man now and such a thing would only make him mad.

"Go on," she encouraged. "Say what you want to say."

Steve lowered his lemonade to the floor. "I have some news
too," he said. "The Army won't take me. Said they don't need any
new men now that the war is over. Plus my sight isn't too good."

Abby wanted to tell him this was good news, but she knew he
wouldn't take well to that.

"You can go in with us then," said Jim. "You're starting to make
some good money."

Steve stared at his brother, and Abby saw a hint of the old competition rise in his eyes again. Part of her liked to see it. Steve had

spirit. But another part of her worried about him. A man so bent on proving himself might go to desperate measures to accomplish what he sought. She felt shivery all of a sudden. Some of that same trait had put her deceased husband, Stephen, in trouble most of his life.

"I'm not staying in Blue Springs," Steve said as simply as if announcing he wanted biscuits for breakfast. Abby sat up straighter. She hadn't expected this. "I've thought about it for a while. Jim got his chance to go away during the war. Now he's come home. By choice, he's decided he wants to live here, dig in his roots. But I've not yet tested myself against anything. I want to see what's out there. It's time for me to make my way in the world."

Abby started to protest, to tell him he needed to grow up some more, but then she knew that made no sense. A man his age could make up his own head.

"You got all you need right here," said Jim.

"That's easy for you to say," said Steve. "You got a wife, a job with some prospects. My job . . . who knows how long it will last. There's no chance in it to better myself."

Jim glanced at Abby as if to ask her to talk some sense into his brother. Abby stayed quiet.

"I want to go to Raleigh," Steve said. "Where Pa grew up."

Abby gripped her apron. A wave of fright ran through her. Steve had always wanted to know more about his pa—his childhood, his parents, how he became a lawyer, why he stayed away from home so much.

Stephen had pretty much left home the year Steve turned two, had died the year he turned ten. Like any boy, Steve had seen nothing but the good in his pa, and Abby never mentioned the bad traits. Stephen had them of course, more than his share in fact. He often talked bigger than he could deliver; he spent years away from home without much cause; he drank and gambled; he eventually ended up in jail because of shady business dealings.

Abby wanted to warn Steve against falling prey to the same temptations that brought down his pa, but what ma would say such bad things about a pa to his son?

"You could go to college in Raleigh," she suggested, trying to keep things positive. "You know I've always wanted that for you and Jim." She glanced at Jim. "'Course with him married and all now, he won't get the chance. But you still can. Maybe Raleigh is a wise thing for you."

Steve scratched his head. "Don't know about college," he said. "All I know is I've lived here long enough. It's time to see what this world has to offer."

Abby took a deep breath. "You planning on staying with your pa's folks?"

Steve shrugged. "Don't know. But I'll go see them I reckon."

Abby folded her hands in her lap. Steve's grandparents had paid little or no attention to them, not when Stephen lived and certainly not since he had died. She barely knew them and felt like they saw her and her boys as beneath them, her marriage to Stephen a mistake from the beginning. Over the years she had learned to live with their standoffish ways, but she hated for her boy to have to face it now. What if they treated him poorly when he showed up at their house? What would that do to him? Already unsteady about his abilities, would their unfavorable treatment push him down even further?

"They are reserved people," she finally said. "Not given much to keeping in touch."

"I know," said Steve. "They never came to see us."

"They might not know what to do with you if you go to their place."

Steve studied his shoes for a second. "They want me to come."

"What?"

Steve stared at Abby. "I reached them by telephone a couple weeks ago," he said. "Told them I wanted to come see them. Grandmother Waterbury said my coming would please them."

Abby's mind whirled. Had the Waterburys come to their senses? After all these years, had they finally realized what they'd missed by staying cut off from their grandsons? A shot of hope ran through her bones, momentarily overcoming her earlier bad feelings. Maybe the good Lord wanted Steve to go to Raleigh. Maybe this would give him the chance to grow up and become a fine man.

Then another idea hit her and the bad feeling returned. What if seeing Stephen's parents caused his late pa's bad traits to show up in Steve? What if something about that place, about Stephen's folks, caused the worst of the pa to settle on the son? Abby pushed away her questions. She had to trust the Lord. No matter her premonitions, Steve was right about the fact that he was a man now. She couldn't keep him tied to her apron strings forever. If he wanted to go to Raleigh, she had to give her blessing and leave the rest to the good Lord.

"I'm glad they want to see you," she said, keeping her voice even. "Please let them know of our regards."

"I'll do that," said Steve.

Jim turned to Steve, and Abby saw the concern on his face. "What about Clack?" he asked. "Thought you said you were going to take care of Ma."

Steve hung his head. "You and Thaddeus will take care of her for now," he said. "Like you said at Clack's place, I'm not involved in this. I see that now, least not directly. I need to, well, I've got to go, that's all. Can't stay around here and be your little brother for the rest of my life. Nothing against you or anything, but a man needs some clearing to make his own way, you know what I mean?"

Jim nodded. "Then it's settled."

"Reckon so," agreed Steve.

Abby looked at Jim. He put his hands on his knees. "I'll throw in with Uncle Daniel. We'll buy up the land fast as we can."

"And I'll go up to Raleigh and make more money than all of you put together," said Steve with a smile. "Come back here and buy you all out."

Abby laughed but it had no joy in it. Steve had no idea what he would face in a place like Raleigh. Plenty of opportunity, yes. But ample temptation too.

"You dream big, brother," said Jim.

"You just watch me," said Steve. "You'll see."

"You can take care of your ma in her old age," Abby said.

"That I'll do," said Steve. He stood and bent over her, gave her a hug. "I'll take care of you, Ma," he promised. "Even from

Raleigh. Don't you worry any about that."

Abby relaxed in his arms and breathed a silent prayer. Her boy had so much to learn. She hoped and prayed he didn't get hurt too badly while he learned it.

CHAPTER
SEVEN

S mart enough to let the law cool down some before he took any
more rocks in his hand, Ben Clack lay low for the next month
or so. Spent most of his time with a bought woman in an old cabin
about seven miles out of Blue Springs. True, he owned a brick
house right close to the town, but what self-respecting highland
man wanted to stay in a place that had glass windows all shut up
against the night air and no crawl space under the porch for his
dogs to sleep?

In a drunk stupor most of the time, Clack hardly noticed as
September moved in and the nights started to chill off. He wore a
long-sleeved flannel shirt over his overalls and a pair of socks under
his brogans. But other than that, not much changed. So long as he
had a woman to cook him up some eggs and grits in the morning
and warm him in bed—that and a jug of whiskey—he didn't bother
much with anything else going on around him.

Every now and again an old moonshining buddy stopped by,
other rough men who measured their worth by how much liquor

they could hold on a Saturday night, by how they held up in a pistol fight, by how many women other than their wives they could bed. Clack knew those days had mostly passed, but it still felt good to swig from his bottle and relive times gone by.

Clack's belly hurt a lot most of the time now, felt like he had swallowed a hot coal, and he figured he knew why. A man didn't drink as much whiskey as he had over the years without suffering from a touch of belly pain every so often. Fact is, a lot of men his age had already passed on to their final reward because liquor had chewed up their insides. Clack knew he probably wouldn't make it for a whole lot longer. Sometimes, late at night, he got the shakes, whether he was drinking or not. Plus he sometimes spit up some blood early in the morning. The way he saw it, Old Man Death had set his sights pretty steady on him.

That didn't scare him much though. His ma and pa and all his brothers had already gone on to the land beyond the mountain, and he might as well go on and join them. Sure, he had that hell thing to worry about, but he didn't really believe much in it. The way he figured it, once a man died, he was just dead, that's all. Like a possum that got run over by a truck. Squashed and gone and that was it. Nothing waited for him past this life, no matter what the preachers shouted. Clack didn't believe it, no sir, not one bit.

About the only thing that bothered Clack about the notion of dying was the fact that he hadn't finished his business with the Porters. Before he ended up as worm food, he wanted to take one more shot at fixing them for good. His pa would like that, his brother Topper too. If it turned out that a body did live somewhere else beyond this old earth, he wanted to meet Topper and Pa with a grin on his face. The only way to do that was to settle things with the Porters once and for all. Even more important, he wanted to feel really fine one more time before he died, and handling the Porters would give him the satisfaction he desired.

He knew the law would surely do him in this time, if not for what he'd done at Jesus Holiness on the night of the Mingling, then surely for any new mischief he created. The old ways of living had ended, no doubts about it. No more rough highland places where a man could cuss and drink and shoot his guns at anything that moved. No more moonshining so as to make any real money. Sure, you could sell some in the dry counties but not enough to buy any judges or keep the law under your thumb anymore. He still had some dollars stashed away but not much more coming in, and he never liked the notion of trying to go straight like Topper had always planned on doing. Ben had no patience for anything like that.

At just after dark on the last day of September of 1945, Ben picked a fresh bottle out of the closet in his bedroom, moved back to the fireplace and fell into a chair. His woman, Betsy by name, had left him for a couple of days to go see her ma. Clack took a swig off his bottle and threw a boot up on the table in front of him. His stomach growled, and he remembered he'd not eaten anything but a biscuit all day. But he felt too tired to get up and fix anything. With Betsy gone, he would just have to stay hungry for the night. He drank again from his bottle, then heard a knock.

"It ain't locked," he yelled.

The front door creaked open and Clack tilted his head. "Come on in," he said.

A man with a stomach the shape of a full-grown watermelon waddled into the room and took a seat across from him.

"Bluey, you dog," said Clack. "Hope you ain't hungry. Betsy ain't here, nothin' to offer you."

Although Bluey looked disappointed, he didn't voice it. "You got coffee?" he asked.

Clack tilted his head to a doorway. "In the cook room."

Bluey headed to the kitchen, came back a couple of minutes later with a tin cup in his hand.

Clack studied his cousin as he sat back down. His round face looked like somebody had burned it on the cheeks and forehead. Flakes the color of flour dropped off his nose every now and again. He wore denim pants, brogans and a brown shirt that didn't quite make it over his stomach. A floppy black hat sat on his head.

"You look awful," Clack said. "How old you gettin', anyway?"

Bluey grunted. "Nigh onto sixty-five. Rough livin' I reckon."

Clack chuckled. "Don't I know it. I reckon I ain't no prize myself."

Bluey looked him over. "You got some bad teeth," he said. "Nose like a hawk's beak, shoulders rounded, eyes all bloodshot and squinty-like. I don't think I'd pick you out for no blue ribbons, that's for sure."

"I'm fifty-nine," said Clack. "No spring chicken no more."

Bluey pulled a bottle from his pants pocket, twisted off the cap and poured the liquid into his coffee. "Reckon the better part of life's done passed us both by," he said. "The way of things, nothin' a body can do about it."

"I got a trial coming up," said Ben.

"When you figure?"

Ben grinned. "Not for a while yet. I got me a lawyer. He's spreading some money around down in Asheville, helping the judge remember he's got better things to do than haul off up to here to handle a small town case like this one."

"You got that kind of money left?"

"I got enough."

Bluey laughed. "Guess you're glad Thaddeus Holston didn't die," he said. "Not even money could help you if you'd murdered him with all those witnesses."

Clack nodded, drank from his own bottle. Silence. Clack wiped his lips. The trial looming, maybe prison to follow, caused his mood to sag. "What you reckon life's all about?" he asked, not expecting much of an answer. "You know, what meanin' does it all have?"

"You barkin' up the wrong tree askin' me that kind of thing," Bluey said. "I don't do much thinkin' about that."

Clack thought on the matter for a second. "I don't either, usually. But something has got into me the last few days. Don't know what exactly, but I just been doin' a lot of studyin' on some things."

Bluey eyed him suspiciously. "You ain't goin' religious on me, are you?"

Clack grunted at that.

"I seen it happen, you know," continued Bluey. "A man reaches a certain age. His stomach turns bad on him and he starts to fear his passing day. A lot of men turn to Jesus about then, I reckon."

Clack sucked off his bottle. "Don't worry about me doin' anything like that. It ain't gone happen."

"Glad to hear it," Bluey said. "It's cheatin', if you ask me. A man raises the dickens all his life, then gets the faith right at the end. Tryin' to escape the eternal lake of fire, that kind of thing. Don't seem right, that's all. Like eating from the meat that another man shot without goin' on the hunt with him."

"That's right eloquent," said Clack.

"I been listening to the radio every now and again. You pick up things."

Clack sipped his whiskey. "So you see no meanin' in any of it? A man just lives his days and passes on? No more purpose than a rat or something?"

Bluey studied the fire. "Maybe there is," he said. "You know, take care of your family, turn your hand to something worthwhile, don't back down from a fight that comes to you, be a man, that's all I figure. If they's anything else, I just ain't smart enough to find it."

"I got no family left," said Ben.

"Women don't take to hard living," said Bluey.

"Not my wife anyway. She ran off to Knoxville."

"Your kids all moved off too."

"Yeah, six of them, don't ever see them anymore. Half done moved out of state even."

"Not like the old days when a man kept firm reign," murmured Bluey.

Clack sighed. Heaviness fell on his shoulders. Sometimes even a strong man faced some sadness. He took a swig of whiskey and pulled up straighter. No reason to let the melancholy get him. "I got business left with the Porters," he said, the thought lifting his spirits.

Bluey nodded. "They always been a sore spot in your gut. From a long ways back."

"My pa hated them. Solomon Porter took his girl, Rose, from him, married her. She had already been promised by her pa to my old man. But she and Solomon fell hard for each other. Her pa broke his promise and Porter married her. Served her right dyin' young and all, the way she treated my pa."

"You put them off their land," said Bluey. "Your pa loved that, I reckon."

"You helped us," Clack reminded, thinking back to the day Laban lost his pa's property through his poor gambling.

"I did my part."

Clack chuckled as he remembered what had happened. Grieved by a schoolteacher who had just turned down his proposal for marriage, Laban had brought his brother Luke up on the mountain to do some drinking. Bluey and a couple of the boys had taken to throwing a knife at a tree target. Laban wanted to try his hand. They let him throw against Bluey, both men putting a small wager on the throw. Laban won the first two throws. Then Bluey upped the bet, put two hundred and forty dollars of liquor money on a tree stump and offered it for the property where the Porter family lived.

At first Laban just laughed. "Not my land to wager," he said.

Bluey kept after him, the other boys too. Laban studied the money, knew he could use it to leave Blue Springs, maybe get some real schooling, impress the schoolteacher who had turned him down, get her to marry him after all. Besides, he had won the first two throws. No reason he couldn't win the third.

He took the wager. But one of the boys fired a gun just as he threw, and the shot threw off his aim just a touch and Bluey won. Turned out Bluey was a nephew of Hal Clack. The money was Clack's. Now Laban's family land was his too.

"We run them off and burned down their house," Clack said. "A fine day, I got to tell you."

"I hear they're gettin' some of that land back," said Bluey.

Clack's brow furrowed. "How's that?"

"You ain't heard?"

"I reckon not."

Bluey sighed, rubbed his hands over his face. "A new man bought up their old property. Guy named Gant. Seems he's come to take the timber off it."

"So?"

"So, it turns out that Daniel Porter knew Gant's pa back in the First War. Don't know all the particulars. But Porter helped Gant's pa somehow. Now Gant's boy feels he owes the Porters something. Word is, he's asked Daniel to head up his logging crew."

"He gives Porter a job. Not that big a deal. That it?"

Bluey looked afraid to tell the rest.

"That it?"

"Not exactly," said Bluey. "For wages, Gant's given Daniel some of his land back. I heard it was fifty acres. Gone let him buy up more too, as he gets money."

Clack's jaw firmed as he listened. "I'm not pleased to hear this," he said.

"I reckon not."

"I'm not gone stand by and let it happen, I can tell you that."

"You staying true to your pa and still hating all of them?"

"That's what I'm doing," said Clack. "Making sure my pa gets his revenge."

"Your pa's been dead awhile now."

"Yeah, but I still know what he would want."

"What you aim to do?"

Clack stood and threw a log on the fire. "I plan to do something about all this—the land, the Mingling too. That's a real abomination, maybe worse than Porter gettin' back some of his land. A Clack child with the Porters, a Porter baby with the Clacks. No way that's a right thing."

"Add the fact that Topper's girl Rebecca married up with Jim Waterbury and they had a baby, it's two times as bad."

Clack waved his hand. "I'll take care of that. All at one time."

Bluey poured more whiskey into his coffee. "You got some reason for livin' now," he said. "Getting back at the Porters."

Clack took a long drink of whiskey. "It's enough to get a man out of bed in the morning. Sure enough is. If I can keep my trial off long enough, I can take care of a lot of things."

"What you plan on doing?"

Clack grinned, leaned closer to Bluey and said, "You just wait and see. It's sure to be right fun, I'll tell you that."

CHAPTER
EIGHT

Steve left Blue Springs late in the afternoon on the second Saturday of October, on a day that had turned off colder than usual for that time of year, a day almost cold enough to freeze the pipes that brought water into his ma's house. After saying goodbye to his ma, he climbed into Jim's car and they headed out. Neither said much as they wound their way down the mountain toward Asheville, where he planned to catch the train. What was left to say? They had gone their separate ways back in '42 when Jim shipped out to war. Since then they had not spent a lot of time together. Although Steve felt some emptiness in his gut that he didn't feel close to his brother anymore, he didn't know what he could do about it. People grew up, moved into their own lives. In the end, everybody ended up alone—no two ways about it. He had learned that from his pa.

Steve balled his fists. He barely remembered his pa, and what he remembered wasn't always too favorable. If he ever had any kids, he wouldn't run off and leave them like his pa had left him.

Jim let him out at the train station at about five o'clock. A light snow had started to fall. Steve pulled his coat around his ears.

"Reckon this is it," he said. "Train here in a few minutes."

"I'll wait with you," said Jim.

Steve shook his head. "No reason for that. You best head on home before this snow settles in, makes the roads too bad to drive."

Jim's shoulders sagged. "I'd rather not leave you alone."

"I appreciate the ride," said Steve. "But I'm a grown man now. I don't need you to take care of me."

Jim stared at Steve, his eyes sad. "I'm not trying to take care of you. I'm just . . . I don't know . . . don't want to leave you, that's all."

Steve tried to relax. All his life he'd tried to keep up with Jim, usually without too much success. But that was his failure, not Jim's. Fact was, Jim had always treated him well. "Look," he said, deciding to make it easier on them both. "I don't want to worry about you driving in this snow after dark."

Jim glanced at the sky. "You might be right."

"Yeah."

The two brothers looked at each other. Steve hated times like this, when he didn't know what to say, when words stuck in the back of his throat.

"You take care of yourself," said Jim.

Steve nodded. "You take care of Ma."

"I will."

Steve glanced at his shoes then stuck out his hand. Jim took it. The two brothers stood on the train station platform, their hands clutching, neither speaking. Steve sensed something large in this, maybe even larger than when Jim went off to war. From this moment on, they would head out on two separate roads, and only the good Lord knew when or if those two roads would ever come together again. But Steve didn't know what to say about it so it remained unspoken. He squeezed Jim's hand one more time and then dropped it. Jim turned away.

Steve watched him go, slipping on his glasses so he could see clearer as Jim climbed into his car and turned it toward the mountain. Over his shoulder, Steve heard a train whistle but for a second he didn't face it. Instead, he watched Jim as his car disappeared. A lump rose in his throat. He swallowed it down, shoved his glasses back in his coat pocket, picked up his bag and pivoted toward the train. Blue Springs lay behind him now. He had a life to live, a fortune to make.

Five minutes later, he climbed onto the train, glanced at his ticket and saw the seat number. Third row from the back, the window seat. A number of people, including a couple of uniformed soldiers, nodded as he passed. Reaching the seat, he tossed his bag down and settled himself in by the window. His heart thumped heavily as the train left the station, and his hands shook a little as he watched the countryside begin to roll by. Except for a trip to Asheville every now and again, he had not done much traveling. He knew he had a lot to learn. But he felt ready for it. Now that Jim had come home from the war, he no longer needed to stay in Blue Springs to take care of his ma. That's all that had kept him there since Jim left. That duty now fell to his brother.

Relaxing some, Steve leaned back and closed his eyes. A pang of guilt hit him about the small lie he had told his ma about calling Mr. and Mrs. Waterbury. Yes, he had telephoned them, told them when he planned to come to Raleigh, the time the train would arrive. But they had not responded quite as positively as he had let on. Still, he was determined not to let that stop him. He wanted to move to Raleigh, and one way or the other he would do it. And if he had told his ma about their reaction, she would have tried to talk him out of leaving until he knew for sure where he would stay. Knowing his weakness when it came to his ma, he would probably have yielded to her wishes. So he had kept his quiet about all he knew.

He turned to his travel bag, pulled it into his lap. He had a hundred and thirty-four dollars in the bag, money he had saved for the last eleven months. While it wouldn't last forever, it would give him a good start. With enough smarts and determination, a man could go a long way with a hundred and thirty-four dollars.

Steve heard footsteps and twisted to see a woman headed his way, a blonde wearing a calf-length black skirt tight at the hips, a green blouse snug at the waist and a black hat that fit stylishly on her head. The woman stopped right beside him, glanced at her ticket and smiled.

"I'm here," she said, pointing to the aisle seat beside him.

Steve jumped up, wiped his hands on his pants, a fine pair of brown wool slacks with pleats. The woman's eyes looked directly into his. The eyes were bluer than anything he'd ever seen, bluer than the sky on a clear May morning. Her boldness surprised him and he glanced down. She wore heels at least an inch and a half high. Without them, she'd be shorter than he was.

"I'm Claire," she said, extending a hand.

"Steve," he said, then took the hand. Her skin was warm and slightly moist.

They sat down. Claire adjusted a black purse in her lap. Steve put his bag on the floor again. A couple of minutes passed. Steve studied the buttons on his shirt, a blue one with a round white collar. A nice gold tie hung from his neck. He knew he looked fine. Yet he still felt awkward, as tongue-tied as the worst hick in the world. Other than a few girls at Jesus Holiness, he had not spent much time with women. Especially ones who wore lipstick as red as what Claire had spread on her lips. He glanced her way, then down again. She had a fine figure, slim but not skinny like so many of the mountain girls.

"You from Asheville?" asked Claire.

Steve shook his head. "Blue Springs."

"Never heard of it."

A touch of shame came on him. "It's not on a lot of maps."

Claire adjusted her skirt. "I'm from Raleigh," she said. "I was visiting my grandparents in Asheville."

Unsure what to say, Steve rubbed his hands on his knees.

"Where you going?" asked Claire.

"Over to Raleigh."

"Business?"

"You could say that."

The countryside rolled by. Steve wanted to melt into the seat. Why couldn't he think of anything to say?

"You don't ride on trains much, do you?"

"Not a lot."

Silence again.

"Not much of a talker either, are you?"

Steve swallowed hard and rubbed his hands on his pants once more. Inside his head, he chided his backwardness. An ignorant highlander—that's what he was. Never been anywhere, never talked to anybody, never accomplished anything. How pathetic!

He looked up and down the train car. Maybe he could move to another seat, one where Claire couldn't make him feel so fumble-mouthed. He spotted a place about six rows up, almost stood to move. But then something grabbed inside his stomach, and he knew if he left Claire now, he might as well get off at the next stop and go straight back to Blue Springs. If he couldn't manage to talk with a woman as friendly as this one, he surely didn't have what it took to make it alone in a place like Raleigh.

Steve decided right then and there that he would not let Claire run him off. He planned to make it in this world, and here he faced his first test. He turned to her and said, "Look, I've not talked to a lot of strange women."

Claire looked at him from under a pair of long blond eyelashes. "I don't think I'm strange," she said, a tease in her eyes.

Steve blushed. "You know what I mean. Women I don't know."

"But you do know me. I'm Claire, Claire Blankenship, from Raleigh."

"I'm Steve Waterbury. From Raleigh too—or about to be."

They shook hands again. "So now I'm not strange," said Claire.

Steve smiled. "No, you're not."

"Good. So now we can talk?"

"Yeah, reckon so."

And talk they did—all the way past Hickory and Statesville, all the way to Winston-Salem, all the way across the state as the day ended and the night passed. Steve told her about his plans to go to his grandparents' place and see if he could stay there until he found a place of his own. He told her about his hopes to find a job in the sales business, because, he said, he could sell about anything, it didn't matter what. She laughed and touched his forearm and told him she could see how that was true, that now that he had started talking, he had a good way with words. People who talk well make good salesmen, she said.

"My ma gave me most of my teaching," he explained. "She taught me and my brother."

"She must be a smart woman," said Claire, admiration in her voice.

"The smartest. She wants me to go to college. But I'm going into trade instead. Maybe own my own business someday."

"But you don't know what kind of business?"

"Nope. Doesn't matter, just so it's mine. Then I'll buy another business, then another. Before long I'll have a regular string of companies, all mine and nobody else's."

"You're going to be a tycoon," she said, laughing.

"That's it, a regular baron of business."

She laughed again and let her fingers linger on his forearm. He liked her so much, he wanted to kiss her. He suspected she might let him too. She seemed so comfortable, like she knew him already. The thought ran through his head that maybe she seemed a touch too friendly, but he dismissed it as an unworthy notion.

As the train rumbled along, Steve tried to get Claire to tell him more about her own life—what she wanted in her future, what she had experienced in her past. Yet, other than a few general things about her father's work with a tobacco company and the fact that she had an older sister and younger brother, she didn't spell out much else. About an hour out of Raleigh the train broke down. The conductor walked around and told them it might take a few hours to get things fixed, so they might as well make themselves comfortable, maybe even sleep awhile. Steve and Claire kept on talking for about another hour, but then they both yawned and said maybe they should sleep some and so they did. About half past five the next morning Steve woke up and wiped his eyes as the train started moving again. Beside him, Claire breathed slowly. He studied her face. It was round and had a small mole on the upper lip near the right side of her mouth. Her lipstick had smeared some, making her appear a little crooked.

Steve suddenly felt uncomfortable. He'd known this woman less than twenty-four hours, yet he had told her things about himself that no one else knew. How odd to be sitting on a train on its last leg to Raleigh beside a woman he'd never met before last night, a woman who now seemed as close as anyone he had ever known. Did the world always throw such surprises your way? Not knowing a person one day, then spending a whole night with them the next?

Puzzled, Steve wiped his eyes, slipped by Claire and headed to the bathroom. A few minutes later, his face washed and his hair slicked down, he moved back to his seat. The train slowed.

He stood beside Claire, unsure what to do. Her breathing seemed lighter than when he left her. Her eyes were still closed. The train slowed more. In a couple of minutes they'd stop. He'd get off the train and go one way and Claire would go another, and he'd never see her again. Steve felt lonely at the thought. He started to wake her and ask for her address, even went so far as to bend over to touch her shoulder. But then he stopped. What made him think she'd give him her address, a backwoods boy like him? She'd treated him nicely while they traveled, but now they had come to her hometown. Surely she wouldn't want him showing up at her house like an old friend. Chances are that would put her in trouble with her folks. What kind of woman gave out her address to a perfect stranger she met on a train? Besides, what if he asked and she turned him down? How embarrassing!

Steve straightened up. Should he at least wake her to say good-bye? No, that would feel awkward. Maybe it was better if he just walked away, climbed off the train and left her behind, asleep, not knowing he left. The train finally rolled to a stop. He carefully picked his bag off the seat by Claire and started to ease away.

"Hey! Mountain boy!" Claire's voice stopped him and he turned to her. "You're not leaving without saying good-bye, are you?" She stood and rubbed her eyes.

"I'm . . . I didn't want to wake you," Steve stammered.

She stuck out her lower lip as if pouting. "You're not very nice."

Steve stared at his shoes, unsure how to respond. Claire moved to him, touched his arm. "Trust yourself," she said. "You got a lot going for you."

Confused, Steve looked into her eyes. He wanted to ask her for a phone number, an address, anything to make sure he'd see her again, but his mouth locked up and he couldn't speak.

Claire moved closer and kissed him lightly on the cheek. His stomach flipped.

"Take care of yourself," she whispered and then stepped back. "And I didn't mean it when I said you weren't nice."

Steve tried again to ask for her address but couldn't get the words out. Claire smiled one more time, then turned away. Steve watched her for several more seconds, until she disappeared from the train car. Sighing, he hung his bag on his shoulder and climbed off the train. Time to move on, he figured. He had a whole future waiting for him. No reason to let one friendly woman keep him from his destiny.

Steve reached the address for Mr. and Mrs. Waterbury at just past nine o'clock, his legs weary from walking the last couple of miles after the ride he had hitched headed in a different direction. The house—a two-story brick place with white columns in a fashionable neighborhood—had two dormer windows jutting out from the attic and sat at the bottom of a hill, its front recently painted. The wide porch looked inviting and warm, the bushes in front thick and lush, although slightly untrimmed. To Steve's surprise, he saw a broken flowerpot on the porch. Dirt spilled over from the pot onto the brick steps.

Steve checked the address again, saw that he had it right. Blowing on his hands against the cold, he stepped to the front door and knocked. Nobody answered. He knocked again. Again no response. He knocked a third time but heard nothing. He stepped to the side and peered through a window. A couple of chairs sat in the room, but other than those, he saw nothing else.

Puzzled, he faced the street. A man walked by, a child bundled up in a brown coat riding a small bicycle in front of him. Steve threw up his hand. "Hey," he called. "This the home of Mr. and Mrs. Beaufort James Waterbury?"

The man stopped and nodded. "Was," he said. "Until about a month ago. But they moved."

Steve sucked in his breath. "They moved?"

"Yeah, real quick-like."

"You know where?"

The man looked suspiciously at him. "Who's asking?"

Steve moved to the man and stuck out a hand. "Steve Waterbury. I'm their grandson. Came to visit them."

The man shook his hand. "Donald Withers," he said. "I don't know where your folks are now." The boy moved ahead on his bike. Withers followed him as he talked. "Sorry I'm not more help, but I didn't know them too well. Just moved in a few months ago myself. Lots of folks coming and going around here these days."

Steve shoved his hands into his pockets. "You think anybody else around here might know where they've gone?"

"Not sure. Guess you could ask around."

Steve pulled a handkerchief from his pocket and wiped his face. Withers continued down the street with the boy. Steve watched him go, his mind at a standstill. This didn't make any sense. He had told his grandparents he wanted to come see them. They had said nothing about moving. He thought about going house to house to see if anybody knew anything. But then he felt the cold against his nose. Maybe he should wait until later in the day when it warmed up some.

He blew on his hands again. He had seen a small store and restaurant about a mile back. Maybe he could go there, get a cup of coffee and figure out what to do next. Situating his bag on his shoulder, he headed back to the store. Okay, so the Waterburys hadn't told him they were moving. Why should they? No reason to expect them to wait around on him. They would probably write his ma soon, tell her where they'd gone. Maybe they had bought a new place, something even bigger and grander than this one.

Steve made it to the store and restaurant about twenty minutes later, walked inside and headed toward a table in the back. A couple of middle-aged men nodded as he passed. He figured he'd get a bite of breakfast and then talk to the folks at the restaurant, see if they knew of Mr. and Mrs. Waterbury, where they might have moved.

He sat down and slipped his bag off his shoulder. Taking off his coat, he opened his bag to stuff it inside. He saw the pouch on the side of the bag, the snap unhooked. His eyes narrowed. He never left the snap unhooked. He laid the bag across his lap, a sudden sense of doom settling on his shoulders. He kept his money in that pouch.

His fingers trembling, he opened the pouch and looked inside. His heart stopped.

Unable to believe it, he searched the space with his fingers, prodding into every corner of the six-by-three-inch pouch. He found one bill only—ten dollars all by itself. But what sense did that make? Why would somebody rob him but leave ten dollars? They wouldn't. So maybe he hadn't been robbed.

Steve racked his brain. When had he opened his bag? Had he left the rest of the money at home? No, he knew that wasn't the case. He'd checked it more than once before he left. Then how had he lost the money?

He shivered. On the train. Claire. He'd left his bag on the seat when he went to wash up after he woke up. But she had slept through all that. But wait! When he returned, her breathing seemed different. Was she awake at the time? Had she awakened while he combed his hair? Had she taken the money and then pretended sleep when he came back? Left him ten dollars as a gesture of parting friendship? Had she marked him as an easy target from the beginning? A dumb mountain boy she could take for all he was worth?

He couldn't believe that. She seemed so honest, so friendly. Maybe too friendly? She hadn't told him much about her background, nothing to go on if he tried to find her. He had her last name, though. He'd go looking for her, get his money back! But then he realized if she had taken his money, she had probably lied about her name so he couldn't track her.

Steve thought of what he'd do if he ever found her. How do you ask a woman if she stole money from you? If she had, then the name was certainly made up. If she hadn't, she'd hate him forever for the accusation. He dismissed the idea of looking for her.

Steve rubbed his eyes. Maybe somebody else stole it. Perhaps while Claire slept, somebody else had seen the bag in the seat, opened it, found his money and taken it.

Yeah, he decided, that had to be it. Somebody else had robbed him. But what difference did it make? He was near broke and without a place to stay in a city bigger than any he'd ever visited.

He glanced around. Could everybody tell what had just happened? That his hopes had just disappeared, his dreams too. Did such a thing show up on a man's face?

Steve pulled out his wallet and checked his money. Nineteen dollars. At least he still had that, plus ten. He tried to figure his next step. Should he go back and report the robbery to the train operators? Yet what good would that do?

He put his wallet back in his pocket and considered just giving up and heading back home. Surely he could get back his old job. He could save up his money again and then try once more. But then he knew he couldn't do that. Go back a failure? Have to admit what had happened, how foolish he'd been? No. No way could he face Jim and his ma with that story.

He gathered up his gumption. Sometimes life threw you a rock. You either caught it and threw it back, or it smacked you in the head and you fell down and never got up. Well, Steve Waterbury wasn't the kind to let a couple of hard rocks knock him down. No sir, he certainly was not.

CHAPTER
NINE

I t didn't take Daniel long to get moved to a spot near the charred chimney of his family's old house. With the weekend help of a few men that Gant sent over from his timber crew, he'd put together a four-room cabin by the time October had about ended. Hauling in a couple of single beds and some kerosene lamps, he made the place acceptable, at least until spring, when he could do better by it. Raymond moved in with him, but Daniel insisted that Deidre stay away awhile longer.

"No need for you to come to so rough a spot just yet," he had said as he left her. "You're too delicate."

"I've put most of my delicacy behind," she told him. "But I got to admit the notion of living without running water or an indoor privy doesn't thrill me much."

"Womenfolk are too soft," teased Daniel.

"You never complained to my face," she said.

"I reckon not. Come to think of it, I take right well to your softness."

Deidre hooked her hands around his waist. "Seems I recollect that."

Daniel kissed her, then he and Raymond headed out. He knew he faced a lot of hard labor, years to build back a respectable house, to head up Gant's crew, to regain something of what the Depression had stolen from him. Although he'd left his bitterness about all that behind, he still mused over it now and again. All a man had could disappear in a jiffy, like smoke from a fire, lingering for a while but then blown away by a swift wind. Of course, most everybody else had lost a lot in those times too. And he still had the eleven acres his pa had bought from Uncle Pierce. It still hurt to have to start over in building any kind of real legacy. Least he got the chance to do it, he thought. Lots of folks didn't. Like his boy Ed.

It didn't take long for Daniel and Raymond to settle into a daily routine. They both rose before daylight every morning, took a cup of coffee made over the coal stove they'd hauled up there and ate a couple of biscuits. After that, they talked over the chores Raymond would do while Daniel headed over to Gant's timber crew for the day. After doing his labor for Gant, Daniel hurried back to pitch in with Raymond working on the house and grounds.

On Saturdays he and Raymond toiled together—putting up smooth planks on the inside walls of the house to cover the cut logs, building up the fence down by the shed, starting a new barn. When the weather turned too bad for the timber crew to work, Daniel brought some of the logging boys home to aid him and Raymond. It wasn't long before he and Raymond had made a lot of headway on things.

The steady toil sat well with Daniel. His body dropped a few pounds of padding that he'd put on over the years. His muscles corded up again like when he was younger. His eyes sparkled like creek rocks with the sun on them. He whistled a tune from time to time as he labored. He had reason again to get up in the morning, and he thanked the Lord Jesus every day.

Truly the Lord had given him a new start. If not for the fact that he still didn't know what had happened to Ed, he might have said his life had reached a time without grief. Back in July, the Air

Force had sent him a telegram saying Ed was missing in action in the Pacific theater. His plane had probably gone down over Japan in the last days of the fighting, and the U.S. government would do everything they could to find him. Daniel figured he was dead. No reason to hold out too much hope. But he had fought in a war too and knew how things sometimes fell out. A man might end up in a prison camp somewhere and not turn up for a long time. Of course, since the war had ended, the soldiers had scouted through all the Japanese prison camps. If Ed was there, he would have shown up by now.

Daniel fought hard to keep his head up about Ed's situation. Men died in wars, no two ways about it. If not for the grace of the good Lord, he would have died before Ed even drew breath. At least Ed had died fighting for a right cause. That gave Daniel some comfort, and he tried to stay strong for Deidre and Raymond.

On the last Saturday of October, on a day covered in blue sky, warm sun and the smell of falling leaves, Daniel started out early cutting down a stretch of trees and underbrush that had grown up over the path that led from Slick Rock Creek to the house. Raymond had headed down to Blue Springs to bring back some canned goods for their food supply and some coal for the stove. By midmorning Daniel had made some good progress on the trail, clearing almost twenty feet. Thirsty, he took a minute, headed to the creek and dipped his hand into the cool stream. The water chilled his lips. He pulled a cloth from his overalls and wiped his brow. Taking off his hat, he bent to the water again, this time on his knees, his face in the creek. The sun warmed his back. A sense of pleasure seeped into Daniel. He took a long drink. Something moved on the other side of the creek. He heard a *click*.

Daniel slowly raised his head. His knees bent under his chest, ready to spring. He saw Ben Clack about twenty feet away, Slick Rock Creek between them. Clack held a shotgun aimed his way. Bluey stood by Clack, a second gun equally at the ready.

"Hold her steady there," said Clack.

Calmly, Daniel stood and raised his hands.

"Long time no see," said Bluey.

Daniel eyed the two men. "I thought you had passed on," he said to Bluey.

"Reckon not," said Bluey. "Just took off from these parts for a time, that's all."

Daniel sized up the situation and decided he couldn't make a run for it. One of the two might miss, but probably not both. Best to bide his time and see what Clack wanted.

"I hear you been throwin' rocks," Daniel said, tilting his head at Clack.

"What makes you so sure it was me?" asked Clack.

"A wild guess, I reckon."

Clack chuckled. "I always said you was smart. Got to give you that."

Daniel studied Clack hard. He didn't seem drunk, no slurred words. If not drunk, then maybe he had no shooting in his head. "You ain't out for no Saturday stroll," he said. "So state your business."

Clack glanced around the clearing. "You doing a lot of hard work here. All by your lonesome?"

"Got Raymond, but he ain't here."

"I heard you come into some good fortune. Gant giving you back some of the land."

"The good Lord has smiled on me, I reckon."

Clack spat a stream of tobacco juice into the creek. "I'm here about the Mingling," he said. "Didn't figure you to take to it. Thought you might fight it as hard as me."

Daniel nodded. "I did at the first. Saw no reason to make truce with your kind. We got too much bad blood between us. Lot of hard feelings, shootings, Sol's injuries, Abby's husband dead, your brother Topper. But then . . . I don't know, the Lord got hold of me and I changed my mind. The Mingling seems like the right thing now. Time to leave the fighting behind, get on with living."

Clack raised his shotgun a notch. "That ain't what I wanna hear," he said. "I expect you to have some sense about this. Help me break this thing up, get those babies back to their rightful families."

Daniel tensed. "I ain't gone throw in with you if that's what you're thinking. What good would that do? Me and you together starting the feud again?"

"The feud never ended!" shouted Clack, his face turning red. "That's where you all got it wrong. The feud don't end until I say it ends!"

Daniel glanced around, tried to figure a way out of the standoff. He spotted the stack of brush he had built from his cuttings. Maybe if he made a dive for that, rolled behind it, away from the shotguns.

"I've left the bad blood behind," Daniel said. "Made a promise to the Lord and my sister. I ain't gone take up against you again. Not unless you give me new cause."

Clack glanced at Bluey. Bluey pulled a bottle from his overalls, handed it to Clack. Clack took a long drink. Daniel eased half a step toward the stack of brush. Clack handed the bottle back to Bluey and lifted his shotgun higher.

"You sound like you gone and got religion on me. That what you're sayin'?"

"I ain't ashamed to admit it. I have come to the Lord. Come back, to say it right. You can too if you want."

Clack spat again. "You've turned loony on me. Thinkin' I'm about to trust in Jesus. What's Jesus ever done for me?"

"Every man has to figure that out on his own. But I can tell you the Lord will take you if you want to get your heart right. I believe that."

Clack turned to Bluey. "Daniel Porter sounds like a preacher," he said. "Preacher Porter. What a sorry day this is."

Daniel shook his head. "I ain't no preacher, but I'm gone stand for the Lord whenever I can." Daniel eased closer to the brush. "I don't know what all happened to you. What hurts your pa put on you; what hard things have made up your life. All I know is that the Lord will help us get through—"

Clack raised his shotgun, slid a finger on the trigger, cutting off Daniel's words. "How much work you suppose a man might get done if he gets shot in one of his knees?" he asked Bluey.

Bluey chuckled. "Not much I reckon. Hard to do much work on a pair of crutches."

"You sure you won't throw in with me?" Clack addressed Daniel again. "Leave all this Jesus stuff behind?"

"I reckon not," said Daniel, his legs poised to jump.

Clack raised the shotgun to his shoulder, his eye lined up with the barrel.

A shot rang out. The water at Clack's feet splashed.

"Hold steady right there!" someone shouted from the ridge behind Clack. "You move and I'll shoot you dead."

Daniel's heart notched up, and he searched the woods for the man behind the voice. Clack took a quick step toward him.

A second shot hit near the toe of Clack's brogans. "That is my last warning!" shouted the man in the woods.

"Who are you?" yelled Clack. He turned and searched the woods above them.

"Don't you mind about that. Just lower that weapon and move away from the creek."

Clack looked at Bluey, who was stepping back from the creek. Clack gritted his teeth.

"I said move away!" the man shouted again.

Clack eyed Daniel. "I gave you your last chance," he growled. "Now it's on your head too."

Daniel waved him off. "Get on out of here, Ben," he said. "Leave me be."

After a last look toward the ridge, Clack lowered his weapon and stomped away, Bluey at his heels. For several seconds Daniel listened to them leaving. Then, his palms clammy, he looked up. There, headed down the ridge, he saw a man he thought he'd never see again. His eyes watered and he brushed them clear. Then he started running, his brogans splashing across Slick Rock Creek, his knees churning as fast as his fifty-three years allowed.

"Ed!" he shouted. "You sorry rascal, where you been?"

Ed reached him in seconds, his face split wide open with a grin. "I been mending!" he answered, in Daniel's arms now. The two of them embraced under a tall oak tree, their bear hug tight enough to cut the wind off most normal folks.

"Mending?" Daniel stepped back for just a second to look at his son, his eyes still wide as if seeing a ghost. Ed had almost no skin on his bones, and his cheeks looked hollow and pale. A scar as wide as a hoe handle ran down the left side of his cheek and into his neck. He held a military pistol in his right hand.

Ed held up his left arm. His hand was missing. "Mending," he said again. "In a hospital over in the Philippines."

Daniel hugged him again. Tears showed up in his eyes once more, and this time he didn't brush them away. His whole body shook—with joy, but also with sorrow at what his son had suffered. Only a man who had fought in a war could understand the horror a body could see, the awful hurts that one human could put on another. God only knew what Ed had endured. Daniel squeezed him as if he feared he might disappear again if he ever let go, as if only his hug could keep him steady in this spot.

"I'm okay, Pa," whispered Ed. "I'm home again."

Daniel sobbed into his son's shoulder. "Why didn't you tell us?" he said. "Let us know you were alive?"

"I was sick for a long time," said Ed. "For a while they didn't know who I was."

"We thought . . . we thought . . ."

Ed patted his back. "I know, Pa. I know what you all thought."

Daniel's tears eased, and after a few more seconds he stepped back and stared at Ed once more. "Why didn't you let us know?" he asked again.

Ed studied his shoes. "I didn't want you to worry until I knew whether or not I'd make it," he explained. "No reason to get your hopes up and then have me pass on and let you down."

"But I could have come to you," Daniel said.

"Not likely. This was best. I'm better now. I'm home, so let's leave it at that."

Daniel nodded. Maybe Ed was right. Either way, he was home. Thanks be to the Lord, he was alive and home.

"You gave me a start there," Daniel said. "Shooting like you did."

"You looked like you could use the help."

Daniel eyed Ed's pistol. "Glad you kept that."

"A man always needs a trusty weapon."

"Up here anyway, so long as Ben Clack is still kicking."

Ed put the gun in the waist of his pants, then bent down to the creek and took a drink.

"How'd you know where to find me?" Daniel asked.

Ed stood again. "I went by the post office. Jensen told me about Gant, your job with him. Rest was easy."

"You go by to see your ma?"

"No, figured to see you first. Didn't want to shake her up."

Daniel hugged him again. "You are a sight for sore eyes."

"You got some coffee?"

Daniel laughed and stepped back. "You can bet on that. Come on up to the house. Get you coffee, then put your sorry self to work. Got a lot to do around here."

The two men headed up the trail. "You figuring on my laboring with you?" asked Ed.

"I thought you might could help," said Daniel. "Of course you always were pretty lazy. Won't count on you too much."

"I can outwork you any day," said Ed. "With one hand too."

Daniel glanced at Ed's stump. "You figure on telling me about that?"

Ed shrugged. "Someday maybe."

Daniel nodded with understanding. Some things a man needed to keep to himself. To say it out loud gave it too much life again. No reason to do that with some memories. Better to keep them boxed in like a rabid dog, boxed in until you could let them go forever. Of course memories didn't always stay boxed. Sometimes they got out in places and at times a body didn't expect. He knew that better than most. Figured Ed might learn it too one day.

"Your coffee any better than it used to be?" asked Ed.

"Good enough for the likes of you, that's for sure."

They reached the house and stepped inside. Daniel poured his son a cup of coffee. Sitting down across from him, he took a deep breath. No matter what happened now, he could face it fine. His boy who was lost was home again.

CHAPTER
TEN

I t didn't take Steve long to find a place to stay or to find a job. A boardinghouse on Jefferson Lane became his residence, and one of the three other young men who lived there told him about a store that needed help selling clothes to the students who attended the state university not far from there.

Taking care to dress well and speak clearly, Steve landed the job and settled in pretty fast to his work at the store and also his new residence. The fall days passed quickly. Steve spent most of his time working as much as the store owner would allow, from opening to closing on many days. At first he mostly just unpacked boxes and laid out the clothes for display, the suits on hangers and rods, the shirts and slacks and other items put out neatly for customers to sort through and find what they needed. After about a month, his boss, a man by the name of Stone, sent him to the floor to try his hand at selling. Working hard to keep his mountain ways hidden, Steve took quickly to dealing with people. Politeness went a long way, he soon realized, and his ma had taught him that real well. Plus, he looked people straight in the eye when he talked to them about a suit or a pair of pants, and those who wanted to buy something seemed to like that.

To his surprise he also found out pretty fast that his grammar and speech weren't as rough as he had imagined. Although he didn't have a lot of official schooling, the lessons his ma had taught him had prepared him fine for the big city. He read well and did his numbers as sharp as anybody else in the store, and that gave him confidence he could make it in this place.

Within a few weeks of going on the floor, he had learned all kinds of selling tips, how to steer the folks toward the more expensive suits, how to tell who had money and who didn't, how to move people from a no to a yes. He learned if a man brought a woman with him, the woman usually made the decision about whether to buy or not and what suit to purchase if they did. All in all, he deemed his early weeks on the job a success. He made enough money to keep up his food and rent, pay off the new suit he'd bought and save a few dollars to boot.

On the last Saturday evening before Christmas, he finished up at the store about six, told Mr. Stone he'd see him on Monday and headed out for the twenty-minute walk back to the boardinghouse. The sun hung low and looked tired. Everything was quiet. Steve fingered the wad of dollars in his pants pocket. It felt good to know he'd made it so far on his own. He didn't need to depend on anybody else—not his ma, not Jim, no one.

Steve passed a church, its tall steeple towering over him. He studied the church for a few seconds. It seemed so fancy—a tall white steeple, smooth red bricks, a row of columns in the front. What kind of church could afford such a fine meetinghouse? Nothing like any back in Blue Springs, that was for sure.

A touch of guilt fell on Steve. He hadn't attended church since moving to Raleigh. Yeah, he had his reasons. The churches here were too high and mighty for one thing. Plus, because he worked six days a week, he needed Sunday to rest and to look for the Waterburys. For several weeks he'd asked all the neighbors around their old house if they knew what had happened to them. Sadly, no one knew anything.

Reaching the boardinghouse, Steve moved up the wood steps. Four rockers sat on the front porch, all of them empty in the winter chill. A car drove by on the street, and a dog barked somewhere in the distance. Steve stopped at the sound and faced the street again. A nudge of loneliness ran through him. Even if he'd done well so far at work, he had to admit that his nights often turned melancholy. With no family nearby, he had nobody around to share his successes.

Steve glanced up and down the street, saw a man and woman walking away from him, their hands interlocked. Tall leafless oak trees framed them as they strode around a corner and out of sight. Steve put his hands in his pockets. Lots of women shopped at his store, many of them single. But most came in with boyfriends or were shopping for one. He hadn't found much chance to meet anybody he might actually talk to.

He knew what his ma would tell him. "Go to church," she'd say. "Find some girls there, good girls."

Steve grinned. His ma had a one-track mind on such things. In Raleigh, though, he had other options. His boss had suggested he try a couple of dancing clubs that had sprung up since the war ended. Stone said lots of men and women met at the clubs, nothing wrong with them at all.

So far Steve hadn't tried the churches or the clubs. The churches were too fancy and the clubs cost money, so he didn't like either one of those options. He thought of Claire, the blonde from the train, and wondered again if she had stolen his money. What kind of woman would do that? Not one from his experience, that was for sure. A Clack woman maybe? But no, not even one of them would have the boldness to take a man's money.

He thought a lot about searching for Claire, only he didn't know what he'd say if he ever found her. "Hello, did you steal my money?" Or "Hello, remember me? I'm the country hick from the highlands." No, he couldn't do that. So he didn't try looking for her, although he still felt her lips on his cheek from time to time, the way her blue eyes looked into his. When those memories returned, his heart fluttered like he'd swallowed a handful of duck feathers, and he wondered if love felt like that. Did it leave you fighting to get your breath, all shaky inside? He didn't know, but he liked it when the feeling came. He hoped that someday, some way, he'd run into Claire again.

Hearing a door open, Steve swung around. A fellow about his size and no more than three or four years older stood in the doorway of the boardinghouse, on his way out. Something about the man looked familiar to Steve, though he couldn't place what. The man eyed Steve as if judging a horse he might want to buy. Steve started to move past him, but the man spoke before he could.

"You Steve Waterbury?" he asked.

Steve inspected the man. Neat gray slacks and blue shirt, brown shoes, hair slicked back in a short brown wave. "Who wants to know?"

The man nodded toward the rocking chairs. "Can we talk a minute?"

Steve's eyes narrowed. "It's a touch cold to sit out here, don't you think?"

"This won't take long."

Steve pulled his coat up some. Why not? He didn't have anything else to do. Besides, he was curious.

They took seats in the rockers. The man shifted to face Steve. Then, his hands on his knees, he stared at the floor. "I know you're Waterbury," said the man. "No reason for you to deny it."

"Okay," said Steve. "But who are you?"

"Allen Baldwin. That mean anything to you?"

"Should it?"

"Nope, not at all."

Baldwin pulled out a cigarette, held it without lighting up. "I hear you've been looking for Beaufort James Waterbury and his wife."

"That's right," Steve said, striving to stay at ease. "What's that got to do with you?"

"What if I told you I knew where you could find them?"

"I'd ask you to tell me what you knew."

Baldwin glanced at Steve, and Steve again sensed something familiar, something about the way he carried himself, the cut of his face, tone in his voice. What was it?

"Why are you trying to find them?" asked Baldwin.

"That's my business," said Steve.

Baldwin nodded. "I guess it is. But I can't tell you anything else until you answer the question."

"Folks where I come from would call you a mighty nosy man," said Steve.

Baldwin smiled. "Nosy sometimes keeps a man out of trouble."

"Or gets him into it."

Baldwin lit the cigarette and stuck it in his mouth. Steve wasn't sure he wanted to tell him anything else until he knew more. "You know Mr. and Mrs. Waterbury?"

Baldwin weighed the question as if answering it might reveal some world-endangering secret. "I know them," he finally said. "They sent me to find you."

Steve moved to the edge of his rocker. "They're still in Raleigh, then?"

"Oh yes, still in Raleigh."

"How did you find me?"

Baldwin pulled from the cigarette. "That was easy," he said. "A former neighbor of the Waterburys called them, told them a young man had showed up at their old house, that he had spent a lot of time visiting in the neighborhood trying to find them. They sent me to talk to that neighbor. He said you had recently come to town, were claiming to be their grandson."

"That didn't tell you where I was, even if I was still in town."

Baldwin flicked ashes into the yard. "You came around every Sunday for a while. On foot. That says you were in town and close by. I started asking around, figured you were in a boardinghouse somewhere, probably one for single men. A married man with children doesn't spend every Sunday looking for his grandfolks."

"You think you're pretty smart, don't you?"

Baldwin shook his head. "Not smart, just logical."

"So you tracked me down. I'm still wondering why."

Baldwin stared at the porch again. Steve noticed it then, the way he dropped his head, the way his eyes didn't want to meet his. His heart notched up at least two paces. But then he told himself that he was wrong, no way could Baldwin be—

"Mr. Waterbury is ill," Baldwin said, interrupting Steve's suspicions. "Right close to dying."

"He sent you for me?"

"Not him. Mrs. Waterbury. She wants to see you, wants you to see him."

Steve gripped his chair and his fingers turned white. "Why now?" he asked. "After all these weeks? They don't even know me."

Baldwin shrugged. "I guess you'll have to ask her that. It's not for me to say. But from what I know, the old man wouldn't let her come to you any earlier. 'Course now he's too sick to do anything about it."

Steve's jaw tensed. What sense did this make? A stranger suddenly showing up to take him to his grandparents? Something about it made him angry, the realization that Mr. and Mrs. Waterbury had known about his coming to Raleigh all along but had just now chosen to contact him. Why should he go at their beck and call? He started to tell Baldwin to leave him alone, to tell him to get off the porch and give him some time to think. At least make them wait a few days, he figured. After all, he wasn't a boy anymore, someone who had to obey when a grown-up snapped his fingers. Yet he did want to see them, to talk to the people who had raised up his pa. He rocked a couple of times, weighing what to do.

"What's wrong with Mr. Waterbury?" Steve finally asked.

Baldwin pulled from his cigarette again. "He's got heart problems," he said. "Not long for this world from what I can see."

Steve noted Baldwin's sadness, and his suspicions reared up again. "What's all this to you? You work for Mr. and Mrs. Waterbury?"

Baldwin flicked his ashes, stubbed out the cigarette and threw the butt into the yard. "Yeah, I work for them."

Steve studied for another few seconds. "What do they want from me?" he asked. "I don't have much money."

Baldwin grunted. "I don't know what they want. Maybe it's just that an old woman wants her husband to see his grandson before he dies. Is that too bad a motive?"

"They've ignored me and my family for a long time. All my life, in fact. Bet I haven't seen them more than ten times since the day I was born. Guess I just find it hard to swallow that all of a sudden they feel the need for my company."

Baldwin stood and faced Steve. "Look," he said, his hands reaching for another cigarette. "If you don't want to come, just tell me. I'll take back the message. I can understand how you're feeling, that they should've come to you as soon as they knew you were here. But sometimes people can't do everything they want, everything they should. If you haven't learned that already, you probably will soon. Sometimes things don't fall the way you want them to fall, don't give us all the choices we'd like. So just tell me what you want me to do, and I'll relay it back and won't bother you anymore."

Steve rocked, his eyes never leaving Baldwin. He felt it for certain now, something so plain he should have known it the instant he spotted Baldwin on the porch. But, as certain as he was, he had to know for sure before he went anywhere.

"I'm going to ask you one more time," Steve said. "And I expect you to give me an honest answer. It's the least you can do given the way you've showed up here, no warning or anything."

Baldwin's cigarette stilled between his lips.

"Who are you?" asked Steve. "What's your connection to me and the Waterburys?"

Baldwin took the cigarette out of his mouth and stared at Steve with a stonelike gaze. "You're bringing up things that don't need to get raised."

"They do for me. It's one of the reasons, maybe the main one, I moved to Raleigh. It's why I've tried so hard to find the Waterburys. I want to know about my pa, his life here, what made him do the things he did."

"That's important to you? Learning about your pa?"

"I hardly knew him," Steve said. "He didn't stay around much. I've always felt, you know, like I missed something, still miss it, some part of me that I have to fill up or . . ."

"Or you'll never quite be satisfied," Baldwin finished for him. "Content and all."

Steve nodded. Baldwin had it right. Until he knew more about his pa, he would always feel empty somehow, not complete.

"You sure you want to hear this?" Baldwin said.

"I'm sure."

"It might make you hurt, more than you want or need."

"I'm a grown man. I can deal with anything you got to say."

Baldwin shook his head as if resigned to doing something he didn't want to do. Steve held his breath. Baldwin threw a leg over the porch railing and, in a nonchalant kind of way, said, "I was born in 1922. My ma's name was Mary Beth, my pa's, Stephen. Truth is, I'm your half brother, eldest child of Stephen James Waterbury."

CHAPTER
ELEVEN

January rolled in snowy and cold, the days short and weak. On the second Saturday morning of that month, Abby walked with Sam down to the general store so she could meet up with Daisy Clack to exchange their babies for the next two days. She had lived in a high state of agitation over the last few months, her spirit uneasy because of her constant fear of Ben Clack and her steady worry over Steve. She had spent more time on her knees praying in the last several weeks than she could ever remember. If the good Lord didn't help her through this, then nothing would.

As agreed, Daisy showed up at about ten with Rose Francis. The two women embraced, then exchanged their babies. Though she wanted to leave immediately and spend the rest of the day with her little girl, Abby held herself back. Because Daisy would be caring for her child for the next three years, she needed to know her better. Besides that, they both had Ben Clack as an enemy now, and there's nothing like a common danger to draw two people together.

She led Daisy to a table in the back of the store, where they served coffee and soda drinks. The two women sat down, their babies in their laps.

"I hope you're well," Abby said.

"I'm percolating pretty good," said Daisy. "And you?"

"Not bad. A few worries here and there."

"Old Ben is still on the loose," said Daisy. Abby nodded. Clack had thrown a rock through Daisy's window too. "You think his trial will come up soon?"

"Probably not until summer. Judges don't like coming up here in the cold."

"Reckon not."

"Ben seems quiet for now," said Abby, her tone hopeful.

"He lays low in the ice and snow," Daisy said, dashing Abby's optimism. "Like the judges."

Abby pulled her coat tighter. "If cold is what it takes, I hope we get a long winter."

Daisy laughed. Abby got them both a cup of coffee. She studied Daisy as she sipped the warm liquid. Like all Clacks, she had brown eyes, hollow cheeks and little flesh on her bones. She was only twenty years old. Her front teeth had a gap in the middle. Typical of most highlanders in her age group, she had little real education.

"Sam is getting big," Abby said, indicating Daisy's baby, now settled into his true mama's arms.

"Rose Francis too," said Daisy. "Though she's a slight child by nature."

Abby stared at her daughter, so still against her chest. A brown blanket wrapped around her shoulders. Her eyes were closed.

"She don't cry much," Daisy continued. "Stays up all day and sleeps all night. Into everything when she's awake."

"You reading her those books I gave you?"

Daisy glanced away for a second. "I do the best I can," she said. "You know I don't do too fine with reading."

Abby touched the younger woman's hand. "I'm not trying to make you feel bad," she said. "Just want my baby to hear words early. You know how much stock I put in education."

Daisy nodded. "I know. You're about the smartest woman in these parts, everybody says it."

"I'm not sure about that," said Abby. "But I do appreciate it when you read to my girl."

"I said I would do it," said Daisy. "So I'm keeping my word."

"And I'll teach your boy. That's my promise to you."

Daisy kissed Sam. "He'll be a smart man someday," she said. "Have a chance to become somebody real important."

Abby smiled. "He's a good baby. He seems to like the night more than the morning."

"That's me for sure," said Daisy. "Love it after dark and hate it when the sun comes up." The two women laughed. "Your girl is starting to favor her pa. All except her eyes. Her eyes are all yours."

Abby nodded. Daisy had it right about the eyes. "How's Eugenia?" Abby asked, thinking of the woman who had first talked to her about the Mingling. "Her health any better?"

"The winter has gone hard on her. Not as young as she once was."

"None of us are," said Abby.

Daisy drank her coffee. "Daniel getting much labor done this winter?"

"Some. Weather shuts down logging, though."

"I hear you all are pitching in to buy up the land."

"Me and Jim, Elsa and Preacher Tuttle. Ed and Raymond too, Daniel's boys. Got about seventy-five acres now, counting the fifty Gant gave Daniel at the start."

"You must be proud."

"We are."

Daisy took a heavy breath. Abby could see she had something on her mind. But, like all highlanders, she refused to prod. A body would speak what she wanted to speak. No use her pushing anything. They sipped from their coffee. Abby wondered how much money the Clacks had these days. In times past they owned most everything. But most of their dollars had come from whiskey making back during Prohibition. With all that long past, had any of them saved any money? Found any new ways to make any?

"You coming to church tomorrow?" she asked Daisy.

"Possible. Wait and see I reckon."

Abby ran her fingers over Rose Francis's brow. "If I don't see you there, I'll meet you here again at five."

Daisy and Abby hugged again and then Daisy left. Abby picked up some flour and sugar from a shelf and walked to the counter to pay up. She heard the door open and looked up to see Jensen, the postman, headed her way.

"Got this for you," he said, holding out an envelope. "Save me a few steps out to your place."

Abby took the envelope and held it up to the light that hung from the ceiling.

"Looks like it came from Raleigh," said Jensen. "Your boy Steve I reckon."

Abby started to tell him to mind his business but she knew it wouldn't do any good. Jensen took it as his right as postman to know people's affairs.

"Thank you," she said.

Jensen waited as if expecting her to open it and read it to him, but when he saw she didn't plan to do it, he turned and left the store.

Envelope in hand, Abby sat back down with Rose Francis. She had heard from Steve only twice since he left, both times by letter. When he'd written her that he had to work the day before and after Christmas and so couldn't come home for the holiday, she had fallen into a deep sadness for a few days, her heart low that her boy had truly moved away for good. In his letters he'd said little she could truly get a handle on, telling her little more than that he'd found a job selling clothes and had settled in at a boardinghouse. She'd written him at least ten times, each time asking for more details, more information. What about Mr. and Mrs. Waterbury? How were they? How had they received him? So far, Steve had said nothing about them. What did that mean?

Now, her hands shaking, Abby ripped the envelope open and eagerly read the one-page note.

Ma,

I'm fine. Guess what? I'm planning to take a new job. You'll never guess what I'm going to do. I'm going to work with Mr. and

Mrs. Waterbury. That's right. I didn't find them at first. But now I have. Mr. Waterbury is sick. Mrs. Waterbury wants me to help with their business. Says if it goes well, I can make a lot of money real fast. I think she's right. Besides, I'll be the boss, or I should say one of the bosses. Won't have to work for somebody else, not like at the store. One thing about the store, though, I got some good new clothes there—suit, shirt, shoes, tie, everything I needed. Now I'm ready for my new job. I keep the clothes real neat, wash the shirt every couple of days. I'm going to stay at the boarding house for now. Three other men about my age live here too. Don't worry, I'm saving my money and staying out of trouble. I'll make you proud, you'll see. Say hello to all, Jim most.

Love,
Steve

Abby read the letter a second time. A hundred questions rose up in her head. What did he mean about not finding the Waterburys? She knew the address he had was correct. And what kind of business were they in? Why didn't he tell her? Why wasn't he staying with them? He was family. Could he make any money laboring for them?

Abby read the letter yet again, and this time it settled her some. At least he had a roof over his head and a job where he earned enough money to eat. She leaned back and faced Rose Francis.

"I don't know how I'm going to do this," she whispered. "Not go crazy worrying about my children."

Rose Francis didn't respond. Abby touched her nose. "I'll end up going loony for sure," she said. "If it's not Jim at war, it's Steve all alone in a big town. And who knows what you'll do when you grow up. You plan on causing me anxiousness too?"

Rose Francis puckered her lips as if to answer but made no sound. Abby tucked Steve's letter into her coat pocket. A ma never knew the future for her children. Maybe that was the only way she survived.

CHAPTER
TWELVE

Steve hurried into the Waterbury house behind Allen at just past dark on the last Sunday of March on a day rainy enough to turn most of Raleigh's streets into rivers. Both men slumped some, and their shoes were caked with mud. Steve took off his shoes as they entered to avoid tracking mud onto Mrs. Waterbury's entry hall rug. Allen kept his shoes on.

Moving through the hallway, they both did what they did at the end of almost every day. They walked to the back room of the house to check on Mr. and Mrs. Waterbury. Again, Steve followed Allen. Although he'd been visiting his grandparents for three months now, he still felt like an outsider most of the time. And, in spite of the fact that he and Allen were half brothers and worked together nearly every day, he still didn't feel comfortable around him. Allen treated him okay, yet Steve still sensed a barrier between them, like Allen distrusted him, like he thought Steve might throw a punch at him at any second. Steve tried to talk to him some, but Allen revealed little, only that his mama had died in 1938 from some kind of flu and that he had no other siblings. He had lived with the Waterburys since his mama's death, gradually taking over more and more of the business as Mr. Waterbury's health failed.

Steve passed off Allen's quiet as the result of a normal rivalry between two brothers and tried to ease his mind by staying out of his way.

They found the Waterburys in their usual spots—Mr. Waterbury in bed, his milky eyes staring at the ceiling, with Mrs. Waterbury beside him, her eyes red from lack of sleep.

The room depressed Steve. It had only one window, and a heavy drape covered it. Maybe it was the mountain still in him. But something about stale air made his stomach queasy.

Allen took a seat by Mrs. Waterbury. As usual, Steve stood. He didn't feel comfortable enough yet to relax in a chair with the Waterburys. Mr. Waterbury coughed and closed his eyes. He seemed more shrunken today, and his breathing took longer per draw. Steve glanced at his grandmother. She wore a gray robe, tattered at the sleeves. Her hair fell in gray strings around her shoulders. She looked ancient.

"Your day go well?" she asked Allen.

He nodded but said nothing.

She pointed to Mr. Waterbury. "The doctor came earlier," she said. "Not much more we can do."

Allen stayed quiet.

"The doctor says it's a matter of days. His heart is worn out."

"He has lived a long time," said Allen.

"Close to seventy years," agreed Mrs. Waterbury.

Silence came again. Steve wanted to leave. He didn't belong here. In spite of his blood connection, these people were strangers, his time with them too short to hold much strength. What right did he have to sit in on such a moment? A man ought to die with people he knew around him, not in front of someone he really didn't know or love. Steve thought back over the last few weeks, to what he had learned about his kin.

Mr. and Mrs. Waterbury owned close to twenty rental houses in some of the roughest parts of Raleigh. Fifteen of the houses sat in the colored section of town. None of the houses amounted to much. Most consisted of about four main rooms, shotgun style, frame dwellings with a small porch, a front room, a kitchen and two bedrooms. Many had some bad places in the roof, so that when it rained like today, the tenants had to bring out buckets to catch the water that dripped through.

Yet the Waterburys charged rents that most of their tenants had trouble paying. That was why they had brought Steve into the picture. He and Allen watched after the houses, not so much to make repairs, because nobody did much of that unless absolutely necessary, but to make sure that people paid their rent.

A lot of the folks didn't, at least on a timely basis. So, as Mr. Waterbury took sick, his business had fallen on hard times. That was why he and his wife had moved from the finer place Steve had visited when he first came to Raleigh to this older, much smaller house.

Steve recalled his first thoughts when Mrs. Waterbury told him they were landlords and asked him to work with them. Pictures of fine homes with green lawns rushed to his mind, homes built in the new ways—electrical work in all the rooms, plumbing in the bathroom and kitchen, maybe even a garage for a car. He saw himself overseeing the upkeep of these homes, maybe even building some from scratch. The idea thrilled him. Help people find a good house for their families, a place where the kids could grow up happy and secure. Give kids what he never had in his boyhood.

To his discomfort, he found out that the Waterbury houses weren't exactly what he pictured. But by the time he discovered that fact, he'd already agreed to their offer of a job. Now he felt unable to back out, that he was obliged to work for them.

He tried to figure a way to leave the room, the death room as he saw it, the room where in a few short days Mr. Beaufort James Waterbury would drop off to glory. Or would he? Steve knew that Mr. and Mrs. Waterbury claimed the Methodist as their church, though he hadn't seen them pay much attention to it. Did they really believe in Jesus if they never showed up at the Lord's house? He considered his own situation. Since moving to Raleigh, he hadn't gone to church either. Did that mean he didn't trust the Lord anymore? He hadn't prayed in a long time. What did that mean?

He wiped his hands on his pants, saw the mud spattered on his socks. What an awful day. Slogging around on unpaved streets trying to collect money from poor black people who could barely make ends meet. What kind of life was this? Better than the one he had led in Blue Springs? One that would please the Lord?

He thought of his ma. He hadn't written her as often as he should, hadn't answered most of the letters she sent. But what could he say without telling too much?

He wondered about Jim. From what his ma said, Jim and Rebecca were doing well, their baby, Porter, too. Well, Jim had it easy, a wife and family, a reason to go to work every morning. He wasn't striving all by himself to make a go of it in a big city that didn't care a whit about a man one way or the other. Succeed or fail, live or die, happy or sad, a city like Raleigh didn't give two hoots about what happened to anybody.

Steve took a deep breath, recognizing the reasons for his melancholy. Loneliness, failure, resentment, like somebody who owed him something hadn't paid up. He knew he had no right to feel that way. Nobody owed him anything. Then why couldn't he stop thinking such sour thoughts?

Mr. Waterbury suddenly jerked, pulling Steve back to the present moment. Waterbury raised up on his pillows and beckoned to his wife with a single wobbly finger. She moved to him and sat down. Waterbury looked past her to Allen, then over to Steve.

"Come here, boy," he whispered.

Steve hoped he was calling Allen but then saw he meant him. Slowly, he moved to the bed. Waterbury cleared his throat, laid a hand on Steve's forearm.

"I didn't want you to come here," Waterbury rasped. "Not my choice to go find you."

Steve nodded. Mrs. Waterbury had sent for him against her husband's wishes.

"I tried to keep your pa's bad deeds a secret from your family," Waterbury continued. "No reason to pull everybody into one man's mistakes, bring his shame on them."

Steve lowered his eyes. He knew the tale. His pa had gotten a girl in trouble. Mr. Waterbury had tried to make him marry the girl, but her ma and pa didn't want him for a son-in-law.

Unable to face the shame of it all, Mr. Waterbury had sent Stephen to Boone to make it on his own. That was where he had met Abby, married her, sired his two sons, Jim and Steve.

"That's why we didn't see more of you boys over the years," said Mrs. Waterbury, helping her sick husband say what needed to get said. "Figured the secret would leak out if you came here too often, if we spent much time with you in Boone."

"I know," said Steve. "You already told me."

Mr. Waterbury patted his hands. "But then, after all those years, you showed up looking for us. I wanted to leave you alone, figured you'd stay a few weeks then go back to the mountains. But you took a job, looked to stay awhile. I said let it go some longer. But"—he glanced at his wife—"she thought otherwise."

Steve looked at Mrs. Waterbury. She dabbed at her eyes. "I didn't want anything to happen," she said to her husband. "Without . . . without him seeing you."

"I'm glad she went against me," said Mr. Waterbury to Steve. "Now that I've seen you, had a chance to be with you every day. You're a fine young man, no doubt about that. A hard worker and smart too."

Steve patted his hand. "I'm doing my best," he said.

"I know," said Waterbury, "and it pleases me." Mr. Waterbury faced Allen now. "Sorry my son took advantage of your mama," he said to him. "He didn't always live by the straight and narrow. Guess I didn't raise him good enough. I'm sorry for that."

"That was a long time ago," Allen said. "No reason to worry about it anymore."

Waterbury closed his eyes. When he spoke again, his voice had become a whisper. "I'm going soon," he said. "But before I go, I got to do one more thing." He licked his lips. "I want Steve to take over our business."

Allen sat up straighter, and Steve saw his fists tighten into balls.

"I'm giving him full authority to handle all my affairs," continued Waterbury. "I wrote it out with a lawyer this morning."

Steve's eyes widened. Allen glanced at him, his face a storm.

Steve opened his mouth to protest, but Waterbury held up a hand to stop him.

"No," he said. "I won't accept any argument. You are my choice. You carry the family name. Now Allen here"—he turned to his other grandson—"he's stayed true to us and we love him. But he . . . well, he's not legitimate. I hate to say it that way but it's true. So . . ." He coughed and his body shook. "So I have no choice in this." He faced his wife, and his voice found a final burst of strength. "I expect Steve to consult with Allen in all important matters. But the final authority rests in Steve's hands. That's the way it has to be." He then sank deeper into his pillows, obviously spent from the effort of speaking.

Steve faced Allen. "I don't want this," he said. "Won't take it."

"You got to take it," Allen said. "It's what he's set up, legal and everything. None of us have any choice."

Steve looked at Mrs. Waterbury. She threw up her hands in defeat. "I tried to talk to him," she said. "He made up his mind."

"Are you going to hold this against me?" Steve asked his half brother.

"That shouldn't matter to you," said Allen. "You got what you wanted when you showed up here."

"This isn't what I wanted."

Allen grunted at that.

"You've got to believe me," insisted Steve. "I had no clue about any of this. I just wanted to know my pa's folks better. Then when you came to me and I met them, well, I just did what I could to help, nothing more or less. How's that my fault?"

"Fault or not, the business is yours now, all of it. You're the true son." Allen said the last words as if spitting out a bad piece of beef.

Steve truly didn't want this. Yet was this what the Lord wanted for him? Was this why he had moved to Raleigh? His ma always said the Lord wanted to guide folks, wanted to give them direction. But he hadn't done any church-going in a long time. Fact was, he hadn't carried hardly any of his religion to the big city. Was that the way a man's faith was? You could pack it up and take it with you like a shirt in a suitcase? Or could you leave it behind like an old pair of shoes you no longer wore? Steve studied the matter for a second, and it suddenly dawned on him that his faith didn't really feel like his own anymore. Mostly it felt like something his ma had handed to him, like a coat for the winter. But now he had shed that coat, not sure if it fit him any longer. Would the Lord guide him if he spent no time in His house? No time in praying? If he wasn't even sure if the faith he'd learned all his life really belonged to him?

"This should go to Allen," he said to Mrs. Waterbury, still unsure of what to do.

"But he says it goes to you," said Allen. "No way to change that."

Steve looked at Mr. Waterbury again. "You sure this is what you want?" he asked.

Waterbury didn't respond. Steve's mind clicked fast. Perhaps this was the right thing. Perhaps he could make things better through this, better for the tenants and for himself too. Perhaps he could move from just renting houses to building them. Lots of people moving into the city these days. A man with some vision could go a long way. Perhaps, if he labored hard enough and thought smart enough, this was just the break he had always wanted. Maybe he could make a name for himself and a pocketful of money at the same time. Allen would get half of it, yeah, that's how it would work. Then he couldn't stay mad at him.

The idea inspired Steve, and he decided why not, he would do what Mr. Waterbury wanted. Anyway, what choice did he have? He turned to Allen. "I want you right beside me," he said. "You know a whole lot more about all this than I do."

Allen hung his head. Steve reached to put a hand on his shoulder, but Allen pulled away.

"You're going to help me, aren't you?" Steve asked.

Allen faced him, his eyes stern. "Seems you don't need my help. Seems you got everything pretty well under control all by yourself."

Steve started to protest again but knew it wouldn't do any good. A man had to make his choices, one way or the other, and what another man said made little difference. If Allen wanted to hate him for this, he couldn't do anything to stop him.

"You should never have come here," said Allen. "Not your place."

Steve saw the anger in his brother, and it suddenly hit him that Allen felt toward him the way he sometimes felt toward Jim. Like he had nothing while Jim had everything. Like Mr. and Mrs. Waterbury loved him more than they did Allen. Like he had to prove himself over and over, that no matter what he did, it never quite measured up.

Steve wanted to tell Allen not to let any rivalry come between them, that they needed each other. But he knew he couldn't do that, couldn't do it any more than Jim could come to him and say it. Until a man earned his own worth, it didn't matter what another man said to him about the worth he already had.

Allen stood and moved to Mrs. Waterbury. After quickly hugging her, he chuckled and left the room.

Steve watched him go, then faced Mrs. Waterbury and said, "He'll get over it, won't he?"

Mrs. Waterbury opened her hands, palms up.

Steve nodded. Who knew what anybody would do next.

CHAPTER
THIRTEEN

Ben Clack met Bluey and two other rough-cut men at a switch-back in the road about four miles from Daniel's place at about one o'clock in the morning on the last Friday night of July. The way Ben figured it, the time was now or never. After nearly a year of postponements and delays, the district judge had finally scheduled his trial to start the last week of August. Not even his money could keep the trial away forever.

Bluey and his buddies climbed out of an old truck, their feet shuffling on the gravel road.

Ben eased up from where he sat on the ground. His eyes searched the truck bed. "I see you got the cans," he said, pleased with Bluey's efforts. "They all full?"

"To the spout," said Bluey.

"Fine work," said Ben.

Bluey and his buddies kicked at the gravel. Ben pulled out his wallet, took six hundred dollars from it and handed the money to Bluey. Bluey handed a third of the money to each man.

"You get the other half when we finish what we came to do," said Ben. "Just like we agreed."

"It's turned off real dry for you," Bluey said, pocketing his money. "No rain to speak of in almost six weeks. About as good as you could expect."

Ben glanced at the sky. Stars blinked down on him. He took a dirty handkerchief from his overalls and wiped his brow. "Reckon the *good Lord* is looking out for me," he joked. "Keeping it dry like this."

Bluey pulled a bottle from his back pocket. "Have a drink to celebrate," he said, handing Ben the bottle.

"Guess I should." Ben drank the whiskey. His stomach tore at him as the liquor hit its spot. He coughed and felt hurt deep in his insides. The way he figured it, he might never face the trial. His cough had gotten worse the last few weeks, especially in the mornings. Lots of times his coughs brought up vile tasting fluid that had blood streaks in it. He thought about going to a doctor but then decided against it. A doctor would just tell him to go to a hospital, and Ben held no liking to that idea. His days were numbered anyway, and he planned on spending them wild and free, not cooped up in a hospital room somewhere. Might as well go to prison.

Ben took another drink. He didn't care that his days were short. Just let him finish up this one last chore and then let matters take care of themselves. He handed the bottle back to Bluey.

"Let's get moving," Ben said. "Need to get this started before daylight."

Bluey hesitated. "You don't reckon anybody gone get hurt, do you? I know Daniel's wife is moved up with him since this spring."

Ben grunted. "If they don't bother us, they won't get hurt."

Bluey took another drink, then pocketed the whiskey. "You want me to ride with you?" he asked Ben.

"No. I'll drive alone."

Bluey eyed Ben for a second. "You sure you wanna do this?" he asked. "It'll start up trouble again for sure."

"As sure as anything I've ever done in my life." Ben laughed. "Don't you worry, I told you it was on me. No one will ever know you or your boys had any hand in it. I promised you that, and you know when it comes to this kind of thing, I'm a man of my—"

Ben coughed and his body shook. Bluey touched Ben on the shoulder. Ben turned away and spit into the gravel. He coughed again, then once more.

"Ye're not a healthy man," said Bluey.

Ben faced Bluey, half-doubled at the waist. "I'm healthy enough to do this," he said. "After that, it don't matter none. It just don't matter."

Bluey nodded as Ben stood up straight again. Bluey motioned, and his men piled into his truck. Then Bluey and Ben Clack climbed into their vehicles and headed up the mountain to finish the work that Ben had planned so many months ago.

———

Daniel didn't notice anything unusual as he climbed out of bed the next morning, slipped on his clothes and went to milk the cow. He didn't notice anything as he took a bite of breakfast either. Fact is, he didn't notice it until afterward, when he stepped out on his porch and pulled out his pipe. He had just started sizing up the work he planned to get done that day when, off to the west, he saw a soft curl of dark smoke rising from the trees in the distance.

His eyes narrowing, he moved to the porch's edge. The smoke looked like it came from a chimney, riding up into the blue sky. Daniel rubbed his beard. No house lay in that direction. What was the smoke coming from?

As he turned to go into the house to ask Deidre what she thought, he caught sight of a second curl of smoke rising off the ridge. More concerned now, he left the porch and stepped into the yard, pivoting in all directions as he walked. Smoke rose from five different sources, all of it drifting up as if at ease with the world.

Not daring to think the worst, Daniel called for Deidre and tried to stay calm. Had some hunters come on his property overnight and set up camp? Was this their morning fire? Or maybe some loggers had strayed off their land and onto his? Why else would smoke come from five different spots? He remembered the thunder he'd heard earlier that morning. Although the sky had produced no rain, there had been flashes of lightning for a couple of hours before first light. Had the lightning started up some fires?

Deidre walked outside, her apron around her waist. Ed followed, Raymond behind him. Daniel pointed to the smoke. His heart pounded. "What you think that is?" he asked.

Ed moved to him, his eyes as busy as Daniel's. "It's fires, Pa. Five of them."

"But how?" asked Deidre.

Daniel tried to sort out what it could be. No logical explanation came to him. Nothing made sense.

"What you reckon caused them?" asked Raymond.

All at once Daniel knew. "Clack!" he yelled and then took off for the barn. "It's got to be Ben Clack! He swore he'd get revenge!"

Ed and Raymond followed him. Daniel shouted back at Deidre, "Take the truck. Go get Sol, Thaddeus, Jim, anybody else you can find! Clack's trying to burn us out again, like a long time ago. Only this time he's after the whole place, not just the house."

Ed and Raymond disappeared into the shed, where they kept the tools. Deidre stood motionless, obviously too shocked to move. Daniel ran to her, took her hands in his.

"This is it," he said. "Clack's last shot at us. We got to take care of this, then we can move on. You understand?" He kissed her hands and looked into her eyes. After a second, she focused on him and nodded. "Go," Daniel said. "Bring back help. It's the only way we can fight this."

Coming to grips with the situation, Deidre shifted into full gear, sprinting back to the house for the truck keys. Daniel ran into the shed. Ed and Raymond handed him a shovel and a pair of work gloves. Ed held a saw and another shovel; Raymond, a hoe, another saw.

"We don't have much," said Daniel, "but we'll do with what we got."

"Least there's no wind," Ed said, checking the sky.

Daniel nodded, grateful for small favors. "We fight them one at a time," he said. "All together until we get help. I don't want anybody getting caught alone with something he can't handle."

Ed and Raymond agreed, and Daniel led them toward the first spot where he'd seen smoke. No way was he going to let Clack burn him out this time. One way or the other—live or die—he would stay on this land.

Sitting on her front porch with a knitting needle in her hand, Abby saw Deidre speed up the street in Daniel's logging truck, the truck almost tipping over as she turned the corner. Abby dropped her knitting and jumped to her feet. Deidre braked the truck and sprang out, her face flushed.

"Fires!" Deidre shouted. "Five fires up on the mountain!"

Abby ran to her and they met halfway down the steps. "Calm down," said Abby. "What fires?"

"Daniel thinks it's Clack," huffed Deidre, her breath short. "Thinks he set them this morning. Sent me to get everybody I can. He and the boys are already fighting them."

"Let me get Sam," Abby said. "Then we'll go to Elsa's. She and Preacher Tuttle can make a telephone call to Sol. Thaddeus is at the school painting the ceiling; Jim's down at the store. We'll need somebody to tell them."

Deidre nodded and Abby left her and ran inside. Pulling Sam from his crib where he lay asleep, she rushed back to Deidre, who had jumped back into the still-running truck. Abby climbed in with Sam, and Deidre sped off. They reached the parsonage of Jesus Holiness in less than five minutes, both of them leaping out as soon as the truck stopped, Sam in Abby's arms.

"Go to the church in case the preacher's there!" Abby directed Deidre. "I'll check the house."

Abby yelled for Elsa as she hurried up the steps and through the door, not stopping to knock. Elsa met her in the hallway, her hair under a kerchief, her apron stained with flour.

"You need to come!" urged Abby. "Daniel's got fires burning on the mountain."

Elsa said she would go to help and followed Abby out the front door. They met Deidre and Tuttle at the truck.

"I'll call Sol," said Tuttle. "Round up everybody from the church I can find."

"Go to the school for Thaddeus," Abby said. "The store for Jim."

Tuttle nodded. Elsa suddenly stopped, her right hand at her throat.

"What?" asked Abby, disturbed by Elsa's expression.

Elsa looked at Sam. "I just had a shudder," she said. "If it's Clack, what's he after?"

"Burning us out again," said Abby. "Simple to see."

Elsa shook her head. "Too simple. What does Clack want more than anything else?"

Abby recognized Elsa's point. She clutched Sam closer, her arms tiring from carrying him, then thought of Rose Francis. "You think Clack's doing this for a feint?" she asked. "Trying to put our attention on the fires so he can get at these babies?"

"I'm not sure," said Elsa. "It just hit me, that's all."

Abby studied it for a second. The notion made sense. Clack had vowed to end the Mingling, probably wanted that more than anything, more than burning Daniel off his land again. If he could do both with one plan, why not try it? Everybody knew the judge had set Clack's trial for August. If he went to jail, he couldn't do anything for a long time, maybe never, since his health had turned so bad.

"I'll stay with the babies," Abby said, reaching a quick decision. "Me and Daisy. If Clack comes, we'll be ready for him."

"I'll get Thaddeus. He can stay too," said Tuttle.

"No," Abby said, her jaw firm. "You need all the men fighting the fire. We don't even know for sure that Ben's coming after the children. For that matter, we don't know for absolute that Ben's behind any of this. You put a rifle in my hand, I can stop Ben Clack if it comes to that. Don't say a word to Thaddeus, promise me that."

Tuttle opened his mouth as if to argue, but Abby shook her head, and he stayed quiet. Abby faced Deidre.

"Go to Eugenia Clack's," she said. "Tell her to send Daisy and Rose Francis to my place. Send William to the fires if he's not already gone to work."

Deidre nodded. Tuttle said to Elsa, "Grab anything we can use at our place. Then take Abby home, pick up all the shovels, buckets, other equipment like that. I'll meet you back there in half an hour."

Everybody rushed out, Abby and Elsa toward the shed at the back of the parsonage. "You really think Clack will come after the children?" Abby asked.

"No way to know," said Elsa. "Just you stay ready in case he does."

Abby remembered the rifle in her closet. She would stay ready; Elsa could count on that.

Ben Clack had stayed up all night, his body wired on whiskey and evil intent. Before the day ended, he would finish his doings with the Porters once and for all. Leaving Bluey at a small roadside restaurant about six miles from Blue Springs, he drove toward William and Daisy Clack's house about an hour after sunup, his body almost shaking with glee. He planned to strike before anybody could stop him, take his vengeance and let the chips fall. He cackled at his cleverness.

It didn't take him long to reach his destination—a small white house about a hundred yards up a gravel road about four miles from town. Parking his car at the end of the road, Clack hauled out of the seat and made his way through the woods to the back of the house. Overhead, the sun warmed his head and shoulders and sweat broke out on his dirty face.

Hiding behind a thick maple tree, he took off his hat and wiped his forehead. His hands were soiled with smoke and mountain dirt, and he smelled like kerosene. He smiled as he remembered setting the fires. So far the only flaw in his plan was the lack of wind. A good fifteen-mile-an-hour breeze to fan the flames would have pleased him greatly.

Clack studied the back door of his niece's house just like he'd done a number of times over the last few months. He knew the routine. Everybody got up at about five-thirty. William left at about seven for his job at the lumber mill near town.

About an hour later, Daisy would step outside the front door to feed their two dogs and sweep the porch. She usually took about five minutes, just enough time for Clack to do his business and sneak out. He glanced at the sky. William had most likely already left.

Staying low, Clack dodged through the trees to the back stoop of the house. Any minute now.

Sure enough, before long he heard Daisy holler out, "Hey, Buster! Tick!" A dog barked from the front porch. Clack quickly grabbed the doorknob, opened it and sneaked inside the kitchen. After a fast look around, he moved down the hall to the two bedrooms on the side of the house. He found Rose Francis in the first bedroom, her crib in the corner. She lay on her side, her eyes open, a cloth doll in her tiny fingers. She wore a plain brown dress and white socks. She rolled over as he entered and jabbered at him in a language he didn't understand.

Clack eased across the room, his ears poised for any sound from the front of the house. Rose Francis smiled as he lifted her out. Her pink fingers grabbed at his nose. He pulled her to his chest. "Friendly baby," he said. "Real friendly."

Rose rested against him as if in her mother's arms. Clack glanced around, saw a full milk bottle and a blanket sitting on a table by the crib. "You about to get fed?" he asked her.

She just looked at him with eyes so like her mama's. Clack grabbed the milk and blanket and rushed from the room. He heard a door opening as he reached the kitchen. Bounding out, he jumped off the back stoop and into the woods. Behind him, he heard Daisy yelling. Knowing he wasn't in any shape to run too far, Clack suddenly stopped, pulled his pistol from his pants and twisted around. Daisy halted when she saw the weapon. Clack waved it at her.

"You best not move anymore," he said. "It would be a shame if I had to shoot you."

Daisy breathed heavily. "You got to give me back Rose Francis," she shouted.

"I don't have to do anything of the sort!" he replied with a grin.

"They'll kill you for this."

"I'm already almost dead."

Daisy wiped her hands on her apron. "Why you doing this?"

"I think you know. I'm the last one left, the only true Clack."

"It won't change anything. The old ways are gone forever."

"I reckon that's true. But if this is the end, let it be one worth telling in days to come."

"Where you taking her?"

Clack grinned again. "You go to Abby," he said. "Nobody else. Tell her to meet me at dark at my spot up by Edgar's Knob. You know where it is." Daisy nodded. Clack continued, "You say anything to anybody but Abby and I'll have to . . ." He looked down at Rose Francis.

"Even a man as bad as you wouldn't hurt a baby," said Daisy.

"I ain't looking to do harm to this child," said Clack. "But you best send Abby."

Daisy looked down while Clack slinked away with Rose.

Less than an hour after Deidre had shown up with news of the fires, Abby stood on the porch and watched as Preacher Tuttle and Elsa left for Daniel's place. Jim and Rebecca rode with them. Two trucks filled with men from Jesus Holiness followed, all of them loaded with shovels and buckets and anything else they could find that might help in fighting a fire. Sol drove one of the trucks, Thaddeus the other. Abby dug her fingers into her arms as they all drove off. Deidre had not found Eugenia Clack at home. That meant nobody had warned Daisy to look out for Ben.

Abby shivered in spite of the sun baking down. A bad feeling ran through her bones. Even though she had a rifle inside, she sensed it wouldn't help her, because Clack would probably not come in such a way that she could shoot him. Somehow he would find another path to gain his revenge.

Taking one more look up and down the street, she headed into the house to the room where Porter and Sam played in a wood pen Thaddeus had made. The two boys looked content as a couple of pups resting on a cool porch. Porter had a small ball in his hands. Sam played with his toes. Abby moved to the boys, touched each of them on the head. She then heard a thump on the porch, followed by someone pushing through the door. Headed for the rifle in her bedroom closet, she rushed into the hall where she saw Daisy coming at her, her face covered with sweat.

Abby immediately guessed the worst.

"I ran . . . fast as I could!" Daisy panted. "To . . . warn . . . warn you!"

"Warn me about what?" said Abby. "Where's Rose Francis?"

Daisy buried her face in her hands and tears began to fall.

Abby's eyes grew wide and she said, "Clack took Rose Francis?"

Daisy nodded, her head still down.

"What's he want? Is he coming for Sam?"

Daisy continued to cry.

Abby took her by the shoulders and shook her. "Tell me what he wants!" she insisted. "Tell me now!"

Daisy looked up, wiped her face and tried to control her tears. "He wants . . . wants you," she sobbed. "Wants you to . . . meet him."

Abby froze. "He wants me?"

"Said he wanted you to meet him at dark at Edgar's Knob. I'm to show you the cabin."

Abby realized what this meant. Clack wanted what he'd always sought, back from the time when she first met him as a young girl, the time he trapped her in the trees, the time he tried—

She pushed away the memory and instead thought about all that had happened since then. Why couldn't Clack let it all go? What evil lived in a man that he could keep such a bad grudge in his heart for so long? For just a second, Abby felt sorry for Clack. Having run off his family by his meanness, he had no love in his life, nobody to give him comfort. What a sad way to live.

She remembered Ben Clack's pa. He had once loved Abby's ma. But Solomon had come along and taken her away from him. Was Ben Clack trying to even the score for his dead pa?

"He's not coming for Sam?" Abby asked, just to make sure.

"Don't think so," said Daisy. "Said for me to bring you to him, to tell nobody else."

Abby weighed her choices. She could go to Daniel's and get Thaddeus, Sol too. But Clack said to tell nobody but her. But what if she didn't go? Could she do nothing, just wait for Clack to come down after her? But he had Rose Francis! And as crazy as he was, he might harm her if Abby didn't follow his orders.

Abby decided she had to do what Clack said. No matter what he wanted, she would give it so long as it meant no hurt would come to her baby girl.

CHAPTER
FOURTEEN

D aniel fought the fire all day long, his jaw set against the hot flames that threatened to burn away what he had so long loved. He stopped for only a few minutes when the folks from Blue Springs arrived, just long enough to divide up the crews and give them some directions. Ed, Raymond, Sol and Thaddeus fought beside him against the largest of the fires, the one closest to his house. The five of them barely stopped all day and then only to drink some water every now and again and take a biscuit and a tomato that Deidre brought them at just past midday. At first, Daniel wondered if they could hold back the fires. With almost no rain in the last few weeks, the underbrush burned quickly, the fire acting like a living snake crawling through it at their feet. They lost close to twenty acres by noon, another ten by midafternoon, another twelve or so as the day started to slant down. But they kept fighting, their shovels throwing dirt, their arms pouring out water from the creek, their feet stamping out the flames when they crawled too close.

By seven o'clock Daniel's face looked like somebody had caked it with black soot, and his clothes were burned and torn to shreds. His shoulders ached. Blisters covered his hands and face. He had trouble breathing too and knew he had swallowed a lot of smoke. Pausing for just a second to catch his breath, he glanced up and down the fire line. It stretched at least three hundred feet left and right, a slow-burning but deadly threat to his land. He raised his eyes east and west to see how much smoke still belched from the other four fires. To his relief, he saw that some of them actually looked smaller, one no more than campfire smoke. He pointed to his left.

"Maybe they're getting a handle on it!" he yelled.

Everybody looked up, their faces grim but hopeful. Tuttle and two other men from the church ran up. "We got ours under control!" they shouted. "Thought you boys could use some help."

Daniel walked over and slapped Tuttle on the back. "You gone do some good around here sooner or later," he teased, suddenly full of hope.

Tuttle nodded and moved to the fire. Daniel turned to his right, where the fire had reached a scrub area, thin on underbrush and filled with rocks and boulders. Daniel pointed his shovel about thirty feet in front of the fire line.

"Let's dig in here!" he called. "Make us a break at these rocks. Maybe we can stop it right here."

Everybody nodded and stepped back to the line Daniel had chosen. Their shovels started digging, their hoes chopping. If they could clear out the underbrush at this barest spot, they might choke off the fire's fuel. It would reach the rocks and the trench they had cleared and, unless the wind suddenly rose up and blew it across the line, the fire would die out.

Daniel's hands burned as he labored. In his bones he realized they had to make their stand here. Even though they were fighting with all their strength, he knew he and the rest of the men couldn't go on forever. Everybody had limits, and the heaviness in his chest and shoulders told him he had about reached his. End it here, he told himself.

The minutes clicked off. Close to an hour passed. Daniel

glanced up every now and again to check on how the others were doing. Gradually their line stretched out to the edge of the fire on both sides.

"Make it wider!" yelled Daniel. "Twenty feet past the line and as deep as we can! We don't want the fire to jump!"

The men doubled their efforts. Daniel's heart swelled. No two ways about it, the Lord had given him some good fellows as companions. He glanced at Ed, busy with his one good hand, and Raymond, now strong as a young bull. The Lord had given him a fine family—two honest, hardworking sons, a daughter of faith and a wife with a heart as big as skillet. If some tree fell on him today and ended his hours on this earth, he could go happy with what had befallen him. True, he had faced some tests in his life and had strayed from the Lord for a time. Yet, in the end, he had come home. No matter what happened now, he could live or die content in his soul.

The trench widened. The fire reached the rocks. Daniel heard a rumbling and looked up at the sky. Clouds had suddenly gathered from nowhere. The breeze picked up a little. Daniel frowned. He didn't need any wind right now. The clouds banked in closer and turned darker. The men on the line glanced up with him, their faces confused. If rain came, fine and good, it would put out the fire. But if they got wind and no rain, then that might spell their doom.

Daniel dug in, his hands moving the shovel in and out of the ground, digging the trench deeper. The wind freshened some more, and he looked up again. The fire jumped up the side of a young tree, and its leaves began to burn. Everybody stopped suddenly, their shoulders slumped as if expecting the worst. Daniel searched the clouds for some message, some sign that rain might soon fall. The wind notched up again. The flames from the fire danced as if happy to feel the wind at their back. Daniel's heart fell.

Then a drop of rain hit his face. Another followed. The rain became a splatter. Daniel smiled. Soon it fell in a sheet, a sudden roar of water dropping down from the sky. Daniel's grin turned into full-throated laughter. The men around him threw their shovels down and their hands into the air as if in worship of the rain that soaked their heads. Daniel raised his hands too. The rain washed the soot off his hands and face. It drenched his clothes, but he didn't care. The rain washed the burning trees and underbrush, smothering everything with cool water. Smoke sizzled out of the ground where the rain hit and, within minutes, nothing remained of the fire. Daniel searched the horizon for signs of the other fires but saw none. Certainly the rain had doused them like it had this one.

Daniel dropped his shovel and turned to Ed. Ed slapped him on the back and then hugged him. Raymond joined in the hug, and Daniel just stood and let it all soak into him. Clack had done his worst, yet the good Lord had sent rain to end his meanness. True, he had probably lost sixty to seventy acres, but given time, that would all grow back. Nobody had gotten hurt, and the cabin still stood.

Daniel stepped back from his boys and faced Tuttle. The preacher moved to him and the two men shook hands. Daniel shook hands with Sol and Thaddeus too, the three of them wearing grins.

"I reckon we did it," said Thaddeus, rain streaming down his face.

"I'm obliged for your help," said Daniel.

"You'd do the same for me."

They faced the others. "Reckon we should get back to the house," said Daniel.

"I could use a bath," said Sol.

Daniel looked at his half brother and laughed. "You needed a bath before you got here," he said.

Sol chuckled as they gathered up the tools. Daniel threw an arm around Ed, and they all headed toward his cabin. About twenty paces down the path, Daniel thought of Ben Clack, and a rush of anger rose up in him. He tried to push it away. No reason to waste time worrying about that awful man. No doubt he had started this fire, but Daniel had no proof of it. Best to let it go, not fall back into any efforts at revenge. The court would take care of him soon enough, the Lord after that.

Daniel patted Ed and kept walking. After another dozen or so paces, another notion hit him. Why had Clack set these fires? To burn him out? Yes. But was that all? If so, why hadn't he set twenty fires? Enough so that even with help, Daniel couldn't have put them all out?

Then it hit him. Abby! Clack wanted to end the Mingling, wanted to start up the feud again.

He stopped and turned to Thaddeus. "Who's with Abby?" he asked. Everybody paused.

"Nobody," answered Tuttle. "We tried to get word to Daisy but couldn't, and Abby wouldn't let us leave a man with her."

"You got to go to her," Daniel told Thaddeus. "I got a bad feeling about this."

Thaddeus looked at Tuttle and asked, "What's the matter?"

"Abby wouldn't let me tell you," said Tuttle, "but Elsa thinks Ben may have used the fires as a feint to get at Sam and Rose Francis."

"You left her alone?"

"She gave me no choice, said everybody needed to come to the fires, you included. You know how she can be."

Thaddeus nodded. Daniel weighed the matter. If Clack had indeed used the fires to keep everybody busy, then he had probably finished his evil work and cleared out from Blue Springs. But where had he gone? Daniel immediately knew the answer. He turned to Thaddeus to speak but then stopped. If Clack had fallen so far as to hurt a couple of babies, he wouldn't hesitate to harm somebody else. Best he handle this alone and keep everybody else out of danger.

"Go home!" he told Thaddeus. "You and the preacher. Make sure Abby is okay."

Everybody moved fast, reaching the cabin in a matter of minutes. Within another five, everybody but Daniel's family had climbed into their trucks and cars and driven off.

Daniel instructed his sons to wash up, and then he told Deidre he had to go back out.

"Why?" she asked. "You've not even eaten."

"I'll take a couple of biscuits with me. Got one more thing to handle."

"You going after Ben Clack?"

Daniel hugged her tight. "It's all right," he said. "It's not out of revenge for the fires. I don't live for that anymore."

"Then what?"

He kissed her on the forehead. "If Clack is after the children, I have to stop him."

"You need help," said Deidre. "Don't go after him by yourself."

"I got to go alone. You know what's happened in my past. Every time somebody faces danger with me, I live and they die. Laban. Stephen. I won't take that chance again."

"But what about you? What if something happens to you?"

Daniel smiled and his heart felt good. "I'm a Jesus man for good now," he assured her. "If something happens to me, I go home to see the Lord. And Ma and Pa, my brothers, Laban and Luke."

"What about me?" asked Deidre, tears filling her eyes as though she were already standing at her husband's grave.

Daniel kissed her on the cheek and whispered, "I'll be back. Don't worry. You know I have to go."

She wiped her eyes. "I know," she said. "You've always done your duty. It's the Porter in you, a strong reason I loved you from the first. You got this honor in your bones, got to fix a wrong if you can."

"Abby is my sister," he said. "I expect she needs me or soon will."

"Go on then," said Deidre. "Just come home safe when you're done."

Daniel stared into her eyes. Oh, how he did love this woman. "The Lord blessed me when He gave me you," he said. "You're still the prettiest woman on the mountain."

"And you're full of blarney," she said with a laugh.

"I love you," he said and then kissed her.

Deidre kissed him back, again and again. He closed his eyes and knew that no matter what happened to him after this, he had come as close to heaven on earth as a man could reach.

CHAPTER
FIFTEEN

At just before seven-thirty Abby and Daisy left Porter and Sam with a couple of older ladies from Jesus Holiness, then used Eugenia Clack's car to drive to Ben's cabin on Edgar's Knob. Daisy drove. It took them close to an hour to reach the spot where they had to park. From there Abby followed Daisy up the narrow trail, slipping from time to time as she lost her footing in the fading light. Neither said much. Sweat broke out on Abby's face, and her breathing labored as the incline grew steeper. In the distance she heard thunder and wished for some cooling rain to come their way. She clutched a cloth handbag to her chest, her fingers outlining the barrel of the pistol that lay inside. Although she hated the notion of using the weapon, if it came down to having to protect her child by shooting Clack, then she'd do it, simple as that.

Abby prayed through most of the hour it took them to reach the remote cabin. Somehow the good Lord had to see her through this. No way she could do it on her own. Truth was, she had no idea what Clack might do. Did he want her there to see him as he hurt Rose Francis? Did he plan to torture her that way? Abby pushed away the idea. No man, no matter how mean, could hurt a baby, could he? Then what? Another idea came to her, but she refused to entertain it. The notion made her skin crawl.

They reached the top of the incline and turned left through a narrow clearing. "Not long now," whispered Daisy.

Abby wiped her face and touched the pistol again. Daisy didn't know she had it. Abby wondered if she could really use it. She prayed again that the Lord would deliver her from the necessity.

A few minutes later, Daisy knelt behind a rock and held up a hand to stop her. "There," she said, pointing to a light about a hundred yards away. "Ben's cabin. Been here close to fifty years, I guess."

Abby studied the shoddy building. A dim light showed out an open window at the front. "How do we do this?" asked Abby. Daisy pushed back her hair. Abby saw her hand trembling. She laid a hand on Daisy's arm. "You love her too, don't you?"

Daisy nodded. "I am a mama," she said. "You taking care of my baby. I should have taken better care of yours."

"Don't blame yourself," said Abby. "You didn't do anything wrong."

Daisy lowered her eyes.

Licking her lips, Abby said, "We got to do this, no way around it. We go to Ben, see what he wants. Get Rose Francis and get out of here." Daisy nodded. Abby sucked in her breath. "Let's go."

The two women walked to the cabin, and Abby knocked on the door. A few seconds later, Ben Clack opened the door. "Come on in, ladies," he said with a smirk on his face. "Let's do us some talkin'."

Her hands clutched to her purse, Abby followed Daisy into the room.

Daniel made his way up the trail to Clack's cabin almost thirty minutes after Daisy and Abby did. Worn out from fighting the fire all day, he found it hard to keep his balance, and his hip hurt like it had a knife sticking in it. He pushed heavily on his walking stick, its sturdy end pushing into the mountain dirt to help him steady his gait. More than once Daniel shook his head as if to make sure he kept things straight. If he'd figured it wrong, Clack might not even be on Edgar's Knob. Yet, after years of knowing the Clacks and their ways, he suspected he had it right. When he wanted to drink and stay out of sight, Ben Clack headed to his shanty in the high reaches of the mountains.

His rifle slung over his shoulder, Daniel dug in harder with his cane. He and Clack had clashed off and on for most of their lives. But something told him that tonight he would settle things once and for all with his old enemy.

Daniel glanced at the sky. The moon blinked at him clear as a silver nickel. For some reason he felt good—clean and content. Whatever the Lord brought his way tonight, he could abide it. Just so nothing happened to Abby or Rose Francis.

He reached the edge of a clearing, paused and stared at the back of Clack's cabin a stone's throw away. A low light seeped out of the shanty. As he had suspected, Clack was here. Now what? Daniel squatted, laid down his cane and rifle and took some water from a small flask in his pocket.

Daniel pocketed the flask, picked up the walking stick and studied it. His pa had carved it years ago, had given it to him as he lay dying of the cancer. Unable to see the cane in the dark, Daniel fingered the carvings like a blind man. He knew them by heart, and his fingers searched for his favorite—the face of Blue Springs Mountain that looked down on their property. Daniel touched the shape of a man's face his pa had carved on the mountain. "The face of God," his folks had always said. A smile crossed Daniel's mouth. Though he had wandered away, the mountain had brought him home just a year ago.

Daniel rested his rifle on his knees. Like all highland men, he took good care of his weapon. He didn't use it to hunt for food as much as in the past, though he still shot a few deer with it, still saw it as much a part of him as his hat. He rubbed his fingers over the barrel. True, he had shot men before, in the first big war and also that night at the Lolleyville jail against the Clacks, but the notion of using it again bothered him. Now that he and Jesus had come to such good terms, did he have it in him to shoot a man again? Even a man as bad as Ben Clack?

A tremble ran through his shoulders. He didn't want to use a weapon against another man again. But what choice did he have? If it came to Clack or his kind, a highlander man had to protect his kin. The good Lord would surely understand that, wouldn't He?

Daniel stood, the cane in one hand, the rifle over his opposite shoulder. He hoped he wouldn't have to shoot Clack. But, one way or the other, he would settle things with his enemy before anybody else got hurt.

Inside the cabin, Clack stood by the back wall, one arm clutching Rose Francis, one holding a rifle. Abby and Daisy sat at a rickety table not more than six feet away, their hands in their laps. Abby's heart pounded so loud she could hear it in her ears. She squeezed her handbag, unsure of what to do. Clack's eyes blazed red, shot full of whiskey and anger. Abby had never seen a meaner man. His heart had turned as cold as a stone at the bottom of a winter river.

"I'll give you back this sorry baby," said Clack, "but only for a price."

"What do you want?" Abby pleaded.

Clack grinned, then coughed violently and doubled over at the waist. Abby edged up in her seat. Maybe she could surprise Clack by—

He seemed to read her mind and jerked up straight, his hands leveling his rifle on her. "You know what I want," he said, catching his breath. "I want you."

Abby's stomach turned queasy. Just as she had feared. It had started a long time ago when Clack had trapped her in a stand of trees. She had run from him that day, but he had never given up. Now, after all these years, he still had the awful idea in his head. She almost gagged. Yet what choice did she have? No matter how high the cost, she would pay it if it guaranteed safety for Rose Francis.

Clack held out Rose Francis as if to hand her over. "This brat goes with Daisy," he said. "You stay here with me. An easy swap the way I see it."

Abby faced Daisy. "Take her and go," she said, her voice weaker than she wanted. Daisy opened her mouth, but Abby stopped her. "Do it," she said. "Now!"

Daisy moved to Clack. He handed the child to her. "Git out of here," he said. "And keep your words shut if you know what's good for you!"

Daisy took Rose Francis and looked at Abby once more.

"Go on," said Abby, standing. "I'll be okay."

Her eyes filling with tears, Daisy hugged her and then went to the door.

"Tell Thaddeus I love him," said Abby.

Daisy glanced back one more time, then left Abby alone with Clack. She faced him, her hands on her handbag.

"Now," said Clack, licking his cracked lips, "you and me got some business to attend."

Abby ground her teeth. Now that Rose Francis was safe, she had no reason to back down from Clack. So what if he had his rifle pointed at her? She preferred dying to what he planned to do.

Coming from the back of the cabin, Daniel heard the front door creak open and ran toward the sound. To his surprise he saw Daisy Clack rush out the door, a child in her arms. Grabbing her, he got the story as to what was going on inside.

"Ben's got Abby," whispered Daisy. "A swap for Rose Francis here."

"Go back to Blue Springs," he said. "Tell Sol. Send him up here. If I can't stop Clack, he'll need to do it for me."

Daisy nodded and ran into the darkness. Daniel faced the cabin, his rifle at the ready. Sneaking onto the porch, he peered into the front window and saw Clack standing over Abby, who was sitting at a round table with her back to Daniel.

Clack had one hand on Abby's neck, the other on his rifle. Daniel moved without thinking, his anger carrying him through the door and into the room, his hands on his rifle, his blood hot.

"Hold on there!" shouted Daniel.

Clack turned quickly, his rifle aimed at Daniel's chest. Abby jumped away from Clack and crouched behind the table. The two men stood face-to-face, rifles poised, neither of them backing off.

"Reckon we got us a standoff," said Daniel.

Without lowering his weapon an inch, Clack coughed and spit into a handkerchief he held in his hand.

Daniel started to pull the trigger to end it right then and there, but something held him back. Maybe he could talk some sense into Ben, he thought.

"No reason for anybody to get shot," Daniel told him. "No harm's been done so far."

Clack stayed still. Daniel saw Abby's hands on her handbag.

"Let's just both put down our rifles. Everyone walk away."

Clack coughed again and his face turned white. "My days are short," he said. "I got nothing left."

"Maybe not," said Daniel. "But that's no reason to finish in such a bad way."

Clack glanced at Abby. "You leave us alone," he said to Daniel. "For just an hour. That's all I'm askin'."

"You know I can't do that," said Daniel. "No self-respecting man could."

"Then I reckon we gone finish things. Right now."

Daniel gripped his rifle tighter. Maybe he'd kill Clack. Maybe Clack would kill him. Either way, he didn't want to do this. But it seemed he'd lost his choice in the matter.

A strange sense of peace suddenly gripped him. Maybe he did have another choice. He measured it for a second, felt its craziness. What sense did it make? None. Yet he felt squeezed to do it, like somebody's hand had him by the shoulders and turned him in a new way. Daniel started to lower his rifle. Clack's eyes widened as he saw the rifle barrel point to the floor.

"I'm not going to shoot you," said Daniel.

Clack rubbed a hand over his face. He glanced at Abby, then back at Daniel. "You gone soft on me," he said. "Didn't figure that of a Porter man."

Daniel's voice sounded strong in the cabin. "I'm not going soft. Just that the Lord don't take to men killin' other men."

"Your brother is gone womanish," Clack said to Abby with a laugh.

Abby kept her eyes on Clack. Daniel saw her set jaw, knew that

look as one of determination. He spoke to Clack again. "You don't
have to stay so angry," he said. "The Lord can free you from all
that."

"You tryin' again to turn me to Jesus?"

"I'm telling you what I've found is true. The Lord cleaned me
of all my hurt, washed it clean away."

Clack shook his head. "It's too late for me," he said. "No more
talk. Time for it all to end."

"It's never too late," said Daniel. "Not this side of the river."

Clack's eyes glinted red and evil. Daniel's hands tightened on
his weapon again. He wondered if he could get it drawn fast
enough to shoot Clack before Clack shot him. No, he realized. He
had made his choice. Now he had to live with it. He saw Clack
twitch, his finger move. Abby moved too, her hands rising up from
behind the table where she crouched. Out of reflex Daniel tried to
lift his rifle to protect himself. A shot fired and Daniel fell backward.

Abby's hands had moved quietly into her handbag as Daniel
tried to talk sense into Clack. She prayed too, prayed that the Lord
would show her what to do, how to protect herself and her brother.
When Daniel lowered his weapon, she wanted to shout at him, to
tell him not to do it. But then she knew he had no choice. Daniel
had turned his whole self over to Jesus, and when her brother did
something, he did it all the way. If he believed Jesus wanted him to
try to reach Clack this way, he would do everything he could to do
it.

But what if he couldn't? What if Clack paid him no attention?

When Clack fired, Abby raised her pistol with both hands. Seeing Daniel fall, she knew she couldn't stand by and do nothing.
Clack would surely try to take advantage of her now that Daniel
was down. After that, who knew what he would do? Who would
stop him if he headed out after Rose Francis again?

Clack rushed to Daniel, his rifle ready for another shot. Abby
squeezed her pistol, her heart torn against shooting. But then Clack
cackled and pointed his rifle at Daniel to finish him off, and Abby

did the only thing she could. She shot Ben Clack dead where he stood.

Daniel lay on the floor, his head cupped in Abby's hands. "I don't hurt much," he said.

Tears streamed down Abby's cheeks. "You're a good man, brother."

"I didn't . . . want to shoot Ben."

"I know," said Abby.

"Thought I could . . ." His voice trailed away.

Abby touched the spot in his chest where the bullet had penetrated. "I don't want to leave you," she said. "But you need a doctor bad."

Daniel raised a hand to his chest, pulled it back red with blood. He had seen wounds like this in the war, knew he wouldn't last long enough for a doctor to reach him. "Stay," he said. "No time for a doc." Daniel tried to rise up but then fell back again.

"You want water?"

Daniel shook his head. "Just tell Deidre I love her, the kids, all of them. Tell them it's okay."

"You did good, Daniel. All these years. Even in the hard times, you never wanted to hurt anybody."

Daniel coughed. "I'm . . . with the Lord."

"You'll see Ma and Pa," said Abby. "Luke and Laban."

Daniel smiled. "I'll like that. Maybe Luke can play me some of his guitar."

Abby lifted him higher. The blood from his wound soaked into her dress. She rocked him, her body a shield against anything else that wanted to hurt him. "You raised a fine family," she said. "Got the land back too."

"I did okay," he whispered, his eyes closed.

"You did fine, just fine."

Sobs wracked Abby. She bent closer to Daniel, touched her cheek to his.

He opened his eyes and stared at the ceiling as if seeing something far away. "I can see the mountain," he whispered. "God's face on it."

"It's always there," Abby said. "Like Pa said."

Daniel closed his eyes again, and this time they stayed shut forever.

SECTION II

1946–1960

CHAPTER
SIXTEEN

Things in Blue Springs settled down for a long time after Preacher Tuttle spoke final words over Daniel's body and the undertaker buried him next to his ma up on the ridge behind his new house. Seemed like the mountain had seen as much fractiousness as it could stand for a while and so decided to give everybody a long respite from anything too heartbreaking.

With Ben Clack dead, nobody saw any need for the Mingling to go on any longer, so Sam and Rose Francis went back to their rightful families.

Ed, Raymond and Deidre strove hard to finish up the house Daniel had started, and they finished it up real stout and sturdy within a year. Then, to nobody's surprise, Deidre decided to move back to Asheville to help her ailing pa live out his last days. Raymond went with her, his quiet strength a comfort to his ma as she continued to grieve over Daniel's death.

Ed decided to stay on the mountain. He took up his pa's old job as Gant's crew boss so he could keep buying back the land.

Before another year had passed, he had built a new barn and fence to go along with his house. In addition, he'd met a woman named Priscilla from over in Brevard and, before anybody knew it, married her and brought her home. Before long they had a boy they named Lester, then a girl named Mary.

As the family had agreed, everybody kept putting their spare dollars in the pot to buy the land, and they made good progress with that real fast. With his head for business, Jim kept up with the paper work on it all, and by the time four years had peeled off the calendar, the family owned almost two hundred acres.

Not everything turned up rosy in those years, though. Some sadness also came. Elsa Tuttle took sick in 1950 and died with the pneumonia in January of that year, her death leaving everybody, especially Preacher Tuttle, with a heavy heart for a long time. For a while, in fact, they thought Preacher Tuttle might just pass on with her. But then, about a year after Elsa's death, his spirits took a turn for the better and he started preaching with his old fire again. Another couple of years moved past.

Eugenia Clack died in the fall of '52, her big body wasted away to no more than skin and bones because of the cancer. When Abby attended her funeral, she thanked the Lord that the wife of a man as mean as Topper Clack had found the courage to help her bring a halt to the bad blood between their families. Except for Daisy and William and their kids, all the rest of the Clacks scattered away from Blue Springs after Eugenia's passing, like leaves falling off a tree.

The country elected Ike Eisenhower as president that year, and more cars showed up on the roads in and out of the Blue Ridge highlands while the Porters and their kin bought up more of their old land. Billy Gant and his crew finished logging on Daniel's land and moved their trucks to another parcel of property not far away. Ed moved with him and kept right on working.

People talked a lot about a place called Korea in those days. Abby and Thaddeus sat by the radio on many a night and listened to news about the fighting. It scared them some that the country might end up in another big war, but they tried not to show it. Thaddeus kept teaching, though now at a fancy brick school the county built in '53. Two other teachers had joined him there, but not Abby. Since she had never finished her degree, she didn't have the required papers to work in a government school. So she stayed at home, taught a few kids who needed extra help and made sure that Rose Francis got all the extra learning she might ever need.

Abby heard from Steve four or five times a year, usually through short letters. Every time he wrote, he told her he felt fine and that, in spite of the fact that he had to spend almost every waking moment slaving in the business Mr. Waterbury had left him, most everything had turned out okay. Abby wanted to take him at his word, but the few times when he actually came home, usually around Christmas, she sensed an uneasiness in him, like he wanted to tell her something but didn't dare. She noticed that he wore finer clothes too and spoke with more and more sophistication and drove a fancier car every time she saw him. Obviously he was doing well. Every now and again he told her he hoped to become a builder someday but so far he hadn't achieved that.

Abby yearned to have a long talk with Steve, to ask him more about his work, his friends, his connection to a church, to talk to him about anything and everything. Yet as a ma she knew that sometimes it was best not to press a child, especially a boy trying to prove his mettle. In spite of the fact that she didn't feel like she knew her son too well anymore, she mostly stayed quiet as the years moved on. From time to time it came to her that her distance from Steve felt similar to the way she and her first husband, Stephen, had ended up and that scared her, but she didn't know how to fix it except to pray and trust the Lord.

Jim and Rebecca prospered through the early 1950s, Jim's mechanical abilities becoming a major asset as cars showed up everywhere. Within a few years he had taken ownership of three different garages in the county. Twelve men labored for him, and he stopped doing the actual labor so he could supervise and handle the paper work. He and Rebecca had two more children—Tommy and Harriet—and their little Porter became a constant friend to Rose Francis, the two of them as close as brother and sister as they grew up.

Time moved ahead—another year, then a second and a third.

With his back bothering him more and more from the gunshot wound he had taken back in '37 from Ben Clack, Sol finally gave up sheriffing and moved with Jewel to a piece of the family land on Blue Springs Mountain. He cut out a clearing, put up a fine frame house and took to farming. Sol's daughter, Katy Ruth, married a Hickory boy and moved to the dairy farm he and his family owned. Sol and Jewel's youngest child, Horace, now twenty-one, joined the Army and shipped out to Texas. Nathan, the oldest, followed his pa's line of work and became a policeman with the city of Knoxville, Tennessee.

Blue Springs didn't grow much in that decade. In fact, as some of the logging started to play out, many of the men who had moved in for that work actually headed away from the highlands. Road building seemed about the only trade that ever brought in any newcomers, although many of them lived somewhere else and only came to Blue Springs every now and again to buy supplies. All in all, the little town stayed about the same.

On her twelfth birthday Rose Francis announced that she wanted everybody to call her "only Rose" from then on, and Porter started calling her exactly that. "How's Only Rose?" he often asked when he saw her at school. "Is Only Rose okay today?" She usually stuck out her tongue at him when he did this, but that didn't seem to bother him much.

Abby reached fifty-six years. Her figure had rounded out some more and the gray in her hair took over for good. Thaddeus's looks followed hers. Everybody said, however, that they still acted like young newlyweds, holding hands as they walked about town, sitting close to each other in church, smiling like they had Cupid sitting on their shoulders.

By the fall of '56 the family had purchased back close to seven hundred acres of their old place, and all but Abby had built themselves a place on the mountain. Jim and Rebecca's house—about three hundred acres away from Ed's—had two stories, a porch all the way across the front on both floors, and a garage right beside it, a place as modern as anything found in Asheville.

Abby did a lot of reflecting in those years, her mind trying to figure whether all the changes had made things better or worse.

Lots of folks called the changes *progress,* and she didn't know that she could argue with that. After all, almost everyone had the electrical now and, except for a few families in the remotest hollers, indoor plumbing too. Many had telephones, and a new thing called a television had shown up in at least a couple of houses down in Asheville, even if not yet in Blue Springs. Education had become real regular for children, what with the schools open almost eight months out of the year now. Better times had surely come.

Yet, at certain moments, when she thought about all the folks that had moved away, Abby wondered just what the word *progress* meant. Did it mean that a family had to scatter out everywhere and hardly ever come together all at once anymore? Did it mean that the same roads that brought in truckloads of fine food and already-made clothes also carried people away, disconnecting them from the land of their birth? Did progress mean that you drove a car with its windows closed up so you couldn't smell the spring rain anymore? Or hear the cry of a whippoorwill at night? Did progress mean that people stopped going to their churches because they had so much, they didn't feel the need for God anymore?

Well, if that's what progress was, Abby wasn't sure it added as much as it subtracted. Either way, she knew she couldn't stop it, couldn't stop the passing of the years or the changes those years brought. So she might as well come to grips with it and take in the good as much as she could.

Abby counted her blessings as she got older, despite her loneliness for Steve. It seemed the good Lord had taken a shine to her family. She did what all highland women of her day tried to do: she cared for her child, tended to her husband, helped out with her grandbabies when she got the chance and volunteered at her church. If she hadn't known better, she would have sworn that at least a little bit of heaven had fallen on her shoulders. Of course she well understood that such golden years didn't last forever. Life always seemed to throw up a rock when a body least expected it. Even so, she spent many evenings on the porch with Thaddeus just soaking in the peace of her middle years. Surely life could not get much better than this.

December came and Abby started preparing the house for the

family to gather at Christmas. Steve had telephoned to say he would come home this year. Abby decided that this year for sure she would take him aside and make him tell her everything. Once she had reconnected with her boy, she could relax for good.

All seemed well. But then Mr. Billy Gant's car got smashed on an icy night in Raleigh, and just like that everything that had appeared so settled for so long turned upside down again.

Abby got the word from Ed. He drove up in his scruffy truck right at sundown just five days before Christmas. Abby knew the instant she saw him that something had gone terribly wrong.

"Sit," she said, leading him to the kitchen table. "Take some coffee."

Ed lifted the cup with his one hand and swallowed hard from it.

"Priscilla and the kids are well?" asked Abby, hoping nothing had happened to Ed's family.

"Yeah, fine. Lester's a mess but healthy as a horse. Mary too."

Abby smiled. Ed took some more coffee. "Billy Gant is dead," he said when he had finished swallowing. "Car wreck last night. Word reached the loggin' crew a couple hours ago."

Abby wiped her hands on her apron, took a seat at the table and tried to gather her thoughts. "Mighty young for something like this to happen."

"He was only forty-one. It's a real shame."

"Life is not predictable," said Abby. "Mr. Gant did right by us for a long time."

"He was a fine boss. Nobody ever asked for better."

Abby sighed. Troubles came when a body least expected them. "When are his services?" she asked.

"Don't know just yet. They do it differently in Raleigh than they do here."

Abby nodded. "You plan on going?"

"I reckon I should. I labored for the man for most of ten years."

"Jim should go too. He took care of all of Gant's trucks and such."

Ed nodded.

"Maybe you two can go see Steve when you go over there," Abby said.

"Yeah, I'd like that. He's doing good?"

"Seems so. Although he's not much to stay in touch. I guess that's the way it is with boys."

"Wonder why he's not married yet."

"He says he spends too much time working to meet many girls."

"That man's laboring too hard if that's the case."

Abby chuckled, poured herself a coffee and studied Ed. He looked so much like his pa, only wider in the arms and face. Plus, he didn't sport a beard like Daniel had most of his life.

"Gant has a wife and kids if I remember," Abby said.

"Yeah, two boys and a girl. One boy is about grown I guess."

Abby wondered if Ed had thought through the possible result of all this. "How much land have we bought up?" she asked.

"Seven, eight hundred acres," Ed said. "Jim knows the exact amount. Most of what Pa wanted."

Abby sipped her coffee. "You reckon Gant's boy will take up where his pa left off?"

"Don't know. Haven't seen him out in the woods much. He's been in school, I think."

"Might have a career other than logging in mind."

"I suppose so."

Ed studied his coffee. "You think he might put somebody else in charge of what we're doing here?"

"Reckon he could. Maybe he'll sell this business. It's a long way from Raleigh."

Ed's eyes widened and Abby knew he hadn't figured through all this. "You really think he'd do that?"

"No way to tell. But you ought to prepare for it, figure out what to do if he does. Life changes in a hurry; you ought to know that by now."

"So long as he gives us a fair shot at buying up the rest of our land, I don't guess I care what he does with the rest of his property. I can find another job, that's for certain."

Abby patted him on the back. Even though he was thirty-four

years old with a family of his own, she felt protective of him. With his ma down in Asheville, he needed some tending and seemed to like the advice she gave him when he asked.

"You're like your pa," she said, "able to do most anything and plenty willing to do it to make ends meet."

Ed took a long breath. "I miss him," he said. "Even after all these years."

"You should miss him. He's your pa."

"I still got his cane."

"He'd want you to care for it."

"Old Solomon did some fine carving on it."

"That he did."

Both sipped from their coffee once more. Outside, the night darkened and the temperature dropped colder.

CHAPTER
SEVENTEEN

J im and Ed left before sunup two days later to attend Billy
Gant's funeral, both of them dressed in the only suits they
owned, Jim's navy blue, Ed's brown. Both wore white shirts and
striped ties.

"Tell Mrs. Gant our family will pray for her," Rebecca said,
handing Jim a lunch bag as he climbed into his two-year-old Ford.
"Tell her we said Mr. Gant was a fine man."

Jim hugged her and headed out. They didn't talk much on the
way and stopped only for gas and to eat the food Rebecca had
made for them. They reached the red brick Methodist church
where they had Gant laid out at just past two o'clock. The funeral
was to start at three. The preacher, a short man with a round face,
said a lot of good things about Gant, and Jim had to agree with
them all. So far as he knew, God had made a fine man when he
built Billy Gant. Too bad the good Lord had seen fit to call him
home so early.

When the funeral ended, the pallbearers hauled the casket to a graveyard out behind the church. Jim and Ed followed the crowd, their hands shoved in their pockets, Ed's stump pushed up against his side. The sky hung gray and cold. A wind whipped across the headstones of the graveyard. The round-faced preacher read some Scripture, prayed some more and then threw dirt over the casket. Gant's wife followed him, doing the same, then their children. The oldest boy, a brown-haired man with a reddish complexion, stayed real close to his mama. He wore a smart gray suit and a blue tie and kept his back straight as he threw a handful of dirt onto his pa's casket. When the family had finished with the dirt, the crowd took their place behind them. When everybody had thrown a handful over the casket, the preacher said a final prayer and then everybody started to talk, their voices low and soft in the winter air. After a few minutes the group headed back to the church, where somebody had laid out food.

Jim found it all real interesting. Back home, they would most likely have buried the body on the man's own property. But here only a few people owned enough property to do that kind of thing. Also, back home everybody would have gone to the home of the deceased to eat. But in a city it might take a good long while for everybody to get there. So instead they set up the food at the church.

As soon as he felt comfortable about it, Jim made his way to the widow, Ed beside him. Although he hadn't seen her in a while, Jim had met Mrs. Gant a couple of times when she had driven to Blue Springs to spend time with her husband. He doubted she would remember him.

In front of her, he took her hand, introduced himself and Ed and reminded her that the two of them had worked for her husband.

"He was a fair boss," said Ed.

"Yes," she said. "He spoke often of Daniel Porter and his family. Said the Porter men labored hard. Said he could trust you to do what you said you would do."

Jim lowered his eyes. He had not come here to hear any praise. He changed the subject as soon as he could. "My uncle Daniel spent some time with your husband's pa in World War I."

"I heard about that," she said. "Men like that know what sacrifice means."

"Your husband sold our land back to us," Ed said. "After he met my pa. He gave us the chance to re-claim something we thought we had lost forever."

Mrs. Gant's eyes widened. "I didn't know that," she said. "He kept most of his business to himself."

Ed nodded. "Yeah, we've bought up close to eight hundred acres over the last decade. Most of what we once owned."

"How fortunate," she said. "I know you're—"

The preacher stepped to Mrs. Gant, and Jim could see they had taken up enough of her time. "We will pray for you," he said. "All of us Porters will."

Mrs. Gant smiled, and Jim and Ed backed away and left the church. A few minutes later they stopped at a small roadside diner to get a bite to eat. When they had finished, Ed cleared his throat and said, "I figure you'll go see Steve now."

Jim wiped his mouth. "I've never been to his house, you know," he said. "Ma had to give me an address."

"You two haven't stayed close, I reckon." Ed said it as a matter of fact, not as an accusation. But Jim felt embarrassed just the same.

"I need to do better by my brother," he said.

"I reckon you ought to see him by yourself," Ed suggested.

"I appreciate your thoughtfulness. Haven't seen him at all in almost a year. But you're still welcome to come."

"I know," said Ed. "But if I go, you two won't get much chance to really say anything, you know what I mean?"

"I'm obliged for your wisdom."

Ed laughed. "I'll just have another cup of coffee or two," he said. "Maybe a piece of that pie." He pointed to a chocolate pie sitting on the counter.

Jim stood and put on his hat. Then he left the diner and headed to Steve's house. It took him about half an hour to find the place. By then it had turned almost dark. Jim chided himself again for never having visited his brother.

Steve met him at the door, his glasses in hand, his tie undone. Jim noticed mud on his shoes.

"Come on in," said Steve. "Long time no see."

Jim shook his hand and the two brothers took a seat in the parlor. Jim took a quick look around. Heavy tan drapes hung on the windows. Dark rugs covered the hardwood floor. A heavy sofa with a velvetlike burgundy cover sat in the center of the room. A clock ticked in the hall. The place smelled musty. Jim knew the situation. Steve lived here with Mrs. Waterbury, took care of the business since her husband's passing. He wondered if Steve really liked it, what with him still young but having to slave at a job all day and care for an elderly woman at night. Did he really enjoy living in a city so far away from his mountain roots? Did he miss anything about home? Not seeing his family any more than he did?

"How long has it been?" asked Jim, trying to start the conversation.

Steve studied a second. "Too long," he said. "Least according to Ma."

"Guess we ought to feel ashamed. Brothers and all, we ought to keep in better touch."

Steve played with the string on one of his shoes. "Life goes by real fast," he said. "Easy to get busy and not see people."

"Ma is looking forward to your coming at Christmas," Jim said.

"It will be good to get back to Blue Springs for a few days," said Steve. He said it flatly as if not too convinced by his own words.

"It's not changed much."

"Probably never will."

The clock ticked. Jim twisted in his seat. "You've changed some," he said, trying to keep the talking going. "Added a pound or two, maybe."

Steve smiled. Jim looked closely at him. Nice britches, hair cut neatly, fine blue shirt and yellow tie. Fancy wire-rimmed glasses. He wondered how a man could shed so much of his past in ten short years. A stranger looking at Steve would never believe he had grown up in the remotest highlands of North Carolina.

"How's our grandmother, Mrs. Waterbury?" Jim asked.

Steve shifted. "She's resting right now. Okay most of the time. Takes spells though, you know. Can hardly walk a couple of days a month. Hurts from a bad back and gets numbness in her legs. The doctor doesn't say much about what causes it."

"You take care of her by yourself?"

Steve took off his glasses, wiped them on the end of his tie. Jim thought he noticed a slight hesitation in him, something not quite right. But he couldn't put his finger on what it was.

"Yeah," said Steve. "Every now and again I have a woman come do some cleaning and cooking. But it's usually just me and her."

Jim nodded. "You seeing any young women? Ma won't like me anymore if I don't ask you that and report back to her."

Steve put his glasses back on. "I'm not a hermit. But you'd be surprised by how busy I stay, trying to make a business run, taking care of things here."

"I don't think Ma will like that answer too much," said Jim with a chuckle.

"Ma won't like anything I answer in that regard until I tell her I've got a fine Christian woman I'm about to bring home."

Jim laughed again. "How many houses you got now?"

Steve edged up on his seat. "Almost forty, and I'm buying and fixing and renting more every year. The profit margin is slim because we have too many people who don't like to pay on time or try to skip out without paying at all, but we're making some progress. A few more years and I hope to start building houses from scratch. Lots more profit in that. You're selling those, see, not just renting. And people buying their own place pay for it a lot better than folks just renting for a few months or so."

"Sounds like you got a good plan," said Jim, noting the excitement in Steve's voice.

"I think so. A little more time and it should do real well."

"Maybe you could take me around to see some of your properties."

Steve glanced at his shoes and Jim thought he saw hesitation in his face. "I take it your business continues to prosper," Steve said.

Jim started to go back to the notion of visiting some of Steve's houses, but something told him to leave it alone. "I'm making it okay," he said.

"More than okay from what I hear."

Jim felt the tension rise. He started to stay something to ease it but knew from past experience that it probably wouldn't help. Steve seemed bound and determined to prove himself as good as if not better than him, and Jim didn't know what he could do to stop that. He lifted his hat off his knee. "I reckon I should head on back home," he said. "Gone be late on the highway."

"You know you can stay the night here," said Steve, relaxing again. "Like I said when you called."

"I appreciate your invitation," said Jim, "but Ed's with me, waiting at the diner. And you know I don't like a workday to pass by without hitting a lick at a chore or two."

Steve smiled. "You're one of the hardest laboring men I ever saw."

"Seems like you do pretty good with that too."

Steve nodded and stood. Jim got the feeling that, in spite of the invitation to spend the night, Steve didn't mind too much that he had turned it down.

"I'll see you in a few days," Steve said, heading to the door.

Jim followed him, moving past a large table in the entryway. "At Jesus Holiness I reckon," he said. "Dinner at Ma's after that."

Steve opened the door. Jim glanced at the hallway table, saw several pictures sitting on it. A couple of the pictures showed Steve and Mrs. Waterbury, a couple more just Mr. and Mrs. Waterbury, a couple with Mr. and Mrs. Waterbury and another man about Steve's age. The other man looked vaguely familiar.

"You were younger then," Jim said, pointing at one of Steve's pictures.

"Thinner too," Steve said.

Jim laughed and moved closer to the pictures. "Who's he?" he asked, pointing to the young man with the Waterburys. Steve quickly picked up the photo and held it with the picture facing his chest. "A guy who worked with them for a while," he said. "But not anymore."

Jim nodded. Something bothered him about his brother's reaction, and he started to ask more about the man in the photo but then decided against it. No reason for nosiness. Jim put his hat on, shook Steve's hand and headed out the door. Steve followed him out, waving as Jim climbed into his Ford and drove off.

Turning the corner, Jim wondered why Steve seemed so guarded. Did the city make him that way? Or had he always shown that kind of streak? A man who didn't want to reveal too much?

A couple of miles from Steve's house, Jim suddenly sat up straighter as he realized what had unnerved him about the man in the photo. He looked a whole lot like Steve. Or maybe more accurately, he favored their pa to a remarkable degree. Jim played out the possibilities in his head. Just a coincidence? A trick of his mind? Or did the man actually have Waterbury blood in his veins? A cousin maybe from some part of the Waterbury family he didn't know about? Or was there something about his pa's past that nobody back home knew, maybe not even his ma? Jim couldn't know for sure either way.

Easing back into his seat, Jim told himself to let it drop. Something didn't add up here. But, like any good highlander man, he didn't see it as his place to go snooping around to find out just what. When and if the Lord wanted it revealed, the Lord would take care of it. Until then, he might as well just let it rest.

Within seconds after Jim left, Steve walked back to Mrs. Waterbury's room. She raised up from the bed as he entered.

"Your brother left?" she asked.

"Yeah," said Steve. "Headed back home."

"I know it's hard on you keeping this secret," Mrs. Waterbury said. "But it's best, don't you think?"

Steve cleaned his glasses on his tie again. Truth was, he didn't like lying to his ma. And he felt like that was what he was doing. Yet he wasn't sure. Was staying quiet about something the same thing as denying it straight out?

"I don't want to ruin my pa's name back home," he said.

"My thoughts exactly," said Mrs. Waterbury. "No reason to drag anybody through the mud, especially a dead man."

"And my ma's happy. Why cause her any undue pain?"

"You're a fine son, Steve."

Steve put his glasses back on. What good would it do to tell this? None that he could see. His pa was dead. People back home believed he died a hero trying to save Uncle Daniel's life. Why ruin that story with a sordid tale of a man who had made a woman pregnant out of wedlock? Why put that burden on his ma and hurt her that way? Only a cowardly man would do that, a man who couldn't bear the burden by himself. Well, he wasn't a cowardly man. Despite his having never fought in the war, he could carry a heavy load as well as the next man. Like a business that had huge debts hanging over it when he started managing it. Like a half brother from a pa who had never done much good for anybody his whole life.

His pa had been a cowardly man. Steve believed that now. Yes, he had made up for it at the end. But until then he had shown no courage at all. He had run out on an unmarried woman, pregnant with his baby. Then he had run out on the woman who became his wife and birthed him two sons. He had left both women with huge responsibilities while he took care of his own needs. He had lied to a lot of people and let people down. He had died penniless, a friendless crook who had failed at everything he had ever tried. Well, Steve pledged he would never become that kind of man.

"You need anything?" he asked his grandmother.

"No, I think I'll just rest awhile."

Steve left the room and walked to the porch. Although the wind nipped cold at his nose, he took a seat in a rocker and stared out at the yard. He had tried so hard in the last decade, had stretched high to take care of things, take care of people, like Mrs. Waterbury. Yes, he could have taken a place of his own, but with Allen moved away and hardly ever showing up anymore, who would care for her if he did?

He thought of his tenants, many of them poor black folks who couldn't afford much. He had fixed up their properties a lot, many times without increasing their rent a single dollar. Yet many still couldn't pay regular.

Standing, Steve walked to the porch rail and leaned over it and took out a cigarette. As for ladies, sure, he invited one out for dinner every now and again, sometimes to a movie. But none of them had interested him much. He lit the cigarette, pocketed his lighter. He thought of Claire, the woman from the train the day he left Blue Springs. He remembered the kiss she gave him as he left her. Something about her still fascinated him. He'd even tried to find her a few years ago, but nothing had ever turned up. He knew it was silly to hang on to her memory, but the woman had smitten him, and sometimes he wondered if he'd ever get over it so he could go on and find someone else.

Steve pulled a drag off his cigarette. He'd done well by most accounts. Accomplished a lot. Sent his ma some money every month. Took care of a sickly woman. Provided as best he could for his tenants. Gave money to the nearest church even though he never attended. Earned a reputation as a man of integrity in the city.

He blew smoke through his nose. He'd done one other thing too, maybe the most important thing of all. He'd kept the one promise he had pledged always to keep. He had not ended up like his pa—a weak man who didn't take care of his family.

Steve stubbed the cigarette on the rail and threw it into the yard. So long as he had anything to say about it, he would protect his ma from the knowledge that her dearly departed husband had fathered a boy she knew absolutely nothing about. His pa had never protected Abby from anything. But Steve would. Even if that meant he had to keep his distance lest she find out the awful secret that his pa's family had kept from her for so long.

CHAPTER
EIGHTEEN

E arly March rolled in clear but icy cold. Abby found herself in the parlor by the fireplace on the first Thursday of the month, some mending in her hand. Just before she sat down in her rocker to get started, she heard a knock at the door. Laying her mending down, she checked the door and found Preacher Tuttle there, his head pulled down into a thick gray coat to keep off the cold. Abby quickly opened the door and let him in.

"Come on to the fire," she said. "Let me get you some coffee."

Tuttle moved to the parlor, Abby to the kitchen. In one way, it didn't surprise her to see Tuttle. Telling everybody that the church needed some new blood, he had stopped preaching at Jesus Holiness the Sunday after Christmas. Since then he had found himself with a lot of time on his hands, time he spent visiting the people closest to him. Yet today was mighty cold for anybody, even a man with no full occupation anymore, to come out. She wondered why he had showed up this morning.

Two cups of coffee in hand, Abby moved back to Tuttle, gave

him his coffee and sat down in her rocker. He took a spot on her sofa.

"How cold you reckon it is?" he asked, sipping the coffee.

"Too cold to be out."

Tuttle nodded, stared into his coffee. Abby studied his face. She guessed his age to be seventy-five or so. The years since Elsa's death hadn't gone easy on him. He had lost weight, despite people in the church keeping him stocked up on plenty of good food.

Tuttle put the coffee cup on the floor between his feet and brushed his thin hair back. Age spots dotted his hands. Abby wanted to comfort him some way, tell him that she loved him, appreciated him for all he'd done for so many folks and for so many years.

"How are you doing since you quit preaching every week?" she asked.

Tuttle smiled. "I don't know what to do with myself," he said. "Still do my Bible reading every morning, my praying. But come Sunday I got nowhere to pour out all I stored up from the week."

"I reckon once a preacher, always a preacher."

"I guess that's why they call it a calling."

"Reckon so."

She took a drink of her coffee. Tuttle stared at his shoes. Abby almost laughed. Although he had preached most of his life, Tuttle still acted tongue-tied sometimes when he was alone with someone, even someone like her that he'd known for years.

"When will the new preacher get here for good?" she asked, trying to help him feel comfortable.

"A couple of weeks. Still in north Alabama right now, near Huntsville. But he's supposed to start preaching regular here some-time this month. He's a young fellow. Full of vim and vinegar. I plan to stay out of his way, not give him any cause to feel threat-ened by me."

"I'm sure you'll be a perfect gentleman."

"Hope the folks like him." He brushed his hair back again. Abby got the distinct feeling that he hadn't come to her on such a cold day just to pass the time. He had something specific he wanted to say.

She decided to push him along some. "You don't usually make house calls on a day so cold as this unless you got something in your craw," she said.

Tuttle glanced at her with a sheepish grin. "You are a smart woman," he said. "I am a touch nervous here. Got me a situation I don't quite know how to handle."

Abby tried to figure what. Somebody at the church needing help that Tuttle needed advice about? His own health maybe? Everybody knew he'd had some kidney problems in the last few years. "I'll do whatever I can," she assured him. "You know that."

He reached over and took her hands. "You're the salt of the earth, Abby. Nobody would argue that."

Abby started to protest but when she looked at Tuttle again, she stopped. Tears glistened in his eyes. From nowhere, it hit her why he had come. Her house—it didn't belong to her. It had belonged to Elsa. For a long time she and Elsa had lived there together. Then, when Elsa and Tuttle married, they moved to the church house, leaving her and the boys at Elsa's place. Elsa let her stay in the house without rent. That was where she had been since. Years ago, after Elsa died and Tuttle inherited all her property, she'd offered again to pay rent to him, but he had refused just as Elsa always had. But now, with Tuttle retired and a new preacher coming to move into the church house, Tuttle needed a place to live. But he didn't know how to tell her.

Tuttle opened his mouth, but Abby held up a hand to stop him. Needing a second to think, she stood, moved to the fireplace and stared into the flames. She and Thaddeus owned no place of their own. He had made a living wage over the last few years, but since they had spent most of their spare money on buying back the family land, they hadn't saved anything to buy a house outright. Maybe they could rent something. But what? Blue Springs didn't have a whole lot of decent houses for rent. What would they do now?

The notion of having Tuttle move in with them came to her but then she quickly dismissed it as impractical. Not enough room for any privacy for any of them if they did that.

She turned back to Tuttle, still sitting on the edge of the sofa. Her heart suffered for him, and she knew she needed to relieve his mind.

"Before you say anything, I want you to know I've been doing some thinking. I'm ready to move out of Blue Springs, maybe build a house up near Jim, our old land, you know?" Tuttle's eyebrows arched. Abby continued, "I figure maybe you should move back here. Since we got the new man coming to the church house, I expect you'll need a place to lay your head. You think you want to come to this old spot?"

Tuttle teared up again. Abby went to him and put a hand on his shoulder. He looked up at her, gratitude on his face. "I love it here," he said. "Didn't want to move away. Could go stay with my eldest daughter, over in Chattanooga. But all my friends are here and I'm a highlander. And this is my only place. I hate to move you out, but . . ."

Abby patted his back. "Don't fret yourself. This is a good thing. Something Thaddeus and I have talked about more than once. We got us an old car now, and with the new road up near our property, we can park it about half a mile away. Thaddeus and Rose can walk down to it, then drive on to school. It's not like the old days when you had to walk all the way into town from up there. We'll do fine. Get Jim and Ed and all working on a cabin, we can move in after a few months."

Tuttle smiled and Abby knew she had guessed right.

"You are the salt of the earth," he said again.

Abby moved back to the fire. "This is good," she said. "Let Rose move back to her origins. Live like I used to live, in the wild of the highlands."

"Except she'll have indoor plumbing," said Tuttle.

"Yeah, that'll be different."

The two of them laughed. Abby pushed back her reservations and decided not to worry. She'd go back to the land of her birth. What could be wrong with that?

———

Abby talked with Thaddeus that night, and he agreed she had done the right thing by assuring Tuttle they would move out as soon as possible. The house belonged to him; he should come live in it. Thaddeus had a little more trouble dealing with the notion of moving up on the mountain. But, after talking through all the options, he agreed they had little choice. Decent rental houses in town were hard to find. Abby would talk with Jim the next day to figure out a way to get a small house built beginning in the early spring. If everybody pitched in, they could start with three or four rooms and add on later.

When Thaddeus and Rose headed out to school the next day, Abby rode with them and Thaddeus dropped her off at Jim's office by the highway. He gave her a kiss as she climbed out. "You sure you want to walk home?" he asked. "I can get you a ride if you want."

Abby smiled and said, "I've walked all over this mountain my whole life. Don't start treating me like I'm an old woman. Not yet anyway."

Thaddeus laughed and then drove away. Abby watched him go. She drove some herself, although she didn't really like to. Unless a trip stretched out past three miles or more, she would just as soon walk. Smoothing down her skirt, she hurried across the driveway toward Jim's office. Several men said hello to her as she passed. She smiled at them and walked up the steps to the small house Jim had built to serve as his headquarters. With four garages and one gas station now, he needed a place to keep everything organized. She found him sitting behind a small metal desk, his brown shirt pressed sharply, his hair slicked back. He had his ear to a telephone but quickly made his excuses and hung up as she entered.

"You're a busy man," she said as he pulled out a chair for her.

"Never too busy for my ma," he said, kissing her on the head.

The telephone rang but Jim ignored it. "What are you doing out here so early?"

She set her purse in her lap. "It's not a social call," she said. "I don't like to bother you while you're working."

He smiled at that, and she counted her blessings that she had such a good son. He and Rebecca seemed so happy. She thought of Steve and said a quick prayer that his life might run as smoothly as Jim's.

Jim leaned back. The phone rang again. He looked at it, shook his head and faced her. Abby decided to get to the point.

"I had a visit from Preacher Tuttle yesterday." She then told Jim what Tuttle came to say, leaving out only the part about how she had actually brought up the matter for him to spare him the embarrassment. Jim nodded with understanding. "So we need to move," she said, concluding the story, "but don't really know of anything in Blue Springs."

"You can move in with us!" said Jim, springing forward in his seat. "We got an extra room. I built the house real big, you know that." He stood and moved to the room's window as he talked, obviously warming to the idea. "Rose and Porter get along great. They'll love living in the same house. And Rebecca and you can work together, take some strain off the both of you." He turned back to Abby, his face beaming.

"I appreciate the offer," said Abby, "but I thought we'd just build our own place. Use the money we've been paying on the land to buy the materials. Get everybody on it, Sol and Ed maybe, and hire a few fellows."

"Well, if that's what you want," Jim said slowly.

Abby pondered for a second, then said, "I think it's best in the long run. You and Rebecca got more than enough to handle without us piling in on you."

Jim nodded. "Maybe. But at least you can move in with us at the start, until we can get you a house built."

She took a deep breath. "That has been a worry to me," she said. "Where we'd go until we got something of our own."

The telephone rang once more.

"Go on and take it," Abby said. "You've heard most of what I came to say."

He smiled and picked up the telephone. She watched him—so professional, so adult. What a fine man he had become.

He suddenly scowled and turned away from her, his mouth pressed close to the phone. Abby wanted to leave so as not to hear his private business, but she had no place to go.

Jim grunted. "You got to be kidding me." Quiet fell on the room. Jim grunted again. "You say your brother stopped by?"

Abby tried to piece together what might be going on. Rebecca's brother Will, never close to anybody in Blue Springs, lived down in

Asheville. Had pretty much let everybody know he didn't care for anything or anybody in the highlands.

"I can't believe this," said Jim. "Got to be a mistake."

Abby stared toward the window, feeling awkward.

"This isn't possible!" argued Jim. "Not after all we've done!" He listened a few more minutes. "Okay," he finally said. "We have to deal with it. But don't worry—this isn't the last word. I can guarantee you that." He put the telephone down and looked at Abby.

"You don't have to explain anything to me," she assured him. "Your business is your business."

Jim stuck his hands in the pockets of his brown slacks and fell wearily into his chair. "I wish I didn't have to tell you," he started. "But given everything . . ." He paused and took a huge breath, exhaling slowly. "It's crazy, just crazy." He stared at Abby and shook his head in disbelief.

Abby's hands tightened on her purse. She knew that good times didn't last forever. Life ebbed and flowed, laughed with you one second and punched you hard in the ribs the next. Something about Jim's posture told her that some ebb now headed her way, a bleakness to follow some of her family's most recent successes. She braced for it.

Jim put his hands on his desk. "That was Rebecca," he said. "Her brother Will visited her today."

Abby recalled all she knew about Will Stowe, real name Wilbur. A lawyer who did a lot of buying and selling of land. Not close to his sister. A dark-haired man with the slouch of his dead pa, Topper Clack. Though she hadn't seen him more than a couple of times in the last decade, something about the man made her uneasy.

Jim went on, saying, "It seems somebody from Raleigh called him, said they needed a lawyer to handle some matters here in Blue Springs. Said they had done some checking and had heard that he knew this area."

"So?"

Jim clasped his hands together under his chin. "Well, it was the Gant family that contacted his office. They want to sell their holdings in this part of the country. Don't plan to look after anything other than what they own in Raleigh."

Abby knew instantly what this meant. The rest of the property from the old family place. Gant had been selling them the land at a reduced rate. Now they'd have to pay market price for it, most likely more than they could afford.

Then she relaxed. They had already bought all but two hundred or so of their old acres. So what if they never got those back? She'd like to bring the whole thousand back into the family but at least they had most of it. They could live on that.

Jim shook his head and she realized there was more. "I don't rightly know how to say this."

"Just speak it out," Abby said.

"When they went through Gant's papers in Raleigh, they of course found where he had owned all our acres." Jim hesitated, cleared his throat. "Well . . . it seems they found the title to the thousand acres, and there's no record of Gant selling us any of the land."

"I'm not following you. We have title to the land we bought, don't we?"

Jim studied the knuckles of his hands. "Nope. Never got any title. Gant told me he and Daniel had agreed he would just deed it all over once we had bought back the whole thousand."

Abby rocked back. "But we've got witnesses! Gant came to my house back in 1945, told us what he planned to do. Gave us that first fifty acres and told us we could buy back the rest as we got the money."

Jim nodded. "We'll go to court, no doubt of that," he said. "But you never know what a court will do. What happened in '45 is a long time ago. All we got is the word of our family, all with reasons to tell the same tale. A judge may or may not believe us."

Abby felt faint. She wiped her brow and tried to think clearly. "What about our records?" she asked. "Surely Daniel kept some, you too."

"Yeah, I got notes of what land we've paid for since Daniel's death. We'll check with Ed about Daniel's records. But again, they're just our word, our notes, nothing that will stand up without some support from Gant's books."

"What about payment?"

"Cash," said Jim. "No real record of it, especially nothing that said we paid him for land."

"Why hasn't any of this come up sooner?"

"No reason. So long as Gant lived, we had an agreement. But now, with him gone and nobody else in on it from his side, that agreement goes by the wayside."

"Can't somebody who worked with Gant testify to what he said to us, how we paid him over all these years?"

"You would think so. I know I paid him face-to-face. A few of his men were with us a couple of times, but we didn't talk much about the deal. I just handed him the money, he took it, we shook and he left. That was about it."

"They check his house in Raleigh?"

"Seems so."

"What about here in Blue Springs—didn't he keep an office here for a long time?"

"Yeah, had a small place up near my house he used when he visited here."

"Anybody check there?"

"Don't know. Guess we should."

Abby took a heavy breath. What a mix-up! But maybe it wasn't too bad. Just because they had a dispute over some property didn't mean anything bad would happen. A couple of days in court and a fair judge would settle the whole thing. But what if he didn't? What if a judge decided against them, allowed the Gant family to lay claim to all the land, sell it from under them even though they had already paid for it?

"What do you think will happen?" she asked.

Jim turned, faced the window. Abby could see he didn't want to answer, to say out loud something that Will had told Rebecca.

Abby stood and walked to him, put a hand on his shoulder. "It's okay, Jim."

"No. It's not," he said quietly. "They want us off the property. Will said he had come to bring that message. That we had to move. Sol and Jewel, Ed and Priscilla too."

The revelation didn't unnerve Abby all that much. She'd lived

too long and seen too many bad things to get spooked by such as
this. "What you figure we should do?"

Jim patted her hand as it lay on his shoulder. "First, we don't
move," he said. "Not without a judge throwing us off."

Quiet fell for several seconds. Abby moved to the window and
looked out. "Seems like surprises come when you least expect
them."

"Guess that's why they call them surprises."

Abby smiled but it had no pleasure in it.

"I guess we could just let it go, then try to buy it back again
since they're selling it," Jim said.

"For the third time? That's just a touch unfair, don't you
think?"

Jim nodded. Abby weighed the situation. She wondered what
this meant for her and Thaddeus, her need to move.

"You will still move in with us," said Jim, thinking along with
her. "But you best do it fast, before the law tells us you can't. Once
you get there, it's harder to throw you off."

"The fact that you've all built on the land—Ed, Sol and you—
that will add some weight to your word that Gant sold you the
property."

"I expect so. Only somebody's liable to say that Gant just let us
live there for a time, while we worked for him. Without clear title,
we just don't know. Especially if somebody really wants us off the
land."

Abby moved back to her son and tried to figure what to say.
Tell him not to worry, that everything would turn out all right? She
didn't know that for certain. Sometimes things didn't turn out all
right. Sometimes bad things turned up, and no matter how hard
you looked, you just couldn't see the reason for them. Yet, she
believed, as her pa used to say, that if you looked close enough you
could see some good come out of all things. That didn't mean all
things were good, though. Just that sometimes God moved through
all the muck and mud to bring out some fresh water. Well, this one
sure looked mighty muddy.

She picked up her purse. Jim looked at her with anxious eyes.
For a second he looked like a little boy again.

"What *you* think we should do, Ma?" he asked. "I'm fresh open for advice."

Abby stared at him and suddenly she knew what they had to do. Although moving back to the family land had always been Daniel's dream and not hers, this was just plain wrong. No way should a family get thrown off of property they had paid for fair and square. When Laban lost the land the first time in his foolish wager, they had no choice. Every highlander knew a man had to pay up, no questions asked, when he lost a bet. But this smelled foul and she just couldn't accept it without protest.

"We fight," she said, her jaw firm. "No two ways to it. This land is ours, bought and paid for. It's ours forever. It's where we should all live if we choose to. You and your family, Ed and Sol and theirs, me and mine." She talked louder now, voicing something she hadn't realized she held so close to her heart. "We've all spread out since the war. And not just our family either. Just about all the young of the highlands have grown up and left, all thinking they've got to go somewhere else to find their fortunes."

She thought of Steve and wanted to cry, but she held back. "Well, we need to keep this spot on the mountain this time, our grounding place, land where we can always return. I got a feeling that everything around us will keep on changing in the next years, changing so fast it will make your head swim. But this mountain won't change; our land will stay the same."

She stepped to the window and stared out. Blue Springs Mountain stood some miles away, yet she could still make out its outline against the clear sky.

"For a long time when I was a girl I wanted to leave this land," she said. "Wanted to leave the isolation, the poverty and ignorance." She shook her head. "But that was a long time ago. I don't know if it's me or the place, but something is different now. We still got our problems up here. Still a lot of poorness, still cut off some from the outside world. I don't know, but it seems to me these highlands are about the only secure thing anybody around here has got left." Her voice dropped to a whisper. "Without our land, we're people without roots, nothing to tie us together. To lose the land now, after all we've gone through to get it back . . ." She turned and faced Jim again. "It would be like losing our ties to everything, who we are as highlanders. You know what I mean?"

Jim went to her, put an arm around her waist. "You always said we could see God's face on our mountain," he said.

Abby nodded. "Without our land I don't know what will become of us. It's where we best see the Lord."

Jim gazed out the window at the mountain with his ma.

"We'll fight for this land of ours," she said quietly.

CHAPTER
NINETEEN

W ill Stowe left his sister Rebecca's house and immediately headed north out of Blue Springs. He drove a bright blue Ford, wore a navy blue suit with a sheen to it and a white shirt and light blue tie, everything fresh and neat. A small smile played on his lips as he anticipated his next move in this most recent game of his. Outside, the sun appeared tired, worn out by the cold clear sky. Will felt good though. After a long time waiting, things had started to turn for the better for him. He pointed the car past the last house in Blue Springs.

As he drove, he recalled the days long ago when as a child he had lived here. He and his sister and younger brother had grown up as unclaimed kids of Topper Clack. When Clack stayed away, they did okay. But when he came around, no one ever knew what would happen. He might cuff them about in a drunken rage or he might hand them five dollars and send them to the store. Such unpredictable happenings could throw off a child's sense of balance. Their mother, though beautiful and smart, seemed to have no power when it came to her man's temper. Except for rare occasions that had to do with her children, she always yielded to his demands.

On one occasion when she did stand up to Topper, she demanded that he pay for her daughter to go to Raleigh and get an education. If not, she said, she would never see him again. At that point, Clack gave in. After all, Elizabeth Stowe had a particularly pleasing look about her, and any man with blood in his veins wouldn't want to give that beauty up just to save a few dollars and keep a useless girl around.

When his sister, Rebecca, moved off to Raleigh to attend school, Will begged her to take him with her. But, still young herself, she had no means to make that happen, in spite of her promises to the contrary. Will hadn't known this at the time and so, as the years passed and Rebecca never did anything to keep her promise, he marked it off as a lack of love. She had repeated her promises every time she came home. She did teach him to read pretty well and even brought him books from Raleigh, but she never got him out of the highlands, and he never forgave her for it. Any true sister would have managed to get her baby brother out of the hellish world of Topper Clack, and yet Rebecca had failed to do that. Obviously, then, she wasn't a true sister.

Left behind to care for himself, Will did the only thing a boy his age could do. He worked hard to please Topper Clack, all in the effort to avoid the smacks Clack liked to land on him.

For a while things had gotten some better. Noticing that his pa had tried to clean up his look, wear new clothes and such, Will had sought the same for himself. In fact, it was during this time that Will had gotten the idea that eventually saved him. After reading in one of Rebecca's books about the famous Scopes Trial that took place in Dayton, Tennessee, in 1925, Will had decided that maybe he could become a lawyer like that Clarence Darrow fellow. And, knowing from his mama that Topper thought he should take his business into more legal areas than moonshining, Will figured maybe Topper would pay for his education, that is if he could become convinced that a true-to-life lawyer might actually do him some good someday.

But then, right before he got a chance to talk to Topper about it, Daniel Porter killed him in the shootout at the Lolleyville jail. That put a real crimp in Will's plans. If not for the fact that Topper had left a sizable wad of money at his ma's house that she kept for herself after he died, Will didn't know what would have become of him and his brother. As it was, his ma used the money to move away from Blue Springs and get them both started to school in Knoxville.

Will went on to become a lawyer like he had dreamed and opened up a practice in Asheville that specialized in buying and selling land. But he still felt real mad at his sister and all the Porters. So when his firm got a telephone call from a lawyer in the capital city telling them that a family over there wanted to sell some property near his old house, he instantly took the job. And then when he found out the family was none other than Billy Gant's and that the property was the exact same land the Porters were now buying back, he just about danced a jig.

At first he didn't know what he would or would not do about it all. Fact was, he still didn't have a workable plan. Still, the idea that the Porters might lose what they had all worked so hard to gain made Will grin with joy. And his sister, well, she had married a Porter, so she deserved whatever came her way. Maybe this would take her down off her high horse a little. Make her pay a little more attention to others.

Will steered his Ford up the last stretch of road leading to the spot where he knew would be best to park. Yes, he had known about the Porters buying up their old land. He kept up with the goings-on in Blue Springs through letters Rebecca sent him. Of course he hardly ever wrote her back. He didn't want her to think she could make up with him so easily. With Will, past hurts stayed put a long time, and eight or nine letters a year didn't even begin to nudge them out.

His jaw set, Will left the car and trudged up the last incline to the Porter land. A few minutes later he crossed Slick Rock Creek and made his way up the clearing toward the small house where Billy Gant used to stay when he checked on the work of his logging crew. Will stayed low now, and quiet. He didn't want anybody to see him approach the house. Probably no one else had thought about doing what he had come to do. Even so, he wanted to make sure. No reason to advertise his presence.

Passing behind a tree whenever he could, he neared the frame house from the back, away from the side where, three acres away, Ed's house was situated. At the door he tried the knob and found it open. He smiled as he stepped inside. Mountain folk didn't much go in for locks.

The air in the house smelled musty. He knew that no one had opened a window or door here for many weeks, maybe months. A thick layer of dust lay over the floors, and cobwebs hung in the corners. He glanced around the room. A small wooden desk sat straight ahead, a wicker basket on the floor beside it. On a table in the corner was a coffeepot, with a dust-covered lamp next to it. Three chairs stood in front of the desk. Overlooking the desk and chairs was a square window.

Will rifled through the desk, found an old ledger, two pencils and a stack of unused writing paper. He scanned the ledger, saw it was empty, then dropped it back into the drawer and turned around, leaving the drawer open. Unsure what to do now, Will inspected the room again, looking for what, he wasn't sure. He noticed a door to his right and walked through it, his feet tracking in the dust. A single bed sat in this second room, a table with a lamp on it beside the bed. The table had a drawer. Again, the room had one window, this one with filthy curtains hanging over it. The window had a small crack at the top, and a light breeze blew through it.

He checked the table drawer and found nothing but a Bible. He ran his fingers over the dusty cover. Such a silly book. Full of tales fit only for women and children. He thought of his late pa, the open contempt Topper had for matters of religion. His pa hated all the nonsense the preachers spouted, all the ranting about "Jesus this" and "Jesus that." Well, Jesus never did a thing for him, never stopped Topper from beating his back with a stick until the blood ran, never made Topper quit hitting his ma when he had too much of the drink.

Disgusted, Will grabbed a handful of pages from the Bible and ripped them out. He crumpled the pages in his fist and threw the wad to the floor. Stupid religion; no good for anything. The breeze eased the crumpled pages toward the corner of the room.

He took a big breath as he looked over the rest of the room. A trunk at the end of the bed produced a few pairs of men's denim pants, some flannel shirts and a pair of worn boots. Will left everything in the trunk, then scanned the room one more time. Nothing. He turned to leave but then stopped. Might as well check under the bed, he thought. Lowering his face, he looked under the cot but saw nothing. He stood and lifted the mattress, just in case. A white folder had been placed between the bottom board and the mattress of the cot. He picked up the folder and searched through it. A couple of letters from Mrs. Gant. A newspaper with a headline about the end of World War II. Another ledger book.

Will opened the book with trembling fingers. He read Billy Gant's signature on the front page. He flipped to the next page, the statement of accounts. It was full of entries. Page after page of business dealings. Names, dates, deals. All the labor of a man of commerce.

His heart beating faster, he scanned the pages looking for the name Daniel Porter. Before long, he found it. The name first appeared in early September 1945. A statement about the fifty acres Gant had granted to Porter.

Will's fingers traced through the list of transactions. Time and time again Porter's name showed up. After 1946, Jim Waterbury's name became the one of record. Dollar amounts. Acreage sold. Dates of the sale. All of it plain and proper and in good order. No court in the land would argue with this record. The Porter family owned almost eight hundred acres.

Will smiled and took another deep breath. His instincts had served him well once more. A good lawyer learned to trust such things, especially the thoughts that came in the middle of the night. A man like Gant would surely keep good records. If not at his home or office in Raleigh then somewhere else, somewhere close by, somewhere where he did his work.

After throwing the bed back together, Will headed out, the ledger firmly held to his side. Fifteen minutes later he reached the

Ford, his breath short from his hurried pace down the incline. He quick opened the trunk and slid the ledger into a black briefcase. Then, using a key attached to a ring of keys he had in his pocket, he locked the briefcase and slammed the trunk shut.

Soon he was driving down the mountain, a wide grin on his face. While not exactly sure what he planned to do with the ledger in his trunk, he did know one thing: he didn't plan to tell anybody that he had it. Not his wife in Asheville, not his brother in Knoxville, not the Gants in Raleigh. And, most definitely of all, not the Porters in Blue Springs.

CHAPTER
TWENTY

S pring settled gently on Raleigh in 1957, the breezes soft and
the rain sufficient but not rough. By the time April rolled in,
the rains had largely stopped and Steve had taken to wearing short-
sleeved shirts on most days, his jacket shed in favor of the sunny
days and warm temperatures. As usual, though, he kept wearing
his tie. A man of his position dare not let his tenants see him without proper attire. That might cause them to disrespect him. The
most important thing Steve had learned in his time collecting rents:
if folks didn't respect you, they tended to avoid paying. Somehow
a tie hanging from the neck of a crisply starched shirt seemed to
remind the tenants that he deserved payment come the first of
every month.

Steve had fallen into a rather predictable if uninspiring pattern
by that April. Work from seven in the morning until six at night.
Go to Mrs. Waterbury's for a bite of supper. Leave her house and
stop in at a gentlemen's establishment about eight. Have a few
drinks, though nothing alcoholic. He'd learned not to drink by

watching what it did to his pa. There he would visit with a couple of businessmen with whom he regularly met, then go home about ten, shower and fall into bed. It wasn't exciting but it was simple and kept him from thinking too much. He liked that part—no time for deep reflection. Just do your job, collect your rents, keep your nose clean and live from day to day. Even at twenty-nine years old, he didn't think it wise to project too far into the future. If growing up during the hard times of the Depression had taught him anything, it had taught him that the future could always change—and usually did.

The first Saturday of April began like most every other day. He climbed into his black Chevy with the whitewall tires, his blue shirt fresh, his yellow tie gleaming, his black shoes clean and polished. With only four tenants slated for a collection visit, he figured to make it home by lunchtime. Afterward he hoped to go downtown and meet a couple of buddies for lunch.

Pulling out of the driveway, Steve turned left at the end of the street and drove west. He had three properties about four miles away, two of them houses he had only recently bought and put up for rent. These particular houses were a touch nicer than most of what he owned, and he expected the tenants—two women about his age, one a nurse named Margaret, the other a lady he hadn't yet met—to pay without much prodding. He loved those people who proved they were dependable, steady and consistent. Over the years he'd worked hard to find these kinds of folks to live in his houses. To do that, he'd also labored to improve the quality of his properties. Now, after his having worked at it the last ten years, they all had a solid roof that almost never leaked, fresh paint within and without and driveways with no mudholes in them.

He had even improved the houses in the Negro section of town. No reason not to treat these folks with respect too, just like he treated everybody else. Steve had hired an old man named Izzy to help him in that section. A former preacher in the area, Izzy lived there in one of Steve's rental properties. Izzy, known as Isaiah in his preaching days, did most of the collections in his part of town.

"Folks here know me," he had said to Steve when he made his pitch for the job. "You just let me live in this good house for nothin', and I'll bring you every dollar owed to you every month of the year."

It didn't take Steve long to accept the offer, and after a year or so, Izzy had become an important man in his operation. Not only did he collect rents, he also took care of complaints and oversaw the fix-ups in the neighborhood. Fact was, when Steve needed anybody to take care of a hard job, he knew he could depend on Izzy.

This morning, though, Steve didn't have any collections to make over in Izzy's area, so he turned left and headed south. Then half a mile down he turned left again. A couple of minutes later he reached the two new houses he'd bought. Wide porches fronted both houses, with trees surrounding them. A sidewalk ran in front and a fence marked out the backyard. A small white shed stood to the right. Steve's chest swelled with pride. He hadn't yet done any building, but he at least had managed to upgrade the quality of the houses he now owned. Soon he'd build one from scratch, maybe do one of those subdivisions everybody seemed so keen on these days.

He parked the vehicle, climbed out and walked to the front door of the first house and knocked. Nobody answered. He knocked again. He heard a groaning sound coming from inside. He waited, not sure what to do. Another groan rolled through the house, and he stepped to the side to see through a window. He saw a sofa and a couple of chairs in front of a fireplace, yet nothing identified the one doing the groaning. Steve thought about leaving. Whatever was going on wasn't his business. But then he realized that the groaning person might need his help, that maybe someone was hurt. What if he walked away and the person died in his house? Maybe even from foul play? That would hurt his business for sure. Most of the folks in this neighborhood owned their houses. What if something bad happened in one of the few rentals? People would not take kindly to that, would want to do away with tenants and properties like his.

He knocked again, louder this time. Another groan sounded from the back of the house. Steve tried the door and found it open. He yelled out but nobody answered. He moved through the front of the house. Another moan sounded. He reached the door where the sound originated. For a second he hesitated. Then he heard voices.

"Hey!" Steve yelled. "Everybody okay here?"

He heard feet on the floor, then the door swung open and Margaret, the tenant he had met, stuck her head outside. She wore brown slacks and a tan blouse. A white towel lay over a shoulder.

"It's my sister," she said. "She's, well, she's delivering, that's the trouble."

Steve shook his head, not understanding.

"A baby," said Margaret. "She's delivering a baby."

Steve's face flushed. "We got hospitals for that!"

"I know. But my sister didn't want a hospital . . . can't really afford one."

"They'll take her. Money or not."

Margaret shrugged. "She asked me to help her with the delivery. What can I say? I'm a nurse, just trying to help my sister."

Steve paused, tried to think. "This is a respectable neighborhood," he said. "Not a place for baby delivery."

"I know," said Margaret again. "But what was I supposed to do?"

"Where's your sister's husband?" he asked. "I'll help him get her to the hospital."

Margaret sighed. A loud groan escaped the bedroom. "I need to get back in there," Margaret said.

"Her husband's not here?" asked Steve.

Margaret shook her head, her eyes down.

"She's not married, is she? That's why you two live together."

Margaret faced him now. "No," she said. "She's not married."

Steve rubbed his chin. What a mess! If this got out, the neighbors would run off his tenants as soon as they could. He thought of lifting the woman off the bed, carrying her to his car and driving her to the hospital before anybody could find out what was going on. But then he thought of Allen, how his own pa had gotten a woman pregnant, how she had delivered her baby without benefit of a husband nearby. Steve made a quick decision.

"Get back in there," he told Margaret. "I'll get a doctor."

"You don't need to do that," said Margaret. "I can deliver a baby just fine."

"Maybe so, but I want a doctor here anyway, just in case."

Margaret's eyes smiled with gratitude.

"Move!" said Steve. "And keep her quiet if that's possible."

Margaret touched his elbow, then turned and flew back to her sister.

Steve went immediately to the telephone in the front parlor and called a lawyer he knew. "Steve here," he said quickly. "I need a favor."

A few minutes later he hung up the phone and hurried back to the bedroom door. He knocked and Margaret stuck her head out again.

"I've got a doctor coming," he said. "Should be here in thirty minutes."

"She's hanging in there," Margaret said. "I think it'll be a while yet. I told her to stay as quiet as she could. Told her a doctor was coming."

Steve nodded, grateful for the help.

"She wants to see you," said Margaret.

"What?" Steve stood up straighter.

"My sister—she's afraid you'll evict me on her account."

"She doesn't need to worry about that," said Steve, not wanting to go into the room. "I'm just looking after my own interests, to tell you the truth. I get this baby delivered safely and get her out of here, nobody's the worse for any of this, the neighbors never know. You see what I mean?"

Margaret laid a hand on his forearm and said, "I think you're understating it. It really doesn't matter to me either way, but my sister says if you don't come in and let her thank you, she's going to scream to high heaven until you do."

Steve grunted. What kind of craziness was this? Yet, if that was what it would take to keep the woman quiet . . .

He agreed, and Margaret led him into the room and over to the bed. The woman lying there had blond hair, damp with sweat. A sheet was spread over her body from the neck down. Her face, though squeezed with pain, looked vaguely familiar. She motioned him closer, and he took a seat by the head of the bed. She stared hard at him. Her eyes were bluer than anything he'd ever seen.

He took a quick hard breath.

The woman said, "I'm sorry we had to meet like this."

Steve found it hard to speak. The woman gritted her teeth and closed her eyes. Another groan, this one quieter than the others, escaped anyway. Steve studied her face, her round forehead, firm chin, full lips. He told himself it wasn't possible, that what he thought couldn't be true.

The groan ceased, and the woman opened her eyes again. "I didn't know where else to go," she said. "Margaret has always been my big sister. She . . . takes care of me. Always has." She then closed her eyes as if to rest.

Steve faced Margaret. "When did she get here?"

"Just this morning," said Margaret. "Planned to move in earlier, but you know, things happened."

"She doesn't look like you," he said.

Margaret smiled. "She's the blond one, like our father. I'm the brunette, like my mama."

Steve nodded. He feared to ask his next question but knew he had to do it. "You know the father of this baby?"

"No, she won't tell me."

"Did you know she was in this shape before she came to you?"

"Yes, I've known for a couple of months. That's why we figured we'd get a place together. Until the baby was born, then she'd go somewhere else."

"And the father's not helping?"

"He gives her a little money, but he said marriage wouldn't do for either of them."

Steve's anger boiled at the man, at any man who would do this to a woman and then leave her.

For several minutes the room fell quiet except for the occasional groan and the sound of Steve's heart pounding in his chest. He stared at the woman on the bed like a man staring at a dream, wondering if it was real. How could this be? He dreaded asking Margaret, knew that if he did, something would happen that he couldn't control. Yet, in spite of his dread, he knew he had to face the matter head on. For some reason, fate or God or something had put this situation right in his hands, and he had to deal with it whether he wanted to or not. He addressed Margaret one more time, his eyes never leaving the woman about to give birth.

"You haven't told me her name," he said.

Margaret stepped over to the bed, put a wet cloth on her sister's head. The pregnant woman opened her eyes, looked straight at Steve. He had never seen such blue eyes, except once, a long time ago, on a train.

"I'm Claire," she said. "Good to meet you."

Steve took her hand and held it tightly. "Steve," he said. "I own this place."

Her eyes widened for just a second as if in recognition, but then a cloud moved across them and her expression dimmed.

Steve could hardly breathe. After all these years, the woman from the train! Was this why he'd never met anybody else that interested him? Nobody who made his heart thump like this? Had the Lord wanted him to wait on Claire? To find her like this so he could take care of her? How strange that she should show up this way. If not God's will, then what? Pure coincidence? But which did he believe? Which did he trust? Did he even believe in God's will anymore? Or God, for that matter?

Unable to answer his questions, Steve just held on to Claire's hand and waited. Let the doctor come, he figured. Let him deliver the baby. Then Steve would decide what to do next.

CHAPTER
TWENTY-ONE

I t took until mid-July for the judge in Asheville to get things situated enough to hold a hearing regarding the rightful owner of the land Billy Gant's death had placed in dispute. Thankfully for Abby and her kin, Mrs. Gant had shown herself a generous woman and had not forced them to move in the meantime.

The Monday of the hearing broke off so hot that the fan Abby carried to keep herself cool failed to do much good. Her blouse, a light blue cotton piece that buttoned in the back, stuck to her back from perspiration. When the judge—a hog-faced man by the name of Hobbert—entered the room and took his seat, Abby wondered how he could stand the heat in his black robe.

The judge grunted, and Abby's heart quickened. What if he threw them off the land? Disallowed their claim to any of it? What would happen to her family? She glanced to her left. Ed, Jim and Sol sat side by side, each of them dressed in their Sunday-go-to-church clothes. Except for Abby, the women had stayed home. Thaddeus had agreed to let Abby come while he took care of Rose.

Abby placed her hands in her lap and tried to stay calm. The good Lord would provide, she knew that. Despite her confidence, she hated the notion of giving up the land she and her kin had purchased. Once, maybe. But twice? No, that wasn't right. She set her jaw, still determined to fight this thing with everything she had.

She looked to her right. Mrs. Billy Gant sat just behind the lawyer's bench, her curly hair touching her shoulders, her hands also in her lap. She wore a navy blue jacket and skirt, a simple but nice white blouse. She had on makeup but not too much. Mrs. Gant glanced at Abby and nodded as if she knew her. Abby wondered if she did.

Hobbert rapped his gavel and everybody faced his way. A man in a black suit announced the case and the hearing started. It took close to an hour. For several minutes Hobbert studied over some papers on his raised desk. Then he called the lawyers—Will Stowe on behalf of Mrs. Billy Gant, and Tom Link, a man Jim had hired from Asheville—to make a statement or two. Stowe stood tall at his bench and told the judge how Mrs. Gant wanted to do the right thing about all this but that she and her family also wanted what rightfully belonged to them. If her dearly departed husband had indeed sold the land to the Porter family, all they had to do was to produce some proof to that effect—nothing more, nothing less.

The judge asked him if all of Gant's records had been searched for any documents to show the truth of the matter either way. Stowe said yes. Gant's home, his offices in Raleigh and in Blue Springs had all been searched, but they came up with nothing to say what was or wasn't done regarding the land.

Hobbert studied his papers some more. Abby focused on Stowe. Something about him bothered her. Like the fact that he didn't look her in the eye when she spoke to him as they entered the courtroom. Like his polished ways. Yes, it was fine to put on a nice suit and look good. People in his profession needed to do that. But something about Will Stowe went beyond dressing nice to match his line of work. He seemed to use his refinement as a perch from which to look down on others, like he had climbed up and over them. Well, Abby knew Stowe's background and it didn't include much that gave him any cause to act all high and snooty.

Abby wondered why Will and Rebecca hadn't stayed in better touch over the years. Though she had never directly asked Rebecca about it, she knew for a fact that the two didn't do much conversing. Did they have something hard going on between them? Did Will look down on Rebecca because she had chosen to marry a Blue Springs boy and settle down with him? Another notion came to Abby, and she sat up straighter as she pondered it. Did Will Stowe see her family as the enemy, like his pa always had? If so, Rebecca's marrying a Porter might stick in his craw just a little. Maybe he stood off some from his sister because he disliked all things related to the Porters.

Her brow furrowed. If Stowe had it in for the Porters, if the feud still burned in his gut, then she needed to pay real close attention to this case. A lawyer with a grudge could do her and her kin some real damage, especially when he held a case that directly affected their life and property.

A twinge of guilt hit Abby. Was she thinking bad things about a man without any cause? Was she holding Stowe's blood against him without reason? After all, he was just a lawyer handling a case. What relationship he kept with his sister wasn't her business. Maybe Rebecca and Will had drifted apart as a natural result of life—one in one direction, the other in another. She knew that happened with folks, even blood relatives. Life just carried people out and away.

Abby's heart ached. Like her and her boy Steve. He didn't write much or call either. She wrote him almost every week. Most of the time he didn't answer. She asked him to come home more often, but he always said his business kept him too involved to break away. She tried to figure out if she had done anything to hurt him, to make him want to stay absent. She couldn't think of anything.

Maybe Steve just never liked Blue Springs. Like his pa, maybe he preferred life in a bigger place. Perhaps Blue Springs reminded him of bleaker days, times when his pa disappeared on him, disappointed him. And so he returned only when necessary because he didn't like the way the place made him feel. Who knew?

Abby waved her fan across her face. She had wanted to leave Blue Springs too. How could she blame Steve for trying to make his way in the world, even if it cut him off from her?

She smiled as she remembered the money Steve sent home every month. All his life he'd said he would take care of her. She would have preferred his presence much more than the money, yet it showed he still wanted to keep that childhood promise.

Judge Hobbert cleared his throat and Abby looked up.

The judge laid down the papers and said, "I see here that Mr. Gant held a business partnership with a Mr. Roosevelt Sweeter, up in New York."

Stowe looked surprised. He turned to Mrs. Gant but she held out her hands, palms up. Stowe faced the judge. "This is new information, Your Honor."

"Shouldn't be," said Hobbert. "It's in the papers here."

Stowe smoothed down the front of his coat. "Yes, Your Honor," he said. "But I must inquire as to the relevance of that partnership."

Peering over his glasses at the lawyer, Hobbert said, "It's not your place to inquire of me. But I'm a fair man. I'll answer you. If Mr. Gant holds a partnership with another person, maybe he kept some of his records there. Have those records been searched for anything germane to this hearing?"

Stowe turned to Mrs. Gant again. She shrugged. Abby could see that the woman didn't know much about her husband's business. Stowe faced the judge. "Not that I know of," he said. "But that doesn't mean—"

Hobbert scowled, which caused Stowe to shut his mouth. The judge shifted his attention to Tom Link, lifting his large hand to indicate to Link he should stand now and give his account.

Link stood—a thin, balding man wearing a gray suit.

Hobbert pointed to his papers. "Says here your clients are claiming about eight hundred acres of land."

"Yes," said Link. "Bought up over the last eleven years."

"You say you got papers to support these claims?"

"Yes," said Link, his tone hopeful. "A list of the parcels and when they were bought."

"Notes kept by the Porter family."

"Yes."

"No independent records?"

Link's shoulders slumped. "No, but—"

"You got witnesses?"

"Yes."

"The Porter family again?"

"Yes."

"No others?"

Link stood straighter. "Yes, your honor. A couple of men who saw Daniel Porter give Mr. Gant money on at least three occasions. I will gladly call them."

"Not today," Hobbert said, waving him off. "Hold that for the trial if it comes to that. Can the witnesses state why Mr. Porter gave Mr. Gant the money?"

Link slumped again. "No," he said. "They didn't hear anything about the reason for the money exchange."

The judge ran his fingers through his hair. He turned back to Stowe and said, "Can you produce anyone to state that what Mr. Link claims is *not* true? That the Porter family didn't buy back this land?"

Stowe looked surprised. "No, not really, but—"

Hobbert held up a hand. "No 'buts' here. Now, Mr. Stowe, do you have any evidence that they didn't buy back the land?"

"Your Honor knows that the party that holds title to a property legally owns that property. No other proof is required. Mr. Gant's family holds the deed to the land. Not the Porter family."

Hobbert nodded in agreement. Stowe beamed his pleasure. The judge said, "How do you explain the fact that three families of Porters have built homes on the property? How could they have done that without the approval of Billy Gant? If they didn't own the land, would Mr. Gant have allowed them to build such permanent structures on it?"

Stowe thought for a second. Abby thought the judge had him stumped.

"I can't answer for why the deceased did or didn't do what he did or allowed," Stowe said. "Maybe he let them build because one of them worked as supervisor of his logging crew and he wanted him to live close by. He may have allowed the others to build but as renters. Perhaps he planned to take the houses from them later.

Or maybe he sold them the acreage where the houses actually sit, a half acre or so. Who can say? The point is not whether they did or didn't build and live on the land. We know they did. The point is, did they own it or not? That is what we don't know. But Mrs. Gant holds the deed to the property. That makes her the legal owner of the disputed land, no matter who built or lived on it or for how long."

Hobbert nodded as if he knew the answer but wanted somebody to remind him of it. He read over the papers in front of him for another couple of minutes. Then he grunted, looked up and faced the courtroom. Abby glanced at Jim. He reached to her, took her hand in his.

"This is a complicated matter," Hobbert said. "On the letter of the law, I have no choice but to accept Mr. Stowe's argument. The holder of the deed owns the property. No two ways about it."

Abby's heart about stopped.

"Yet," continued the judge, "we've got other circumstances here, circumstances that complicate the situation. People already living on the land, houses built. That tells me something went on here that we don't exactly understand, that the relationship between Mr. Gant and the Porter family went beyond mere employer and employee connections." He paused to take a breath. Abby's hopes rose. "I hesitate to throw families out of the houses they've built until I can know more of what put them there. Until I can make absolute certain that there are no records anywhere to show one way or the other what happened." He looked at Stowe, then at Link.

"So here's what I'm going to do. I'm going to leave this matter open for now. Give us time to check on this partnership in New York. In the meantime, I'm going to allow the families already on the land to stay there. But they can't build anything else, can't change anything from the way it currently is. Mrs. Gant, on the other hand, can't sell the land to anyone else, can't make material changes to the disputed property. Until we can get a bit more information, we will leave things as they are today. After consultation with the attorneys and a look at the court docket, we'll make some determinations about the future dispensation of this case." With that, Hobbert took off his glasses, rapped the gavel on his bench, stood and left the room.

Abby faced Jim. He looked confused.

Link turned to them. "It's okay," he said. "About as good as we could have hoped."

"Everybody stays put?" asked Jim.

"Exactly. Nothing changes."

Jim nodded. Abby took a big breath. Link started gathering up his papers.

"But what about you?" Jim said to Abby.

"What do you mean?"

"You, Thaddeus and Rose got nowhere to go. We were going to build you a place up near us, remember?"

Abby tried to appear unconcerned. "We'll find something," she said. "We don't need much space."

Jim shook his head. "It's not right. We bought that land, all of it."

"I know. But it's okay; we'll be fine." She heard movement behind her and turned just as Mrs. Gant reached her. Abby's eyes widened.

"I'm Louise Gant," she said, extending a hand. "Billy Gant's wife."

"I know," said Abby. She took the hand and shook it. "Your husband was a good man, and we're sorry for his passing."

Mrs. Gant smiled. "He spoke fondly of Daniel Porter," she said. "But he never said anything to me about all this business. Mr. Gant didn't believe in talking about such matters at home."

"I know the type," said Abby, glancing at Jim. "Closemouthed men."

Mrs. Gant smiled again, and Abby felt good about her.

"I wanted you to know I'm not feeling hard toward you for your stance on this," said Mrs. Gant. "I'm not trying to take something if it doesn't belong to me, but I got to do what's right for my family."

"I don't resent you either," Abby said. "You're just trying to protect what's yours."

"I'm glad you feel that way. It would be easy for us to dislike each other. I don't want that."

"Neither do I."

Mrs. Gant stepped to her, and Abby opened her arms. The two women embraced for just a second, then stepped back.

"I will check on the matter in New York," said Mrs. Gant. "I was not aware of my husband's connections there."

"Seems like your lawyer knew but didn't want to speak of it."

Mrs. Gant shrugged. "Lawyers. Who knows when it comes to them."

Abby smiled. Mrs. Gant didn't know that her first husband, Stephen, had been a lawyer. Yet she was right about one thing. She didn't know about Will Stowe. So maybe she or someone else should do some checking on him.

CHAPTER
TWENTY-TWO

For the rest of the week and into the next, Abby's uneasiness about Stowe continued. True, he'd said that all of Billy Gant's offices had been checked. But what did that mean? Could she trust him? What if he'd found something in Gant's Blue Springs office that would help her family's case? Would he have brought it forward? Maybe not.

Her suspicions increasing by the day, Abby visited Jim at his office the next Friday and asked him if he would make a short trip with her the next morning.

"You want to go up to Gant's place, don't you?" he asked.

Abby smiled. "You got a mind like mine," she said. "Are we wicked for wanting to check if Stowe's been tellin' the truth?"

Jim shrugged. "Just cautious," he said. "Rebecca's said more than once that Stowe holds no love for any of us, not even her."

"Why you think that is?"

"Rebecca says he holds it against her that she didn't take him when she moved away to go to school when she was a kid."

"That's many a year to keep a grudge."

"Yeah, but you know the Clacks—they harbor hurts a long time."

Abby had to agree that was true. "Let's go up to Gant's place in the morning," she said.

Jim nodded. "Maybe we should keep this to ourselves."

"My plans exactly. If we get in any trouble for it, no reason for Thaddeus or Rebecca to end up in the same boat."

"The law would go easy on you," Jim said with a smile. "No prior convictions."

"We can do it quick and easy," Abby said.

———

Saturday dawned, and Abby left Thaddeus and Rose in bed and met Jim at Jesus Holiness just before seven. The trip took just less than forty minutes, the last ten up a dirt road so overgrown that tree branches brushed against Jim's truck as they drove. They talked only a little. Jim asked about Steve, and Abby told him she hadn't heard much lately.

"That's normal for him, isn't it?" asked Jim.

"Pretty much," said Abby. "I worry about him some."

Jim turned the truck up a steep incline. "I fear sometimes that I ran him off from here. The older brother, always besting him at things, you know how that is."

"Like a couple of bears," agreed Abby. "The smaller has to leave the territory to make his own way."

"I wish he lived near us," Jim said. "I miss him."

"He seems right successful. Sends me money on a regular basis. Even telephoned me when he heard about the situation with Preacher Tuttle. Told me he had a place in Raleigh where I could live, asked me to come with Thaddeus and Rose."

"You don't plan to take him up on that, do you?"

"Oh, no, I've spent my time off this mountain. Thaddeus is happy here, me too. No reason to leave."

"Good," said Jim, a wide grin on his face. "Because I've got a surprise for you."

Abby touched his elbow. "I've had enough surprises lately."

"This is a good one," he said. "I visited with Preacher Tuttle a couple of days ago."

"Don't go bothering him," she said.

"Not bothering him. Making him an offer."

Abby sat up straighter. "What kind of offer?"

Jim pulled the truck to a stop. Abby saw they had reached the spot where they needed to get out and walk. Jim faced her. "I bought his house from him."

"What?"

"His house. Gave him more than a fair price for it. You don't have to go anywhere. You're free and clear right where you are."

Abby's heart raced, and she started to hug Jim. But then she held back. What would Thaddeus say?

"I talked to Thaddeus before I did it," Jim said as if reading her mind. "Didn't want to hurt his pride or anything. Asked him to pay me back, regular dollars every month like at a bank, only I won't charge him any interest."

"You can afford to do this?"

"I'm doing real well," Jim said.

"You keep pretty quiet about it."

Jim glanced down. "No reason for boasting," he said. "But don't worry, I can take care of my ma."

Abby didn't know what to say. "Where will Tuttle go?" she finally asked.

"We checked around. There's a small house off Main Street. It's a rental now, but he thinks he might can buy it now that he's got the money. Plenty left over too—he liked that about the deal."

"You've thought of everything, haven't you?"

"I sure tried to."

Abby suddenly thought of Steve and realized he might not like it that she took Jim's offer but not his. "Your brother might not take to this," she said.

"I'm sorry for that," he said. "Surely he'll understand that you didn't want to move all the way to Raleigh."

"I hope so."

Jim patted her hand.

"You're a good son," Abby said.

Jim smiled, then leaned over and kissed her on the cheek. "And you're the best ma. It's the least I could do."

Abby blushed at her good fortune.

"We best get going," Jim said.

Abby nodded. Jim climbed out of the truck and she followed him. The air hung dry, the day already hot. Abby wiped sweat off her face as she looked around the area. The trees were still thick, in spite of Gant's crews having taken out a lot of lumber over the years.

"Gant didn't clear-cut," she said. "I always liked him for that."

"Mr. Gant loved these mountains," said Jim. "Said he wanted to cut them the right way so they would produce more trees in years to come."

Jim led Abby up the road and into a tiny clearing where a plain but well-built house stood, the front overgrown with bushes and tall grass that had come up since Gant's men had last worked the place. The two of them stepped onto the porch. Abby heard a bird calling. She took a deep breath; the air smelled sweet. Such a peaceful place, the highlands of her birth. She suddenly ached to move back here, to leave town with all its noises, even as small as it was. She loved this land, she realized. It moved in her, made her who she was. How could she ever have thought she could live somewhere else? The highlands belonged to her and she to them.

Jim moved to the door, pushed it open and stepped inside. After taking a look around, Abby joined him, quickly glancing around the room. A small wood desk sat straight ahead, a wicker basket on the floor off to the side. A coffeepot and lamp sat on a table in the corner. There were three chairs in front of the desk and a window on the wall behind the desk.

Jim went to the desk and searched it. Abby watched as he picked up a dusty ledger.

"Anything there?" she asked, stepping to his side.

Jim shook his head as he flipped through it. "Nope, nothing." He put it back in the drawer. Abby saw a few pencils and a stack of writing paper. Jim examined the paper, then put the stack down and closed the desk.

The two of them stepped back and searched the room with

their eyes. Nothing jumped out. Some dusty footprints on the wood floor but not much else. Abby noticed an interior door that led to a second room. She walked over and swung the door open. A single cot sat in the room, a table and lamp beside it. The table had a drawer in it. The room also had just one window, this one with curtains hanging over it.

Abby saw crumpled pieces of paper in the corner of the room but she moved first to the table. A Bible lay on top. She lifted the Bible and thumbed through its pages. "Look at this," she said, turning to Jim, who had followed her into the room. She handed him the Bible.

Jim took it. "Pages torn out," he said.

Abby moved to the wad of papers on the floor, picked up several and studied them. "Somebody tore these out," she said. "That's strange."

Jim put the Bible back down. "Mr. Gant seemed right religious to me."

"Came to Jesus Holiness some," agreed Abby. "Wonder why he'd do this?"

"Don't figure he did," said Jim. "Somebody else for sure."

"But who?"

"No way to tell."

The wrinkled pages in hand, Abby watched Jim as he checked the rest of the room.

"Over here," Jim said. He pointed to a trunk at the foot of the bed. They quickly searched it but found nothing but some men's denim pants, a couple of shirts and a pair of old boots. Abby set everything back in the trunk.

Disappointed, she scanned the room one more time. Nothing. Jim checked under the bed. He then lifted the mattress and saw a newspaper and a paper folder. He handed the newspaper to Abby and flipped open the folder.

"A couple of letters," he said.

Abby looked over the newspaper, saw the headline declaring the end of World War II.

"Nothing in here," Jim said.

"Here either."

They replaced the items and laid the mattress flat again.

"Looks like all we got is the torn Bible," Jim said.

Then Abby noticed the boot prints in the dust just like in the front room. "Somebody came through here," she said, pointing at the prints. "Not too long ago."

"But who?" Jim said. "Mrs. Gant maybe?"

"Not unless she's got a mighty big foot," said Abby, nodding toward the boot prints.

"And something against the good Lord," Jim said.

"You think it was one of Gant's workers?"

"Could be," he said, "but why come in here and tear up a Bible?"

"That one's a mystery," Abby agreed. "Who's mad at the Lord that we know?"

Jim shrugged. "Hard to say."

Abby thought of Will Stowe. Although he had done nothing to hurt her, she just didn't trust the man. He seemed so distant, so standoffish. An angry man, she figured. But what motive did he have to do them harm? They had never done anything to him. True, as soon as he sold their land, he earned some dollars for his work. Was that enough to make a man keep evidence that might prevent him from earning a sale? Did a dollar rule him that much— enough to make him take such a chance? If discovered, he could lose his law practice, at least for a while.

Abby started to say something, but not wanting to bring Jim into this, she thought better of it. Stowe was his brother-in-law, after all. Until she had some kind of proof, she had no right to make such an accusation.

CHAPTER
TWENTY-THREE

Steve never told Claire that he had met her on a train a long time ago, and she never indicated that she remembered him. At first this bothered Steve. Was he that forgettable? Yet he knew he'd changed much in the decade since he left Blue Springs. Thirty years old now, he had gained about fifteen pounds and dressed a whole lot better now. He'd let his hair grow longer too and kept it slicked back with hair tonic. Besides that, he'd lost all of his mountain speech patterns, and he never said his last name around her. So why should he expect her to recall meeting him a decade ago?

No longer bothered by Claire's poor memory, Steve moved to another feeling—anger. With nothing to contradict his belief, he still figured Claire had stolen his money back on the train. She'd made his start in Raleigh a tough one. Truth was, he had almost given up and gone back home. What if he had? What a disaster that would have been!

Again, as time moved on, Steve found reasons to let go of his resentment. If Claire hadn't stolen his money, would he have taken a room in the boardinghouse? Would he have tried so hard to find the Waterburys? Would Allen have found him? Would he have ended up running the Waterbury business, making it the success it had become?

Steve didn't know. Did God have some hand in all of this? Maybe He had put Claire on that train for a good reason, for things to go like they had so Steve would take the steps he needed to take in order to end up where he was.

In the weeks and months after Claire birthed Franklin David, Steve gradually gave up asking questions for which he had no answers, and he also gave up his misgivings about Claire. No matter what had happened in the past, he found it impossible to stay mad at a single woman and her newborn child. Steve wasn't sure, but maybe he was trying to make up for what his pa had done to his ma, the way he had run out on her and her boys. All he knew was that a man had treated a woman poorly, and something about that brought out every ounce of tenderness that lived in his heart.

Every now and again he wondered about the father of the baby. What kind of man was he? How could he leave this woman alone to handle such a heavy load? An awful man, he decided.

At times Steve wondered about Claire too. What kind of a woman let herself get in such a fix? What kind gave her favors to another man without benefit of marriage? Well, Steve knew of the kind, but somehow Claire didn't seem to fit that pattern. She seemed more respectable than that, a touch wayward maybe yet not one who shared her body with just anyone at any time. No, if he had to guess, which is all he could do at this point, Steve figured that whoever had fathered Claire's child had probably taken advantage of her. Not that he forced himself on her or anything, but maybe he wooed her in untoward ways, wore down her defenses with his charm and guile until she thought she loved the man and eventually yielded herself to him.

Of course Steve remembered how Claire had approached him on the train, her friendly ways and all. But, somehow, that didn't cause him to think any less of her. Obviously her pregnancy resulted from a liaison with a man who had betrayed her love and trust; that was it for sure. It could be that thinking this way proved he wore blinders when it came to Claire, but he couldn't help it. That's the way he saw it.

All through the rest of 1957, Steve did everything he could for Claire and Franklin. Bought new clothes for the both of them. Refused to take any rent money from her or Margaret. He brought in a crib and bassinet and put them in a room he had made into a nursery. And he paid all of Claire's medical bills.

Using his business as an excuse, Steve made only one trip home that year, just long enough to see his ma for a day in early December. He knew he ought to stay longer and at least visit Jim and Rebecca for a spell, but he felt so odd at home these days, like a fish thrown up on a creek bank, all out of his rightful spot. Truth was, he had two reasons for staying away from home that year. One, it made him real mad that his ma had taken Jim's gift of Preacher Tuttle's house after turning down his offer of a place in Raleigh. Of course Steve understood why his ma didn't want to leave Blue Springs. Why should she leave the highlands? But it still frustrated him that Jim had bought the house without asking him to help pay for it. Didn't Jim know he made a lot of money these days, that Raleigh was growing by leaps and bounds and he now had close to sixty houses under his care?

The only reason he could figure that Jim hadn't asked him to pitch in was that Jim wanted all the credit. Jim had always been that way—the big brother taking care of the younger, the war hero everybody admired and loved, the man who stayed home and took care of his ma while the younger boy left her high and dry on her own.

Well, Steve saw no reason to go home and listen to everybody praise Jim for all his accomplishments. He had some accomplishments too, even if nobody back home knew about them. One thing he didn't do, no sir, he didn't brag about all he did, no matter how successful.

Mostly though, Steve didn't go home that year because he wanted to stay close to Claire and Frank. When December reached the halfway point, he hauled in a Christmas tree and decorated it with peppermint hooks and red bows. Then he bought Claire a new green dress, almost the same color as the one she'd worn on the train when he first met her. After that, he purchased Frank a wooden horse for him to ride just as soon as he got old enough to sit up straight on it.

On Christmas Day Margaret cooked up a fine dinner: fried chicken, mashed potatoes and gravy, fresh biscuits and assorted vegetables bought at a store around the corner. Steve wore his best suit, a tan pinstripe. Claire had put on the green dress he'd bought her.

All through dinner Steve watched her and Franklin. She did so well with the boy, handled his every need. Her face glowed with happiness as she fed him, held him, laughed at something he did. Steve marveled at her show of love for the boy, wondering if a man's love could be as deep. Or was a man's love something that could come and go? Or maybe not come at all? Was that what caused a man to leave his child? Did he not love the baby from the beginning? Maybe that was why his own pa had never stayed long with him and his family. Steve shook his head. The same old questions.

He focused on Claire. Such a fascinating woman. She'd never spoken of the man who had fathered her baby, and Steve never asked. He figured that if she wanted to tell him, she would. Until then, what did it matter? What mattered was her presence right here and now and his desire to stay with her and provide any help he could.

When they had finished dinner, Margaret stood to clear the table. Steve pushed away and wiped a napkin over his mouth. Frank started crying and Claire lifted him to her chest.

"Sounds like he's ready for a nap," he said.

Claire smiled at Steve, then headed to the bedroom to put Franklin in his crib. Steve's eyes never left her. As she disappeared from the room, Steve suddenly realized that he had fallen in love. Just like that, he loved Claire and Franklin. No two ways about it.

Jolted by the realization, he stood, helped Margaret with the dishes and then left her in the kitchen and went to the parlor where a fire burned in the fireplace. He couldn't do this, he told himself, couldn't fall for a woman with a baby. What would his business associates think? What would his ma think?

He stared into the fire, his emotions a jumble. What did it matter what someone else thought? If he loved Claire and she loved him, they could just ignore what others might say about it.

Steve rubbed his chin. Did Claire love him? She'd never indicated anything of the sort. Yes, she smiled and thanked him every time he did something nice for her or Frank. She touched him often, like she had on the train, her hands on his forearm, his back and shoulders, touches of affection and appreciation. But none of that really meant that she *loved* him.

Steve thought again of Frank's father. Did Claire love him? If not, then why had she given in to his advances?

He tried to figure what to do next. Declare his feelings and see what she said? What if she laughed at him, called him silly? He couldn't even imagine the embarrassment.

But what if she returned his feelings? Was he ready to marry her? He didn't know. So what should he do? No clear path came to him. Claire entered the room and he turned to her. She took a seat on the sofa by the fire. Steve watched her, his head hurting from the tension he felt inside. He didn't know that much about her. Had never asked her about her parents, her background, how she had ended up living in one of his houses just as she reached the time of her delivery. It all seemed so strange. Did that mean that God had stepped in to make it happen? Otherwise, why had it all come to pass the way it had?

"Claire?" he said.

"Yes?" She smiled at him, and her eyes sparkled.

He took a seat on the sofa beside her. "I need to talk to you," he said. She tucked her feet under herself. Steve glanced down, then back up. "Are you happy here?"

She furrowed her brow, looking confused by the question. "I suppose so," she said. "Frank is healthy. Margaret likes her job at the hospital. I stay busy with the house, with Frank." She smoothed down her dress.

Steve took her hands. "That's not what I mean," he said. "Are you happy?"

She shrugged and said, "I'm not sure what happiness is anymore. I'm a woman with a baby but no husband. I don't have much of an education. I depend on my sister for my upkeep, at least for now. Yet, I have a good place to live. My baby laughs a lot, and I have a good mind and a strong body. The future looks better than the past. What's not to be happy about?"

Steve took a deep breath.

Claire smiled and patted his hands. "And I have you. The kindest man who ever lived."

Steve blushed and looked at his shoes.

Claire continued, "I don't know why you've taken care of me the way you have, but I'll always love you for it."

Steve looked in her eyes and his heart fell. The look on her face spoke of a different kind of love than he wanted from her. It spoke of the love a friend feels for another friend, not the passion that one needed in order to marry someone and settle down forever.

"Who's the father of your baby, Claire?" He asked the question without thinking, before he could stop himself.

She shook her head. "I'd rather not bring him up."

"Does he know about Frank?"

Claire nodded. "He knows."

Steve stood and moved to the fireplace. "Has he seen the boy?"

"Yes."

Steve swung around back to Claire, suddenly angry. "Does he come here during the day when I'm not around?"

Claire seemed to shrink. She hung her head. "He's been here a few times, yes."

"Do you love him?" Steve wanted to know.

"I told you—I don't want to talk about him," Claire said. "But he *is* Frank's father. I don't think it's right to keep him away if he wants to see his son."

Steve took her by the shoulders. "Is it the baby he comes to see?" he asked in a loud voice. "Or you?"

Claire shrank more, her shoulders pulling in, her arms wrapped around her sides.

"Are you and he—?" Not able to finish the question, Steve let go of her. Suddenly he felt like a fool. All this time he had cared for Claire, provided for her every need. But she had continued to see the man who had deserted her, the man who had . . . He went to the fireplace and picked up a small shovel by the wood stack and poked at the fire. Soon his anger left him, and he felt sadder than he'd felt since a small boy. "I'll never understand women."

He heard Claire stand and move to him. She laid a hand on his back. "I'm not with him," she said. "I'm here . . . with you."

He faced her, his mouth firm. "I love you," he blurted.

She gasped and folded her arms around her waist.

"I said I love you," he repeated.

Claire nodded. "I heard you," she whispered.

Steve held his breath.

She put a hand on his waist. "I'm sorry; I guess I'm just surprised."

Steve chuckled. "I guess you don't understand men too well either," he said. "How much more obvious could I be?"

She laughed nervously. "I don't know that I can say what you want to hear right now," she said. "I just had Frank, and his father is still . . . well, it's just too soon to start over with someone else. I hope you understand."

Steve picked up a piece of wood and tossed it onto the fire. "I know," he said, standing straight again. "And I didn't come here tonight planning to say any of this to you. But something . . . I don't know, I just had to say it, that's all."

Claire put a hand back on his waist. "You know I care for you. But it's just too early. I need time."

"You think it's possible, though?" he asked. "You might love me, someday?"

She smiled, stood on tiptoe and kissed him lightly on the cheek. "It's possible," she said. "Just not right now."

Steve took her hands and raised them to his lips. Claire hadn't promised him anything, yet somehow that didn't matter. He had loved her from the first time he saw her. And, somehow, someday, he'd make it so she loved him too.

"I can wait," he said. "As long as it takes."

"You're a fine man," she responded.

Steve closed his eyes. Claire respected him. If nothing else, he at least had that.

CHAPTER
TWENTY-FOUR

June of 1958 turned off real hot. School shut down for the summer, and Thaddeus and Abby spent most of their mornings in the garden behind their house. In the afternoons they liked to read or listen to the radio while they sat on the porch. On Saturdays Abby always did her shopping, picking up at the general store what they couldn't grow.

On the second Saturday of that month, she hoisted a couple of sacks into the back of the ten-year-old Oldsmobile Thaddeus had bought, climbed behind the wheel and drove toward home. A sense of peace rolled through her. Life had turned out just fine. Yes, she still had some worries about Steve, and they still had a mess in dealing with the land because the judge hadn't made any final determination about it. But all in all, she didn't have too many complaints. Thaddeus made a decent living, and except for some stiffness in her back every morning and some heartburn Thaddeus sometimes suffered when he ate more than he should, neither of them had any health problems.

She turned left on her street, her mood high. Almost thirteen now, Rose showed every sign of turning out a wonderful woman. Smart as any child in school, she loved to read and sang with a clear soprano voice that made people turn her way when they heard her down at Jesus Holiness. Though she hadn't filled out as a young woman yet, people often spoke of her fine looks, how her hair and eyes took after her ma, her lips too, full and round. A number of boys stopped by the house after school on most days, and Abby had to shoo them away at dark or they would stay long into the night.

To Abby's relief, Rose paid the boys little attention. The only boy she seemed to like was Porter. They thought of each other as cousins, even though Porter was actually Rose's half nephew—the son of her half brother. She liked him because he took to a lot of the things she liked—books and baseball and music and radio programs that talked about history and kept them up with world events. As far as Rose was concerned, boys other than Porter were but a nuisance. She had big plans, she sometimes told Abby, college for sure and maybe even more. Perhaps she'd go to the college in Boone like her ma had. Or maybe she'd go off someplace even more exotic like over to the university at Chapel Hill.

Abby smiled as she pulled into their driveway and climbed out. Thinking of Rose and all the possibilities for her future always made her smile. A bird chirped. Abby brushed her hair back. Thaddeus stepped onto the porch, his face a dark scowl.

"Where you been?" he asked.

"Down at the store," she said, opening the back door and taking out the groceries. "Like I do every Saturday morning."

Thaddeus grabbed a sack. "It doesn't matter," he said, heading back into the house. "I'm just glad you're home."

Abby followed him to the kitchen and placed her sack on the table. "What's going on?" she asked, concerned by his demeanor.

"Not sure," said Thaddeus. "But it's Rose. She's not feeling good, hasn't gotten herself out of bed yet."

"That's not like her," Abby said. She left the groceries and followed Thaddeus to Rose's room. "She usually tears out early on Saturday, all set to find Porter and head downtown."

Rose lay still on her bed, her forehead damp with perspiration, her auburn hair splayed out on her pillow. Abby rushed to her.

"I feel funny," said Rose.

"You hurting?" Abby asked, touching her forehead, then her arms. She felt warm, definitely had a fever.

"Some," said Rose. "My head mostly, throat some too. And I feel all weak. My legs—it's like a bee stung them. They're numb below the knees."

Abby ran her hands over her child's thin body, looked closely at her eyes. They seemed paler than normal, like somebody had dimmed the light just a little.

"Probably got some fever from something," Thaddeus said. "Give it a day and she'll feel all better."

Abby nodded, but something about the way Rose looked made her feel uneasy. Her skin had a washed-out color. "I expect you're right," she said, trying to convince herself, "but maybe I'll just drive her over to Doc Spencer for him to take a look. I got to go that way this afternoon anyway."

"Whatever you think," said Thaddeus. "You want me to go with you?"

"I reckon not. I know you got things to do."

It took less than fifteen minutes for Abby to load Rose into the back of the car and drive to Spencer's place, a two-room office in the back of his brick house about a mile out of town. To her relief, she found him home.

"Wait here," said Spencer, pointing Abby to a small sofa in the outer room of his office area. "Let me look this pretty girl over."

Abby took a seat and laid her hands in her lap. Rose had never had a sick day in her life—not an earache, not a fever, not a stubbed toe. "She's charmed," Preacher Tuttle had said a couple of times. "Like the Lord sent a few extra angels to watch over her."

Abby stood and moved to the window. No reason for nerves, she thought. Children take sick all the time. But not Rose. For her to take sick meant something bad, Abby just knew it. She'd had too much happiness lately and knew that life didn't stay that way forever. Just when you least expected it, some trouble always stuck its head up.

The minutes seemed to last forever. Abby prayed for Rose. Nothing else entered her mind, not the problems with the land, not Will Stowe, nothing but her child. After what seemed like an hour, she heard a door open and turned to see Spencer and Rose walking out of the examining room. Rose wore a blanket around her shoulders and was holding a wrapped red lollipop.

"Have a seat right here, child," Dr. Spencer said. "I want to talk to your mama for a second."

Rose sat and pulled the blanket closer. "I want to save this," she said, holding up the candy, "till I feel better."

Abby hugged her. Spencer motioned Abby into the examining room, pointed her to a wood chair as they entered. Abby licked her lips.

Shaking his head, Spencer began, "I don't know exactly what we're looking at here, but I think maybe we need to get her down to Asheville for some more testing."

"Asheville?" Abby's heart raced. Going to Asheville meant something serious.

The doctor glanced at the floor, then back at Abby. "Look, I reckon I need to just say it out plain. I'm thinking Rose may have the polio virus."

Abby didn't grasp it right away. Polio? What sense did that make? Her child was healthy, always had been. "I don't understand," she said. "Rose took that new Salk shot about a year ago."

Spencer fingered his stethoscope. "The shot isn't always effective," he said. "Still so new and all. They're working on making a vaccine you can swallow now, which they hope will be better. But it could be years before that's ready."

Abby shook her head, still not wanting to believe what she'd heard. She knew that thousands of folks had suffered from polio in past times, that parents kept their kids from swimming holes in the summer when the epidemic got bad, that polio caused all manner of paralysis, sometimes even death.

"I don't know for sure," said Spencer. "Her symptoms, though—fever, headache, numbness in her lower body—all give me cause to want to check her more closely, just to make certain."

Abby nodded, trying to take in the situation. Yet it all seemed outside of her somehow.

"I need to make a call down to Asheville," the doctor said, "and get it set up for you to go on down there right away. Time is important with something like this."

Abby stared at Spencer. "Will it kill her?" she asked, voicing her worst fear.

Spencer took her hands in his. "Polio comes in different strengths," he said. "Sometimes the symptoms pass with no long-term effects. With others, a person will have some paralysis for a few weeks, maybe months. I've even read of some cases where a person suffered paralysis for several years, and then it all just went away. We just don't know right now."

Abby pulled her hands away. "It kills some kids, doesn't it?"

"Every now and again, but not usually. So don't even think that. Does nobody any good."

Abby thought of Thaddeus. Spencer had just delivered news strong enough to crack open the world, and Thaddeus hadn't even heard it. How strange that he didn't know this awful thing while she did. She tried to focus again on Spencer, but his words sounded a long ways off, like a man speaking in a dream from one side of a river to the other.

"We'll get her to Asheville," he said. "See what the doctors there have to say, see how things develop."

Abby nodded yet her mind drifted. So many years of good had passed. She had married the man she loved. Her sons were doing well. She had a daughter of beauty and intelligence. On the whole, she had more blessings than she could count. But now this, her baby girl. Abby could barely think the word *polio* much less say it.

She clenched her hands. Everything and everyone but Rose faded into the background. She would not let polio take her child away, Abby decided. *Lord,* she prayed silently, *do whatever you want with me, whatever you want with the land, anything I own. But please leave my baby be, that's all I ask. Just see Rose through this—that's what I want. I never asked much for myself, you know that's true. But I'm asking you for this, begging you for it. If you see fit, please let this not kill my child.*

"I need to make the call," Dr. Spencer said. "Why don't you go get Rose, drive her home, pick up a few things. Meet me back here as fast as you can."

Abby nodded and then hurried from the room. She found Rose lying on the sofa, her lollipop still in her hand, her face pale. Abby took her by the hand and left the office. In the car, she kissed her baby. Her cheeks felt hot. Driving home, Abby wiped tears away and told herself to stay strong. The Lord wouldn't let this awful thing happen, she told herself. Surely the Lord wouldn't.

CHAPTER
TWENTY-FIVE

By the time they reached Asheville, Rose's fever had spiked up and her headache made her cry. The doctor in Asheville, a man named Durwood, did a quick check of her throat, extremities and eyes and immediately admitted her in the hospital. By the next morning Rose cried out when anybody so much as touched her. Dr. Durwood told Abby and Thaddeus that the tests had shown Rose indeed to have the polio virus.

"We need to keep her still," Dr. Durwood said. "Wrap her in moist warm towels. See how it progresses. The next seventy-two hours are critical."

"What else can we do?" asked Abby.

Durwood shook his head. "Not a lot, I'm afraid. We'll take care of your daughter. Get yourself a room close by. You can see her in the morning for about an hour, then again in the afternoon."

"I want to stay with her," Abby insisted.

"Can't do it," the doctor said. "Hospital policy."

Gritting her teeth, Abby left the hospital with Thaddeus and called Daniel's widow, Deidre, and informed her about what had happened. Deidre told them right off that they should come to stay with her, that she wouldn't hear of them going to a hotel. Glad for her generosity, Abby and Thaddeus drove to Deidre's house, hauled in what few belongings they had brought along and took a room on the second floor. Abby didn't feel much like talking, and Deidre seemed to understand, giving them free rein to come and go as they pleased.

On the afternoon of her third day in the hospital, Rose took a turn for the worse. Her breathing became labored. Dr. Durwood telephoned Abby and Thaddeus at Deidre's house and told them to rush over. He met them when they entered the dark room where Rose lay deathly still. Warm towels covered her legs and arms.

"The polio is affecting the muscles that control her breathing," Dr. Durwood said. "I think we best put her in the iron lung."

Abby almost fainted. She knew about the metal contraption named the iron lung because she'd spent a large part of the last two days in the local library reading all she could about polio. A man named Philip Drinker had come up with it—an airtight metal tank that enclosed the polio patient's body. When polio victims became so paralyzed that they could no longer breathe on their own, the motors of the iron lung changed the air pressure inside the tank so as to force air in and out of the lungs. That way they kept breathing and stayed alive.

"You think she's that far gone?" Thaddeus asked.

"She's lost some use of both legs," said Durwood. "Her right arm too. All of it may come back, we're not sure. But the paralysis seems to have moved into her chest now, the muscles that keep her lungs going."

"That's why she needs the iron lung," Thaddeus said, as if explaining it to the doctor.

"It's a precaution," Durwood said. "And remember, even if she goes into it, that doesn't mean anything long term. Some folks use the lung for a long time, then get better and live normal lives."

"Do it," said Abby. "Do what you have to do."

Durwood nodded and within a couple of hours he and a nurse had slid Rose's slender body into the iron lung. Immediately the machine started helping her breathe. Abby's heart almost broke. That day passed, the night after it, then another day and another night.

Near the end of the week, Thaddeus headed back to Blue Springs to take care of some things at the house and bring Abby back some fresh clothes. When Abby wasn't with Deidre, she stayed with Rose every minute that the hospital rule allowed.

After a week of obeying the hospital rule that she not see Rose but twice a day, Abby finally decided she wouldn't put up with that anymore and started staying almost twenty-four hours a day. If they didn't want her there, they would have to hog-tie her and throw her out. Every now and again a nurse would look at her funny, but after a couple of days they just shrugged and treated her like she belonged there.

Everything closed down around Abby, and the next seven months passed by in a blur. She had only one focus, one reason for living—to aid Rose any way she could. To tell it true, she couldn't do much but just sit and talk to Rose in the dark room, read a little when the nurses opened a window blind for a few hours early in the morning.

The days passed slowly, one after another, one day bleeding into the next, the days into weeks, the weeks into months. Visitors came to see her and Rose from time to time. Ed and Priscilla, Sol and Jewel, Preacher Tuttle, Jim and Rebecca, Porter too.

Rose especially liked it when Porter came on weekends and told her about all her friends or read books to her from school. Watching the two together, Abby's eyes always moistened. Would Rose ever again climb a tree with Porter, wade in the creek with him, sit by a radio and listen to the singers wail out their music? Would she live to see the friend she loved grow up and become a man? Would Porter ever see Rose get married or bear a child? Abby knew she was really asking this for herself, but it didn't hurt as much asking it this way.

Steve dropped by from Raleigh on two occasions, once in October and once near the Christmas after Rose took sick. Mrs. Gant even checked in on her once, her soft voice assuring Abby that everything would turn out fine.

Abby politely visited with all of them, yet she stayed so focused on Rose that her heart didn't connect much to anybody else. The year ended; a new one began. Thaddeus visited whenever he could, but since he had to teach to make a living, he only got to come on the weekends.

January of 1959 rolled through and soon February started. Abby watched Rose every day and prayed for her recovery. The iron lung covered her like a suit of armor, its noise an engine that kept her alive. Nurses worked with her legs every morning, massaging them, moving them up and down, turning them out and back, first in one direction then in another. When they weren't there, Abby did the work for them, careful not to hurt Rose as she stretched the leg muscles. The nurses told her they could see some progress in Rose, said her muscles had responded some, gotten stronger. Abby wasn't so sure. From what she could see, Rose's thin legs still held little strength.

"You're too close to it," Thaddeus said when he saw her that first weekend of February. "But she's able to do more, that's the truth."

Abby nodded, but she wouldn't let herself believe in any progress. To do so meant she had to raise her hopes, to let her mind think Rose might actually recover. She couldn't go that far just yet, no matter what anybody else said. If she let herself believe that Rose was getting better but then it failed to happen, she didn't think she could take it.

As the days went by, Rose gradually began to breathe for longer periods outside the iron lung. On good days, she now managed to stay out of the lung for about four hours a day, almost twice as long as when she had first started using it. The nurses told Abby that meant she had regained some use of her chest muscles, another sign that maybe the worst of the paralysis had passed, that maybe she would start some real recovery now. Abby smiled weakly at the nurses.

On Friday of the third week of that month, Abby left Rose's room after helping her stretch her arms and legs and headed to the hospital cafeteria to get a cup of coffee. Five minutes after sitting down, she saw Dr. Durwood coming her way. From the straight line he made toward her, she knew he had something to say. She braced herself for the worst. Durwood took a seat across from her and got right to the point.

"We think it's time to move Rose," he said. "They got a place in Raleigh that's doing great things with therapy. Now that she's out of the iron lung as long as she is, she can do some more work on her extremities."

"What kinds of things they doing?" Abby asked.

"Braces, exercises, surgeries."

"Surgeries?"

"For those that need it. They graft muscle from one spot to another, from places where muscle is still good to places where it's all shriveled up."

"You expect Rose will need any of that?"

Dr. Durwood shrugged. "Not sure, maybe not. She's making some progress without it. They'll try the braces first, get her on her feet again."

Abby pictured her baby on braces. She'd seen other kids, adults too, fighting to stay upright on the metal contraptions. She wondered if they hurt, the metal pieces stuck to the legs like they were. "Rose is so thin," she said. "Won't braces hurt her bones?"

"Some people don't take well to them," he admitted, "but others do just fine. Your girl has a strong spirit about her, and I believe she'll get on real well."

Abby smiled. Durwood spoke the truth about Rose. In all her time in the hospital, Abby had seldom heard her daughter complain. "I got a son in Raleigh," she said. "Maybe I can stay with him."

Durwood patted her hands. "I'm sure he'll be glad to have you."

Abby took a deep breath. If Dr. Durwood thought this was right, how could she argue? "How long you think we'll need to spend in Raleigh?"

"As long as it takes," he answered.

A nurse approached them. "You got a visitor," she said to Abby. "The waiting room at the end of the hall past your daughter's room."

Abby excused herself and walked to the room. A minute later she smiled as she saw Mrs. Billy Gant moving toward her. "Thank you for coming," Abby said. "You're most kind."

Mrs. Gant waved off the compliment. "You're in my prayers," she said.

Abby motioned for her to sit, and they took spots on sofas opposite each other. Mrs. Gant smoothed down her skirt, a navy blue pleated one that reached to mid-calf. She wore a hat that matched, the brim wide but not overly so. Abby liked the woman, had liked her from the first time they met.

"How is Rose today?" asked Mrs. Gant.

"They say she's getting stronger," Abby said.

"What do you say?"

Abby stared at Mrs. Gant, wondering if she wanted her true feelings. Why not? "I say she's a thirteen-year-old girl who might never walk again, with or without braces. What does it matter if she's getting stronger if she never gets strong enough to make any real difference?"

Mrs. Gant clasped her hands in her lap. "I can't imagine how hard this is."

Silence fell. Mrs. Gant fingered her purse, a black leather bag with a big buckle. Abby suddenly sensed that Mrs. Gant had a specific reason for the visit, something other than checking on Rose. She thought of the land for the first time in weeks and realized that surely Mrs. Gant had heard something about the situation in New York in the last few months.

"You got news for me, don't you?" Abby said.

Mrs. Gant nodded. "We finally got all the estate in order," she said. "The bank in New York let us look through Billy's papers there. We had to go through the courts—all very complicated." She lowered her eyes.

"You didn't find anything to verify our claims to the land?"

Mrs. Gant shook her head. "Nothing. I'm sorry."

Abby shrugged. What did it matter? If Rose never walked again, what did anything matter? Yes, she wanted the land, believed her family deserved it after so many years trying to buy it back. But in light of what Rose faced every day, none of it seemed too important anymore.

"What will you do now?" asked Abby.

"I'll have to put the land back up for sale," said Mrs. Gant. "Mr. Stowe says the prices are good right now, and I'm not rich enough to just sit on it."

Abby thought of Stowe for the first time in months. She still didn't trust the man but didn't know anything she could do about it. "I guess all my kin will have to move."

Mrs. Gant played with the buckle on her purse. "I'm sorry about that," she said. "I don't know what else to do."

Abby pushed her hair back. "Well, we all have to do certain things we don't like sometimes. Just part of life. You'll get in touch with my family about this?"

Mrs. Gant nodded and started to stand. But then she stopped. "Look," she said, "given all that your family is going through, let me see if we can put off this sale for a little while. I've got another parcel or two in the mountains that I can sell first. No matter that Stowe says I should sell yours as soon as I can."

"He said that?"

"Yes. He seems real eager about your property. I guess he thinks it will sell high, give him a bigger fee for the transaction."

"You know he's brother to my son's wife, don't you?" Abby asked.

Mrs. Gant smiled. "He never said anything. But your boy Jim told me. Seems Mr. Stowe and his sister don't see eye to eye on much."

"I don't think Stowe is pleased with her choice in husbands. The matter goes back a long way, bad blood between Mr. Stowe's pa and all my family. Except for Stowe, it seems pretty settled now."

Mrs. Gant's eyes narrowed and she asked, "You think Stowe has some grudge against you?"

Abby studied on whether to say anything. What if Mrs. Gant ran back to Stowe with her words? Would that matter? Abby decided it wouldn't. "You remember at the hearing when he said that all of Mr. Gant's properties had been searched for papers, anything that would tell us about his businesses?"

"Yes."

"Did anyone go with him when he checked your husband's office up on Blue Springs Mountain?"

"I'm not sure, but what does it matter?"

"Well, Jim and I went up to where your husband made his office while he labored here. Somebody had already gone through the place, only we don't know who."

"You think Stowe might have taken something he shouldn't have?"

Abby lowered her eyes. "I feel bad saying something with no proof to back it up," she said. "But something bothers me about it. We found a Bible all torn up. Stowe's pa, Topper Clack, didn't take much to religion."

Mrs. Gant thought a second, then said, "That's pretty skimpy. Not much basis to distrust a man on that."

"I agree."

Silence fell again. Abby wondered how she could find out more about Stowe but realized she had too much to worry about with Rose to do it. "I'm taking Rose to Raleigh," she said, changing the subject.

"I can visit you there," said Mrs. Gant.

"You're kind to check on us," said Abby.

Mrs. Gant stood to leave. "I'll hold off selling the land as long as I can," she said. "And I'll see what I can find out about Mr. Stowe."

Abby thanked her and then Mrs. Gant left. Abby walked back into Rose's room to tell her they would be heading to Raleigh soon. As she did, she also made a mental note to phone Jim and tell him what Mrs. Gant had just told her about Stowe's eagerness to sell their land.

CHAPTER
TWENTY-SIX

When his ma first called to tell him she had to come to Raleigh because of Rose's needing treatment, Steve wanted to kick up his heels and rejoice. Now his ma could see how he had succeeded, how much money he had made. But then he paused and realized how complicated all this could become. How could he keep his ma away from Mrs. Waterbury? From Claire and Franklin? From the worst of the properties he owned that he didn't want anyone to see?

Steve stewed on the matter for days and finally reached a conclusion. He wouldn't tell Mrs. Waterbury his ma had come to town, and he'd tell his ma that Mrs. Waterbury was too sick to see any company. That should take care of it, and he wouldn't even have to tell a lie. Mrs. Waterbury *was* sick, and not saying anything about his ma didn't technically violate the truth.

Satisfied, Steve picked out the best empty rental he had, got a couple of his men to clean it and paint it up fresh and white, and moved his ma into it the first week of March. She thanked him over and over again and offered to pay him rent, but he told her to keep her money, he wouldn't take a penny of it. She thanked him again and unpacked her bags in the main bedroom, then bought some groceries for the kitchen and packed them all away. When she'd finished that, she asked him to take her to the hospital to check on Rose.

At the hospital, Steve kissed Rose on the cheek and told her she looked good. The truth was, though, he felt awkward around her because, even with their being blood kin, he had left Blue Springs when she was but a baby and so he didn't feel like he knew her too well. Rose didn't seem to notice his awkwardness and, despite her leg braces and loose skin on her arms, smiled at him with a look so bright you would have thought he'd just bought her a new pony. A few minutes after their arrival, a nurse came into the room and said that Rose needed to go downstairs for her therapy. Steve told his ma he needed to head out too. Abby gave him a quick hug and thanked him yet again for letting her stay in one of his houses.

"I'll pick you up after dark," he said. "Take you home then." Abby nodded and Steve left the room.

After that, the days settled into a steady routine. Steve drove his ma to the hospital as he left his house every morning, and she stayed there all day. He returned around suppertime to bring her back to the house. He usually stayed with her for supper but then begged off soon afterward. "Got to check on Mrs. Waterbury," he always explained. "She's not in good health."

More than once Abby asked about going to see her, but Steve always put her off. "She's not up to company," he said. "I'm sure she'd like to see you, but it can't be helped."

"Tell her of my prayers," Abby said.

Steve said he would and he kept his word. When he got home, usually around nine each night, he always informed Mrs. Waterbury that his ma prayed for her. Mrs. Waterbury never responded much to this, and Steve felt glad about that. No reason to bring the two women together. Nothing good could come of it.

After checking on Mrs. Waterbury, Steve usually drove by to see Claire and Frank. He'd moved them to a house closer to his, a quaint brick place with a yard full of trees and a white fence to keep a dog. He stayed there until almost midnight each day, the time mostly spent on the porch with Claire after Frank had gone to sleep. After telling her the one time that he loved her, Steve never said it again. She knew how he felt. If and when she wanted to respond to it, she would. If not, he'd just have to wait.

Weeks passed, then months. Abby stayed so busy with Rose that she didn't interfere much with Steve's daily routine. Summer rolled in, hot and sticky with moist days and nights. Steve labored hard all day, his mind occupied with plans to fix this house and buy that one, with pressures to collect overdue rents and get more out of the tenants. For the most part, the business stayed stout. Yes, he had problems every now and again. Cash stayed pretty tight because he constantly borrowed money to buy new houses and fix them up, as he had to do that before he could rent them out and start paying back the banks with the rent money they produced.

Sometimes he stretched right to the edge of what he could financially manage, and the banks put some pressure on him to keep the payments timely. That made him nervous. Men like his pa had gotten into real trouble stretching their dollars past the point they could go, and the notion that he might do that caused him many a sleepless night. Yet, without taking some risk, he knew he wouldn't ever make any progress. A man had to step to the edge of a cliff before he could see how to make it to the other side, that's all there was to it. So long as he kept his footing and labored hard, he could make it, he figured. Steve believed that. Men like his brother, Jim, proved it. Nobody ever got anywhere without taking some gambles.

The summer ended. September reached its halfway point. Steve finished up with work on the second Friday of the month, a rainy day full of thunder and lightning. His feet muddy from tromping around collecting rents with Izzy in the Negro sections of his properties, Steve climbed into his Ford just after dark and headed toward the hospital to pick up his ma. He felt unsettled as he drove, a feeling that often hit him after a day with Izzy. In spite of his best intentions, he had never done as much as he wanted to improve the properties in that part of town. Time and time again he had meant to take more money and fix up the worst of the places, put on some new roofs, patch the bad plumbing, the sagging porches, maybe even tear down and rebuild some of the houses. Yet he never seemed to get enough money to do everything. He had fixed many things. But not enough, not ever enough.

Steve listened to the thunder rolling. Sometimes a man's best intentions never got fulfilled. Like his plans to start going to church again. With his ma's presence, he felt more and more guilty for that oversight. On Sundays she always insisted that he take her to the Baptist church about half a mile from her house, a congregation more like Jesus Holiness than any other she had found in Raleigh and close enough to attend without too much trouble. She'd told him that it didn't matter that she didn't know anybody there; she knew the Lord and that would do just fine.

Steve knew she wanted to ask him why he had given up the practice of churchgoing. But, like a good highlander, she didn't pry, just shook her head a little as she climbed out of his car and walked toward the front steps of the Baptist church.

Turning left, Steve's heart fell even lower. Not only did he feel guilty about not going to church every week, but he also felt low about Claire. A lot of time had passed and yet she still showed no inclination to marry him. He'd begun to wonder if she ever would. If not, he just didn't know what would happen. At age thirty-two now, he didn't want to wait much longer. Over the last year or so, a loneliness worse than anything he had ever felt had settled over him, a loneliness that left him feeling empty, that gnawed at his insides. Sometimes, when he felt his worst, he thought about buying a bottle somewhere and seeing why so many men liked to drink. He knew his family's thirst for the drink, of course, the way it had almost destroyed his uncle Daniel, the way it had caused so much pain for Laban, an uncle he had heard of but never known. A hunger for whiskey seemed to run in his family like the blood in their veins. His pa had loved his liquor too, in a more sophisticated way than Laban or Daniel, but just as destructive. Steve didn't want that kind of thing to happen to him and so far had kept the temptation at bay. Yet, at times, only the bottle seemed to offer him any comfort.

Lightning flashed outside, and Steve pushed away his bad

thoughts. He reached the hospital just as his ma was stepping out of the building. She hurried to the car and then shook her shoulders to fling off the rain before climbing in.

"A fractious night," she said.

"How's Rose?"

"Making progress, I think," Abby replied. "Doctor says she might can go home soon, maybe for good if she can get a little better with her braces."

Steve smiled briefly. No longer having to use the iron lung, Rose had passed the stage of danger between living and dying. Now she just had to find out how much better she might get. Would she ever walk without braces again? Would she ever regain all the use of her hands? Nobody knew.

"Maybe she can make it home by Christmas," Steve said.

"Thaddeus would like that for sure," said Abby. "I don't know how that man has stayed so patient with all this."

"Because he loves you and Rose," Steve said.

Abby rubbed her shoulders. "I sure do miss him."

"It won't be much longer until you can all be together again."

"Sure hope that's true."

They turned right and drove down the street toward Abby's house, silence between them. Steve pulled up in front of the house. His ma turned to him, put a hand on his arm. Steve faced her, his heart hurting with sadness. Something inside told him the time had come to do something different with his life, to make some changes. His ma seemed to know it too, maybe had known it for a long time.

"I don't want to speak out of turn," Abby said. "I just want you to know I hope you find somebody someday, somebody to love you, somebody you can love. You need that—all of us do."

Steve started to tell her about Claire. Suddenly he wanted to tell her about everything—about Allen, about all that had happened to him since he left Blue Springs, about how lonely he felt, how guilty and sad. All at once he felt like a scared six-year-old boy again, and all his responsibilities felt heavier on his back than a boulder from Slick Rock Creek back home. He wanted to tell his ma about his troubles and let her carry some of the load for him. He opened his mouth to speak but then something told him to keep his quiet. How could he pour his troubles on his ma when she already carried the burden of Rose's poor health? No good son would do that, no good man. Steve closed his mouth. He needed to handle his own life, not trouble his ma with it.

"You're right, Ma," he said. "I do need somebody."

"I hope you find her," she said.

"Thank you for your concern," he said, his jaw set with the decision he'd just made, "but you got enough on your mind these days. I'm doing just fine."

Abby studied him as if not sure whether to believe him or not. Then she let it go. "Thanks for the ride," she said. "I'll see you in the morning."

Steve gave her a kiss on the cheek, and she climbed out of the car. He watched her until she disappeared into the house and flipped on a light. Then he turned the car and headed back into the rumbling night. At the end of the street, he turned left instead of right as he usually did. Mrs. Waterbury would have to wait awhile, he decided. He had another stop to make first.

He pulled up in front of Claire's house about ten minutes later. The rain pounded down on the car's roof. He told himself to stay calm but found it difficult. The time had come to find out if Claire would ever love him. He'd put it off long enough. If she said yes, he'd kick up his heels and live happily ever after. And if the answer was no, he'd take a deep breath and move on. But one way or the other, the time had come to make some decisions.

His shoulders hunched against the rain, Steve jumped out and headed up the walkway. A flash of lightning cut the sky, and he rushed even faster. Rain rolled down his forehead and into his eyes. He ran up onto the porch and knocked loudly. The thunder clapped. The electricity in the house flickered and then the lights went out. He peered in through a window but saw nothing. The lights blinked and came back on. The night suddenly settled for a second, the rain easing to half its former volume. Steve heard feet moving inside the house. They sounded heavier than a woman's feet, heavier than Claire's. He leaned toward the window. Lightning flashed, causing the house's interior to go dark again.

Steve knocked again and started to open the door. "Claire!" he called. He heard the steps again, this time the unmistakable steps of a man. He thought of an intruder, a thief! He shoved open the door and stepped inside, his body tense with the thought of protecting Claire and Frank. "Claire!"

He heard voices coming from the back of the house and rushed that way, his body wet with rain and perspiration, his eyes searching the dark to avoid hitting something. Another notion ran through his head, but he quickly pushed it away as unworthy. He reached the kitchen a second later and pushed the door open. Lightning cracked, and he saw Claire's frightened face in the sudden glare of light. The kitchen door stood open, rain blowing through it. Claire ran to him, her arms open.

"You're here!" she said, her voice loud against the storm.

Steve rushed by her to the door. Claire followed him, her hand on his arm as if to pull him back. Steve stared into the yard. The lightning flashed again, and he saw a man running away from the house. Something about the man looked familiar to Steve. He tried to figure out what as he flew down the steps after the stranger. But the man had disappeared over the fence and into the street. Steve knelt to the ground, his knees in the muddy grass, his heart breaking. Tears rushed to his eyes. Though he hated to admit it, he at least knew the truth now. Claire didn't love him, never had and never would. All this time and she'd continued to see the man who had fathered Frank.

Steve had no doubt the man wasn't an intruder. An intruder didn't talk to a victim as he ran from a house. A lover did, one making plans for his next visit.

The storm finally stilled and the rain stopped. Steve stood and wiped his face. Okay, he thought. He would leave Claire behind and look for another reason for living. If she didn't love him, maybe somebody else could. He turned back to the house. Claire walked down the steps toward him.

"Steve?"

He waved her off. "It's okay," he said. "You never made me any promises."

"It's not what you think," she said, her tone pleading. "Let me explain."

Steve started to move past her, but she grabbed his arm and held him still. "No!" she said. "I won't let it end this way."

"It never began," Steve said, his voice stronger than he expected. "You know that. You needed me, so you let me stay around. But you didn't love me, still don't. You've never pretended otherwise. I've got to hand you that—you've never lied about anything."

Her hand strong on his forearm, Claire peered into his face and said, "You're wrong. I *do* love you, more than you'll ever know. But it's far more complicated than that. I wish I could tell you everything. If you'll let me, I will."

Steve studied her eyes, saw sincerity in them. But then he hesitated.

Claire's fingers dug into his arm.

"It's too late," he said. "Too much has happened."

"I won't let you leave me," she said.

"Don't worry," he spat. "I'll still let you live here for free, will still give you some money every month. I care too much about Frank to throw you out."

Claire's face clouded. "You're so bullheaded!" she said. "And so ignorant sometimes."

"I come from the mountains, remember? None of us from the highlands are too smart."

"Oh, you're smart, all right," said Claire. "Just not about the right things, matters of the heart."

"Well, you're certainly the one to talk about the heart! Such an expert in that, you are."

Claire dropped his arm, her patience obviously having worn thin. "I don't claim to be an expert in anything," she said. "But I do know one thing."

"And what's that?"

She stood squarely before him now, her eyes focused directly into his. He glanced down, but she reached up and touched his chin, tilted it back up where she could see his face. "I know I love you," she said. "And that I want to marry you."

Steve shook his head. "What about your man, the one who just ran from here?"

"He's gone," Claire said. "For the last time."

"Why do you say that?"

"Because I just told him I never wanted to see him again, told him to stay away from me from now on."

Steve's eyes narrowed. "I don't trust that."

Claire took his hands in hers. "Look," she said, "I know you've waited a long time, and I've not told you everything I should. Maybe that's best; some things we should just keep to ourselves. But I'm telling you this now and it's the truth—I'm finished with my past, am ready to start a new future, a future with you and Frank."

Steve's heart battled against itself. He wanted to believe her, wanted to more than anything he'd wanted in his whole life. But how could he? From the first time he saw her, she'd remained a mystery to him, a mystery with all kinds of dark secrets. Yet here she was now standing before him and pledging her love. How could he turn her down? How could he step away from the possibility? Yes, it brought some risks. But life always did. Turning away from Claire brought risks too, the risk that he might never find anyone to fill the loneliness inside, the ache in his heart.

"You're sure about this?"

"As sure as anything I've ever known."

Steve took a big breath. He felt tingly all over as he realized that, in spite of what he didn't know about Claire, one thing he did know—he loved her. For now, that would have to do.

"I've got one more question for you," he said.

She dropped her eyes. "Please, don't ask me his name," she pleaded.

Steve tilted her chin up. "No," he said. "I got another question. Will you marry me?"

Claire smiled and his heart soared. "Yes."

He kissed her then, and for the moment at least, every worry he'd ever felt disappeared.

CHAPTER
TWENTY-SEVEN

S teve and Claire got married two weeks later in the Baptist
church that Abby attended every week. Although greatly surprised that Steve had a girlfriend, much less one he had made a
sudden decision to marry, Abby kept her concerns quiet when
Steve told her the news and asked if maybe the preacher at her
church would do their nuptials. No place for a ma to say too much
to a grown man about whether or not he should marry such and
such a person. Yes, it bothered Abby that Steve hadn't told her
about Claire until now; yes, it bothered her that Claire already had
a son by another man whom nobody knew. But what could she do
about it—pull Steve aside and tell him that this marriage had *Trouble* stamped all over it? What good would that do? She'd told Steve
she wanted him to find somebody he loved, somebody who would
love him in return. If he loved Claire and felt that she loved him,
they might do just fine.

Abby knew that any marriage, no matter how clear of difficul-
ties, faced a lot of struggles. Just look at her and her first go at it.

That marriage had turned out far from perfect. Even if she had faithfully stuck it out until Stephen's death, it had taken all her trust in God to do it.

The day of Steve's wedding turned out extra warm for early fall. About fifty people, including Jim and his family and Ed and Sol and theirs, joined Claire's parents from Richmond, her sister, Margaret, and brother, Peter, and a few of Steve's employees in the small sanctuary for the ceremony. Sitting in her wheelchair with her steel braces on her legs from the knees down, Rose attended with Abby, she and Porter constantly talking as they took spots near the front.

Abby prayed silently as Steve and Claire stood before the preacher—prayed that the Lord would pour out His favor on them, make their lives full of joy. She prayed also that Steve would return to his faith, that he'd come back to Jesus and lead Claire and her son with him when he did.

It puzzled Abby what had happened to Steve's trust in the Lord. From what she could see, he hadn't strayed off into any pit of sin, didn't do any carousing with women, any drinking or gambling. But he never went to church, never touched a Bible that she could see, never did anything to give evidence to any true faith. How did that happen to a person? To a man who had grown up with the Lord? Where had she failed him to cause him to turn out this way?

The preacher finished the vows, and Steve kissed his new bride. The ceremony ended and then everybody headed back to Steve's house to enjoy some cake and punch. Abby rode with Jim and Rebecca, Porter and Rose. Tommy and Harriet rode with their uncle Sol and aunt Jewel. At Steve's place they all piled out and headed inside. Abby stood behind a punch bowl that Steve's office secretary had set up. The people stepped by and she filled each glass. Near the end of the line, Mrs. Billy Gant made her way toward Abby. Abby smiled when she spotted her.

"Glad you could come," Abby said. "Other than a few folks I've met in the church, you're about the only friend I know in Raleigh."

The two women embraced. From behind, Abby heard steps, then turned to see Steve approaching. "You doing okay, Ma?" he asked. "I can get somebody else to serve the punch if you want."

Abby waved off the suggestion. "Let me introduce you to my son," she said to Mrs. Gant. "This is Steve, the happy groom."

Steve shook her hand. "You make a handsome groom," she said, "and your new wife is lovely."

Steve nodded proudly. "Prettiest girl around, except for my ma of course."

Abby smiled, and it seemed everything had a glow of joy around it. She faced Mrs. Gant again. "Your family is well?"

"Yes. I'm much blessed by that."

"Nothing more that a mama wants than to see her family happy and healthy," said Abby.

Mrs. Gant nodded. Abby handed a woman a glass of punch. Mrs. Gant stayed still. The woman with the punch moved off. Abby sensed tension in Mrs. Gant. She figured she knew what it was but didn't think she should say anything.

"I hear you deal in real estate," Mrs. Gant said to Steve.

Steve sipped his punch. "Some," he said. "Mostly rental properties. Lots of folks moving into Raleigh. I buy, fix up and rent. Got close to a hundred places right now."

"I'm impressed," said Mrs. Gant. "You're really doing well."

Abby saw Steve swell with pride, and he looked more like his pa than she had ever seen him. A wave of fear washed over her. She hoped Steve didn't get too pleased with himself. Such pride often led a man to his downfall.

"You are the one who's impressive," Steve said. "All you own, here and in the mountains too."

"It was all my husband's doing," Mrs. Gant said. "He and his pa before him."

"Either way, it's still valuable property. What you plan on doing with what used to be ours?"

Abby saw Mrs. Gant wince. She wished Steve hadn't asked such a blunt question. She'd told him of course that Mrs. Gant had put off the sale of their land for a long time. But since then, nothing else had been said.

"Maybe we should speak of that another time," Abby suggested. The preacher then moved to her, and she greeted him and handed him a glass of punch. Mrs. Gant sighed and Abby heard her resignation. Something had obviously changed since the last time they'd talked. The preacher turned away when somebody called his name. Abby faced Mrs. Gant.

"You seem anxious," Abby said.

"I'm sorry," said Mrs. Gant, "we can talk later if you want."

"No," Abby said, focused now. "Go ahead and tell us your news."

Mrs. Gant sipped her punch. "It's simple really," she said. "Mr. Stowe has sold the rest of our mountain property. All I got left is what was yours."

"So you need to sell ours now," Steve said.

"Exactly."

Abby felt faint and took Steve's arm. "I knew this had to happen sooner or later," she said. "But today isn't a good day to hear it."

"I don't guess there is a good day," said Steve.

"I wish I could wait longer," Mrs. Gant said, "but I don't know what else I can do except drop my claims in court. I've thought of that, believe me. I've got kids, though, and they don't know about all this. I feel like I have to do right by them. If we had any proof of your claims, any at all . . ."

"Don't you fret," Abby said. "We've already talked this over. You're not doing anything wrong."

"But I feel so bad."

"You've given us ample time," Abby said. "More than anybody else would have."

"It'll take several months to find a buyer, I'm sure," said Mrs. Gant. "But you probably need to tell your family."

Abby nodded. Jim, Ed and Sol would have to find new places to live. All their labor on their farms would be for naught. Sadness crept into her bones. "Is Mr. Stowe already looking for buyers?" she asked.

"I'm afraid so, although I suspect it could take until the spring for him to find one."

Abby nodded. In the spring. By then she and her family would have to give up all claims to the land of her ancestors, land her pa and ma had scraped all their lives to acquire, land that gave her and her kin a place to call home. What would happen to them all when this land slipped forever from their grasp, she didn't know. All she knew was that she felt helpless to do anything about it, and that was the most awful feeling of all.

After Mrs. Gant walked away, Steve poured his ma a glass of punch and escorted her to a seat. "Rest awhile," he told her, "and don't let any of this bother you. Today is a day for happiness." Abby nodded. He waited a moment for her to relax, then saw Claire headed his way.

"You go on," Abby insisted. "I've kept you long enough as it is. Besides, I need to check on Rose."

Steve kissed her on the cheek and then moved to Claire.

"Your ma all right?" Claire asked him.

"Yeah. Just a big day, you know. All this took her by surprise."

"I guess it did. She's not too sure about me, is she?"

Steve took Claire's hand. "My ma will love anybody I love," he assured. "She's like that—not a woman to cast judgment on another person."

"She's a woman of deep faith, though."

"Yes, that's true."

"Such women can get mean when they come across a sinner like me," Claire said.

"All that's behind us," Steve said. "Time to forget it and move on. And my ma isn't a mean woman. You don't have to worry about her."

Apparently satisfied, Claire nodded toward Mrs. Gant and asked, "Who's she?"

"Just a friend of ma's here in Raleigh."

"I saw you and your ma talking to her a long time."

Steve stared at his bride. "You're a nosy thing, aren't you?"

Claire shrugged, then said, "You don't have to tell me if you don't want."

Deciding it didn't make any difference, Steve said, "It's a long story, but she's the woman who holds title to all my family's property back home. We owned it years ago, about a thousand acres in all. But then, back in 1908, an uncle of mine—a man named Laban, my ma's brother—lost the land in a wager. Later on my uncle Daniel and everybody went in together to try to buy it back from Mrs. Gant's husband. They paid for eight hundred acres. But after Gant's death, a lot of things got mixed up. Turns out my folks didn't have any deed to it. Now Mrs. Gant claims she owns it, and without any proof from our side, she's right. Now she plans to sell it."

"Did you help buy it back too?"

"No. I moved here and left all that behind me."

Claire studied the situation a second. "Is it valuable?"

"All mountain property is valuable."

"How expensive is it?"

"I don't know exactly. Haven't done anything with highland land."

"Why don't you check it out?"

"Why should I?"

"Think about it."

Steve studied his wife. What did she mean? Then it dawned on him. He had told her how much he wanted to care for his ma, how he wanted to make up for his pa's failures. What better way to do that than to get back the land and give it to her? He mulled the matter over. Was this what Claire wanted him to figure out?

Another notion came to him, something Claire knew nothing about. If he did manage to get back the land, it would prove once and for all that he was as good a man as Jim. Nobody would ever again compare him to his older brother and see him coming up short. Not that anyone had done that publicly anyway. But he felt it all the same.

Steve considered his finances. He stayed stretched most of the time. Could he afford to purchase the land? He wasn't sure, yet he at least needed to find out what it might cost him.

"Maybe I should get in touch with Will Stowe," he said.

"Maybe you should," said Claire.

"You're a fine wife."

"Don't you forget it," she replied with a laugh.

Steve smiled. He had a beautiful wife and a smart one too. If he could somehow buy his family's land from Mrs. Gant, it would prove he was as much a man as his brother and a whole lot more of one than his pa. The idea of that pleased him, pleased him a lot.

CHAPTER
TWENTY-EIGHT

His ma took Rose home about a month later and within three weeks after that, Steve got things in order enough to take a couple of days off to go to Asheville to meet with Will Stowe. Not wanting Will to know his identity—after all, Stowe did have Clack blood and might jack up the price if he knew that a member of the Porter family had interest in the property—he sent Izzy and Claire to make the first contact. The two went to Stowe's office while Steve waited in the car a few blocks down the street.

"Tell him you read the sales notice in the Asheville newspaper," Steve advised Claire before she left. "Tell him you're not sure of your interest, but you want to know a price."

"I can handle it," Claire said.

"I'll stay by her, Mr. Steve," said Izzy. "Don't you worry yourself."

His nerves tight, Steve watched them walk off. What if Stowe put an impossibly high price on the property? What would he do then? His finances were stretched about as far as he could press them. He squeezed his fists and tried to calm some. But he found it hard. His nerves were taut, and he bit on a thumbnail as he wondered about Claire, how she would hold up. Over the last few days she had seemed awfully quiet, especially in the mornings. Her color had turned paler too. Just the other day he had found her sitting at the kitchen table, her head in her hands. When he walked in, she quickly wiped her eyes with her apron, jumped up and busied herself at the sink.

"You okay?" he had asked.

"Oh, it's only a woman thing," she assured him, "not a matter for your concern."

Not wanting to push, he let it go. Yet, loving her as he did, everything about her was a matter for his concern.

Will Stowe watched Claire Waterbury and Izzy walk into his office at precisely four o'clock, their punctuality a credit to the man he knew had sent them. He smiled behind his hand as they took seats across from his desk, Claire with her hands primly clutching her purse, Izzy ramrod straight, his hat in his hands. Steve Waterbury thought he was so smart sending his wife like this, trying to hide his identity. But Stowe knew a thing or two about how to handle business, and the first rule of property dealing said you should know the people who acted as though they might want to buy from you.

When the request for this meeting had come to his office four days ago, he had immediately started checking on the person who had called, one Claire Blankenship of Raleigh. The telephone people in the capital city had given him an address. Then a lawyer friend had driven to the house and watched it a couple of hours, saw a man go in and stay. A quick check of the address showed that a Mr. Steve Waterbury owned it. Mr. Waterbury turned out to be the husband of the woman named Claire. Stowe, of course, knew the name Waterbury. After all, his sister had married one.

Stowe cleared his throat. "I'm glad to hear of your interest in the property I have for sale," he started. "It's prime land. A fine stream, Slick Rock Creek, runs through it. The land has pretty much been cut of its timber, although the previous owner did not clear-cut it. Before long, another harvest of good trees will come mature. Still got a lot of game too, if you or your family likes hunting or fishing."

Claire glanced at Izzy. "We're here to begin discussions," she said. "We're not sure that we'll end up making any offer."

Stowe scowled as if concerned, though inside he remained calm. He knew some things about Steve Waterbury. A few phone calls in and around Raleigh and a whole lot of information had come to light. Waterbury owned many houses, yet most brought in only a meager amount of rent money. His income, though fairly steady, stayed stretched because he tended to put every dollar he made back into his business. True, Stowe didn't know why Steve hadn't come to him directly. If he wanted the land, why didn't he just come straight out and say it? Pride maybe, or not wanting to admit the family would have to purchase the same land twice? Or did he just not want to deal with a man of Clack origins? Stowe suspected that, in spite of his thin capital, Steve Waterbury wanted this land far more desperately than his wife now cared to say.

"I'm anxious to show you the land," Stowe said. "I think you'll want it more once you've really seen it."

Claire looked Izzy's way again, then said to him, "We're not ready to see the land just yet. Just interested in knowing your starting price."

Stowe took out a handkerchief and wiped his brow. People tried so hard to play innocent. Of course they didn't need to see the land. Steve Waterbury already knew it well. Smiling, Stowe put away the handkerchief. Even though he seldom saw his sister, she wrote him at least once a month, obviously trying to make up for the way she'd treated him in the past. In these letters, she occasionally mentioned her husband's younger brother. So when he'd found out that Steve Waterbury's wife had called to set up this meeting, he immediately drove up to Blue Springs, spent a day or so nosing around and asking questions about Jim and Steve. What he'd learned intrigued him a lot. From what he could tell, Jim was everybody's favorite. A war hero, a successful businessman, an elder at Jesus Holiness Church. That left Steve as the lowly second brother who had been forced to leave town to get some breathing space for his own life.

Stowe knew the type. Steve was surely jealous of his older sibling and wanted to prove his mettle. A good motive for buying this land. Purchase it and then give it to his ma, bought and paid for, the younger brother doing for her what the older had failed to accomplish. How obvious.

Of course, only a man of Will's superior intellect could have figured this out so easily, only a man of his background and experience.

"I have a reasonable price on the land," he said. "And it's not negotiable."

Claire set her purse on her lap. "Everything is negotiable," she said.

"Oh, is it?" Stowe looked closely at the woman. An exceptionally attractive woman, he decided. Was she saying something he hadn't figured yet?

"You just give us a price," Izzy chimed in, "and we'll move on and let you be about your business."

Stowe looked at Claire and started to say something but then let it drop. He took up a pencil and note pad, wrote a figure on it, and turned the pad so Claire could see it. She studied the number for a few seconds, then looked at Stowe. Her face had paled some, and he thought he detected perspiration on her upper lip.

"That's at least twice what the land is worth," she said, her voice sounding a bit shaky.

Stowe shrugged. "Land is worth what a man will pay for it."

Claire laid her hands flat on his desk and seemed to draw up her strength. "I hear tell the Porter family already paid for it once."

Stowe sat up straighter. The woman had gumption, he had to give her that. "What do you know about any of that?" he asked.

"Oh, not much. I just did some checking, that's all. From what I hear, the courts had some confusion about all this. Kept the sale of this land on hold for a long time. Maybe that confusion will crop back up again, tie this sale up once more."

Stowe relaxed. She didn't know anything that common street talk hadn't already revealed. "Not likely," he said. "Nobody ever produced any evidence to back up the Porters' story."

"No evidence?"

"Nothing ever showed up. I know. I searched myself, and there's no proof of any kind."

"I hear they're honest people."

"Not my concern. I'm just doing a job."

Claire nodded, and Stowe suddenly got the distinct impression that she looked tired, that she had spent all the energy she possessed.

"That's your final price, then?" she asked. "No negotiating?"

He smiled big at her. "Oh, maybe there's a little leeway."

Claire arched an eyebrow, then stood and headed to the door, Izzy right behind her. Before leaving, she twisted back toward Stowe and said, "I'll give it some more thought. See if negotiating is possible."

Stowe watched Claire go. Something about her puzzled him. One second she appeared strong, the next weary, the next strong again. What a strange woman. He stood and walked to his window. A couple of seconds later, he saw Claire and Izzy exit his building and head up the street. Stowe smiled. One thing he had to say about the Waterbury men. They sure knew how to pick their women.

Back in the car, Steve watched Claire and Izzy approach. When they had slid onto the seats, he immediately drove away. Only when they had left the block did he glance at Claire. Her head rested on the seat and she looked spent.

"Well," he said, too concerned about the meeting to worry much about Claire, "what did he say?"

Claire wiped her brow. "He knew who I was," she said. "Had the price twice as high as it ought to be."

"You sure of that?" He looked in the rearview mirror at Izzy.

"He seemed mighty sure of hisself," agreed Izzy. "And that price is mighty steep."

Steve glanced back at Claire. She had her eyes closed. "You okay?" he asked.

She waved him off. He turned the corner and headed out of Asheville. "You reckon we could stop a minute?" Claire asked.

Steve looked for a place to pull over, saw a stand of trees a half mile ahead. "You all right?" he asked again.

Claire rolled down the window and stuck her head out. Steve reached the trees and braked the car. Claire jumped out and rushed to the side of the road. Steve followed her, Izzy behind him. At the base of a tall maple, Claire bent double at the waist and lost the contents of her stomach. Steve ran to her, a handkerchief in his hand. Claire retched once more.

"I see a stream," Izzy said, looking past the side of the road. "They's a bottle in the car. I gets some water." He ran back to the car then down the bank. Claire raised her head, and Steve wiped her face with his handkerchief.

"You look pale," he said. "I'm sorry I sent you to Stowe. Didn't have any idea it would upset you like this."

Claire smiled weakly at him. Izzy ran back to them and in his hand was a bottle filled with creek water. He handed it to Claire. "This will freshen you some," he said.

Claire poured the water over the handkerchief and wiped her face with the wet cloth. "That's better," she said. "Thank you."

"Let's get back to the car," said Steve. "You can rest there."

The three of them climbed back into the car.

"I didn't know it would bother you like this," Steve told her again.

Claire laid a hand over his. "That's not it," she said. Steve gave her a puzzled look. Claire turned to Izzy and said, "Best you step out a minute." Izzy quickly removed himself from the car. "I'm not sick because I saw Will Stowe," Claire said. "Although that might do it for normal women. Truth is, I'm with child."

Steve rocked back. "But we've just been married a few weeks," he said.

"It doesn't always take a long time."

"It's just . . . so unexpected."

"Yes."

Steve thought of what it would cost. "I might have waited a while if I'd had the choice," he said.

"But we don't always get a choice," Claire said.

Another idea hit Steve, the notion that Claire had said yes to his proposal all of a sudden, the stormy night he'd caught Frank's father at her house. Had she—?

He shook his head to rid himself of the thought. No, that couldn't be true. This was his baby. How dare he think otherwise. Claire wouldn't treat him that way, wouldn't lead him to believe this baby was his if it wasn't. Steve put his hands on Claire's. His eyes softened as he looked into her face.

"I'm a little surprised," he said, "but that's okay. It's fine. We're going to have a baby and I'm glad."

Claire squeezed his hands and kissed him on the cheek. "You're a good man," she said. "As fine as they come."

"This baby will have everything," Steve said. "We'll give him everything he needs and then some."

"What makes you think it's a he?"

"Oh, it's a *he*," Steve said. "No doubt about it."

He took her in his arms and held her tightly, forgetting for the moment his plans to buy back the family land and his worries that maybe some other man had fathered the baby now growing in his wife's womb.

CHAPTER
TWENTY-NINE

To Abby's great relief, no buyers for the land came forward all that winter or early spring of 1960. That gave everybody some time to make new living arrangements. Ed and Priscilla decided to rent a place about four miles north of Blue Springs and gave the owner a hundred dollars to hold it for them until April. Jim got some men busy working on a house right beside his garage on the highway. And Sol and Jewel put down a deposit on a frame house just two streets down from where the sheriff's office sat. Although nobody had moved just yet, they had things in order for when the time came.

Abby watched it all with a deep grief in her heart. In spite of everybody's best efforts, it looked like they would have to move after all. About the only solace she had was the fact that they weren't leaving the area, not moving to another town like Steve had done.

In the second week of March, on a windy day with a weak sun, Jim called Abby at just past two o'clock in the afternoon. From the tone in his voice, she knew immediately that he needed to tell her bad news. He got right to the point.

"Mrs. Gant just called me," he said. "It looks like she's got a buyer for the land."

Abby stuck a hand in her apron pocket. "She have a date to settle it?"

"The tenth of April, I think."

"Not long."

"My place won't be finished," said Jim.

"You can stay with me a few months if need be," Abby said.

"Might have to take you up on that."

Abby hesitated, still unable to believe that it had finally come to this. Her distrust of Will Stowe rose up again. "I just can't believe that Gant didn't keep some records somewhere."

"The only man who knows for sure is Will Stowe. But he says nothing showed up."

Abby couldn't help thinking that something about Stowe made him a sorry risk. He had too many reasons to want harm to come their way. And now they were at the end of their rope. So long as things had stayed put off, she had managed to leave her suspicions at bay. But now the time had come to do something.

"I reckon there's no way to check on him, is there?" she asked.

Jim chuckled. "Not unless I break into his place and go through his files."

Abby laughed too but not too hard. "You think he's hiding something?"

"I've always thought that."

"Me too."

"What are you saying, Ma? You want me to—"

"I'm not saying to do anything," said Abby. "Just wondering how we can find out about Stowe when he won't come clean with us."

Jim chuckled again. "You beat all, you know that."

"I just don't trust the man."

"Let me see what I can do," Jim said. "Maybe I need to threaten him or something."

"I'm *not* suggesting bodily injury," Abby said firmly.

"No, Ma. I know you're not."

After Jim hung up the telephone, he immediately placed a call to Steve. To his relief he found him in his office.

"Hey, brother," he said. "Just wanted you to know—Mrs. Gant has found a buyer for the land. Looks like it'll take place sometime in April."

"Thanks for the information."

"You're welcome." Jim said good-bye and hung up. He picked up a pencil and bit on its end. Unless he did something now, he'd never know. Mrs. Gant would sell the land and they would do just fine. But what if Stowe had kept it on false pretenses? What if he had withheld information and cheated them? They'd never find out, and Stowe would get clean away with it.

Jim checked his watch. He had at least two hours' worth of work to finish, then he needed to go home and have a bite to eat. After that? Well, it was now or forget it.

He stood and moved to the window behind his desk. He'd never done anything illegal in his life and didn't like the notion of doing it now. Neither could he stand the thought of letting Will Stowe get away with something he just knew he had done.

Jim stuck his hands in his pockets and made a decision. After midnight, he decided. Then he'd make a trip down to Asheville, down to Stowe's office.

After Steve had hung up from talking to Jim, he called Claire at home. "I have to make a decision," he said, "about whether or not to make an offer on the Blue Springs land."

"Can our finances handle it?" Claire asked, her voice tired.

"Not sure. I need to go to the bank, check with them."

"You're good with those kinds of things," she said. "So whatever you and the bank decide, you know I'll support it."

"I appreciate your trust," Steve said. "It means a lot."

"I'm too sick to worry about it," Claire told him. "Delivering babies is no easy work, I can tell you that."

"You're good at it though," Steve said. "Maybe we ought to have seven or eight."

"Not if I've got anything to say about it."

"I'll call you later."

He set the receiver back in its cradle and leaned back. If he did pay Stowe's price for the land, it would take years until he could find enough money to build any new homes. Years before he could make improvements on the properties in the black section of town; years before he could relax any and feel he had some breathing space related to his business. Was it worth it?

Steve weighed the matter for several seconds. A long time ago he had boasted that someday he would come back to Blue Springs and buy them all out. Nobody had believed him. But he had gone off and made something of himself, had shown that he had as much business smarts as Jim, maybe more. Yet nobody back home knew it. About the only thing they knew was that he'd married a woman who had a boy with no husband and that she already had a second child on the way. Although nobody had said anything, Steve could guess what some of them were surely thinking: that maybe this baby wasn't his, that maybe his wife had decided to marry him because she had a new baby on the way and still with no man to care for them. Steve knew that was what people had in their heads because sometimes that was what he had in his.

Pushing off the idea for now, he tightened his tie, grabbed his suit coat off the chair back and stood. If he hurried, he could still get to the bank today and see what kind of collateral he'd need to borrow the money to make a down payment on the land. Yes, Stowe was asking way too much for it, but like he said, the land's value exactly matched whatever somebody would pay for it.

Jim arrived in Asheville at about three o'clock in the morning. Parking his car two blocks from Stowe's office, he took a swig of coffee from a Thermos, capped the coffee and then stepped out of the car. After checking the street for signs of life, he eased to the front of the building that housed Stowe's law office. At the door he pulled out a small screwdriver and hammer, punched out the door lock and slunk into the dark hallway. For a second he felt guilty, but then he took an envelope from his shirt pocket and laid it and the five dollars it contained on the floor by the door. Whether or not he found anything at Stowe's office, Stowe could buy a new lock with the money.

Jim shoved the hammer and screwdriver back into his pocket and pulled out a small flashlight. He headed up the stairs just inside the building. From past talks with Rebecca, he knew Stowe kept his office on the second floor. At the top of the stairs he moved down the hall as he read the names on the doors. On the last door on the right he saw Stowe's name. Out came the screwdriver and hammer again. Another couple of jabs and the lock to Stowe's office cracked open. Jim set a second envelope with five dollars in it on the floor and slipped inside.

Careful to keep the beam of the flashlight away from the windows, he made a quick study of the room. At least three offices ran off the center space. Jim raised the light to the glass doors, saw Stowe's name on the door to his left. He walked to it. To his relief he found it open and pushed through. His light ran across the floor, up and over the front of a large desk that sat in the middle of the room. A couple of file cabinets were placed behind the desk.

Moving quickly, Jim crossed to the file cabinets, screwdriver and hammer ready. The cabinets weren't locked. His flashlight in hand, he flipped through the files, one after the other, thumbing through them as fast as he could while remaining thorough. It took him close to an hour to get through both cabinets. He found nothing helpful.

He turned to the desk and started opening drawers, his flashlight shining on the contents of the middle drawer first, then the ones on the left. Still nothing. Jim paused and wiped his brow. Only a couple of drawers to go. He moved to the right side of the desk and opened the top drawer. It was empty. He licked his lips and focused the flashlight on the bottom drawer. It was locked. He went to work with his screwdriver and hammer. The drawer opened. He put an envelope with another five dollars on the desk and then trained the flashlight back on the drawer's inside. Near the bottom he found a thick file marked *Gant*.

He yanked it out and laid it on the desk top. His flashlight moved across the papers. Though not versed in legal matters, it didn't take Jim long to recognize the subject matter of the papers. They contained notes on Stowe's meetings and conversations with Mrs. Gant, a couple of copies of a map that outlined the property dimensions, a deed to the land and some notes on his meetings with potential buyers.

Jim's eyes widened when he saw the name Claire Blankenship on one page of notes. Apparently Steve had made at least one trip to Asheville to talk to Stowe.

Jim stuck the paper back into place and flipped to the next group of papers. This stack referred to the hearings regarding the property and Stowe's preparation for these hearings. He hurriedly read through the papers. About halfway through them he found what he wanted—a dusty ledger with the name Billy Gant on the front. Pages of handwritten notes were inside the ledger, and Mr. Gant's signature showed up on the bottom of the pages.

His hands trembling, Jim read enough of the ledger to know it proved everything he and his family had told the judge. Gant had kept records of their purchases, and here was the evidence.

He tried to figure why Stowe hadn't just thrown the ledger away. Cockiness maybe? A feeling that no one would do what Jim had just done—break into his office and go through his files? Or maybe he thought he might actually need the notes someday. If Mrs. Gant had turned out to be a dishonest person, maybe he would have used the material to control her, make her do his bidding. Who knew why a man like Stowe did the things he did? Perhaps he just liked the fact that he had the goods the Porters wanted and every now and again it gave him a perverse pleasure to open the ledger and look at it, to remind himself that he held the upper hand against his enemies. In any case, it didn't matter. Jim had the ledger now.

Jim grinned in anticipation of his next meeting with Stowe. After all these years of feeling cheated, he now held the evidence that proved him and his family as honest folks. Stowe would hate him for this. But sometimes life had a way of evening up the score.

The ledger in hand, Jim hurried out of the office, careful to close all the doors as he left.

———

Steve drove almost all night to reach Blue Springs by sunup. The way he had it figured, he wanted to stop in to see his ma for a couple of hours, tell her what he planned to do and then take her to Asheville. The thought of seeing her face when he told her of his plan kept him awake as he traveled. Nothing would please his ma more, least nothing outside of Rose putting away her braces and starting to walk on her own again.

At just past six he pulled up in front of his ma's house and shut off his car. A light glowed from the front room. Steve sat a second in the car, basking in the thought of his upcoming announcement. What a fine day, he decided, one unlike any other in his whole life. His ma would see today that he hadn't turned out at all like his pa. Not that she had ever said he had, or even that she'd ever suggested that he might. But she had to have worried about it, hadn't she?

Steve wiped his hands on his pleated pants and congratulated himself once more. He had outdone his pa in a lot of ways. He'd taken in a woman with a baby instead of leaving one behind. He'd built up a business rather than letting one become destroyed. He'd labored hard to make a living instead of grabbing for the easy way out.

It was now time to go to his ma and let her know his good news. Out of the car, Steve was striding toward the door when he heard a truck headed his way. Facing the truck, he saw Jim behind the wheel, the truck's headlights bobbing up and down as he pulled into the yard. Surprised, Steve waited for the truck to stop. Jim's face creased when he saw him.

"What are you doing here?" Jim asked, killing the engine.

"I could ask you the same thing."

"I live here. Least not far from here. I came by to see Ma about a matter."

"So did I."

The two brothers studied each other. Steve shuffled his feet and looked away. Somehow he knew Jim had come about the same matter that brought him here. "You found something, didn't you? About the land?"

Jim held up the ledger. "I searched Stowe's office," he said. "I know I shouldn't have, but I did."

"Your searchin' give you what you were looking for?"

Jim nodded. "You here to buy the place from Stowe, I reckon."

"Yeah. Thought I'd tell Ma before I drove down to Asheville."

"You won't have to spend your money," Jim said. "Good news."

Steve grunted, shook his head. "Don't worry," he said. "You all bought the land fair and square. I'm glad you found the proof."

"Come on in with me," Jim said. "She'll be glad to see us both."

"No, I best go on home. Ma won't understand why I'm here, and I'll feel silly telling her."

"Tell her you found out about the ledger. It's not a lie; you just did."

Steve waved him off. "No," he said. "It's best not to stretch the truth like that."

Nodding, Jim said, "You know, we ought to get together more."

"Reckon that's true. But life is real busy, you know that."

"Your missus well?"

"Yes. Just waiting on the baby."

"That'll keep you busy soon enough."

Steve scratched his head. They had done enough small talk. He could see this was Jim's moment, not his. Once again Jim had come to the rescue and gotten to play the hero. No matter what he did, he'd never live up to his brother. He turned to leave. Jim stuck out his hand and Steve shook it.

"You take care, brother," Jim said.

"You too."

Back in his car, Steve watched Jim step through the front door. Even though he knew he should feel glad because his family would soon have their land back and he wouldn't need to pay for it, he still felt beat. Just when he had victory in his grasp, Jim had showed up to take it away.

He started the car and put it in gear. At least he had Claire. No matter what happened to him in Blue Springs, he could count on Claire waiting on him when he drove back to his house in Raleigh.

Jim and Abby decided to visit with Stowe first thing that morning. "Talk to him before you tell anybody else," Thaddeus advised as they all sat at the table early that day. "Don't bring anybody else into it until it's all settled."

"I'll want to call Mrs. Gant right after we get through with Stowe," Abby said. "I want to be straight with her."

"For sure," said Jim.

Stowe met them at the door of his office when they walked in about two hours later, his face carrying a look of anger along with a worried frown. "Have a seat," he said with a gruff voice as he led them into his office. "There." He pointed to two wood chairs across from his desk. Abby and Jim obeyed. Stowe sat down behind his desk. "I think I know why you're here. When we arrived this morning, we found evidence of a theft in our offices last night. Rather crude method, but effective."

Jim studied his shoes, while Abby stared straight at Stowe's face.

Clearing his throat, Jim confessed, "I took your ledger. No reason to fool around about it."

Abby thought Stowe might fall off his chair. The veins in his temples swelled up and turned purple. "You had no right!" he stammered. "I'll have you arrested for breaking and entering, theft, a whole list of charges! You just wait and—"

"Hold on!" Jim barked back at Stowe. "Don't you make threats you can't back up. If you turn me in, I'll just produce the ledger to the police. Then you can explain to them how you've been keeping evidence wanted by the court, evidence which you testified at a hearing that you had no knowledge of, where you told the judge you checked all the appropriate places for proof but hadn't found anything, no such documents. See how a judge takes to that lie you spoke."

Stowe jumped up from his chair and leaned over his desk, his face a dark cloud. "You think you're so smart, don't you?"

Jim shrugged. Abby stared at the man. "You should be ashamed," she said. "Lying all this time, pretending you were an honest lawyer. Against your own family too!"

"You're no family of mine!" he spat. "You nor my sorry sister either."

Abby bit her tongue to keep from saying something she would

later regret. When she spoke, she kept her tone even. "I feel sorry for you, Will Stowe," she said. "You're a lonely, angry man. Cut off from your only sister, a sister who surely loves you, who wishes to know you better."

"She left me a long time ago," said Stowe. "Left me on my own."

"Rebecca loves you," Jim said. "That's the truth."

Stowe eased off and sat back down. He buried his face in his hands. After a couple of seconds, he glanced back up at them. "Look," he said, "I know when I'm licked. Let's not take this any further. I won't act to convict you of any crime if you'll let me go to Mrs. Gant with this, tell her I made another check up at her husband's cabin, just to make sure, you know. She'll believe me. She half wants to just give you the land anyway."

"I'm not giving this ledger back to you," Jim said.

Stowe waved him off. "Keep it," he said. "I'll tell her I gave it to you, for safekeeping, to prove I've got nothing to hide."

"I don't like lying," Abby said.

"You don't have to," Stowe assured. "*I* will talk to her. You just keep quiet about what happened. Otherwise I'll have no choice but to go to the law and have your boy here arrested for breaking into my office. He can show the authorities the ledger and I'll pay as a result, but so will he. My way lets us both off the hook."

Abby looked at Jim. She thought maybe they should come clean with Mrs. Gant. But Stowe did hold some power here. Maybe they could do it like he described, so long as she didn't have to lie to anybody. "Okay," she finally said. "But if she asks me anything straight to my face, I won't tell her a lie."

Stowe nodded. "I understand. You know my position."

Jim stood and Abby followed. Stowe shook his head at them. "This won't end here," he said.

"I reckon it won't," Jim said. "Seems like it never does."

"Eventually I'll find a way to get even," threatened Stowe. "Maybe not like the old days, but it'll hurt just the same."

"Do your worst," Jim told him. "We've always managed to survive."

"So have we."

"I hope you find what you're missing," Abby said. "I expect it's the Lord."

"I'll have none of that in my office," Stowe said.

"The Lord still loves you," Abby said.

"You're getting loony in your old age," Stowe said. "Trying to tell me about your Jesus."

"Don't call my ma names," Jim warned, "unless you want real trouble."

Abby took Jim by the arm. "Come on," she said. "I take no offense at anything said by a Clack."

When they reached Jim's car, Abby paused and looked at her son. "I'm not believing this," she said. "But it looks like we have finally managed to get back the land."

"All but two hundred acres," said Jim.

"You reckon Mrs. Gant will sell that to us?"

"No reason to think she wouldn't for a fair price."

"The Lord is good," Abby said.

"And mysterious," Jim added. "After all these years. Wonder why it took so long?"

"I guess you should have broken into Stowe's office a long time ago."

Jim laughed. "Reckon so."

———————

Driving back to Raleigh, Steve knew he shouldn't feel angry with Jim. Yet, try as he might, he couldn't stop himself. The miles passed bitterly. He stopped once about halfway home to get a bite to eat at a small roadside restaurant, but the food tasted bland and he had little appetite. Back in the car, his anger at Jim turned against himself. It wasn't Jim's fault he always did things right. It was his own fault that he never did things quite as well. No reason to blame his big brother for his own failures.

By the time Steve reached the outskirts of Raleigh, the sky had turned a dull gray and light rain had begun to fall. Steve's mood dropped even lower. Now he felt resigned, down on himself worse than he could ever remember. He had struggled so hard to make people around him proud, particularly his ma, to show he had overcome his pa's sorry ways. But nobody knew anything about it, least not the people who mattered most, the folks back home.

Steve almost smiled at the irony of it all. In spite of his efforts to escape his background, he still cared deeply about what his family thought of him. Problem was, he had so little control over any of that. They thought what they thought, and he couldn't do much of anything about it.

He'd done a lot of good things, though. Had taken in a woman with a child and had treated her boy as his very own. Had given money to a number of charities in the city, sent dollars home to his ma every month for many a year, provided for a sickly woman, provided better housing to the poor folks who rented from him. And he had tried hard to live the straight and narrow. No, he didn't claim any perfection, he knew better than that. Still, he lived a clean life, a lot better than most. So where was his reward? Why didn't he feel any contentment or peace inside? Why hadn't God allowed him some joy for all his efforts? A man who lived clean and did right deserved some favor from the Almighty, didn't he? Shouldn't that put him at least a few rungs up on the ladder toward heaven?

Weary from thinking so much, Steve turned down the street that led to his house. He leaned forward to see through the swiping of his windshield wipers, anticipating the moment when he'd step inside his front door and hug Claire and Frank. They would make him feel better, just touching their warm skin, smelling Claire's hair, playing with Frank. Steve's spirits lifted a little. Claire loved him; he knew it. Frank too. Heaven knew he loved them.

Steve pulled into his driveway and parked the car. The rain dripped off his face as he ran for the cover of the front porch. Nearing the steps, he heard shouting, what sounded like the voice of an angry man. He shoved open the door and ran inside. He saw Claire in the living room, a man's hands on her shoulders, his back to Steve. Claire glanced to Steve, her eyes wet with tears, and something else as well. Fear. It took a second for the scene to register with Steve, for him to realize what was happening, but then he knew it beyond a doubt. The man's back and stature looked familiar to him, like that of the man he'd chased from Claire's house the night she finally said she loved him.

Frank's father! Steve knew it for sure. Maybe too the father of the baby Claire now carried in her womb? Enraged, Steve rushed the man, grabbed him by the shoulders and jerked him away from Claire. The man wheeled around to face Steve. Steve staggered backward when he saw the man's face. Though no one had thrown any punches, he felt like somebody had clubbed him in the stomach with a boat paddle. He found it hard to breathe. His arm reached out for something to give him support. He touched the wall, felt his body sag toward it then slide down to the floor. He looked to Claire, but she had turned away, her arms wrapped around her waist, her chin low. The sound of her sobs filled the room.

Steve looked back at the man, his mind reeling. How could this be?

The man chuckled, and his eyes sparkled with satisfaction.

"Claire?" Steve said, hoping she'd give him an explanation that would somehow make sense.

She pivoted toward him and shook her head, her eyes filling again with tears.

"I've come for her," said the man.

Steve wanted to die. After all these years, now he knew. Everything he loved most was lost. He turned to the man. "It's been a while," he said, his voice ragged. "You've stayed out of sight."

"Oh, I see Mrs. Waterbury every now and again, when you're not around."

Steve pulled himself off the floor and onto a chair. The man sat down across from him. Steve took a deep breath and stared straight into the eyes of his half brother, Allen Baldwin.

CHAPTER
THIRTY

It took some time for Steve to pull himself together enough to
keep his emotions in check. His shoulders square, he decided to
find out the truth once and for all. "Did you play me from the
beginning?" he asked Allen. "From the time I left Blue Springs?"

Allen shrugged. "You told the Waterburys you were coming to
Raleigh. Mr. Waterbury didn't want that. He asked me to do what
I could to keep you away. I sent Claire to find out what she could.
Didn't have a plan at first, figured we'd come up with something as
things unfolded."

"And did you?" He faced Claire now.

"Yeah," she said. "I took your money. Thought that would
make you tuck tail and run."

"Country boy with no money surely couldn't make it in the big
city for long."

"Something like that," said Allen. "But you surprised us."

Steve grunted. Allen continued, "You stuck it out. Got a job.
Kept nosing around until you found us."

"Did Mr. and Mrs. Waterbury move to keep me from finding them?"

Allen smiled. "No, we didn't go that far. They had been down on their luck. A number of tenants had moved out without paying, a house burned down, several things happened that forced them to take a smaller, less expensive house. Just happened to occur about the time you came their way."

Steve shook his head. In a way it all made a strange kind of sense. Looking back, he could see the clues. Claire had seemed to know so much about him. Plus, she was far too friendly for a complete stranger. Yet he still had a number of questions.

"Were you and Claire . . . back then, were you—"

"No," Allen said, shaking his head. "We'd gone out a few times, but nothing serious."

Steve turned to Claire. "Why'd you do it?"

Wiping her eyes, she answered, "I didn't mean to hurt you, Steve. I knew Allen, cared for him. The way he explained the situation, it made sense for you to stay out of things. Mr. Waterbury didn't want you here. Didn't want you to find out about your father and what he'd done. In a way, I thought I was protecting you."

Steve nodded. It made sense. Allen and the Waterburys had their lives, and he had his. What good could come by mixing them? He thought about his ma. He'd done exactly what Allen and the Waterburys had tried to do: kept a secret from somebody. That was what they had wanted. That was what he'd managed to do. How could he blame them for their actions when he had done the same thing? He looked Allen in the eyes.

"Once I got here, things turned bad for you," Steve said matter-of-factly.

Allen shrugged again. "You worked hard and you had a good head on your shoulders. Mr. Waterbury saw that. That and you had the family name."

"I didn't want what he gave me."

"Maybe not, but you didn't turn it down when he offered it."

"I tried."

"If you say so."

Steve started to protest but then knew it wouldn't matter. What had happened had happened. Nothing he could say could change anything now. "When did you two. . . ?"

"Not until years later," Claire said. "Fact is, I moved back to Richmond for a while, not returning to Raleigh until 1954 or so. Ran into Allen again, and we started seeing each other."

"Then Franklin came," Steve filled in. Claire dropped her eyes. Steve faced Allen, his face reddening. "Why didn't you marry her?"

"Because I didn't have anything to offer her," he said. "You know what I've done the last few years, drifting in and out of town, never in one place for any amount of time, never settling on a decent job. I didn't want the ties, the responsibility of anything like that. If I couldn't keep work, how could I expect to take care of a family?"

"So you figured it was better for her to bring a child into the world by herself, is that it?"

For the first time, Allen showed some sign of remorse. He rubbed his hands together. "It wasn't that simple," he said. "She didn't want me either."

Steve's eyes widened and he glanced at Claire. She bit her lip. "I knew Allen real well by then," she said. "Too well, if you want the truth of it. Although we had . . . you know . . . well, I realized I didn't want him as a husband. Figured he couldn't change, would never settle down with one woman, to a steady business of any kind. Decided I'd rather have a child alone than to marry him and end up in a divorce somewhere down the road."

Steve paused to think. Something here didn't fit. Allen had come for her. Didn't she plan now to go with him?

"You've taken good care of her and Frank," Allen said, breaking his thought.

"You sent her to me when it came time to have Frank?"

Allen nodded. "I knew you'd provide for her. I got to give you that. You've shown yourself dependable, caring for Mrs. Waterbury like you have, especially the way you've handled the business."

Steve waved him off. "What if I hadn't recognized her?"

"Oh, I knew you'd recognize her. A man doesn't forget meeting a woman like Claire. Especially when the man meets her his first time out of the backwoods."

Steve took a breath. So many things had been directed toward him without his knowledge. So many things dictated by someone else. He wondered about that. Did the Lord act the same way? Move things around on the checkerboard without anybody ever seeing the plan behind it until it had already happened, until the person looked back on it through a rearview mirror?

He faced Claire once more. "Why did you marry me?" he asked.

Claire reached for his hand, but he pulled it away. She stood and moved to the window. Steve wanted to go to her and put his arms around her, only he couldn't get himself to do it.

"I married you because I love you," she said, turning back to him.

"I find that hard to believe," he said.

"I can understand that now," she said. "But it's true, I mean it. Sure, when I first came to you, I didn't love you. But I didn't know you then. Over the years, the way you've cared for me and Frank, the way you've loved us . . . how could I *not* fall in love with you?"

"You wanted what I could provide," he said bitterly. "What Allen here couldn't give you, I did. Security, a good life for you and Frank."

Claire moved to him and stood by his side. He turned away. She touched his shoulder, but he wouldn't face her. "Yes, I admit it," she said. "I like it that you can give us all that. But that's not why I married you, not why I stayed."

Steve shook his head. His heart wanted to listen while his head told him to ignore her words.

Allen stepped over to Claire, placed his hand on her shoulder. "I love you," he said. "And I can take care of you now. I've taken work in Wilmington. I love the country down there. A partner and I bought an old hotel a couple years ago, fixed the place up. We've done well. Lots of folks headed to the water these days. We're going to expand now, buy ourselves another hotel."

"Sounds like a good plan," said Steve, his fire gone out as he faced the inevitable.

"What if I don't want to go?" Claire said, the question directed at Steve. "What if I want to stay here with you? Will you have me?"

Steve wanted to shout *Yes!* Wanted to tell her the past didn't matter, then take her in his arms and hold her so tight she couldn't breathe. But he knew better. The past did matter.

"What about the new baby?" he asked. "What about that?"

Claire lifted her chin so she could stare into his eyes. "This baby is yours," she said.

Steve wanted to believe her, but he found that wasn't possible. She had betrayed him in the past. She could just as easily do it again. He looked at Allen and asked, "Is she telling the truth?"

"She's your wife," Allen replied. "Don't you believe her?"

Steve pulled away from Claire and walked to the window. The rain outside trickled down the windowpane. He didn't know what to believe. But one thing he knew—he couldn't figure this all out right now. He needed some time, some distance from everything and everybody in this room. For a long moment he stood still and watched the rain fall. Claire and Allen waited behind him. He tried to sort through his feelings. He knew what he wanted to do. But how could he trust Claire when she had shown herself so unworthy of it? To take Claire back, to trust her about the baby, to forgive her of her deception meant giving up his pride, the one thing that had always kept him going when nothing else did.

He thought back to his boyhood days, to when other boys had kidded him about not having a pa. He'd never said anything to anybody about those awful times, when it seemed he'd die from shame. Sometimes he wondered if Jim had felt the same way. From what he could see, Jim had done just fine. But not him. He had hurt from it, had hurt so bad that he had puffed out his chest and sworn that nobody would ever make fun of him again. Not about something he did and not about something somebody close to him had done. A man could take a lot of things, but if he kept his pride, he could survive them all.

Though still confused, Steve turned to Claire and Allen, his hands in his pockets. "I think it's best if you both leave."

Sobbing now, Claire ran to him with her arms outstretched. Steve ignored her pleas as she clung to him. "I want to stay," cried Claire. "You know I love you."

Steve forced himself to stay strong. Tears didn't mean a whole lot to him anymore. As a boy, he'd cried enough tears to fill up Slick Rock Creek. Yet, for all his crying, his pa had never come back home.

Claire finally let go and stepped back. "Where will I go?"

"You can stay here," Steve said. "I'll move out. Even though it's over between us, I'll let you and Frank stay where you're happy."

"You can go with me," said Allen. "I've got a home for you and Frank now, the new baby too."

Claire wiped her eyes, then looked back and forth between the two men. "I don't know what to do."

"It's your choice," Steve said.

"I want to stay here. But in the same house with you, not alone." She stared at Steve as if expecting him to say something. What could he say? Obviously she didn't really love him. Why should he go on making a fool of himself for a woman who had used him so?

"You can do half of that," he said. "Like I've already said."

Claire took a step his way. "Steve?"

"You used me, Claire," he said. "Only a fool would let you do it again."

"Listen to him," said Allen. "He doesn't want you anymore. I do. I love you, you know that."

She looked up at Steve one more time, her eyes pleading. But he didn't waver. Sometimes a man had to stand up to the hurts, face them down. Otherwise they would just plain kill him.

Claire finally nodded and then took a step toward Allen. Steve's heart broke, but he didn't dare let them see it lest they think him weak.

SECTION III

1961–1974

CHAPTER
THIRTY-ONE

The years after Abby's family finally got their land back passed quickly. Jim and Ed helped her and Thaddeus build a house on the mountain not far from theirs, and the two of them took Rose and settled in up there like they had never left. The house—an eight-room, two-story frame dwelling—sat on a hill that faced Blue Springs Mountain, porches running all the way across the front on both floors, four rocking chairs decorating it on the bottom, with two chairs on top.

Abby faced a lot of happenings in those years, some of them good and happy, some sad. Most of the hard news came from Raleigh. Although Steve refused to tell her the reason, she found out pretty fast about his troubles with Claire.

"I left Claire, Ma," he said the day he called to tell her the news. "I'm sorry to have to say it, but it's true."

She almost told him he couldn't do it. A man didn't just up and leave his wife and baby, no matter what the cause. Steve's pa had done that to her, and she wasn't sure she could abide her son doing it to another woman. But then she bit her lip and stayed quiet. A ma had a lot of say in the lives of her children, but Steve was a grown man, and if he chose to do this, she had to let it go even if she didn't like it.

The truth was, Abby hadn't felt good about the marriage from the beginning, and when she found out within a few weeks of the nuptials that Claire had already come up with child, something suspicious rose up in her head. She knew she shouldn't feel that way, but something about Claire made her uneasy. Obviously Steve had found out some news that made it impossible for him to stay with her. Abby wanted to ask him what that was, yet she kept her quiet. If Steve wanted her to know, he'd tell her, she figured.

"I'm still going to take care of her and the children," Steve had told her. "I won't leave them without any means."

"I'll pray that you two will get back together," Abby said.

"You are welcome to do that," said Steve. "But you might not should get your heart set on it."

The years moved on. Abby slowed some in her sixties, her back starting to hurt from arthritis, her bones creaking a touch when she climbed out of bed every morning, especially on cold days. And her hair turned completely gray. Jim teased her that maybe she should dye it from a bottle. She just smiled and said, "No thanks. What color the Lord gave me, I reckon I will keep."

In spite of her physical ailments, Abby kept real busy, her time split between tending her house, working her garden and serving at Jesus Holiness Church. When night fell and the chores were all finished, she sat in her rocker and hummed as she busied her fingers with sewing. On most evenings Thaddeus sat beside her and read.

Abby loved these quiet times with Thaddeus. With age creeping up on him too, he retired from his teaching in 1965 and took to helping her more on the farm. What with crops to grow and barns, fences and sheds to keep up, he found plenty to lay his hand to do. Occasionally he complained of a little chest pain, but the doctor said his heart seemed fine, that they shouldn't worry too much about it. Abby tried to follow the doctor's advice yet sometimes found it hard. So long as she had Thaddeus beside her, she could face anything, no matter how bad. But if something ever happened to him, well, she couldn't even think about that.

Some folks did pass on in those years, including Daniel's widow, Deidre, down in Asheville. A virus gave her pneumonia before the doctors could stop it. Then, a year later, Sol fell victim to cancer. Mrs. Waterbury in Raleigh died next, from plain old age. Abby mourned them all but especially Deidre and Sol, whom she knew a whole lot better than Mrs. Waterbury.

Abby tried to keep it all in a right perspective. Nobody's life lasted forever, and she trusted that, because Deidre and Sol had lived their lives striving to follow the Lord, they were now at peace with Jesus. She hoped the same was true for Mrs. Waterbury.

In contrast to the sadness caused by Steve's problems and the deaths of some folks she loved, Abby experienced a great deal of joy in other places. Rose moved off in 1963 to go to college at the university in Chapel Hill. With her love for books she decided to study English and teach when she had finished.

Having almost completely recovered from the polio that had hit her so hard in '58, she had long since left her braces behind. She still had a slight limp, but only those who knew her well really noticed it. That didn't mean, though, that the polio hadn't left its mark. While she couldn't have identified the cause if somebody asked her why she had the personality she had, the polio had touched her soul as much as her body, had made her more sensitive to others, more prone to watching out for the underdog, the broken and the feeble. When she saw people hurting and hungry, she took it upon herself to do what she could to help them. When she saw someone beating up on someone weaker, she became furious and wanted to take a poke at the bully.

She and Porter kept close while she attended college. With him over in Raleigh working on earning a business degree at the state college, Porter set her up with guys, and she did her best to find him a girl to measure up to her standards. Both failed in their matchmaking efforts, however, though neither held it against the other. They loved each other like brother and sister, and some bad blind dates couldn't change that.

After college Rose moved to Asheville to teach, and she and Porter drifted apart some. But she still felt connected to him and knew that, even if they didn't see much of each other anymore, they still had a friendship that nothing could ever break.

The nation's politics in the 1960s made Rose sick at heart. She cried for two days when the president got shot in Dallas. Watching a television that Jim had given her ma, she shouted at the screen when she saw grown men standing in school doorways to keep black children out of their classrooms. Later, she got just straight out angry the day she heard a gunman had killed Martin Luther King Jr. in Memphis while he stood on a hotel balcony. Rose decided right then and there that something had to change if her country was to ever feel good again.

Abby and Thaddeus were pleased that Rose had taken up teaching after college. True, Abby didn't always agree with some of Rose's political views, but she still swelled with pride that she stood up for what she believed. Woman or no, she refused to take a back seat to anybody when it came to expressing her opinion.

Abby also felt good about Jim's achievements. His auto-repair business boomed, and in 1963 he decided to get into car sales as well and opened his own dealership. A second one, over in Hickory, started up in '66. He and Rebecca became leaders in the Blue Springs community, their good sense and generous support of town causes bringing them respect and appreciation.

Their children grew up solid and steady, Porter leading the way. When he got old enough he started working after school with his pa and then some years later headed off to college in Raleigh. At the college he decided he wanted to serve his country and defend it against Communism, so he joined up with the ROTC. By the time he graduated in 1968, he'd decided to enter into the military full time.

Rose tried to talk him out of that choice but had no luck. "My pa fought in the Second World War," he had said to her one August day as they sat together on Abby's front porch. "He met my ma overseas. Besides, how can I turn my back on my country now? We've got to stop the Communists before they take over the whole world."

She sat there arguing with him for a long time, yet he wouldn't budge, so Rose finally gave up. They went their separate directions for a while after that, him heading into the Marines as an officer, her staying in Asheville to do her teaching.

A couple of times Rose talked to Abby about Porter, hoping her ma would take her side and press Porter to get himself out of the military.

"You know this war in Vietnam isn't right," Rose said every time they talked about it. "We're fighting for the wrong reasons and in the wrong place."

"I don't know much about the politics of the war," Abby always replied. "But I know the men in our family. They tend to fight when their country calls on them."

"But what if their country is corrupt? What if it's sending them to their deaths for no just cause?"

"You'll need to take that up with Porter," Abby said.

Rose usually let things drop there. She apparently didn't want to do anything to widen the distance between herself and Porter.

To Abby's relief, Rebecca's brother, Will Stowe, stayed silent during those years, at least as it came to them. Through the grapevine she heard he was doing well in his law practice. Then, in 1964, he spent a lot of money running for the state legislature and managed to win. After serving a few years in that spot, he decided to go after bigger game and ended up getting some powerful men in the western part of the state to back him for a campaign for Congress. With their dollars as his support, he got elected in '68 and prepared to take office soon after the new year.

Thaddeus felt uneasy about him having so much power. Abby told him to let it go, saying, "Stowe's surely got more important things to do than to bother with us. We're little fish to him."

"I don't know," countered Thaddeus. "A man like Stowe keeps a long memory, and you folks always seem to get the best of him. Best to keep your eye open when it comes to Will Stowe."

Abby had to admit that was true but figured it wouldn't do much good to let it bother her too much. So the years passed. Christmas of 1968 arrived and the weather turned off cold and snowy. Abby worked in the kitchen for several days to fix food for all the family that had promised to come. Thaddeus hauled in stacks of firewood even though they now had an oil furnace that heated the whole house.

"Don't strain yourself," Abby said, noting the big logs he carried inside. "You're not so young as you once were."

"I'm not a cripple yet," he said as he wiped his hands. "And I still like a good fire on a snowy day. No matter if I need it or not."

Abby smiled and patted him on the back. "Some things just don't ever change."

"Thank goodness for that," said Thaddeus.

Abby nodded in agreement. So much had changed. They now had roads all over the place. Lots of houses had put in window air-conditioners and in the summertime kept their houses like large refrigerators. Almost everybody had a telephone now and most owned televisions. Many of the highland women had taken jobs that earned real wages, most in towns several miles from their homes.

The nation beyond Blue Springs had changed even more. Every day the newspaper, radio or television brought all kinds of distressing news. Politicians were getting shot, the war in Vietnam was becoming more deadly, the colleges were boiling over with protests by the students, with riots breaking out in cities like Los Angeles and Detroit. At times Abby wished she could just close her eyes and pretend none of it affected her, though she knew she couldn't do that. True, most of the happenings didn't hit right at her, but Rose and Porter and the rest of her family had to deal with them all the time. That bothered her more than anything, for what concerned them concerned her.

On Christmas Eve everybody attended church at Jesus Holiness and then drove up to Abby's place. Abby and Thaddeus took everybody's coats as they piled inside. Jim and Rebecca and Harriet got there first—their youngest at sixteen—and Tommy, home from school in Boone. Rose came in next, then Ed and Priscilla and their kids, Lester and Mary, both grown and living in Greensboro, neither of them married yet. Steve arrived last, his glasses covered with frost from the cold.

Thaddeus led the men to the parlor, while Abby and the women took the food they had brought for the meal to the kitchen. A couple of minutes later Jim joined the women, moved to the stove and stuck his finger in a bowl of mashed potatoes. Abby slapped his hand.

"Stay away!" she scolded.

"But I'm your son," he said. "And Rebecca doesn't cook as good as you."

Rebecca moved behind him. "I heard that," she said. "Guess you want to sleep on the sofa tonight."

"Not if you want the expensive present I got you."

Rebecca laughed. "What am I going to do with him, Mrs. Abby?"

Abby threw up her hands. "Men," she said. "What can we do with any of them?"

Everybody laughed. About an hour later they all sat down at the table, Thaddeus on one end, Abby on the other. Food covered the table.

"I'll say grace now," Thaddeus announced. Abby looked at her family. Almost all but Porter had gathered.

"Please remember Porter in your prayers," Jim said.

Thaddeus nodded. They all knew the Marines had him stationed in Charleston, South Carolina. He had said he didn't know whether he could get leave and make it home.

"The young woman he's been seeing as well," added Rebecca.

Abby smiled. Porter had told his ma and pa that he had met a girl named Blanche and he liked her a lot, and even if he did get a few days' leave, he might go to her house and visit with her folks instead of coming home.

"Any other special prayers?" Thaddeus asked.

"Marla and Raymond," said Ed, mentioning his siblings.

Thaddeus took Abby by the hand. Everybody else grabbed the hand of the one sitting next to him and together they formed a circle of hands. Then all bowed as Thaddeus led the prayer. After he had given thanks and prayed for those family members not present, he ended by saying, "Father, we thank you especially for your Son, Jesus, for the salvation He gave us, for the grace we feel every day. We pray your blessing on this day. Amen."

"Amen," everybody echoed.

Hands moved to the food. Bowls passed from one to the other. Butter spread on biscuits and corn bread. Sweet tea poured out of pitchers. Forks clattered. Mouths went silent of speech as everyone ate.

Abby ate too, but not quickly. Her heart was filled with joy. So many good things had happened to her family. She shivered as she thought about the past. Times hadn't always been so good. What could go wrong now? True, Steve hadn't found all the joy she wanted for him. But her family had more money than they could spend. And they had their land, the last of the original two hundred acres now bought and secured. Jim kept the deed to all of it in a safe down at his office.

Abby wiped her eyes. Daniel would feel proud today, glad for all they had accomplished, even in the face of life's heartaches. Something rose up in Abby then, the feeling of a content mother, pleased with all her children. But something else came too, a sense that she couldn't rest easy with the way things were. Life had never let her do that, at least not for long. At age sixty-eight she had lived long enough to know that something always came to offer another challenge.

She spread her napkin in her lap and said a short prayer. Whatever it was that might come next, she needed the Lord to face it. She reached for a piece of corn bread then heard the front door swing open. She stood, her heart racing. A second later Porter burst into the house. His Marine cap was held under one arm, his uniform crisp and neat. A slender dark-haired woman held to his other hand. Her eyes were bright and a touch nervous. Rebecca jumped up and ran to Porter, Jim right behind her. Abby waited until his ma and pa had hugged him and then she went to his arms and hugged his neck.

Porter stepped back and tugged the woman at his side to the center of the room. "Ma, Pa," he started, "everybody, I want you to meet Blanche. She's from Charleston."

They all smiled at Blanche and she beamed back. Abby embraced her. Jim and Rebecca did the same, then Rose and the other women.

"Glad you came to visit us," Abby said. "You are always welcome in our home." She took Blanche's coat and hung it on a hook by the door.

"It's good to bring her here," Porter said. "For her to meet everybody."

"Come on and let's eat," Jim said. "Food's getting cold."

"Tell us everything," Rebecca said.

"Come sit by me," said Rose. "I need to tell Blanche a few things about Porter that I expect she doesn't know."

"I can't sit by a hippie," Porter said. "No matter if she's the prettiest hippie I've ever seen."

"This hippie has the ham right beside her. So if you want any, you'd better set yourself down next to me," Rose said.

"I guess my country will forgive me."

Everybody laughed as Porter took the spot by Rose, with Blanche on his other side. The food was passed to Porter and Blanche, and for a few minutes everybody went back to their eating. But then, after Porter had made a first pass at his plate, Jim started the questioning.

"How long did it take you to get home?" he asked.

"About seven hours," Porter said. "Charleston to Columbia, Columbia to Greenville, Greenville on up."

"You still driving that Mustang?" Thaddeus asked.

"Nothing else. She's a mean machine. Blanche loves it." He bit off a biscuit, took up a glass of tea.

"How long are you home?" Rebecca asked.

Porter smiled at his ma. "I got a week," he said. "Figured to stay here a couple of days, then go to Blanche's folks for the last three or so."

"Maybe I can get some work out of you," Jim said with a smile. "You can wash a few cars for me, change some tires."

"That would be the first time in years he's done any work," Rose said. "He used to brag how much you paid him for how little he did."

Porter looked at her like she had revealed a national secret. "Traitor!" he protested.

"I guess I'll need to work you extra hard," said Jim. "Or you'll need to pay me back some money."

"Money I've got," Porter said. "Been saving for years. You need money, come to me, I'll loan you some."

Blanche leaned close. "I may need some of that money," she said, her tone teasing.

"At what interest?" Jim said.

"Only twice what the bank gets," said Porter.

Everybody laughed again. Then the room quieted and the attention shifted to Blanche. Abby knew everybody wanted to know more about her but didn't want to appear nosy. Blanche glanced at Porter, her hazel eyes full of love. Abby studied her. She wore a long tan skirt, a white peasant blouse, a flowered sweater over it. Her hair fell long on her shoulders. Blanche touched Porter's elbow, and Abby sensed a closeness between them, something more than just sweethearts. Without thinking, she looked at Blanche's hands, wondering about a ring but saw none. Porter put down his fork and cleared his throat. Abby held her breath.

"We're married," said Porter as calmly as if asking for another biscuit.

The room turned silent. Jim glanced at Rebecca. Rose sat up straight.

"Yesterday," Porter said. "In Charleston. We wanted you all to be there but we didn't have time for that."

"But my folks were present," Blanche said. "They approve. We hope you do too."

"It's mighty sudden," Jim said, his face dark.

"Not as sudden as you and Ma," said Porter. "I've known Blanche for seven months now."

Jim glanced at Rebecca.

"He's got us there," Rebecca said.

Jim chuckled and the tension eased. "The men in this family sure know what they want," he said. "When we see it, we do go for it."

"You couldn't even see me," Rebecca said, referring to the war injury that had put Jim's eyesight in jeopardy. Thankfully he had later regained all his vision. "Had to take my word about my looks."

Jim laid down his fork, stood and moved to Porter. "Congratulations, son," he said, extending his hand. "We're happy for you."

Everybody stood and Rebecca hugged Blanche. Jim followed her, Abby and Rose and all the rest too. When they had finished, everybody took a seat again. Jim took Rebecca's hand and kissed it.

"A man needs a good woman," he said, looking at Porter. "Glad you found one."

Abby glanced at Steve, who had his head down. She wondered how he felt about all this.

"You might need to get a station wagon instead of that Mustang," Rose said. "You're a family man now."

Porter smiled. "You might be right about that. We're wanting kids real fast."

"No rush on that," Jim said.

Porter nodded. "We'll see."

"How long you think you'll stay in Charleston?" Jim asked.

Porter looked down at his plate, not answering. Something about his manner suddenly bothered Abby.

"They'll probably send him to Washington soon," Rose teased. "Let him hang out at the Pentagon and at taxpayers' expense."

Porter laughed but not as easily as before.

"That right?" pressed Jim. "You going to Washington?"

Porter took another bite of biscuit. "I'm headed overseas," he said. "Got my orders last week. One reason me and Blanche decided to go ahead and get married."

"Where?" Jim said.

Everybody at the table tensed.

"Let's talk about this later," Rebecca said, "after we finish eating."

"No," Jim said. "We need to talk about it now." He faced Porter. "Where they sending you?"

Porter glanced around the table. "Okinawa," he said. "But only for six months or so. Then I'm going to Vietnam. I volunteered."

Abby saw Rose set her fork down and stare at Porter. "I don't understand you," she said. "We've got no business over there."

Porter sighed. "We've been over this time and time again. You know we don't agree, won't ever agree."

"Only an idiot would volunteer for Vietnam," Rose said. "Or serve in the military for that matter." Rose turned to Blanche. "I apologize for my feelings," she said, "but I don't want my nephew mixed up in all this."

"It's okay," said Blanche. "I agree with my husband. He's a soldier. I support him in this."

Porter looked at his wife, his eyes grateful, then to his pa and finally back at Rose. His face became stern. "You can call me an idiot," he said. "We've been teasing each other all our lives. But Pa here served in the military too, and he's certainly no idiot."

"His war was different," Rose said. "You know it."

"Not to me it wasn't," said Porter. "A man's country calls him and he goes, simple as that."

"Even if no one can tell you exactly why? Even if nobody can explain what we're fighting to defend?"

"I know why. To protect our way of life."

"I haven't seen any Vietnamese attacking us over here. Seems you're going a long way looking for a fight."

"I'm not looking for a fight. Just serving my country."

"Your country is sending you and a whole lot like you to an early grave."

The table fell completely silent. Abby glanced at Jim, then at Thaddeus. How much longer should they let their children go at each other this way, especially with a newcomer at their table? Jim shook his head as if to tell Abby to stay out of it. She took a breath and decided to remain quiet.

Looking around the table, Porter asked, "How many of you feel like Rose? How many of you believe this is all crazy, all wrong?" No one moved. "I'm waiting," he said. Nobody responded. He faced Rose again.

"They don't agree with you," she said. "But they're too afraid to say it."

Porter took a deep breath. "That may be so, but I'm going anyway. It's all set. You can either support me or not, it doesn't matter. I wear this uniform with pride. I'd think you would appreciate my efforts for our country."

Rose touched his forearm. "I just want you alive," she said. "No matter what happens in some country halfway across the world. Let them deal with their own problems; we've got enough here, don't you think?"

Porter patted her hand. "I'm a soldier," he said. "And my country is at war. That's all there is to it. No way out of it now, even if I wanted, which I don't."

Rose looked blankly at her plate. Abby glanced at Jim and Rebecca.

"We're behind you," Abby said to Porter. "Don't you ever question that."

Rose sighed heavily then laid down her napkin and exited the room. Abby started to call her back but then decided to let her go. A grown woman now, Rose had to make her own way. Abby turned back to her food. A few minutes later the meal ended. That night passed, then the next day. The day after that, Porter and Blanche left for South Carolina, and about two months later Porter headed overseas.

CHAPTER
THIRTY-TWO

Over the next months Abby did a lot of praying. Not only did she have the folks on her usual list—her family and friends, her pastor and his wife—but now she added Blanche and Porter for an extra measure of intercession. Having a grandson on his way to Vietnam scared Abby, more so because she knew from personal experience that war made no distinction between folks. Good Christian men were hit with bullets and shrapnel as quickly as sorry, mean-hearted heathens. To complicate things even further, Blanche had telephoned them in May to inform everyone that she had a baby on the way, due sometime in November. In normal times, such news would have given Abby good cause to kick up her heels and take to her sewing. But somehow, with Porter so far away, it instead made her uneasy. What if Porter never made it home? What if his baby grew up and never got to see his pa?

Not wanting to dwell on such gloomy matters, Abby poured herself into her daily work. Though much slower now, she kept her hands plenty busy. Summer rolled in hot and dry, and the Fourth of July came and went. The newspaper carried stories of students in the nation's big cities rallying against the war. Abby and Thaddeus talked about all the unrest in the country, how it had affected everybody, their family included. Rose believed in one side of things, Porter the other. How could anybody know the right thing anymore?

Given her family history, Abby wanted to believe what her government told her. Yet Rose had done much traveling and knew more than she did. If Rose said the country had no business in Vietnam, maybe it didn't. With Porter over there fighting, however, even thinking such a thing felt like betrayal to Abby.

They got word from Porter every month or so as the dog days of August passed and he left Okinawa and headed for Vietnam. His first assignment there called for him to stay in a reserve unit in Saigon to protect an air base. His letters expressed his frustration with this. Like most soldiers, especially those seeking a career with the military, he wanted to see the action.

Abby knew that officers saw appointments to the front line as the best way to advance their careers, move themselves up in rank. She also knew that time spent on the front line meant danger, possibly injury or death. She prayed more every day. Soon September began, and on the first Friday of the month Abby found herself sitting on the front porch after cleaning up the breakfast dishes. A stack of shirts and blouses lay in her lap, all of them needing repair. The sun warmed her face. A blue truck drove up and parked, and she saw Jim hop out of it. He wore fine navy slacks, a white shirt and clean black boots. His hair, though slightly gray, was combed in smooth waves. Abby smiled. In the last year Jim had taken to stopping by every morning on his way to the office. He stepped onto the porch and wiped his face.

"You looking warm," Abby said. Jim took a rocker and leaned forward. The screen door opened and Thaddeus walked out. "Jim's here," she said, stating the obvious. Thaddeus said hello, then took a seat on the porch swing.

Abby looked at Jim and knew from the way he was sitting that he hadn't come for a social call this morning. She thought immediately of Porter, and then Steve. Had something happened to either of them?

"What's on your mind, Jim?" she asked.

Jim reached into his shirt pocket, pulled out a folded sheet of paper and handed it to her. "Read this," he said. "Guess we should have expected something like it sooner or later."

"Is it bad news?" Thaddeus said.

Jim looked at Thaddeus and nodded.

Abby opened the paper and quickly read through it. When finished, she set it in her lap and started rocking gently. "When did you get this?" she asked.

"Last night when I got home. It came in the mail."

Abby passed the paper to Thaddeus. "What you reckon we should do?" Abby asked Jim.

"What can we do? It's official enough. The government gets what it wants; everybody knows that."

Abby stared out into the yard. A squirrel chattered by the oak tree to her right. Watching the squirrel, Abby pondered why it was that life never seemed completely tied down, how the edges kept coming loose at the corners. She glanced at Thaddeus. He handed the paper back to her and shook his head. He looked tired all of a sudden. No wonder. This kind of news would make anyone tired.

"You figure to just let this happen?" Abby said, looking to Jim.

"You know I'm not one to give up on things," Jim said. "But how do we fight it?"

Abby read the paper again. She figured she knew the source of this latest trouble to come their way. "You know who's behind this, don't you?" she said.

Jim shrugged. "My guess is somebody in Washington got together with some folks down here, maybe in Raleigh, and decided to make this happen."

"And who do we know in Washington?"

Jim studied a second. "You thinking of Will Stowe?"

"Who else you figure would want to do us harm?"

"But we don't know that anybody wanted to do us any harm," Jim said. "Maybe things like this just happen, you know, without anybody planning to hurt anyone in particular."

"I don't believe things just happen," said Abby. "Not anymore. Somebody's usually pulling on the strings, leading this one to go here, another one to go there. Sometimes it's the Lord pulling, and sometimes it's the devil. But either way, somebody's pulling."

"You saying we got no choice in what we do?"

Abby smiled at her son. Sometimes he still seemed like her little boy, waiting for his ma to point him in the right direction. "No, not that at all," she said. "I said somebody's pulling. But I believe people can pull back, choose to go off in other directions, mix up all the strings if they want."

Jim nodded. "So, you're saying the Lord pulls and we get some choice in whether or not we want to follow the Lord's tugs?"

"Exactly. Or the devil's."

"You figure this is Stowe's doing?" Thaddeus asked.

Abby hated to accuse a man of anything, yet it seemed too coincidental to her. "I believe if we look under this rock, we'll find Will Stowe crawling around beneath it."

"You think we should fight it?" Jim asked.

"Maybe, maybe not," Abby said. "In cases like this, they always pay the families, right?"

"I don't know a lot about it, but I think so," Jim said. "You mean we just take our dollars and let it go at that?"

Abby nodded. "That's one choice."

"Not one I like."

"I expect not."

"If it *is* Stowe," said Jim, "I reckon I'd just as soon kill him."

"Don't go talking like that," Abby reproved. "Those days are past. Besides, he's your wife's brother."

Jim shook his head in disbelief. "Why can't he just let bygones be bygones?"

"He's carrying a powerful grudge," Thaddeus said.

"Definitely not a happy man," Abby said.

"You think we could go to court, get it stopped?" Jim asked Abby.

"That's possible. Or we could see about getting somebody in Congress to take the matter in a different direction."

Jim weighed the matter for several seconds. Abby laid her hands on her stack of clothes. She suddenly felt weary. How long would the trouble between the Clacks and her kin go on? How long would

Will Stowe hold his grudge against them?

"Maybe we should just let it go," Thaddeus suggested. "Not take the bait he's thrown our way."

Abby looked at him, her spirit rebelling against the idea. "Just let him win?"

Thaddeus rocked in the swing. Sweat covered his face, and Abby worried about him for a second. He seemed so tired lately, like he didn't have much energy left. "I don't see it as winning or losing," he said. "But so long as you keep reacting to his actions, you're playing his game. If you just let it go, take your dollars, he'll lose all power over you. You can wash your hands of him forever."

"But the land's rightly ours," said Abby.

Thaddeus shrugged. "Seems to me it's the Lord's," he said. "Won't belong to any of us for too long."

Abby looked at Thaddeus with a stern expression on her face. Yet she decided to keep her tongue still.

"You're right about that," Jim agreed. "For now, though, the land is our family's, and I don't plan to let Stowe take it from us— not without a fight." Thaddeus shrugged again and kept rocking. Jim faced Abby. "I'll need to do some telephone calling," he said. "See what I can find out about all this, get some more details."

"You do that," she said.

"These things take a long time to happen," Jim said. "I've read about it in other places. Years sometimes."

"I expect so," said Abby. "Lots to handle."

Jim stood and brushed off his pants. "I'll keep in touch," he said.

"Say hello to Rebecca for me," Abby said.

Jim waved good-bye and started walking toward his truck. Thaddeus stood and went back into the house. Picking up the paper Jim had given her, Abby stared at the official stamp of the United States Government at the top of the notice. After reading it once more, she shook her head and closed her eyes. The government had given them official notice of a federal plan to build a dam half a mile below their property. The dam would harness the waters of Slick Rock Creek and many other creeks and streams that fed off the mountains in and around their part of the state. By damming up these waterways, the notification said, the government could then provide "hydroelectric power" to the region. That and flood control.

It all sounded reasonable, of course. At times the streams and creeks did cause heavy flooding some miles below them, and the electricity provided by such a dam could make for cheaper power. But all that came at a high cost, especially to the families that lived on the land the water would cover. Of course, this wasn't that many folks, probably thirty or forty families, which added up to a hundred and fifty people or so.

Abby looked out from her front porch. Blue Springs Mountain stared down at her. She couldn't see it from her porch, but Jim's house sat to her left about three hundred acres away, Ed's about two hundred to her right. Since their last tussle with Stowe, they had made their homes here. She had settled in for life. But now this. If the government went ahead and built its dam, it would flood this part of the valley, would send water through the front doors of all the houses around here.

She took a deep breath. All her life her family had fought for this land. Could she let it go now, without another fight?

Standing, Abby stepped to the edge of the porch. She thought of Porter, off somewhere in Vietnam fighting for his country. She thought of Steve, down in Raleigh, fighting to make his business a success. She thought of Jim, headed back to his office, fighting to leave a legacy for his children. Seemed like everybody was always fighting for something.

Weary of it all, she sat down on the steps. How long could a person go on fighting? she wondered. Didn't there come a time when a body should just accept things as they came, not struggle against them anymore? Did the Lord want her to join in this fray one more time, stick up for what belonged to her and her kin? She just didn't know.

She looked up at the sky. "What do you want, Lord?" she asked. "Just tell me and I'll try to do it."

Receiving no firm answer, she rested her chin in her hands and propped her elbows on her knees. Sometimes, no matter what you did, a body just didn't know.

CHAPTER
THIRTY-THREE

As usual, Steve went to his ma's place for a couple of days during Christmas of 1969. And, as usual, he made his excuses and headed back to Raleigh soon afterward. The trip gave him a chance to study on all the changes that had taken place in the last few months. For one thing, everybody acted more tense since Porter had gone to Vietnam. The nation's anxiety about the war seemed to have invaded his ma's house as well, and nobody laughed as much as they had in the past.

In addition, Porter's wife, Blanche, had moved into Jim and Rebecca's house since the birth of her baby, a boy she had named Todd in honor of her father. Although she wasn't sure how long she would stay there, Jim and Rebecca had more room in their place than her folks did, and she liked the idea of getting to know her husband's family. What better time to do it than now?

Another reason for the tension came because of the latest threat to their land. To tell it honest, it didn't bother Steve that much. After all, he'd not spent any of his money on the property. Why should it matter to him if they flooded it? Of course he didn't like the notion that his family, especially his ma, would have to move again. But other than that, he had no dog in that fight and so decided to leave it alone.

Arriving back home, he switched on the lights in his dark house, went straight to the furnace to turn it on and then sat down at the kitchen table. He was dead tired. Going to Blue Springs always wore him out, made him feel like a stranger having to talk to people he didn't know too well. At home he always felt like he had to measure up, like he had to make sure everybody understood how successful he'd become. Sometimes he wondered if it was even worth it.

After resting a few minutes, he walked to his office located at the back of the house and pulled out a black ledger. As he had done at the end of the calendar year for almost twenty years now, he spent the next couple of hours adding and subtracting his gains and losses from the previous year. When he had finished, he put the ledger away and moved back to the kitchen. His shoulders sagged as he made coffee, poured himself a cup and sat back down at the table. In spite of all the progress he'd made in the last decade, he still saw no way to begin building new houses. Even though he had more than ninety houses for rent, it took almost all his money to keep them in proper repair. Plus, his bank loans ate up a lot of funds in interest payments.

He sipped his coffee. Somehow or other, he had to do something different this year. He thought of the money he sent to his ma each month. What if he kept that and used it instead for business expenses? His ma had told him over and over that she didn't need it. But what man didn't try to help his ma, even if she didn't want his aid?

Steve stood and walked to the window. A light snow had begun to fall. He knew his motive for sending money to his ma wasn't all that pure. True, he wanted to make sure he did his part to care for her, but he also liked the notion that the dollars he sent her showed he had done well for himself in the big city, that Jim wasn't the only one of her sons who had what it took to succeed in the world.

Sighing, Steve went to the refrigerator, pulled out some cold cuts and a loaf of bread and, while not really hungry, started making a sandwich. His feelings toward Jim weren't good. What grown man still worried that his brother might best him? Yet something still gnawed at him, made him unable to let go of his old feelings of lowness, what people nowadays called "inferiority." Would he ever get over that? He didn't know.

He thought of all the good things that had happened to Jim in the past year. His boy Porter had married, his daughter-in-law had moved to Blue Springs and given them a grandson. In addition, Porter had told them in a letter that he'd been promoted to captain and would soon begin a tour in combat. Steve didn't agree with Porter's eagerness for such hazardous duty, but he could certainly understand it. Even more, he envied the father of such a brave son. What man's chest wouldn't swell for having a boy who faced danger so readily, his uniform full of ribbons and pins from his excellent service to his country?

Steve reflected on his own situation. He had no real wife and no children of his own. In fact, he had no reason for pride in anything but his business. What a failure he'd become.

Sipping his coffee, Steve thought back over the last few years. After leaving Claire and Frank, he had spent most of his energies laboring away at his business. It's what he'd always done best, one of the few things he could do without getting in trouble with people and their confusing ways. He went to Blue Springs less and less often in those days and then only for short amounts of time—a day or so to see his ma was usually all. Sometimes he saw Jim on these trips. When he did, he felt all tangled up inside, like he knew he ought to feel close to his brother but somehow just couldn't.

Then Mrs. Waterbury died, in 1964, and Steve mourned her loss, not only because she had taken him in and treated him well, but also because she had become his last close link to any human being. When he buried her, he lost his last contact with regular conversation, his last touch with someone who took him just as he was. Loneliness bore down on him a lot in those years.

Every now and again he dated some woman somebody had told him about or whom he'd met going about his daily routine. But he never had more than three or four dates with any particular one.

More than a few let him know in no uncertain terms that they could get real interested in him if he would like. Still, none of them attracted him that much.

Truth was, Steve still thought a lot about Claire, even saw her some from time to time. He still owned the house where she lived and he still provided money for her and her two boys. To Steve's surprise, Claire had never moved in with Allen. While puzzled by that, still he never got up the gumption to ask her about it. In another unexpected twist, Claire never bothered asking him for a divorce. Fact is, she plain out told him she didn't want one. So, legally, they stayed husband and wife.

When she gave birth to her second son, Robert Travis by name, Steve stopped by to check on her and bring the boy a new crib. His curiosity getting the better of him, he studied the boy's face for a long time. Unable to make out any recognizable traits, he left the house and tried not to think about it. In the times he'd seen the boy since, he deliberately ignored him so as not to torture himself with questions about the child's parentage.

Steve depended more and more on Izzy as the years passed, mostly to take care of things in his own neighborhoods. He set Izzy up in a nice house, bought him a late-model Ford Fairlane and paid him a decent salary. One thing Steve had learned was that merit carried its own reward, or at least it should. Except in his case. For despite all his efforts, life hadn't treated him too well, hadn't given him too much of a reward.

Tired of his reflections, Steve focused again on his present problems. He needed to save some money if he ever wanted to build new houses. He thought of the house where Claire lived. It was one of his best and yet she wasn't paying him any rent. She kept telling him she wanted to pay, but he wouldn't hear of it. Although he wouldn't live with her as her husband any longer, he wouldn't abandon her and her boys like his pa had abandoned his family so long ago.

Another possibility occurred to Steve. Mrs. Waterbury had left her house in his name and Allen's. He could go to Allen and demand that he pay him for his half of the place. If he didn't, then he could sell the place, give Allen his share of the proceeds and move to a smaller house. That would raise his bottom line some. But at what price? Allen already detested him. Did he want to take the chance of making things even worse between them?

One final notion boiled up. He gave a yearly donation to an orphanage through the Baptist church where he and Claire had gotten married. Should he stop that? But his ma had taught him to give because some people needed aid. So whenever he thought about keeping those dollars, he would imagine a child walking through winter without proper shoes and knew he couldn't refuse that need.

The telephone rang, calling Steve out of his musing. He picked up the receiver.

"You home, Mr. Steve?"

Steve started to make a smart remark at Izzy's dumb question but held back. "Yes, Izzy, got back a little while ago."

Izzy hesitated and Steve found himself suddenly attentive. Izzy had never called him at home before. "What is it, Izzy?"

"I don't suppose you drove by any of your properties today, did you?" Izzy asked.

"No. Is there a reason I should have?"

"I don't rightly know how to tell you this."

"Just say it," said Steve, holding his breath.

"Well, maybe you ought to meet me at my house."

"Tell me now," Steve insisted.

Izzy breathed heavily into the phone. "We had a fire," he said. "This morning, right before light. I wanted to reach you at your mama's place, but I didn't have a number to call."

Steve squeezed the receiver. "What kind of fire?"

"Don't know how it started. But one house took to burning, then another, and nobody could put it out."

Steve's head hurt. "How many?"

"Eight houses in all," said Izzy. "You know how they's all jammed in there together down on Bird Street, one after another, without hardly any space between them. Once that fire took hold, it just licked from one to the other. Took the fire department forever to show up."

Steve pictured the street in his mind. Separated by no more

than ten to twenty feet between them, the houses were shotgun-style wood frames with narrow porches attached to their fronts, one room leading into the next all the way through to the back. He hated the houses and had planned to eventually tear them down and build something better on the property. He rubbed his temples. "Anybody killed?" he asked, his voice shaky at the thought.

"Thank goodness I can say no to that," Izzy answered. "A few injuries, but nobody dead."

"What kind of injuries?"

"Well, Mrs. Hattie Rakes got some burns on her legs and a couple of folks took in some smoke. Other than that, everybody seems fine."

"Where's Mrs. Hattie?"

"She in the hospital, one of the others too."

Steve wiped his mouth. A large black woman, Mrs. Hattie had little money, certainly not enough to pay for a hospital stay. Somehow he'd have to come up with the money to pay her bills, probably the other person as well.

"You say you don't know how it started?" Steve said.

"No sir, just that it began in that one empty house we got down there, that one next to the end, you know?"

"Yeah, the one with the bad roof."

"That's it. Glory be nobody lived in it."

Steve's brow furrowed. "If nobody lived there, then how did it begin?"

"That is a mystery," Izzy said. "You reckon maybe somebody snuck in there, spent the night or something? Maybe tried to start a fire to keep off the cold?"

"Hard to say."

"I reckon so."

"Anything left of the houses, anything we can salvage?"

"Not much I could see," Izzy said. "They's pretty much burned right down to the nubs."

Steve tried to think what to do. With it already dark, he knew he couldn't see much this time of night. Besides, what could he do about it now? Nothing, that's what. "Everybody find a place to stay?" he asked.

"Yeah. Folks up and down the street took in a couple of the families, the church a few more."

Steve rubbed his head again. "I'll see you tomorrow then, first thing in the morning."

"Right. First thing," said Izzy. "Oh, and Mr. Steve?"

"Yes?"

"I'm mighty sorry to bring you such sad tidings."

"That's okay, Izzy."

Steve hung up and moved to his kitchen table. Leaning on it, he tried to sort out the situation. With the houses worth so little, he hadn't bothered to insure them. Yet the rent they brought in made a big difference in his profit and loss statements. Without those tenants paying every month, his loans would quickly become hard to pay. Unless he was careful, he might need to borrow more money just to keep up with his credit interest, much less the principal.

He wondered how much Mrs. Hattie's hospital bill would come to. More than he could afford to pay, that was for sure. Overcome with weariness, he collapsed into a chair and gripped his coffee cup as if trying to crack it with his bare hands. From out of nowhere, a hard, lonely life had become a whole lot harder.

CHAPTER
THIRTY-FOUR

For almost a year after her family got word that the government wanted to move her kin from their homes and flood their valley, Abby spent many of her waking hours trying to figure how to stop that from happening. With everybody pitching in some dollars, they got Jim to hire a lawyer to represent them in court. Three different hearings, spread out over several months, followed. With Thaddeus at her side, Abby attended each hearing.

She worked hard to follow all the arguments. Basically her side argued that, because their family had owned the land off and on since the 1800s, they ought to get to keep it. No government had the right to just come in and take from them what they had labored so hard to buy and build. The other side nodded agreeably when her lawyer spoke but then took a whole different line when they got their chance to speak.

"The government works for the good of the majority," the opposition countered, "not just the few. The government will pay a fair price for the land or give those affected a parcel of acreage equal to what they currently own. Nobody here wants to take advantage of anybody else."

Listening intently, Abby found herself more and more angry at the proceedings. How dare anyone come to take from them what they had earned. No matter about the majority! What about the individual's rights? The individual's history? The individual's property?

Over the next few months she found it hard to clear her mind of the matter. At night she had trouble falling asleep. More than once, she thought of Will Stowe and wished ill on him. The man had deviled her family for too long. Why didn't the Lord take care of him? Although she knew she shouldn't get so angry about it and didn't like that she did, she discovered herself to be more and more stirred up, more and more fractious.

Thaddeus noticed her mood and commented on it one night in late June when, while cleaning up the kitchen, she dropped a plate on the floor and stomped her foot in anger.

"You're a touch brittle these days, aren't you?" he asked gently as he helped her pick up the shattered glass. "Anything I can do?"

Abby started to argue, but then, with a sudden recognition that she hadn't experienced in a long time, she knew he had it right. Rising from the floor, she threw away the broken plate, sat down at the kitchen table and laid her head in her hands.

"I don't know what's come over me," she said with a sigh. "But I'm mad, just plain mad."

Thaddeus laughed. "Not something *I* did, I hope."

Abby looked up at her husband. He was such a kind man. She touched his cheek. Over the last few years he had aged a lot. Complained more often with his chest pains. His doctor had done some tests recently and said he had some troubles in his heart but not enough for any kind of surgery or anything.

"It's not you," Abby said. "It's that Will Stowe."

Thaddeus took her hand and kissed it. "You and yours have fought that man for a long time," he said. "You reckon he's worth all the energy you've wasted on him?"

Abby started to speak but then hesitated. Something about Thaddeus's words clanged in her head. She *had* used a lot of energy being mad at Stowe. Had let bitterness against him build up in her heart.

She hung her head. What could she do? The man kept after them, agitating her and her family. Could she let all that go? Let him win?

Puzzled, she sat up straighter and pondered the matter further. The notion of letting Stowe get away with his latest trick got her blood to boiling. What would her pa think? Or Daniel? Jim and Ed?

Abby rubbed her hands as something else ran through her mind. The Lord mattered more than anybody or anything. What did the Lord think about all this? What did He want her to do? Did the Lord expect her to give up this grudge against Stowe, this latest battle with him? She didn't know, at least not yet.

"I best finish up in here," she said, surveying the kitchen.

"I'll help," said Thaddeus.

The weeks moved ahead, and Abby kept stewing over her dilemma. From what she had seen so far, it looked as though her family had little chance in the courts. Official after official had told them that they didn't have much power over something like this. If the government wanted to, they could declare your land condemned property, give you a fair price for it or swap out other land for what you owned. If you didn't take their offer, they could come in with marshals to remove you and all your belongings. And if you resisted, they could arrest you and throw you in jail.

"The government works for *all* the people," one of the judges had said. "This action, though flooding a few families out, will nevertheless provide protection from more widespread floods and cheaper power for all. Try to see it for the good it does."

Abby understood the logic of it all, yet that didn't make her or anybody else in her family any happier. To her surprise, most of the other families affected by the plans for the dam had gladly accepted the government's offer and signed over their property.

"They gave me money and some new land," one of their neighbors said when Abby asked him why he didn't join her and her kin in trying to get the project stopped. "I never saw so much cash in my whole life."

Abby had to accept the man's choice. Just because her family had prospered and didn't need a lot of cash, most of the other families on the mountain still owned little of any value. The prosperity that had come to the country in the 1950s and '60s had not settled on everybody's front porch. As one man said it, "Lots of folks around here never knew when the Depression hit or when it ended." Truth was, many highlanders still lived on a hand-to-mouth basis.

Near the end of August 1970, at Jim's suggestion, Abby opened her house for everybody to gather to hear the latest developments. On a day so hot the dogs didn't want to come out from under the porch, all the family living on the mountain crowded into her parlor to decide what to do next.

Taking a spot in her rocker, Abby took a second to look around the room. Thaddeus sat beside her by the fireplace, Rebecca on the sofa, and Blanche, with baby Todd in her lap, rested in a recliner.

Abby smiled at Blanche. She had traveled to Hawaii in May to visit Porter while he enjoyed two weeks' leave. Now she had another baby on the way. Ed's wife, Priscilla, sat beside Blanche. Ed was sitting on the edge of the fireplace hearth, and Jim stood.

Abby turned to Jim and nodded. After briefly repeating what had happened over the last few months, Jim gave everybody the chance to ask questions.

"Maybe we ought to go to Washington," Ed suggested. "See what we can do there. Get a politician or two on our side."

Jim shook his head. "It'd be a long shot," he said. "As you all know, Will Stowe sits on the congressional committee that deals with projects like this. He'd try to block us at every turn."

"We sure he's behind this?" Ed asked.

Jim shrugged. "That's not easy to pin down. But the exact location of a dam like this is always a little flexible. They could go a little higher or lower on the mountain. A dam built a half mile higher would miss us completely. I talked to folks from Stowe's office. They denied any direct connection between Stowe and us, said the congressman would never dream of such a thing."

"You didn't go see Stowe, did you?" Ed said.

"Nope. Didn't see the point. He'd just smile and deny everything, then laugh at me after I left his office."

"Maybe we ought to take him down a peg or two."

Abby shook her head. "Ed, that kind of talk won't help us any," she said, "no matter how much we want to stop this."

"She's right," said Thaddeus. Abby raised an eyebrow. Thaddeus usually said little in gatherings like this.

Everybody faced him. "I'm not exactly sure I should say anything," he said. "The land means something different to me than it does all of you."

"No need to say that," Jim said. "You're one of us."

Everybody agreed. Thaddeus took a breath. "Okay," he said. "I've been doing a lot of thinking about this, and I, well, I'm not sure we're dealing with it right."

"What do you mean?" Abby said.

"The land," he said. "Your family has fought for it for a long time, Abby. Your pa, his family before him—they bought it up, scratched out a living on it. You know the story, how you got it, how you lost it." Everyone nodded. Thaddeus continued, "After the war, everybody saved their money to get it back. We've all poured a lot into re-claiming this land."

"The fight has taken a toll on all of us," Jim said. "But we all agreed to the effort, every one of us."

"And now this thing with the dam happens," Thaddeus said. "Whether Will Stowe is behind it or not, we're up against the same issue again, the issue of the land. We're fighting to keep it, spending our lives pursuing it."

Everyone nodded again. But Abby heard something deeper in her husband's words, a warning of some kind, and she wasn't sure she liked what he was getting at. "Where you going with this?" she asked, her tone sharper than she meant it.

Thaddeus wiped his brow, and Abby noticed his face looked a little flushed. "I'm not getting to the point, am I?" he said. "Guess that comes with getting older. Anyway, here's what I'm wondering. I'm wondering if we've made an idol of this land. You know—we've held it up as the one thing we had to have. The truth is, though, there's only one thing we have to have, and that's the Lord. Anything else is just so much stuff added on, like ornaments on a tree if it's good stuff, or lint on a dark suit if it's bad."

"But we've paid for this land!" interrupted Jim, obviously not happy with the direction Thaddeus had taken.

"I know," Thaddeus said. "And I'm not faulting anybody for what we've done. I've been a part of it myself. I don't know, but as I've gotten older it just seems maybe we've put too much focus on it."

"That's easy for you to say," said Ed. "Your family didn't own it from the beginning like ours."

Thaddeus looked sad. Abby noticed his breathing had gotten quicker. He didn't like conflict.

"You're right there," he said to Ed. "That's why I hesitated to speak. You all are my family, but, well, I'm still an outsider on this thing."

"You're just tired," Jim said. "I can understand that. Nobody's begrudging you your feelings. But we can't just give up now, can we?" He turned to Abby for a response.

Abby folded her hands in her lap. One part of her rebelled against what Thaddeus had just said. Giving up sounded too easy. And, never one to give up, she didn't like the notion of starting now. Yet something else in her felt that maybe Thaddeus had hit on a truth. They had all spent much of their lives struggling to hold on to the family land. But was that what the Lord wanted them to do? She felt torn by the question, unable to give an answer.

"I don't know," she finally said. "I'm not ready to say yet."

"It's just property," offered Thaddeus. "Houses and trees and barns and—"

"But it's *our* property!" Ed argued. "Bought with our own hard labor."

Thaddeus looked down at his hands. Abby saw them shake a little as he stuck them under his arms. "If we let it go, the government will give us more land, pay us a fair price to get new houses built."

"I don't want a new house," said Ed. "I want to live where my ma and pa lived, want to keep what he fought all his life to keep. My pa's buried up there, my ma, others of the family. You plan to dig them up and move them to a new place, disturb the dead? Or should they just flood them and cover over their graves?"

Abby saw that Thaddeus had stirred up a hornet's nest, and she regretted that. But she didn't know that he should back down. If he didn't, where did that leave her? She wanted to defend her husband, but she didn't want to give up the land without a fight.

"You two don't have to get involved," Jim said, looking from Thaddeus to Abby. "We're not asking you to do any more about it. We'll take care of it."

Thaddeus turned to Jim, then Ed. "I'm not saying you have to agree with me," he said. "And I won't feel hard against you whatever you do. I just ask you to think about one question real good."

Everyone quieted to listen. Thaddeus took a big breath and winced a little as he exhaled. Abby wondered if his chest was hurting him again.

"Are you so set on keeping this land because of what it means to you or because of the fact that you think Will Stowe has somehow bested you?" he asked. "That's what I've been wondering lately."

Jim studied for a second, Ed too. "I admit to some of that," said Jim, "but I'm not ready to say that's all it is."

"That's fair," Thaddeus said.

"So what if it is that?" questioned Ed. "We've wrestled with the Clacks all our lives. The notion that Stowe pulled this off against us riles me. I don't want him to get away with it. Do you?"

"I don't think it matters what he does or doesn't get away with," Thaddeus said. "Stowe has to answer to the Lord for his life, we for ours." He turned to Abby. His eyes looked tired. "Aren't you weary of the bitterness, the anger he causes when you think of him? It seems to me you've held it too long."

"So you think we should just walk away from our land?" Jim said.

Thaddeus sighed. "No," he said. "I haven't come to that conclusion yet. But don't we all want to rid ourselves of our harsh feelings about Stowe? Don't you think the Lord wants us to do that?"

Thaddeus reached for Abby's hands. She turned to him. His face was flushed from the effort of his talking, and sweat covered his forehead. She patted his hand. It felt clammy and a little cool. Although she didn't know yet if she agreed with his conclusions, she did agree that she wanted to shed herself of her bitterness toward Stowe. Thaddeus smiled weakly. Then, before she could catch him, he pitched forward, his head landing on her shoulder before she could move.

"Thaddeus!" she cried. He didn't respond. She quickly lifted his head and saw that his eyes had closed.

"Someone get some water!" she shouted. "And a wet towel!" Everybody moved, Jim to her side to check Thaddeus's pulse.

"He's breathing!" Abby said.

"Pulse is there!" said Jim. "Weak though. Let's get him to a hospital."

Some seconds later Blanche handed Abby a wet cloth, which she used to wipe the sweat from Thaddeus's face. Ed then took Thaddeus by the shoulders, with Jim grabbing his feet. Abby followed as they rushed outside to Jim's car. Sitting beside Thaddeus as they sped toward Asheville to the hospital, Abby realized that life guaranteed nothing—not the next day, not the next minute, not the next second. She kept herself from crying as they hurried down the mountainside. Right now she needed to focus on praying. If something happened to Thaddeus, she would have plenty of time to cry then.

CHAPTER
THIRTY-FIVE

The next four days passed in a black fog of fear. Abby spent the time in the hospital in Asheville. Rose came by after school every day, and the two of them sat by Thaddeus's bed and held each other's hands and talked and prayed. Abby didn't say much, her words quieted by the gravity of her husband's condition. Thaddeus stayed unconscious most of the time. After undergoing surgery for clogged arteries in his heart, he had been heavily medicated.

"He's basically a healthy man for his age," the doctor had explained to Abby just before the surgery. "Fortunately the attack he suffered didn't do extensive damage to the heart muscle. If we can get him through the surgery and the next few days after that, he should do pretty well."

Abby's eyes streaked red due to lack of sleep. Even though she knew no one lived forever and that Thaddeus had lived his seventy years to their fullest, she still felt cheated by this illness. What if he died? They needed at least another ten years together. Surely the

Lord would give them that. After all, they hadn't married until they were in their forties. It just didn't seem fair. Yet she had to admit, even if God gave her and Thaddeus a thousand years together, it still wouldn't be enough.

A lot of people passed in and out of Thaddeus's room and wished her well, but they felt a long way off to Abby, almost as if she watched them from across a road. She talked to them and was always polite, but mostly she focused on Thaddeus.

To Abby's relief, Thaddeus began to wake up at the end of the fourth day, and she saw how well the doctors had done their jobs. He'd survived. With every day now he opened his eyes a little more and kept them open a little longer. On the eighth day he smiled at Abby and squeezed her hand, and she felt for the first time that he might make it out of the hospital and one day sit on the porch with her again. She took a deep breath and thanked the Lord. That day passed and then another, and Thaddeus gained a bit more strength each day.

Abby did a lot of thinking in her quiet hours by his bed. Mulled over where her life had taken her, what she had experienced, what she wanted to do now. Peculiar, she decided, how folks can go for years and just let the days slide by without taking stock of things, without keeping a firm grip on what a body really needed. Then something like a heart attack comes along and says, "You better pay attention! Nobody gets to live forever, so you best spend the time you have living for what's most vital."

Abby faced that now and spent a goodly number of hours questioning her attitudes of the last few years and wondering what changes she needed to make for the next ones to come. Whether the good Lord gave her and Thaddeus another ten days or another thirty years, she had to make sure she treasured every minute.

Near the end of their third week at the hospital, she and Rose left Thaddeus for a short time to get some food in the hospital cafeteria. Sitting at the table, a piece of chicken and some cabbage and corn bread on her plate, Abby said to Rose, "This kind of situation puts some things in their proper place."

Rose squeezed her hand. "Seems like you've always kept things in their proper place."

Abby shook her head. "Reckon not."

"What do you mean?"

Abby laid her napkin on the table. "I got some things I need to do, things I need to fix."

"That's true for everybody."

Abby waved a finger at Rose. "Don't keep letting me off the hook," she said, a touch peeved. "You're trying to make me a perfect woman. I'm anything but that. I've let Steve stay gone too long, for one thing."

"He's made his own way, that's for sure," Rose said.

"I don't mean I can bring him back to Blue Springs. But we've had a distance between us; I don't rightly know why. It grieves my heart. He's my son and I miss him, have missed him for years. If the good Lord gives me time, I want to see if I can repair that. Another thing," Abby continued. "Our land—the dam they want to build—I'm trying to figure what to do about that."

"It doesn't matter to me," said Rose. "I'd like to keep it, but it's not ours in the long run anyway." Rose took a drink from her tea glass.

"Exactly," Abby said. "Like Thaddeus told us just before this happened."

"You think you can just give it up, after all you've been through?"

"I don't know. But I've got to make sure it's not an idol, like Thaddeus suggested. He showed me that."

"It would gall me some to think that Stowe got the best of us after all."

"Me too, more than you know. Maybe that's a sin too—pride. What difference does it make if Stowe takes some satisfaction out of flooding our lands? The Lord will judge his heart someday. That ought to satisfy us."

"Ma, you're a good woman," Rose said with a smile.

"I want to finish my college too," Abby said, ignoring the compliment.

"That would be great!" Rose sat up straighter. "You think you can do it?"

Abby shrugged. "After Thaddeus comes home, then we'll see.

It's something I always regretted, not finishing what I started. Maybe it's too late now but I want to see if I can go back." She ate a bite of corn bread. Someone walked toward them and she raised her head. Jim! He wore a scowl on his face, and Abby knew immediately that something bad had come up. She pushed up from the table as he reached her.

"It's Porter," he said, not bothering to sit down. "He's MIA."

Abby looked at Rose.

"He means Porter is missing in action," Rose said.

Abby sagged in her seat. "When?" asked Abby.

"A couple of days ago," said Jim. "The military waited that long to see if he might show up. That happens a lot. A soldier gets separated from his platoon and then drags back in later."

"But not this time?"

"No."

Abby covered her face. Rose patted her back.

"Where's Rebecca?" Abby wanted to know.

"At home with Blanche," Jim said. "They're holding up as well as you could expect. I told them I had to let you know, then I'd come right back home."

Abby nodded, relieved that Rebecca and Blanche had each other at a time like this. She focused on Jim again. "I thought the war was winding down," she said. "Thought our boys were starting to come home."

"They are. The president's pulling back forces every day. But the fighting isn't over yet, not by a long shot. As the soldiers hand over the war to the South Vietnamese, somebody has to keep an eye on the enemy, engage him in hit-and-run battles to cover the transition. You can't just up and leave."

"Why not?" Rose said. "We never should have gone there in the first place."

Jim looked hard at her.

Abby caught Rose's eye and said, "Maybe now's not the time to raise such issues. Let's save that debate for another day."

Rose dropped her eyes. "Sorry, Ma," she said. "It just breaks my heart—all the men over there, so many dead, missing, maimed."

Jim sighed. "I know it's a lousy war," he said. "But my boy is fighting it. That's what matters to me, what should matter to you."

Rose nodded.

"They tell you what might've happened to Porter?" Abby asked, changing the subject.

"Not exactly," said Jim. "It's pretty easy to figure out, though. Porter was doing scouting patrols, in an area near the Phu Loc Valley. Small groups of Marines—seven at a time usually—drop in by helicopter to spend five or six days keeping an eye on enemy movements. They're not big enough to engage the enemy really. If they had to fight, their odds wouldn't be good."

"That's about as dangerous as it gets," Rose said.

Jim nodded. "The terrain is treacherous too," he said. "Grass grows as tall as an elephant. A man can get lost in there if he gets separated from his buddies. And it's mountainous, cliffs all over the place."

Abby studied her son. He knew more about this than she had realized. "Porter tell you all this?" she asked him.

"It's soldier talk," he said. "Porter sends us letters, one for me, one for his mama. He tells me things he doesn't tell her and vice versa."

Abby smiled, grateful that Jim and Porter had kept so close to each other.

"I just can't believe that he's, well, that anything has happened to him," Jim said. "It doesn't seem possible."

"He's strong and he's smart," Rose said. "He'll come through this, you just wait and see."

"They might have captured him," said Jim. "He could be a prisoner right now."

"Like Ed," Abby said, her hopes rising. "When the war ends, he'll come home."

"That could be a long time," Rose said.

"True, but better than never," Abby said.

"Or he could still be out there, all alone, trying to find his way back to his buddies," Jim said.

Abby reached for his hand. "I know how you feel," she said.

"You went to war too, you know. I waited for word, waited to know what had happened to you."

Jim wiped his eyes. "He's just got to come home. I don't know what I'll do if he doesn't."

"How do they get out," Rose asked, "after they finish their mission?"

"The helicopters come back and get them," said Jim, his voice firming some as he focused on his explanation. "The soldiers radio in their position, set out smoke flares. The helicopter lands and they jump aboard."

"So if he's got a radio. . . ?"

"And if he's still alive, they might still find him."

"We've got a lot of reasons to hope," Abby said. "Let's not forget that."

Jim wiped his eyes again. "I best get back to Rebecca."

"Thanks for coming to tell us," said Abby.

"Thaddeus still making progress?" Jim asked.

"Go home to Rebecca," Abby said. "Thaddeus is doing fine."

CHAPTER
THIRTY-SIX

Abby called Steve several times and told him she wanted to come see him as soon as she could, but it took almost three months for Thaddeus to gain enough strength for her to feel comfortable with leaving him alone. Steve told her he would visit with her when he came home for Christmas. Abby figured that, with everybody else around, Christmas wouldn't be a very good time for them to talk so she told him no, that she wanted to come to Raleigh. He asked her what she wanted to discuss. She replied, "I'll tell you when I get there." He didn't press her any further.

November turned out cold but clear. On the first Saturday of the month Abby met Jim at just after sunup for their drive to Raleigh.

"Rebecca will check on Thaddeus later today," he told her as she climbed into his car and placed a picnic basket filled with food in the backseat.

"I hope she knows not to baby him," Abby said. "He'll get fractious if he feels like he's being babied."

"Don't worry, she won't baby him," said Jim. "You know that. He seems to be doin' pretty good these days."

"The doctor says he's had his overhaul, should do fine for another hundred thousand miles or so."

"Maybe he can keep up with you again."

Abby smiled and they settled in for the drive. The highways they sped over amazed her. Who would have believed that in her lifetime a body could go from a small town like Blue Springs all the way to the capital city in less than six hours? She could remember a time when it took almost a day and a half of good walking just to travel to Asheville, much less Raleigh. She shook her head at all the changes she saw before her.

During the drive, Jim told her that the government had called and said they hadn't found Porter's body, which meant the Viet Cong may have captured him.

"I pray that's the case," Abby said. "Least that way, he's still alive."

Jim gripped harder on the steering wheel but said nothing else.

"How's Blanche doing?" she asked.

Jim smiled. "Everybody is fine. Hard to believe Blanche is only a few months from having a second child. Swears it's a girl this time. Maybe she'll look like you—auburn hair, brown eyes."

"Mine's not auburn anymore," said Abby, fingering her gray hair. "That was a long time ago."

"Not so long," Jim said.

"Longer than I like to think."

Jim smiled again, and Abby laid her head back to rest. The trip went by quickly. Abby tried to rehearse what she wanted to say to Steve, but the words didn't come easily. How do you tell a son you've failed him? That you've let time and distance close you off? That you've spent so much time focused on your own problems that you haven't given enough care to his life?

Abby closed her eyes and tried to forgive herself. She'd faced a lot of trials in the years since Steve moved away. The feud with Ben Clack, all of Daniel's troubles, trying to get the land back, raising Rose, helping her survive the polio and then gain the ability to walk again. Hard times had knocked her around a lot, and she had every excuse in the world for not keeping up with her son. Yet she still felt guilty. Somehow she should have stayed close to her boy, should never have allowed such a gap between them.

Abby wondered why things had developed as they had. Did Steve blame her for his father running off the way he did so long ago? Or did it have more to do with Jim? Did Steve think she loved Jim more than she loved him? True, Jim had always stayed close to her. But that didn't make her heart any softer toward him than toward Steve. Any mama knew that. She loved Steve in a different way than Jim but not any less.

The sun reached its halfway point as Jim stopped to fill the tank with gas. Abby opened the picnic basket, and they ate ham sandwiches and apples under a stand of pine trees.

"We're running some early," Jim said. "What time is Steve expecting you?"

"I told him sometime between two and four," said Abby. "Give me at least two hours with him."

"Well, that's fine because I've got plenty to do," Jim said.

Abby nodded. Jim had set up a meeting to talk with some men about the possibility of opening a car dealership in Raleigh.

"You will call before you come back?" she asked.

"Just like we agreed."

"You can visit with him after I've had a chance to say my piece."

"Okay."

Soon they were pulling back onto the highway. An hour and a half after that, Jim dropped her off at Steve's house. She watched him drive off. He was a good man and a faithful son. What grief he must feel about Porter, she thought.

A light wind gusted, and suddenly chilled, Abby realized she'd left her coat in Jim's car. Wrapping her arms tightly around herself, she turned toward Steve's house and hurried to the front steps. She knocked on the door but nobody answered. She knocked again with the same result. Walking to the side of the porch, she lifted an empty flowerpot and found the key where Steve had told her to look if he wasn't home when she arrived. Back at the front door, she inserted the key, opened the door and stepped inside. The house smelled clean and looked tidy. She walked slowly through the hallway to the kitchen.

With nothing else to do, she decided to make a pot of coffee. The smell of hot coffee soon filled the house. Abby checked the clock in the kitchen; she had arrived an hour early.

Coffee cup in hand, she took a seat at the table. She sipped the coffee, her fingers around the cup for warmth. A few moments later she stood and moved to the hall to look for the thermostat to turn up the furnace. She didn't see one. Making her way down the hall, she came to an open door that led to a bedroom. She stuck her head inside. The bed was made, the room spotless. She chuckled. Steve had always kept things real neat.

Unable to locate the thermostat, she decided to get a sweater from Steve's closet. She crossed the room and opened the closet door. A row of suits filled the rack, each suit spaced evenly from the next. She glanced past the suits. Shirts lined up beside them, then slacks. She checked the shelf above the clothes but saw no sweaters. She bent slightly and noticed a small trunk on the floor below the suits. Maybe he kept sweaters there, she thought. She reached for the trunk, lifted the lid and saw a stack of manila folders piled on top of a stack of sweaters. Abby started to grab a sweater and leave but then, curious, she hesitated. Part of her knew she should take the sweater, close the trunk and remove herself from her son's closet. But another part wanted badly to open the folders and see what lay inside. Maybe the contents would reveal something important about Steve, something she needed to know to help her bridge the gap between them. She lifted one of the folders and started opening it.

Then, knowing she had no business going through someone else's personal belongings, she stopped herself, dropped the folder back into the trunk and took out a sweater. As she did the stack of folders shifted and a picture frame fell out of one of them. Abby began sliding the picture back into the folder when her breath caught. She wanted to put the picture away, but the young man looking back at her demanded that she stare at it for at least a few seconds. Abby's fingers tightened on the sweater. The man in the picture looked like her late husband, Stephen, yet it wasn't him.

Then who was it? The couple with him were clearly Stephen's parents. They hadn't changed much since Abby had last seen them. Why did Steve have this picture?

Her heart pounding, Abby pushed the picture back into the folder, shut the trunk and then the closet door and left Steve's bedroom and went back into the kitchen. Unless she missed her guess, Steve knew a secret he long since should have told her.

From the minute Steve walked into his house, he sensed something was different. At first he figured it was the smell of the coffee drifting out from the kitchen. But when he entered the kitchen, he knew it was more than just his ma's presence. He'd been expecting her to come. He could see something was up from the way his ma looked at him as she went to hug him, the way she stepped back and moved to the table after the short embrace.

"You have to wait long?" he asked her. He sat across from her at the table, the coffeepot in his hand. He poured himself a cup.

"About forty minutes," she answered, her eyes fixed on him.

"You cold?" He motioned to the sweater around her shoulders.

"I left my coat in Jim's car."

Steve took a sip of his coffee, wary for some reason he couldn't identify. "So, is Jim off swinging some big business deal?"

"He's looking to start a dealership here."

"Times are hard," Steve said with a shrug. "Not a good economy for most folks to start up something new."

"Jim seems to know his business."

Steve looked away. He had to admit the truth of what she said. Jim seemed always to succeed, no matter how tough it became.

"How are you doing?" Abby asked.

He gave her a half smile and said, "I'm good. You know, staying busy."

Abby sipped her coffee. Steve stood and walked to the refrigerator to get some cream. He felt his ma's eyes on him. Why had she called to arrange this meeting? What did she want? He found the cream and returned to the table, poured it into his coffee.

"I reckon I should get right to the reason I came," Abby said. "You know I wanted to see you alone, wanted to talk out some things with you." Steve stared into his coffee. Abby continued, "I've done a lot of thinking since Thaddeus turned ill. About lots of things. Things I've done, things I ought to have done." She sighed, then moved ahead. "I know I have not done as well by you as I should have. Have not worked hard enough to stay close like a ma should."

Steve shook his head. "Not true," he said. "You have been a fine ma, none better anywhere."

"I knew you'd say that, but in my heart I can't accept it. I should have found a way to keep us more connected. It's my responsibility. I'm the parent, the one who should know better than to let years go by with no real relationship. I should have insisted that you come home more, should have come here and visited, should have . . ." Her voice trailed off.

Steve's heart about broke at the thought of his ma feeling guilty because of him. Yes, he had moved to Raleigh to make his own way. But then he had found Allen Baldwin. Wanting to keep that secret hidden from his ma, he had largely cut himself off from his roots. He'd managed to survive all these years, except he hadn't succeeded nearly as much as he wanted. Fact is, with banks charging such high rates for interest these days and the cost of everything going up with inflation, he didn't know how much longer he could hold on and pay his loans. Add Claire's betrayal to all that, and it made for a mighty heaviness heaped on top of his shoulders.

"Nothing's your fault, Ma," Steve finally said. "You've done all you could. Life gets complicated sometimes, that's all, and more so than anybody could ever have imagined. People don't mean to drift away but it happens. Seems natural almost—the world changes, people move away, even sons from their ma."

"But they shouldn't," Abby said. "The ma shouldn't let that happen."

Steve took her hands in his. "I'm okay, Ma," he said. "You need to believe that."

"Are you?" she asked, her eyes searching his. "Are you really okay? You're separated from your wife and the boys. You live here alone, work all the time, hardly ever see your family."

"I have all I need," he insisted, although he didn't say it with much sincerity. "I have friends."

Abby took a deep breath. Steve watched her, hoping she had finished with what she'd come to say. Nothing bothered him more than such emotional scenes as this. Leave things alone, he figured.

Abby reached inside her sweater, pulled out a picture frame and stood it on the table. Steve's eyes widened, and his heart felt like it stopped.

"You want to tell me who this is?" Abby asked.

"Where did you get that?"

"I was cold and needed a sweater, found one in the trunk in your closet. This fell out."

"You went snooping in my belongings?"

"Nope, just looking for a sweater, like I said. But I found this."

Steve picked up the picture. After all these years, she had found it. "I wanted to keep it from you," he said. "Didn't want to hurt you."

"I am a tough woman," said Abby. "Everybody says so."

Steve smiled. "He's Pa's other son. He found me after I moved to Raleigh." He told her the story then, all of it. How Mr. Waterbury gave him his business just before he died. How Allen got mad and then disappeared. How he'd shown up later as the father of Claire's children.

"That's why I left Claire, Ma," he said as he finished. "She betrayed me. How could I stay with her any longer?"

Abby studied her hands for a long time before she answered. When she finally looked up, she said, "Keeping secrets is hard."

"I didn't like coming home," said Steve. "Didn't like it when you came here either. Feared you'd find out. Every time I saw you, it reminded me of what I knew that you didn't. I didn't want it to spill out somehow."

"I could have handled it," she said. "Maybe I could have gotten to know him, loved him even. If only I'd been given the chance."

Steve hung his head and said, "I feared that most of all."

"What?"

Steve looked back up. "That you would love him. I had enough competition for that."

Abby's eyes watered. Steve rubbed his chin. What he had said was true. He didn't want his ma loving Allen Baldwin. But now he had said enough and would make no more revelations today.

Abby touched his arm. "I'm sorry if you ever thought I didn't love you as much as Jim."

"I'm the most like Pa," said Steve. "Everybody always said it."

"You look like him, yes, but you're a lot different too."

"I am?"

Abby smiled at her son's foolishness. How could he not see it? In some ways, he was just the opposite of his pa. "You don't drink, gamble," she said, "and you labor hard, nothing lazy about you. You're almost always honest, except for this one thing." She pointed to the picture. "Your pa didn't own many of those traits. I hate to say it but it's true."

"But you married him," Steve said.

Abby nodded. "I loved him," she said. "But he was a weak man. The Depression knocked the good in him to the side, knocked the bad to the front. He never got over it."

Steve stood and moved to the window. "I don't know what to do," he said. "About a lot of things."

"I know how you feel."

"I love Claire."

"Then go to her and tell her that."

Steve's jaw tightened. "I can't do that," he said. "Too much water has passed under the bridge."

"Don't let your pride keep you from doing the right thing," Abby said.

"She birthed two babies by another man. I can't trust a woman who did that."

"We can do a lot of things by the grace of the Lord."

"I haven't paid much attention to that in a long time."

"Maybe it's time you did. Maybe it's time you turned back to your faith."

Steve stared out the window. "I'm not a bad man," he said. "Do a lot of good things."

"I know," said Abby. "You've done well by me, even when I kept telling you I didn't need it. But that's not the same as living for the Lord, you know that. A body's not justified by the works of his hands but by the grace of the good Lord."

"You've always been a good preacher."

"Just live by grace, that's all you need."

"I reckon I'm not ready for that."

Abby stood, went to him and put her hand on his back. "You'll never know true joy until you come back," she said. "You know that as well as I do."

He turned and hugged her close. "You're a good ma," he said, stepping back. "But there's some things not even you can fix."

"Not saying I can. But I know the Lord can fix anything."

"Not this."

Steve hugged her one more time, then reached for the coffeepot and poured them both a fresh cup. She tried to move the talk back to more serious matters another time or two in the next hour, but he refused to let the conversation go that way. By the time Jim came, they hadn't much else to say to each other. After just a few moments with Jim, Steve looked at his watch, announced that he had an appointment he needed to keep and that he would look forward to seeing them at Christmas. Abby and Jim didn't argue. Just minutes later they climbed into Jim's car and drove away. Steve stood at the door and watched them leave. Then, closing the door, he walked back inside, took a seat at his kitchen table and buried his face in his hands.

Leaving Steve's place, Abby told Jim she had one more stop she needed to make before they headed home. "Claire's house," she said when he asked her where she wanted to go.

"You're not nosing in Steve's business where he doesn't want you, are you?" Jim asked.

"I'm his ma," she said. "And I'm seventy years old. I can nose where I want."

Jim raised his eyebrows but didn't question her any further. "You got an address?"

"No—we need a telephone directory. A restaurant might have one."

A few minutes later they found a restaurant, where they each ate a hamburger and then looked up Claire Waterbury in the phone book. "Got it," said Jim. "Now we need directions."

The waitress gave them directions as they paid their bill. "Maybe twenty minutes from here," the waitress said. "Easy to find."

"I want to see her alone," Abby said once they were back in the car.

"You're mighty mysterious," said Jim. "What's this all about?"

Did she have any reason to keep this a secret? wondered Abby. How much would it hurt Jim to know that his pa had fathered a child out of wedlock, that he had a half brother who lived in Raleigh, a half brother who had sired two children by Steve's wife? She glanced at Jim. He was a strong man, a war veteran. What could she say that would shake him?

"Turns out your pa had a woman before me," she said quietly. "You have a half brother by the name of Allen. He's in Raleigh."

Jim looked hard at her and then back at the road. "How do you know that?"

"I saw his picture, found it at Steve's house. When I asked him about it, he admitted the truth."

Jim maneuvered the car around a sharp curve. "That explains it," he said.

"Explains what?"

"A long time ago, a picture I saw, back when Pa's folks were still alive. A young man that looked like Pa standing with them."

"That's the picture I found," Abby said.

"Why didn't Steve tell us?"

"Said he didn't want to hurt me, didn't want me ashamed of your pa, didn't want to run your pa's name through the mud."

Silence fell. Jim stopped at a red light, turned right when it changed. "What you plan to say to Claire?" he asked.

"Don't really know. But Steve loves her, that's for sure."

"Maybe Steve ought to tell her that."

"Probably. But if he won't, maybe I should."

Less than ten minutes later they reached the address from the phone book. Abby turned to Jim. "Say a prayer for me," she said. "That I'll know what to say, how to say it."

Jim nodded, and she got out and headed up the walkway. Claire quickly answered the door when she knocked. Her eyebrows arched when she saw Abby.

"Come on in," she said. "Mighty cold out."

Abby stepped into the front room. Though the room felt warm, she still shivered. Nerves, she thought, fearing that she would mess things up.

Claire pointed her to a sofa. Abby sat while Claire took a seat in a straight-backed wing chair. "I haven't seen you for a long time," Claire said. "Would you like some coffee or something?"

Abby shook her head. "I won't stay that long," she said. "But I just had to talk to you."

Claire pulled her sweater closer around her shoulders.

"It's about Steve," said Abby. "I fear for him."

"I do too," Claire said. "He's alone too much."

Abby looked at her fingers. They were white from the cold. "He says you betrayed him."

Claire rubbed her hands on her knees. "I did," she said. "A long time ago. I've admitted that to him, asked his forgiveness. Only he won't let it go, won't move past it."

"He says you have two children by his half brother, that even after you were married, you . . ." Abby found it impossible to go on, to say such an awful thing about another person. Even knowing it was true, it didn't seem right to just speak out such a harsh thing.

Claire stood and moved to her fireplace. Abby watched her, admiring the strength she saw in the woman's bearing. She had dignity, Abby thought, no matter her faults. Claire faced her again, her face firm.

"You need to believe me when I say this," Claire began. "I did some bad things when I was a young woman; I know that and will not try to hide them. But I put all that behind me later. By the time I married Steve I had straightened my life out. That didn't change. I stayed true to him, no matter what he says."

"But what about your second boy?"

Claire angrily shook her head. "I tried to tell Steve," she said, "but he wouldn't believe me. Robert Travis is *his,* not Allen's. I didn't see Allen again after I married Steve, except the times he came by to see Frank. You understand what I'm saying? I didn't *see*

Allen again, not a single time. I put all that behind me, stayed true as a good wife should. I loved Steve, wouldn't have done anything to hurt him. He did so good by me, by Frank. How could I betray his love? I couldn't, wouldn't! I loved him I tell you." She wiped her eyes and turned away.

Abby weighed Claire's words. She sounded so honest, so sincere. "I want to believe you," said Abby. "But Steve's my son and he tells a different story."

Claire faced her again. "He's just stubborn," she said. "Too proud for his own good. If I loved Allen so much, why didn't I marry him when Steve put me out? He begged me over and over again, but I said no."

Abby studied the argument. It made sense.

Claire stared at her as if she could convince her by the sheer power of her eyes. "Here," she said. "Come with me!"

She took Abby by the arm and pulled her up. Abby stiffened for a second but then decided to go with her. Whatever she wanted her to see must be mighty important, she figured.

Claire led her down the hall to the back of the house. Standing by the kitchen window that overlooked the fenced-in backyard, Claire pointed to the two boys tossing a football back and forth. "The smallest one," she said. "He's ten. He remind you of anybody?"

Abby's heart jumped. The boy looked just like Steve when his age, had the same build in his shoulders, the same shape of chin and head. But then she remembered that Allen had Waterbury blood in him too. Who was to say that the resemblance didn't owe to him rather than to Steve?

"He looks like a Waterbury," Abby admitted. "So does Allen."

Claire's lower lip trembled. "You don't believe me either?"

Abby hung her head. "I don't know what to believe."

Claire's eyes lit up, and Abby could see she had thought of something else. "Come with me," she said. Again Abby obeyed, hoping all the while that Claire could prove what she was saying to be true, could prove beyond any doubt that Steve had fathered this boy, that his marriage to Claire had produced something so fine as that good-looking child.

Claire led her to a telephone in the front room. Abby sat back on the sofa while Claire dialed a number. A few seconds later Claire spoke into the phone for a minute, then handed the receiver to Abby.

"It's Allen," she said. "Ask him about Robert."

Abby hesitated, but then figured she'd come too far to turn back now. "This is Abby Holston," she said into the receiver. "Steve Waterbury's ma."

"I'm Allen Baldwin," he said. "Figured I'd be talking to you sooner or later."

"I regret that it's later, but there's nothing I can do about that now."

"Claire says you have something you want to ask me."

"Yes. I want to know if you fathered her second child," Abby said. "I expect you know why I want to know that."

"I can take a guess."

"Are you his father?"

There was a pause, and Abby realized that no matter what he said, she still wouldn't know for sure. Yet somehow she figured he would tell her the truth. What reason did he have to lie?

"No, the boy isn't mine," he finally said. "I tried to tell Steve a long time ago, but he didn't believe me, didn't want to believe me."

"You're not lying to an old woman, are you?"

"Got no reason to do that. Claire showed me she didn't love me anymore, not in a marrying kind of way. I've moved on, have married a good woman. Claire loves Steve, much as I hate to say it."

"Why don't you like my son?"

"He took something from me, something I deserved."

"What did he take?"

"Ask him."

Abby took a full breath. In spite of her doubts, she felt Allen had told her the truth. Now she had to find a way to convince Steve of it. She focused on Allen again. "I want to meet you," she said. "Do you think we might could do that?"

"I think we can arrange it," he said. "Maybe after the new year."

"I can tell you some things about your pa," she said.

"I'd like to hear them. At least the good parts."

They each said good-bye, and Abby hung up and looked at Claire.

"Do you believe me now?" asked Claire.

"I think so," Abby said. "How do we convince Steve?"

"Will it really matter if we do?" Claire said. "He seems bent on leaving all this behind."

"I'll see what I can do," said Abby.

Claire moved to her and threw her arms around her neck. "I love your son," she said. "That's why I never got a divorce. I want to go home to him."

"I want that too," Abby said. "Now we've got to find a way for him to want it as much as we do."

CHAPTER
THIRTY-SEVEN

All his worries aside, still Steve felt freer that year as he arrived home for Christmas. He knew why too. With the secret about Allen out in the open now, he could relax some, at least on that front.

As always his whole family gathered at Jesus Holiness on Christmas Eve, filling four rows in the tiny church's sanctuary. Sitting beside his ma, Steve leaned back on the hard pew and tried to relax. Maybe he could make some changes, he figured, such as talk to Jim, see if they could get close again. He glanced at his brother, noted the gray that had settled into his hair since he had heard that Porter was missing. His shoulders had stooped as well, as if pushed down by sadness.

Steve thought of Robert Travis and wondered what he looked like. Since he usually mailed Claire the money he gave her, he hadn't seen him in almost a year. He tried to imagine what it would feel like to have a son who went off to war and just disappeared. No doubt such a thing would probably crack a man's heart right in two.

A quartet stood and began to sing. Not really listening, Steve interlocked his fingers and looked down at his shoes. He felt bad for Jim. If it turned out that Porter was dead, no amount of business success could make up for that. Steve thought about praying for Porter and Jim, but he hadn't prayed in a long time so it didn't feel right. So he raised his eyes instead and stared at the ceiling.

The quartet finished their song, and the preacher—a short, bald man named Stanfill who had just started in November—approached the pulpit and asked everybody to stand to sing along with a hymn. Steve tried to focus on the song's words but didn't find much success at it. He kept thinking of all the things he wanted to do better in the coming year. Like not feel jealous of Jim anymore. No matter what happened to him, no matter if his business failed completely and he had to start all over again, nothing could hurt as much as losing a son.

The hymn singing ended after which Stanfill prayed and the deacons passed wicker baskets up and down the pews for the offering. Steve grabbed ten dollars from his wallet and dropped it in the basket as it moved past him. His ma smiled at him and he patted her hand. Maybe he should take her suggestion and start going to church again, he thought.

After the deacons had finished, Stanfill stood, opened his Bible and began to preach. He took off talking about all the changes that had come in the last few years.

"We've never seen so much change," he said. "All around us. Some of it's for the good, I got to admit that. We got better medicine these days, better roads and cars. And air-conditioning. All of us are glad that's come our way, aren't we?"

Some people replied, "Amen."

Stanfill kept on about all the changes, lots of it for the good. Then he shifted. "But I got to tell you, some of the changes make me right nervous."

"Amen," the crowd said.

"Some of the changes cause a great upsetness in the center of my soul. I mean we got changes in the family, too much divorce going on around here."

"Amen."

"And changes in politics, people going against their government and government going against their people."

"Amen."

"Changes in the churches and in the society. People saying that God is dead. That's the kind of changes we're facing these days."

The people started squirming in their pews.

Stanfill continued, "These changes will lead us down a dark path, a path cut clear by the devil. A path that looks pretty when we start down it, but one that will lead you to hell in a hurry if you stay on it."

Steve shifted in his seat. Stanfill's head reddened as he preached on.

"We've seen the kinds of heartache this path will bring to us. The heartache of war, the heartache of racial unrest, of broken families, of hard economic times. You know this heartache; you've seen it up close. It's grabbed you by the throat and squeezed you hard."

Steve nodded. He knew some of that heartache and so did his family.

"People try all kinds of things to cure their heartache. They take drugs. They try free love. They think always having money in their pockets will fix it. Or getting everyone an education. Do these things and you'll take care of the heartache and find true happiness. But do you think any of that will work?"

Steve took a deep breath. He had tried a lot of things to find happiness. So far he didn't know that he had found it. But what was happiness, anyway? As Stanfill forged ahead with his preaching, Steve drifted. Who did he know who seemed happy? he wondered. His business associates in Raleigh? The people who lived in his houses? His neighbors? He looked up and down his pew and saw his ma, her eyes focused on the preacher.

His ma seemed happy. Despite all her troubles, somehow she looked to be at peace with things. Steve glanced past her to Jim, who also had his attention on the preacher. Rebecca sat beside him. Even with their grief over Porter's coming up missing, strangely they appeared content.

The preacher's voice moved to full throttle. Steve realized

something: People who lived out their faith were different. Like his ma, they were at peace. No matter what trial came their way, folks who trusted the Lord seemed able to put their arms around it, face it with their chins firm and hands steady. Not that trials didn't knock them down and bring tears to their eyes. But they somehow managed to get through the tears and find joy on the other side.

"Jesus is the same," Stanfill shouted, "yesterday, today and forever! Everything else changes, everything else passes away, but Jesus remains the same. He is always good, always loves us, always willing to forgive us and let us come home. No matter what changes come to you, whether good or bad, Jesus is always the constant for your life. That one whose birth we celebrate tonight, the same who grew up to be a man, who was and is the Son of God, is the redeemer of all the world, including everybody in this place here tonight. If you'll stay with Jesus through all the changes in your life, He will stay with you. Do you believe that? Do you?"

"Amen. Amen."

The sermon ended and then the congregation sang once more. Afterward, Stanfill said a closing prayer. A few minutes later the people gradually left and headed for their homes. Still stewing over the preacher's words, Steve drove slowly up the mountain to his ma's place. So much had changed in his life over the years, and he knew he hadn't always handled the changes as well as he should have, yet he didn't know whether he believed Jesus was the way to make his life any better.

Abby rode back to her house with Thaddeus, Jim and Rebecca. Rose followed in her car, Ed and Priscilla in theirs. Heavily pregnant, Blanche had gone to Charleston to see her folks for the holidays. Abby prayed silently most of the way, her heart anxious about what would happen in the next hour or so.

"You think I've done the right thing?" she asked Thaddeus as they passed the mailbox and turned onto the gravel drive.

"It's too late to worry now," he said. "You did what you thought was right. It's in the Lord's hands now."

Abby leaned on his shoulder, grateful for his recovery. What would she do without him? They climbed out of the car and trooped into the house. After hanging up everybody's coats, Abby joined her family in the front room. A hallway clock tolled out nine o'clock. Abby glanced at Thaddeus, then Jim and Rebecca and Rose.

"I'll get some coffee," Rebecca said. Abby nodded and, for once, didn't follow her into the kitchen. Everybody took a seat, Steve on the fireplace hearth. Abby heard a knock at the door. Thaddeus moved to the door while Abby lowered herself in a rocking chair next to Steve and laid a hand on his back. He turned to her, curiosity on his face.

"I need to tell you something," Abby said. "I invited somebody to come see us for Christmas this year."

Steve pulled back a little. "What are you talking about?"

Thaddeus stepped into the room. Abby kept her eyes on Steve and said, "Look at me." Steve obeyed. "I invited Claire," she said. "And Franklin and Robert." Steve jumped up, his hands shoved into his pockets. Abby saw his eyes dart past Thaddeus. Claire and her boys stood behind him. Claire's mouth trembled. "I asked them to come," Abby said. "They're family, like all the rest here."

Steve glanced around as if looking for somebody to rescue him. Abby could see him struggling, wondering what to do, how to respond. *Give him courage, Lord,* she silently prayed. *Help him to get over his pride.* When he spoke, she knew immediately the Lord hadn't answered her prayer, at least not yet.

"Please take the boys out," Steve said to Rose. "I think there's some cake in the kitchen."

Rose looked at Abby, and Abby indicated she should do what he asked. Ed, Priscilla and Rebecca followed them. When they were gone, Abby led Claire to the sofa and sat down beside her.

Steve stayed by the fireplace, his jaw firm. Abby held Claire's hands. Steve stared at the floor. "You're my ma," he said, "and I know you're trying to make things better, but you had no right to interfere this way."

Abby weighed her words carefully, desperate not to make things any worse. "I did what I thought best."

"How do you know what's best for me? How could you do this?"

Abby looked at Jim. "We all talked about it," Jim said. "We all love you."

Steve stared at his brother. Abby could see him struggling, trying to control his feelings.

"So you all got together and decided what to do for poor old Steve, is that it?" he said. "Pitiful Steve over in Raleigh, all by himself. Maybe we can lend him a hand since he can't take care of himself."

"It wasn't that way," said Jim.

"You've tried to take care of me all my life," Steve said. "But you've failed to remember one thing—I can take care of myself! I left here a long time ago. Somehow, even without you, I've managed to make it. I know that's a surprise to all of you"—his eyes swept the room—"but I've done okay. Maybe not as good as Jim here, but still okay. I didn't need your help with any of that, and I don't need your help with this!"

"You've got it wrong," Abby said. "We're your family, that's all. We wanted you to know we care."

Claire stood then and moved to Steve, but he turned away. Claire stepped back and said, "I love you, Steve. I've tried to tell you that." He waved her away.

Abby could see they were losing him. Her desperation to keep that from happening pushed her to speak without thinking. "That boy in the kitchen eating cake belongs to you," she said. "Claire swears it and I believe her. All you've got to do is lay aside your pride and take one look at him—really look at him and you'd see it too. He's you all over again."

"You ought to do right by your boy," Jim said.

Steve's face darkened, and Abby knew that Jim's words had made things worse. Steve walked over to his brother, stood face-to-face with him. "I'm a grown man," he said. "I don't need you telling me how to run my life."

"You're too stubborn for your own good," Jim said.

Steve balled his fists. Abby stepped between them and studied Steve hard. "I fear the Lord will need to break you," she said. "I see nothing else that will soften your heart."

Steve looked at her as if she had stuck a knife in his ribs. Abby clapped a hand over her mouth, stunned at what she'd just said to her boy. Yet it felt right somehow, almost as though the Lord had shoved the words into her mouth.

"I don't know that things can get much worse," Steve finally said.

"Oh, things can always get worse," Abby said. "Just you wait and see."

Steve shrugged. Seeing that her words had hurt him, Abby tried to find a way out of the dead end. "Maybe it was a mistake to ask Claire here," she said. "You can blame me for that. It was my idea, not anybody else's."

She took Steve's elbow and he relaxed a little. He looked at her, and she saw pain in his eyes. She remembered a time right after his eighth birthday, a day when a dog he loved had died. That same look had entered his eyes that day. She had taken him in her arms and held him as close as she could and told him she loved him and that everything would turn out okay. After crying for a while, he had finally pulled back, wiped his face and went out again to play, his grief soothed. She wanted to take him in her arms now and hold him until his tears had ended, but he was a grown man now and she knew he wouldn't stand for that anymore. That made her heart hurt bad.

"I'm too old to have my ma try to fix my life," Steve said.

"I'm sorry if I embarrassed you," said Abby. "Guess a ma sometimes noses where she shouldn't."

"You would never have done something like this to him," Steve said, nodding at Jim.

"She's said she is sorry," Jim said. "Why don't you respect that and let it go?"

"I'll let it go," Steve said. "No problem with that." He turned away from Jim and headed toward the door.

Abby followed him, tears in her eyes. Claire trailed her, Thaddeus too. Steve pulled his coat from the closet. Claire rushed to him and grabbed on to his sleeve. "I'm the one who should go!" she cried. "I'm the outsider here, not you."

Steve pulled away from her. "Not true," he said. "I've been the outsider for a long time, the only one who moved away. The rest of the folks here are highlanders, mountain people. I'm like my pa, a city man through and through. And I'll take care of myself—alone! You got that?" He glared at Claire, then at Abby, Thaddeus and Jim, who had joined them in the entryway. "I don't need all this! Never have, never will."

Tears coursed down Abby's face. It was obvious she'd ruined everything by inviting Claire to her house for Christmas, by interfering with her son in a way no ma should ever do. She stepped closer to Steve and, gripping the front of his coat, cried, "Please, I beg your forgiveness for my meddling! I love you. I only wanted to help. Don't hold this against anybody but me. Not Jim, not Claire, just me!"

Steve looked at her and she saw his eyes momentarily soften. His hands covered hers, and his words fell gently as he said, "I don't hold this against you, Ma. I know your motives are pure. But I already told you once, some things not even your love can fix. You know that's true. It was true with Pa and it's true with me."

Abby leaned into him. He caressed her back. "I love you, Ma," he whispered, "but you got to leave this be."

She buried her face in his coat. "Don't leave," she pleaded.

"I got to," he said. "That way Claire and the boys can stay. I'll be all right. Don't worry about me." He gently pushed her away and stepped back. She wiped her eyes. Steve looked at Claire. "Stay here," he said, "and let the boys enjoy their Christmas."

Claire opened her mouth to speak, but Steve put a finger to her lips to silence her.

"I'll see you in Raleigh," he said. "Maybe in a few weeks."

Then he left. Abby stood in the doorway with Claire, and together they watched him drive away. She realized that Steve had it right; some things even a ma's love couldn't fix. Some things only the power of the good Lord could change.

CHAPTER
THIRTY-EIGHT

During the next three years, Abby only saw Steve four times—once each year for Christmas and the time she drove with Jim and everybody to Raleigh when he opened his car dealership there. She fussed at herself over and over in those years, her guilt piling up for bringing Claire home and for trying to force matters between Claire and Steve. She tried to explain in the monthly letters she sent Steve, letters he answered with only a few short words scribbled on a piece of note paper wrapped around the checks he kept sending. As much as she apologized, she sensed he never quite forgave her. Sensed it from the way he kept his reserve when she talked to him on the phone, from the way he stayed away from home except at Christmastime.

In spite of her heavy heart about her son, Abby made the most of her days. Thaddeus kept gaining strength, and while the doctor warned he wouldn't ever do all he'd done before, nobody much noticed. "I'm supposed to slow some," Thaddeus said every time he got an ache or a pain. "I'm as old as dirt." Abby always laughed at this but she knew deep down that nobody could count on anything anymore. Time eventually caught up with everybody.

Matters with the land kept swinging out and back in those years, the plan to flood their property seeming to move ahead one minute and then going in reverse the next. "Politicians try to do things like this with as little upset as possible," explained Jim, who kept them all abreast of the latest developments. "But every time they announce something about where they're putting the dam, they knock some group's nose out of joint. That group then complains to their congressman, and he slows things down for a while until they calm some. Then they move ahead with what they planned in the first place."

"So it looks like things are still on track for the dam to flood us out?" Ed asked.

"Reckon so," Jim replied. "Maybe after the war ends for good, there will be more money for projects like this one."

Abby listened to all the discussions and tried to stay involved in them, but something in her didn't care so much anymore. If not for the fact that her family had labored so hard for the land and for so many years, she didn't even know that any of it would matter. Let Will Stowe win this, she figured. So what? When they all died, which would come soon enough no matter if they all lived to reach a hundred years, the land would pass on to somebody else. Nobody owned anything, not really, not even her own life.

Porter's fate kept her up late many a night in those years. Nobody had heard anything from him. The government still had him listed as missing. And, since nobody had found any traces of him, they all held out hope that he would turn up in a prison camp after the war ended. Everybody did his best to keep Blanche from getting too down. With two babies now—Lisa Abigail having come in March of 1971 to join her brother, Todd—Blanche stayed with Abby and Thaddeus about half the time and in Charleston with her folks the rest.

Thankfully the war gradually wound down for the Americans and peace talks made some headway. In fact, by the time January of '73 rolled off the calendar, the powers in Washington had reached a peace agreement with the North Vietnamese. Everybody in Abby's house sighed with relief and said an extra prayer that when the enemy released its prisoners, Porter Waterbury would walk out among them.

That didn't happen. When the North Vietnamese opened the prisons on February 12 and the American POWs were escorted onto airplanes to be flown either to nearby hospitals or to air bases back home, Porter did not appear. But then a military official from the government told Jim and Rebecca that he had good reason to believe that the enemy still held some prisoners and that they shouldn't give up hope just yet. They all held to that word as hard as they could.

"We don't know yet," Jim said whenever anybody asked about Porter. "Things are still in a mess in Vietnam. Remember how long it took for Ed to show up. Let's give it a few more months."

And so 1973 moved past, winter to spring and spring to summer, summer to fall. The nation's economy went from bad to worse, and some folks talked about a new depression. Abby worried about Jim and Steve, but more about Steve. Though she didn't care much for all the negative talk, she knew enough about business to realize that high inflation meant high dollars paid on loans, and she just hoped Steve hadn't gotten in too far over his head. A lot of her worry came from the fact that during the fall of '73, Steve stopped sending the monthly checks that he'd been mailing to her every month since 1946. What bothered her wasn't the fact that she didn't get the money anymore but what that might say about Steve's finances. Had he gotten so broke that he couldn't send the checks? Since he had taken such pride in doing it in spite of her protests, the absence of the checks might mean something bad.

Most folks talked a lot about President Nixon in those days. A few defended him, said that regardless of his faults he had also done many good things. Then it was found out that some of his men broke into a building called Watergate some time past, and every day seemed to prove a little bit more that he had tried to cover up the bad acts of the men on his payroll. Abby and Thaddeus watched it all with a tired sadness. "A man makes a mistake, he ought to just go on and confess up to it," said Thaddeus more than once. "People will forgive a repentant man but not a lying one."

Abby nodded and hoped and prayed the country could get through it all. Seemed like bad times came in waves. Both her family and her country were about up to their necks in waves high enough to just about drown them. To make matters even worse, a group of men over in the Middle East decided to slap an oil embargo on the United States, and before anybody could do anything to stop it, gas lines had formed at service stations around the country. Soon after that, people started talking about how the country had better get used to it—the hard times were here to stay.

"This will go rough on Jim," Abby said to Thaddeus a few days before Christmas. "With gas prices going up, the cars he sells won't be so popular anymore."

"Foreign cars get better gas mileage," Thaddeus added. "Everybody wants one of those these days."

Abby kept a close eye on Jim as Christmas approached. He had managed to stay strong through all the fears about Porter and had said nothing to her about the economic situation, but she knew that every man had a breaking point. She worried about another matter too. They had finally gotten notice about the plans for the dam. According to the papers, they had to move out by May. The government wanted to start moving dirt in July at the latest. For a man who had a lot of good fortune go his way for a long time, Jim now had more heartache than almost anybody could take.

Abby also worried about Steve, maybe even more so. With people losing their jobs left and right, how long would it be before some of his renters reached the point where they couldn't pay? She knew from what he had said in the past that he had mortgages on most if not all of the houses he rented. If people couldn't pay him, he couldn't pay the mortgages. Would the banks go after his houses if he got behind on the mortgages, like they had done to her and Stephen so many years ago? Would the bad economy destroy Steve's business, the only thing he seemed to care about?

She thought of Claire and her sons. Convinced that Robert was her grandson, Abby had kept in close touch with them the last three years. Claire had started dating a man from her office back in the summer. He wanted to marry her, yet so far Claire had put him off. How much longer could she wait for Steve to come to his senses and come back to her? Should she wait at all?

Unable to do anything but pray, Abby forced herself to make plans for Christmas. Everybody would come home as always. Steve would make his annual trek to Blue Springs, maybe out of obligation, but he'd be there all the same. Abby tried to think of some way to close the gap between her and her younger son.

The week before Christmas arrived Abby wrapped presents and bought extra food. Thaddeus loaded in firewood. Snow started to fall and soon covered the ground with white. Everything fell quiet in the world past her front porch. Abby sensed something different in the air as she cooked and cleaned, as she made ready for one more Christmas. She stood on the porch every morning that week, the air still, almost as if the earth had slowed down to pay attention to what was about to happen. Abby thought maybe her imagination had gotten the better of her, yet something in her bones told her things would change this year. Try as she might though, she couldn't tell whether the change would please her or make her cry.

———————

Steve sat at his kitchen table, his tie loosened, his shirt unbuttoned. Izzy sat across from him, his face covered with patches of a gray beard. Steve held a letter in his right hand and a cup of coffee in his left. Throwing the letter on the table and rocking back in his chair, Steve said to Izzy, "Looks like they might finally have us. Demanding a hundred and sixty-two thousand dollars by December 27 or they start foreclosure procedures."

"It's been a hard year," said Izzy, his tone all sympathy. "Nothing like it since nineteen and twenty-nine, I reckon."

Steve exhaled heavily. "The Depression took down my pa," he said. "Guess the apple don't fall too far from the tree after all."

"What you gone do, Mr. Steve?"

Steve weighed his options. "I can ask the bank for more time and try to sell all the houses."

"You think they'll wait for their money?"

Steve shook his head and admitted the truth. "This is the third time this year they've threatened me," he said. "I put them off twice already. Even if they gave me another extension, we couldn't get much right now for the property. Real estate is in the dumper."

Izzy took off his floppy hat, rolled it around on his fingers. "Anywhere else we can turn for a loan?"

Steve thought of Jim but instantly dismissed the notion. Even if he knew that Jim had the money, which he didn't, he wouldn't even consider the idea. Better to end up broke than to crawl home to his older brother and have him bail him out. "I've tried at least four other banks," he said, "but when they see my financial statements, they clam up real quick. Money's hard to come by these days."

Izzy rubbed his forehead and said, "I could see if some of the folks could gather up a few dollars. You've done real good by them for a long time, given everybody a fair shake, more so than most men. Who knows what a new owner will do? The folks in my neighborhoods will help if they know you need it."

"Thanks," Steve said. "I appreciate it. But I don't think they can raise the kind of money I need, no matter how generous they are."

Izzy set his hat on his head. "You'll have to turn your properties over to the banks?"

"I expect so. That's my collateral."

"In regular times your houses are worth a whole lot more than a hundred and sixty-two thousand."

"They won't get all of them," said Steve.

"You plan on keeping this one?"

"I hope so."

"And the one where Mrs. Claire and her boys live?"

"If I can. And the one where you live too."

Izzy nodded. "A whole lot of folks will find it hard to get another place for as little as you made them pay. Guess the new year will go tough on more than a few."

"I'm sorry but there's nothing I can do."

Izzy stood and patted him on the shoulder. "Nobody's blaming you," he said. "You did as much as you could. Charged us less than you could have for a long time. That's part of what got you in this trouble—your good heart."

Steve waved him off. "Go on," he said. "You'll need to start looking for another job."

Izzy patted him once more and then left the room. Steve kept sitting there, his hands at his sides, his eyes glazed. Outside, the sun dropped until it disappeared. Steve didn't notice. For him, the sun had dropped when he opened the letter and read it. All his dreams had died in that moment, every hope he'd ever known. He picked up the letter once more and moved to his bedroom. At his dresser he opened a drawer and pulled out a second document. His eyes moved from one paper to the other, the first document detailing the bank's demand that he pay up or they would foreclose, the second telling him that Claire had finally decided to take him up on his long-standing offer of a divorce.

He thought of Robert. Was the boy really his son? Claire and Allen said so. But he still had his doubts. Allen might have lied to protect his wife from knowing that he had a son by another woman. Papers in hand, Steve moved to a window and stared out. His ma had told him about three years ago that things could get worse. At the time he hadn't believed her. Now he held the truth of her statement. He balled up both letters and held them in his fists. His ma had also said the Lord might have to break him. Well, he didn't know if the Lord had done it or not but he sure felt broke.

He laughed out loud at the pun. He felt broke all right, and in more ways than one.

CHAPTER
THIRTY-NINE

He would have avoided it if he could have found a reasonable excuse. Failing that, Steve drove home for Christmas four days later, his heart a jumble of emotions—embarrassment one second, grief the next. Circumstances had fallen in such a way that he had no choice but to do something different with his life. But what?

The banks would get all but a couple of his houses. Should he sell the couple he'd still own and use the money to move away and get a fresh start somewhere else? That seemed to make sense. Move away as far as possible from all his troubles. Start over in a new place where nobody knew his past. But where? California maybe? Or Florida? He'd always wanted to see more of the country. A lot of people said Arizona or Colorado held good prospects. Maybe he would go there.

With the decision to move pretty well set, Steve's spirits rose some as he arrived at home about midday Christmas Eve. Just get through the holidays, he told himself. You won't have to do it again for a long time. One last Christmas at home because you don't want to hurt your ma's feelings. Then afterward go home, settle up with the banks, sign the divorce papers for Claire, sell any leftover belongings and hit the road. Who knew when he would have to come back. Maybe never.

His ma met him at the door while Steve was stepping onto the porch.

"I'm so glad you're home," she said, her tone somewhat tense. "We need to talk."

Steve noticed a gleam in her eyes, a look that scared him for some reason. Obviously she had something on her mind. Dead set against any more of her advice, Steve firmed his jaw.

"Come in," Abby said, taking his coat. "We got a good fire going."

Steve smelled the burning wood and, despite his attitude, calmed some. Nothing like the glow of a fireplace to make a man feel snug. He followed his ma into the house and took a seat in a rocker. She put up his coat, got them both some coffee and then sat down across from him in front of the fireplace.

"Where's Thaddeus?" he asked.

"Taking a nap," said Abby. "He's gotten lazy in his old age."

"I'm sure he's been working to get things ready for us to come," Steve said. "Give the man a break."

Abby laughed. "I guess I'm too hard on him."

Steve drank coffee and squirmed uncomfortably. It felt strange to think that after tomorrow he wouldn't see his ma again for a very long time. He heard her sigh and so looked up. He wondered what she wanted to tell him. Go back to Claire probably. He didn't want to hear that again. Claire wanted a divorce. Even if he wanted to go to her, the time for that had passed. Steve decided he might as well get some things out in the open.

"I plan to move," he started.

"What?"

Steve knew he had surprised her, though the gleam hadn't left her eyes. He wondered at her cheerfulness. "I'm closing down my business," he said. "Times have made it too hard to keep going."

There, he had said it, not the full truth but enough to make plain why he had to move away.

"You don't have to do that," Abby said.

"I have no choice. Besides, I'm tired of my work, the stress of it all. And Claire wants a divorce. I don't reckon I should refuse her. Nothing left for me here."

Abby sank back in her chair, and the gleam in her eyes disappeared. "I knew she was seeing a man," she said. "But I hadn't heard about the divorce."

"I reckon she didn't want to hurt you," Steve said.

"She still loves you," Abby said.

"A divorce says otherwise."

Abby stood and moved closer to the fireplace. She took up a long stick and poked at the burning logs. "This complicates things," she said, turning back to Steve. "But maybe there's still time."

"Time for what?"

Abby pulled her rocker up close to Steve, took his coffee cup and set it on the hearth. After sitting down, she took his hands. "Izzy called me," she said. "Told me about the bank situation."

Steve froze.

"He wanted me to know," she said. "He said I should take extra care with you this year."

"Izzy is a meddler," said Steve, his face reddening with embarrassment. "You should pay no mind to anything he says."

"He's your friend," Abby said.

"How much did he tell you?"

"Just that the bank had given you notice."

Steve hung his head. "I'm a failure," he said. "Like Pa. Nothing more to say."

The room became quiet. Abby patted his hands. "Everybody fails sometimes," she finally said. "It's part of life. Nothing sinful about it, it just happens. Sometimes something we did causes it, sometimes not. Sometimes things just gang up on us, like a bunch of dogs on a rabbit. Nothing the rabbit can do to stop it."

Steve grunted. "I did it to myself," he argued. "Tried to do too much with too little. Kept pushing things, borrowing more and more money to buy more and more houses. Always trying to do more and more. Trying to succeed, to prove myself."

"You're a man," said Abby. "Men like challenges, like to shoulder heavy loads, build things. Nothing wrong with that."

Steve pulled away, stood and moved to the fireplace. One part of him wanted to believe his ma, to accept her comforting words. But another part said he couldn't forgive himself so easily. A failed man always caused his own failure, no two ways about it.

"It doesn't matter either way," he said. "Whether I caused it or not. It's done and there's nothing here for me anymore. I plan to move as soon as I can settle up in Raleigh." He turned back to his ma, moved to her side and knelt. "I'll keep in touch, Ma. But I got to leave here, I know that now. I need a new place, a place where I can figure out what I want."

Abby stared at him, the gleam having returned now. "You don't have to move."

"You already said that."

She smiled at him.

"What?" he said. "What's going on?"

"I've got your money," Abby said.

Confused, Steve eased back into his rocker.

"The money you sent home every month," said Abby. "I've got it all, almost every dime since 1946, plus the interest it's earned over the years. I checked two days ago, after Izzy called."

Steve heard the words but they still didn't register.

Abby continued, "You sent me fifty dollars a month for the first three years, then a hundred a month the next four. After that you notched it up a lot. Five hundred dollars a month for close to fifteen years, a thousand a month the last five. With interest it's close to a half million dollars."

Steve lost his voice for several seconds. His mind reeled as he gripped his coffee cup tighter.

"You hearing me?" Abby asked, breaking the silence.

"You kept all that money?" Steve said.

"I kept telling you I didn't need it. I spent a little every now and again, when Rose got polio, when she went to college, but I kept the rest of it. It's all there—yours for the taking." Steve rubbed his eyes, still not sure whether to believe any of this. Abby laughed. "You could have used this money to pay your bills over the years," she said. "No reason not to do it now."

"But it's *your* money," said Steve. "I gave it to you."

"I never wanted it. Still don't. I want you to take it back."

Steve rubbed his eyes again. A half million dollars! A man could do a lot with that. Then again, what difference did it make now? One thing he had learned out of all this—he couldn't make any success out of anything. What made him think he could do any better with this money than he had with all the other money he'd made over the years?

"I can't take it," he said. "I'd just lose it like I did the rest. I'm just like Pa, a failure. I've lived my whole life trying to prove I'm not anything like him, but the truth is I'm him made all over again."

"But you're not," Abby insisted. "Can't you see that? The very fact that you sent me money all these years proves it. Your pa wasted everything he ever earned, always tried to make a show. You haven't done that. You've given away more than you've ever kept for yourself. And you've worked more hours in a month than your pa would labor in a year. You're nothing like him."

Steve stared at the fire. Something worse than losing money gnawed at him now, yet he didn't know if he could say it. To say it stamped him forever like his pa, an awful man. His pa had failed so miserably. To say it put him right there with him.

"Believe me, you're not your pa," Abby repeated.

"But I ran out on my kid," Steve said, his body shaking. "No matter how much money I gave Claire, nothing can fix that." Saying the words broke him, and he slumped over in grief.

Abby moved to his side. "It's not too late," she whispered. "Claire still loves you."

"She's asking for a divorce," Steve moaned.

"But she loves you."

"You don't know that."

"Only one way to find out."

Steve pulled himself together for a second. "I can't do that now," he said. "Too much time has passed. She's with a new man."

"She'd leave him if you'd go to her," said Abby. "So long as you're breathing, there's still time to fix this. Look at me and Thaddeus. You're about the same age that we were when we finally got together."

"I don't know. I can't start over now." He wiped his eyes.

"Why not?"

"I've hurt too many people."

"You've helped more than you've hurt."

Steve brushed back his hair. What should he do? Would Claire take him back? Should he take the money from his ma, go back to Claire and beg her to forgive him? He didn't know.

"Help me, Ma," he said. "Help me know what to do."

A knock sounded on the front door. Abby turned to it then back to him.

"I'm okay," he said. "Go on and see who it is."

"You sure?"

"Yeah. I need time to think anyway."

"Hang on just a second," Abby said.

Steve took a deep breath then decided to follow her as she walked through the front room and opened the door. Thaddeus joined them, looking refreshed after his nap. A tall man in a faded green military jacket, fatigues and scuffed black boots stood on the porch. A handlebar mustache covered the man's upper lip, and long hair hung past the collar of his jacket. A nasty red scar cut across the left side of his face.

"Can I help you?" Abby asked.

The man stuck out a hand and Abby took it. "I'm Skeet," he said. "Looking for Jim Waterbury."

"I'm his ma," said Abby. "He's a short ways further up the road. You're one house short."

"You reckon he's home?" Skeet said.

"Probably at work," said Abby. "Usually closes about three on Christmas Eve."

Skeet hesitated, and Steve got the distinct impression the man had news but didn't know how to say it. "I can take you down to see him if you don't want to wait," Steve offered.

"That would be good," Skeet said.

"You mind me asking your business with him?" Abby said.

Surprised at her directness, Steve stared at his ma.

Skeet paused but only for a second. "I just got home a few months ago," he said. "I served time in a Hanoi prison with a man named Porter Waterbury."

CHAPTER
FORTY

As Abby rode with Steve, Thaddeus and Skeet on their way to Jim's office, it took every ounce of her willpower to keep from asking Skeet what he knew about Porter. Was Porter alive? Still in prison in Hanoi? Her imagination ran in all directions. Gritting her teeth, she managed to keep her questions at bay. When they arrived, she hurried from Steve's car, up the steps and into Jim's building. The others followed close behind. A secretary met them as they entered.

"Is Jim busy?" Steve asked her.

"Hang on a second." The secretary walked over and picked up a telephone. Abby glanced at Skeet, trying to guess his news. Good or bad, she couldn't tell, but his eyes looked tired and a touch haunted, like they had seen things no one ought to see. Abby feared the worst. The secretary ushered them to Jim's office. Jim smiled at Abby and hugged her, then shook Steve's hand.

"I was just about to quit for the day," he said. "Christmas Eve and all."

"This is Skeet," Abby said. "He came by our place looking for you a little while ago. Didn't want to wait for you to get home."

Jim's eyes narrowed some but he shook Skeet's hand and motioned them all to have a seat. Abby eased down and folded her hands in her lap. Skeet perched on the edge of his chair, his military jacket drooping toward the floor. Jim sat behind his desk, his brown leather chair creaking as he rested himself in it.

"Skeet came with news," Abby started.

Jim's face lost all its color.

"I spent time with Porter Waterbury," Skeet said, "in a prison in Hanoi."

Jim looked at Abby, his eyes round. "We haven't heard from Porter in a long time," he said.

Skeet lowered his head and said, "I hate to bring you this news. But he asked me to come . . . if he didn't make it. . . ." His voice trailed away.

Abby saw tears pool in Jim's eyes. For a long time nobody said anything. Jim's phone rang five rings but he ignored it. Tears ran down his cheeks. Abby's heart ached. She wanted to go to Jim and hold him like she had done when he was a child and something hurt him.

Then Jim stood before she could move and turned to face the window behind him, his hands shoved into his pockets. "You're saying my son's dead," he whispered.

"Yes. I'm sorry," Skeet said. "We were in prison. Had a guy named Weed with us, a grunt all shot up in the legs, not able to move much. One of the guards had a mean streak, didn't like it when any of us didn't hop to real fast when he said something."

Jim wiped his eyes with the back of his hand and turned around. Skeet kept talking.

"One day the guard told us we had to move out so they could clean up our area, wash out the stench. I bent down to pick up Weed, but the guard didn't think I moved fast enough. The guard kicked Weed in the face. Porter went after the guard, knocked him down, grabbed for his weapon. Another guard fired off a couple of rounds at Porter. Hit him in the chest. He lived three days. With no real medical care available, he didn't have a chance. I held his hand, did all I could, promised him that if I made it home, I'd come here and tell you what happened."

"They bury him?" Jim asked.

"Don't know," said Skeet. "They just took his body away and I didn't see him again after that."

Abby watched Jim and silently started praying for him. Prayed for Rebecca too. Prayed for Blanche and Todd and Lisa.

Jim stared at the floor. After a long moment, he moved back to his seat. "Wars kill good men," he said.

"Your boy was a good man," said Skeet. "He died because he tried to stand up for somebody else."

Jim nodded.

Skeet reached inside his jacket and pulled out a folded piece of tattered cardboard. "He asked me to give you this."

Jim quickly stood and walked around his desk.

"It's a note," Skeet said. "He wrote it the morning before he died." He handed the note to Jim. Jim took it and stepped back to the window and unfolded it. Abby waited while he read it. When he finished, he folded it back up and wiped his eyes again.

"I need to see Rebecca and Blanche," he said.

Abby said, "We'll go now."

Jim went to his ma and sagged onto her shoulder, his body shaking. Abby held him for a long time.

Finally Jim pulled away and said, "Porter fought for his country. For a land he loved. A man can die for a lot worse reasons."

"Here's his dog tags," Skeet said, reaching into his jacket once more. "He asked me to bring them home to you."

Jim took the dog tags, squeezed them tight in his hand.

Skeet looked Jim in the eye. "You should be proud of him," he said. "I never knew a better friend, a better Christian either. He spoke Scriptures to us, kept us going strong."

"You'll spend Christmas with us," Jim told Skeet, his tone indicating he'd accept no argument. "Tell us everything about every second you spent with Porter."

"It would be an honor. Porter sure loved his family, this place here in the mountains. It's all he ever talked about."

Jim smiled weakly, and Abby knew he would somehow get

through this. As hard as it hurt, a believing man like Jim still knew how to survive.

"Let's go home," said Jim. Abby nodded and everybody headed to the door. "You ride with me," Jim said to Skeet when they reached the parking lot.

"Thaddeus and I will go with Steve," Abby said.

Jim nodded and Abby climbed in. Jim handed her the cardboard note from Porter. "Read it," he said. "Tell me what to do when we get home."

So Abby took the note from him. Soon they were heading toward their mountain. She just held the cardboard note for the first mile or so, her mind too numb to read it. She glanced at Steve, wondered what was running through his head. How did he feel about all that had just taken place? Steve hadn't said a thing during the time in Jim's office.

She reached over and patted his arm. "We'll talk soon," she said. "Just need to get through the next few hours."

"I'm okay," he replied. "We need to take care of Jim and Rebecca right now, Blanche and the kids too."

Abby nodded. Steve pointed the car north. Settling into her seat, Abby let her eyes turn to the cardboard. Smudges covered its jagged edges, and she wondered if the smudges were blood. Had Porter's lifeblood dripped onto the cardboard as he wrote his last words?

The words were simple, written in a scraggly hand.

The Lord is with me. I am okay. Blanche, babies, I love you. Pa, keep our land, whatever you have to do. It's what holds us together. I'm cold. Bury my tags on the land. Love, Porter.

Abby leaned back and closed her eyes. Once again death had squirmed its way into her family. Once again she had to look to her faith and her family to see her through.

CHAPTER
FORTY-ONE

S teve joined everybody but Jim and his family at Jesus Holiness that night. He didn't pay much attention to the service. Instead, his mind kept drifting to other places and other matters. The word of Porter's death had shaken his family in ways he didn't think anything could. His ma's shoulders had seemed to stoop sharply all of a sudden, almost as if the bad news had bent her permanently in the middle. Jim and Rebecca's faces took on a pale and vacant look, and Rose, for maybe the first time in her life, failed to find words to speak. Blanche, of course, took it harder than anybody. She collapsed when she read Porter's note, her body falling into Jim's arms like a rag doll. They immediately put her to bed and called in a doctor who gave her some medicine to help calm her.

Steve felt the grief too, a dull ache in his stomach. All his life he had seen Jim as the indestructible one, the one blessed. Everything he had ever tried had succeeded. He seemed to have immunity from anything bleak. Steve had always envied that about his brother and had wondered why Jim received such fortune while others did not. But now that blessing had turned to a curse, had taken him out and given him a thrashing as hard as anybody ever had to endure.

When the church service ended, the family quietly piled into their cars and headed back home. When they got to Abby's they all moved inside. Jim and his family soon joined them. As hard as it was, they needed to hear any stories Skeet had to share. Abby prepared coffee and cake, and they sat around and ate and talked, their voices somber. Skeet took most of the spotlight, telling out all his experiences with Porter. They had spent close to two years in prison together, he said. They had suffered together through some of the toughest conditions imaginable. Yet they had found times to laugh too, times to hope and dream, to talk about their families and about God.

Steve watched Jim closely as Skeet wore out his stories, yawned and said maybe he should try to sleep a few hours. Jim showed him to a room and then went to bed himself, and everybody else followed suit. Nobody slept much that night.

Christmas Day dawned bright and cold. The morning found Steve drinking coffee at the table with the others, his head full of questions, his heart aching from all the hurt he'd felt in the last few days.

About midday everybody gathered in the living room again, their eyes weary and red. When they had settled some, Jim stood up and waved everybody quiet.

"This is a hard day," he said. "The hardest I have ever faced. We now know that Porter is dead. We hoped otherwise but our hopes didn't prove out."

Steve rubbed his eyes. Jim seemed so strong, stronger than he himself could ever have been. Where did he get the strength?

"Porter left us a last wish," Jim went on. "I have talked to Blanche about it and we are in agreement. We plan to honor Porter's wishes and bury his dog tags here on the land."

Steve sat up straighter. What sense did it make to bury the only thing they had left of Porter on land they had to vacate within a few months?

"We're only here until May," said Thaddeus.

Jim shook his head. "Not if I can help it," he said.

"But we've got no choice," said Thaddeus.

"A man always has choices," Jim argued. "My boy left one last wish. I plan to honor it if I can."

"But how?" Abby asked.

"I have a plan," Jim said. "Least the first notions of one."

"You care to let us in on it?" Thaddeus said.

Jim shook his head then looked over at Steve. "Just Steve," he said. "I plan to tell him."

Steve's eyes showed his surprise. "I'm not sure what I can do," he said.

"You got some contacts in Raleigh—people I need to meet."

"I'm leaving Raleigh," Steve said. "Soon as I can."

Jim raised his eyebrows.

"I haven't had a chance to tell anybody but Ma," said Steve, "but I've had some troubles with my business. Time to move on."

"When you plan to leave?" Jim said.

"Two weeks if all goes well."

"You leaving your son too?"

Steve gritted his teeth to keep from showing his anger. Yet when he spoke, the words came out sharper than he meant. "I don't think that's your business," he said.

Jim moved to no more than two feet away from Steve, looked him face-to-face and said, "I'm sorry if I spoke out of my place. I don't mean anything by it. It seems, though, the time has come for us to stop dancin' around the truth. I . . . I just lost my son." He stammered for a second then said, "But you still got one."

"You don't know that," Steve said.

"Yes I do," said Jim. "So do you if you'll get honest. You've seen the boy. Ma says he's your image up one side and down the other. Everybody in this room agrees with me."

Steve looked down.

"I need your help, Steve. But even if you won't help me, you need to go home to your boy. Don't let both of us lose a son this Christmas." Tears formed in Jim's eyes, and his voice choked as he said, "I had no . . . choice in losing mine. You still got a choice over whether or not you'll lose yours."

Jim made some sense, Steve had to admit that. But he still couldn't do it. "Claire plans to marry somebody else," he said.

"Doesn't matter," said Jim, firming up his words. "He's still your boy, whether Claire's your wife or not. As your brother, I beg you, don't lose your boy."

Steve glanced at Abby. "Jim's right," she said. "Robert needs you. You've labored all your life to prove you're not your pa, and you're not. But if you desert your boy now, you'll never know that for certain and you'll never forgive yourself."

Steve found it hard to breathe. Everybody watched him. He wondered how Porter's death had put so much attention on him. Why couldn't they leave him alone, let him finish up his business in Raleigh and leave this place forever?

"Claire will forgive you," Abby said, now at his side. "Like I said before, she loves you."

"It's not too late," Jim added.

Unable to control his emotions any longer, Steve rushed from the room. Maybe he would change his mind and maybe not. If he did, it would be because *he* decided to, not because his brother or his ma or anyone else had pushed him into it.

The family buried Porter's dog tags later that afternoon, all of them gathering on the ridge behind Jim's house just as the sun started to fall. They wore heavy coats pulled up tight against the cold wind, and their breath puffed out in gray bursts as Jim, Rebecca and Blanche carried out the last request of their beloved son and husband.

"Here are the tags," Blanche said. Dark circles had formed under her eyes from crying.

Rebecca received the jewelry box Blanche handed her and carried it to Jim, who stood by a two-foot-by-two-foot hole he had dug earlier through the snow and the hard ground. Jim took the box and lifted out the white handkerchief that covered the tags, unwrapped the tags and held them up for everyone to see one more time.

Standing with his family, Steve tried to decide if he should go back to Claire and try to start over with her or leave and begin anew in a different place. Accept the money his ma offered and use it to rescue his business or decline her offer and strive to make it on his own. Take Jim up on his request for help with his secret scheme or turn down his brother and probably throw away the last chance the two of them had for any real closeness.

The thought of moving somewhere else, somewhere far away, was tempting. It felt easier, less risky. Heading off to a new town meant he could leave behind all the hurts of his past.

A cold wind whipped across his face. If he left, he knew he'd never come back. Why should he? Jim wouldn't want to see him again after he turned him down. Claire would marry and he'd lose her forever. Chances were his ma wouldn't live too much longer. Could he just walk away and never see them again?

Jim laid the dog tags back on the handkerchief, wrapped them and placed them in the box. Then he handed the box to Blanche. She held it a few more seconds and then set it carefully in the hole in the ground. Jim lifted a shovel of dirt and spilled it over the box. Tears filled Blanche's eyes. Steve glanced at his ma. She stood by Thaddeus, clinging to his side. What would his ma tell him right now? He looked up at the mountain looming over the ridge. The mountain that had always stood there, least as long as anybody could remember. The last of the sun glanced off the stone outcropping on the mountain's face, and Steve remembered the old story.

A person can see God's face on the mountain, the legend said.

Steve knew that his grandpa Solomon had gotten lost one time when a boy and had climbed to the top of the nearest tree and searched for the mountain. When he saw it, he climbed back down and followed it home.

Any time you get lost, just find God's face on the mountain and it'll show you the way home again.

Tilting his head, Steve searched the mountain for God's face but saw nothing. He tried again but still no image presented itself. He chuckled to himself. Maybe everybody else could see God's face cut into the bald, but he couldn't. He turned back to the hole.

Thaddeus pulled a Bible from his coat pocket and started to

read. He began, " 'We know that all things work together for good to them that love God, to them who are the called according to his purpose.' "

While Thaddeus read on, Steve wondered how God could do good out of any of this.

" 'What shall we then say to these things?' " Thaddeus read. " 'If God be for us, who can be against us? He that spared not his own Son, but delivered him up for us all, how shall he not with him also freely give us all things?' "

Steve thought of Porter, a son lost to Jim and Rebecca, a husband and father lost to Blanche and her kids. He thought of Jesus, a son lost to God. But Jim and Rebecca had not willingly given up their son. God had—at least that's the way the Bible described it.

Steve pictured little Robert in his head. How could he just move away and leave him?

" 'I am persuaded that neither death, nor life, nor angels, nor principalities, nor powers, nor things present, nor things to come, nor height, nor depth, nor any other creature, shall be able to separate us from the love of God, which is in Christ Jesus our Lord.' "

He tried to imagine that kind of love, the kind that stayed with you no matter what. Had he ever experienced that kind of love? Not from his pa. His pa had left him a long time ago, had deserted him, had let hard times and weak character separate himself from his sons and wife.

Steve wiped his eyes. It still hurt that his pa hadn't loved him enough to tough it out, to stay and take care of his family. What kind of pa did that? Not one he wanted to follow, that was for sure.

Thaddeus finished with the reading, and then Jim poured another shovelful of dirt over the jewelry box. Steve shifted his feet as he tried imagining what God was like. Was God like a pa? Maybe so. But his own pa had deserted him. Had God deserted him? It sure felt like it.

Something quaked in Steve's heart. Was his lack of a connection to God tied to his feelings about his pa? The notion shook him. The Good Book said that God never left folks. But his pa had left him. From that time on, his sense of God had changed. He hadn't noticed it at the time, had been too young to figure it out. But he had felt alone after that, cut off from almost everybody and everything. From that year forward, he had started to pull aside from other people, had begun to depend more and more on himself and less and less on others around him. He didn't trust people as much. Didn't trust God as much either. Somehow when his pa left he had decided that God must have left too, must have deserted him forever. If God was like his pa, he knew for sure he didn't want to follow Him.

Steve dropped his head. The moment had come for him to make a decision. He couldn't put it off any longer. Since the time he was a boy, he had felt alone. Sadly he still did.

Thaddeus said, "Let us pray," and everybody but Steve bowed. Steve looked at his ma. She had on a long black dress, buttoned at the neck. Her hair was pinned back in a gray bun. Her face looked downcast yet remained strong, steady.

Suddenly Steve's heart warmed. Although his pa had left him, his ma never had. His eyes widened as a new idea hit him. His ma's love had never deserted him. He rolled the notion over in his head. His ma's love had been as constant as God's, had stayed with him through everything. All these years, no matter what happened, his ma had never turned against him. She had loved him with a love as steadfast as anything on earth, as strong as the mountain above them.

He realized then that some people saw God's presence on the face of Blue Springs Mountain, while others saw God's steadfast love in the face of their pa. That was fine and good. But he saw God in the face and in the love of his ma.

Something in Steve broke loose all at once, and his shoulders relaxed and his heart slowed. A sense of peace like he'd never felt before rolled through him. He smiled for the first time in a long while. He saw that he'd been searching for God in the wrong place for many years. God could show up in a ma as well as in a pa. God was everywhere that somebody loved somebody else, everywhere that somebody stood by somebody else, everywhere that somebody kept praying for somebody else.

Steve heard the amen, and then Jim covered the jewelry box with a last shovelful of dirt and patted it down with his foot. Steve moved to his ma and put a hand on her shoulder. She turned to him, and he bent and wrapped his arms around her.

"You're the face of the Lord to me," he whispered. "The face of the Lord." She glanced up, confusion in her eyes. "I'll explain later," he said, "after I do whatever it is Jim wants me to do."

"You're staying then?" Abby asked.

Steve smiled and hugged her again. "I'm home," he said. "No reason to go anywhere else."

"You need to go to Claire and those boys," Abby said.

"I hope she'll still have me."

"I believe she will."

"Thank you for not quitting on me," said Steve.

"I never even considered it."

"I love you, Ma."

"I've never had a doubt to the otherwise."

CHAPTER
FORTY-TWO

Steve and Jim left for Raleigh two days later, on a day unseasonably warm. After stopping by his bank to deposit a check large enough to keep his creditors satisfied for a long time, Steve brought Jim to his house, telephoned Claire and asked if she would meet with him. She agreed, so Steve left Jim and drove over to her house. She met him at the door, her eyes questioning. Once they were seated in the living room, Steve went right to the point.

"I want you to come home," he said. "Plain as that. I love you and the boys."

Claire rocked back. "This is a shock," she said.

Kneeling before her, Steve took her hands in his and said, "I know I have a lot to explain. Something happened to me on Christmas Day, something good. I've made my share of mistakes in my life but I don't intend to make the mistake of losing you and the boys. That's one mistake I could never get over."

"But another man has asked me to marry him," Claire said.

Steve dropped his eyes. "If you love him instead of me, I'll step aside. But I'll still want to see Robert. I know he's mine—always have."

Claire raised her chin and sighed. "I'll need some time to think this through."

Steve's heart sank. He'd come too late. "That's not what I wanted to hear," he admitted. "But I can't blame you. I've been a fool." Resigned to his fate, he stood. "Guess I should go. Jim's at my house."

"Jim?"

"Yeah, there's something we got to do."

"You two are working together?"

"Funny, after all these years . . ." Steve shook his head. "You remember when you and I first met?"

"Of course," she said. "On the train. Allen sent me."

"He's a sneaky one, isn't he?"

Claire laughed.

"I loved you from the first second I saw you," Steve said.

"You were too young to know anything about love."

"You're wrong there." Silence fell. Claire wiped her eyes. Steve said, "Maybe we could go on another train ride someday. Start all over."

"You said Jim's at your house?" Claire said, changing the subject.

"Yeah. He's got a scheme, hopes to save our land from flooding—you know, what we've been fighting."

"Glad you two brothers are together again."

"I've missed him."

Claire stared at him. "Something has happened to you, hasn't it?"

Steve shrugged. "I love you," he said. "I want to spend the rest of my life proving that to you, to the boys."

Claire folded her arms. Steve turned to go and she followed him.

"I'll give you time," he said, trying to stay hopeful. "As much as you need."

She saw him out the door, and a minute later he was driving toward home. Most likely he wouldn't get Claire back and that broke his heart. But he wouldn't let it destroy his resolve to live a new and different life. And he would still take care of Robert, no matter that Claire married another man. His chin firm, he climbed out of his car and headed up the steps of his house. Jim met him there.

"Claire called," Jim said. "She said she has taken all the time she needs."

Steve's heart dropped. She had quickly dismissed him. But what did he expect?

"She said she had an urge to go on a train ride. Said you would understand what she meant."

"A train ride?"

"Yeah."

Steve laughed—a full-throated roar. Jim looked at him as if he'd lost his mind.

————

It took Steve and Jim about ten days to arrange things in order to carry out Jim's plan. A couple of lunch meetings with a real estate lawyer who had worked with Steve over the years. A number of telephone calls between the lawyer and Will Stowe's congressional office in Asheville.

"Yes," said the woman they finally reached only a few days into the new year. "Congressman Stowe is still in town for the holidays and hasn't returned to Washington yet."

"I'd like to arrange a meeting," the lawyer said, a stocky middle-aged man by the name of Buddy Staples, who had a stomach like a washtub and a head of spiky brown hair.

"I'm sorry but because of the holiday the congressman isn't available," the secretary said. "He's not keeping office hours."

"It's about the dam up past Blue Springs. I think I can save the taxpayers some money. Surely Congressman Stowe is interested in that."

The secretary hesitated, obviously unsure what to do. "I'll call the congressman," she finally said. "That's all I can do."

"Here's my number," said Staples. "Call me when you hear from him."

A day later, Staples heard back from Stowe.

"Congressman Stowe here," he said. "How can I serve you?"

Staples cupped the phone and grinned at Jim and Steve, who sat at a table in his office. They picked up connected phones so they could listen in.

"I represent some clients here in Raleigh. They do construction work—earth moving, road building, engineering, things like that. They'd like a shot at helping you get your dam built."

Steve nodded. Staples had told no lies. He did represent clients who did that kind of work.

"I'm afraid I can't help you," Stowe said. "Those contracts were awarded months ago, through the government."

"I appreciate the situation," Staples said. "Bureaucrats and all that. But I also know sometimes a man of influence like you can cut through the red tape and make things happen. At least that's what I've heard."

Steve glanced at Jim. They had told Staples to flatter Stowe.

Stowe cleared his throat. "Look," he said, "I don't know who you are but I'm a busy man and I'm on vacation. I usually don't do much business this time of year. If you want to make an appointment with me, call my offices and we'll see what we can arrange. But for now—"

"I understand," Staples said, cutting him off. "But do the names Jim and Steve Waterbury mean anything to you?"

Stowe fell quiet. Steve grinned. Staples had played it perfectly.

"How do you know them?" asked Stowe.

"Steve Waterbury is a bum who owes me money," Staples answered.

Steve had to fight to keep from laughing.

"I hear he owes a lot of people."

"You hear right."

"Okay, but what does that got to do with me?"

"I've done my homework," Staples said. "And I hear you want to get this dam finished as soon as possible, before anything else can happen to slow it down, perhaps even stop it in its tracks. Like any good congressman, you don't want that. You don't want to lose those jobs for your good constituents in these hard times. Plus, if

my information is correct, you've got a little history with Waterbury and his kin, wouldn't mind letting this dam settle up some of
that history. I promise that if you hook up with me, we'll get this
project over with faster than anyone else can do it. My guys are
champing at the bit."

Steve chuckled under his breath. When Jim had told everyone
what he wanted to do, their ma had made them promise they
wouldn't tell any lies. If Stowe messed up, he'd have to do so on his
own. To best a bad man by deceit made you as low as him.

"You do it fair and square," she had said, "or don't do it at all.
The Lord won't honor those who cheat."

Following her advice, he and Jim had told Staples to keep to the
truth. So far he had done so. If Stowe fell for their ruse, they would
get the project over with, only in a totally different way than he ever
suspected.

"So you're saying you want me to throw some of the construction dollars your way, is that it?" Stowe said.

"We'd like it all. But if not that, even a little will make a difference. We're talking about millions of dollars here," said Staples.

"What do you get out of it?"

Staples laughed. "I'm a lawyer; we always get our cut. That and
the pleasure of seeing Steve Waterbury get what's coming to him.
Lot of satisfaction in that, you know."

"Can't argue there."

Staples waited for the congressman's answer. Steve could picture Stowe weighing the situation. So far though, Stowe hadn't
asked the one question they needed him to ask. Stowe cleared his
throat, and Steve tensed. Would he take the bait?

"Sounds like you've thought this out," Stowe said.

"Of course I have," said Staples.

"It'll take a lot of doing to change the contracts. A lot of hours."

"I hear you've got the power to make that happen pretty fast,"
Staples said.

"It's not a question of power," said Stowe. "It's a question of
my time."

"Of course," Staples said. "Your time is valuable, no doubt.

More valuable than most anybody's. I can assure you we'll remember that, no questions at all."

Stowe hesitated. Steve wondered if he suspected anything. But when he spoke Steve knew he'd fallen into their trap.

"Maybe we should meet," Stowe said.

"Maybe we should," said Staples. "When?"

"Tomorrow. At a restaurant named Lucinda's, there in Raleigh. You know the place?"

"Sure. One of the best restaurants in town."

"How does four o'clock sound?"

"Fine."

"You come alone," said Stowe. "Nobody else."

"See you there." Stowe hung up. Staples turned to Steve and Jim. "You think he'll go for it?"

"We'll know tomorrow," Jim said.

"We best call Ma," said Steve. "She said she wanted to know if it happened."

―――――

Lucinda's had two levels of seating, and at exactly three forty-five the next day Steve and Jim led Abby to a table on the second floor behind a round wood column, a vantage point that allowed them to see the bottom floor without being seen themselves. Steve's heart pounded as he pulled out a chair, took a seat and checked his view to the first floor. A waiter appeared and gave them each a menu. Steve looked at it but didn't feel hungry.

"Is Claire well?" asked Jim, apparently trying to make conversation to keep the tension down.

"Great," Steve said. "Soon as this is over, we're going away for a few days."

"A train trip, I suppose," Abby said.

Steve smiled at his ma. After calling her yesterday, she had insisted that Ed drive her to Raleigh. She had arrived about noon. The waiter appeared and they ordered tea to drink. Steve wiped his hands on his pants. He needed to say something to Jim, something he hadn't yet said in the swirl of the last week. Now seemed the right time. Steve laid his hands on the table.

"Look," he started, glancing from his ma to his brother, "I got something I need to get off my chest." Jim and Abby put down their menus. Steve continued, "It's not easy but . . . well, I'm sorry for all the years . . ." his voice trailed off and he looked at his ma again. She smiled but said nothing. Steve turned back to Jim, who wiped his mouth, then spoke.

"I'm the one who should apologize," Jim said. "I didn't come to you like an older brother should have. I just let you go, didn't do much to help you. Life just got so busy . . . you know how that happens."

"I felt pretty small," Steve said, not willing to let Jim take the blame. "Next to you, I mean. Thought I had to go and prove myself."

"I know," said Jim. "But I didn't know how to convince you to let up, to tell you how big you really were, how talented."

"I failed at a lot. You never failed at anything."

"I got more breaks is all."

Steve shrugged, admitting that what Jim said was partly true. "Wonder why?" he said. "God's favor, you think?"

Jim shook his head. "Who knows. But that seems a touch unfair if you ask me. Why would God show more favor to me? I never did anything to deserve it."

"I guess it's not a matter of deserving," said Steve. "God chooses and favor happens." He thought of Izzy, then Allen. Both of them had reasons to say God had not favored them nearly as much as He had favored him. And what about people born in places where they didn't have enough to eat, where children died of starvation before they turned a year old. Why did God favor him more than them? Guess some things he would never figure out. "We're brothers," Steve said. "That's what matters now."

The waiter appeared and they ordered. Afterward Steve extended his hand across the table, and Jim shook it. Abby smiled at them. Steve knew that no matter what happened in the future, he and Jim would never again let go of each other.

Buddy Staples arrived at Lucinda's and had just stepped inside when immediately he felt a man at his shoulder. The man had a darkly shadowed face and hair slicked back with cream. He wore a well-pressed gray suit with a white shirt and blue tie.

"I'm Will Stowe," the man said, his hand stretched out. "Congressman Will Stowe."

"I recognize you from a picture I once saw in the paper," Staples said as he shook the congressman's hand. "You doing well today?"

Stowe grunted. A restaurant host then led them both to a nearby table. Staples sat down, Stowe across from him. A waiter appeared and asked for their drink orders. Once the waiter had left, Stowe shifted forward in his seat and said to the lawyer, "I don't have a lot of time and I'm not one for socializing with strangers. So let's do our business and take our leave."

Staples nodded. "You're right. I offered you a business proposition, plain and simple."

"I checked on you since yesterday," Stowe said. "So far, you're legit. Turns out Waterbury does owe you money, close to thirty thousand dollars."

"You work fast."

"I have too much to do to fool around with fakes. But you're not one, so let's talk."

"Okay, here's the deal. My guys need your help. They'd be real grateful if you could see your way to their view of things."

Stowe glanced around as if looking for spies. Seeing none, he faced Staples again. "How grateful?"

Staples pulled an envelope from his pocket, held it up for a second, then laid it on the table and slid it over to Stowe. "This grateful."

Stowe tugged at his tie, then put a hand on the envelope, pulled it over and slipped it into his jacket pocket. "How much?"

"Ten thousand," Staples said. "Ten more will be available if and when the new contracts are awarded. Ten more every three months after that, so long as the job lasts. A small price to pay for the time of such a hardworking congressman like yourself."

"Your men can work fast I hope," said Stowe, ignoring the comment.

"Faster than anyone else."

"I want this done," Stowe said. "I want dirt moving by June, no later."

"Soon as you get me the contracts, they'll go to work the next day."

"I'm already on it. Made some calls this morning."

The waiter showed up, and Staples ordered a steak. Stowe waved the waiter off.

Leaning closer to Staples, Stowe asked, "What kind of man is Steve Waterbury?"

Staples sipped from his water glass. He didn't want to lie. "He's a good man," he said. "Just not a lucky one, least not so far."

Stowe grinned. "Neither is his brother," he said. "Not now anyway."

"Why do you hate them so much?"

Stowe shrugged. "I'm not sure. Just seems right, you know. Like a dog and a cat—just seems natural they don't like each other." Stowe stood to leave. "I'll be in touch," he said.

"I trust you will," said Staples.

Stowe walked off as the lawyer leaned back in his chair. A couple of minutes later, Jim and Steve appeared and sat down.

"We saw him take it," Jim said.

Staples nodded. "Hook, line and sinker."

"You'll call your brother," Steve said, hardly believing what had happened.

"Brother Richard," Staples said. "Head of the Federal Land Management Committee in Congress."

"The committee Stowe's trying to take over," Jim said with a laugh.

"Exactly," said Staples. "My brother hates Stowe at least as much as Stowe hates you. You boys get your pictures?"

Steve pointed up to his ma, who was still sitting at their table. Abby held up the camera. "About two dozen shots," Steve said. "Glad the place is well lit. The one where you held up the envelope should turn out just fine."

Staples chuckled and said, "Well, this wouldn't stand up in court, but it should scare Stowe plenty. Our word and my brother's against his. Pictures of him and me in a restaurant, passing an envelope across the table."

"He'll have no more leverage in Congress," Steve added. "Given all that's happened with Watergate, just the threat of this kind of scandal can kill a man's career."

Jim smiled.

"You think your brother will be able to stop the dam from getting built?" Steve asked Staples.

"He'll begin an investigation. That will slow up the dam, maybe for years. You know how the government is with things like this. Who knows what'll happen later. But if federal money stays tight, this will probably shut it down for good."

"So this is the end of it?" Jim asked.

The waiter came with the steak and set it in front of Staples. He picked up his knife and fork, then looked at Steve and Jim. "Only the Lord knows the end of it," he said. "Although I wouldn't doubt if it's the end of Stowe."

Steve looked at Jim and they both grinned. They had done it. A sense of peace ran through Steve. He looked up at his ma. She smiled down at him. He smiled back and waved to her. "I think I'll go home to Claire now," he said. "We got a lot to talk about."

"I'll take Ma home," Jim offered. "Back to Blue Springs."

Steve nodded. Blue Springs. Suddenly he realized how much the place meant to him. The highlands, the land of his family, the land that had always held them together. "I'll bring Claire soon," he said. "And Franklin and Robert too. I want them to know our mountains."

"See you soon," Jim said.

"Yeah," said Steve. "Real soon."

"You boys don't mind if I eat my steak now, do you?" Staples said.

Steve took out a couple of twenty-dollar bills and dropped them on the table. "Enjoy it," he said. "On me."

EPILOGUE

Granny Abby opened her eyes and smiled gently. I wiped her brow with a wet cloth. Her hands trembled as she reached out to touch my face.

"I am some tired, Lisa," she said. "I reckon I should stop the story for now."

I stepped back and laid the cloth on the table by her hospital bed. "It's clearing up," I said, nodding toward the window. "Looks like the sun's coming out."

Abby smiled again but weakly. I moved closer to her, my heart heavy. Her doctors had said that the fluid around her lungs and heart had built up to a dangerous level. It was obvious she didn't have long to live.

"I want to tell you something," she said, "before I take my rest."

She reached for my hands. Her flesh felt cool, like most of the blood had drained from it.

"You don't need to fret yourself," she said. "Whatever comes of all this." She moved her eyes across the room to indicate all the medical equipment in her intensive care unit.

"You're doing fine," I lied. "You have to tell me the rest of the story."

"You know the rest," Granny whispered. "You were alive for it, remember?"

I nodded, realizing the truth of what she said. My memory went back to about 1975. Even though a great deal had occurred in those years, most of it seemed mild compared to what Granny had faced during her long life.

With the money Granny Abby had given him, Steve paid off his creditors and kept his business going until the economy turned. Then, with his newfound capital, he made some wise investments. His rentals became profitable, and within ten years he had started building, as he'd always dreamed of doing. Eventually he paid Granny Abby back and made a pile more money for himself. Now he owned property all over the state. His faith stayed strong over the years, and he gave a lot of his money away, much of it to a local orphanage. With Claire at his side, they raised Frank and Robert. Robert was close to finishing his preparations to become a pediatrician, while Frank had become a high-school football coach in Sanford.

Jim and Rebecca—my grandpa and grandma—took a long while to get past my dad's death. But, strengthened by their love for the Lord and each other, they endured their grief and came out on the other side. With the help of the lawyer Buddy Staples, whom he hired as his company lawyer the year after he met him, Jim eventually acquired four new car dealerships and a string of auto parts stores that spread out over four southern states. His boy, Tommy, took over the business when Jim retired in 1986 to hunt and fish. And Harriet, their daughter, married a baseball player and moved to St. Louis.

To everybody's delight, Buddy Staples moved to Asheville and ran for Congress in '82, beating Will Stowe in a runoff. After that, Stowe pretty much disappeared from the area.

Rose continued to teach school in Asheville. She married a high-school principal in '78 and won Teacher of the Year for the whole state in '87. She and her husband now have three girls living within twenty miles of them, one married, one single, and one in college.

His heart worn out, Thaddeus died in 1985, four months after the state teachers college Granny had attended so many years ago gave her an honorary degree. Jim and Steve told her the school gave her the honor because of her efforts over the years to educate mountain children, but she said it had more to do with a large donation the two of them made in her name than anything else.

Granny Abby weathered Thaddeus's passing better than most had expected. She cried a lot the first year, but never in despair. "I know where he's living," she said more than once. "Expect I'll join him by and by."

Ed died in 1991 when his liver went bad on him. His wife, Priscilla, passed on two years later. Their kids and grandchildren had spread out all over east Tennessee and western North Carolina by then, the memory of their pa a strong bind that they never lost.

I thought of the rest of Granny Abby's family. Like all families, some had done well while others had found life one hard struggle after another. On the whole, though, most had managed well. Only one of her descendants had suffered through a divorce, and most everyone had become a believer in the Lord. In spite of the fact that a lot of them no longer lived on the mountain, their loyalty to God gave them a tie that kept them connected. Granny Abby's legacy was largely responsible for this strong family, and I wondered what would happen when she passed on.

"You got at least a few good years left," I said to Granny Abby, forcing myself away from the consideration of her dying.

Granny licked her lips. "Don't blow smoke at me," she said. "I know what's going on here. The doctor doesn't call in the family unless a body's time is drawing nigh."

I squeezed her hand. "I need you to stay on awhile. I feel like I've finally gotten to know you again. I don't want to lose you just yet."

"You'll do fine," she said. "Just need to clear up a few things in your head, that's all."

I nodded. I had found out so much in the last few days, so much about my family, about myself, about Granny Abby. But had that changed me? Would it make any difference in my life? I didn't know but I certainly hoped so. I had so much I needed to change; Granny Abby had shown me that. But could I do it?

Granny Abby closed her eyes. A vein throbbed slowly under the skin over her left ear. "I got one more thing you need to hear," she whispered.

I leaned in to make sure I heard every word. "What's that?"

"It's all passing," she said.

"What do you mean?"

"All of it," she continued. "The years God gave us—the troubles that come with those years, the joys too."

She paused, and I saw how much this talking took from her, like a siphon drawing her energy. I wanted to tell her to be quiet, to save her strength, but I knew her well enough now to know that whatever I said wouldn't matter. If Granny Abby wanted to talk, she would talk until she decided to quit, and nothing I said could stop her.

"Not just our lives either," she said. "Everything else is passing too. The trees in the woods, the flowers that bloom in the spring, the fish and the animals we hunt and eat. None of it lasts."

She licked her lips. I felt confused, and sad too. I knew she was right. But if nothing lasted, what difference did anything make? Why should we try to live right? Why should we try to please the God that Granny Abby trusted so much? "That's not very encouraging," I said.

Granny opened her eyes and patted my hand. "Oh, I'm not bleak about it," she said. "Not at all. Just saying we shouldn't put our trust in anything of this life, anything that won't last."

I saw it now, what she wanted me to hear. "The Lord," I said, "only the Lord lasts."

"You got it right," she said. "Think about Blue Springs Mountain, rising high over all of us."

I nodded and said, "Your pa used to say you could see God's face on it. He followed it home once when he was a boy and got lost."

"We lived beneath that mountain all our lives," said Granny Abby, her voice gaining strength as she spoke out. "It's the most solid thing in these parts, the most permanent. Thousands of folks have lived and died in its long shadow. But one of these days, a long time from now for sure but one of these days, that mountain will cease. The wear of time—the wind and rain and ice and sun—all of that will bring that mountain down and it will become nothing more than a grain of sand you can put on the tip of your finger.

"When that happens, when you and I and your kids and grand-kids and great-grandkids have all breathed and ceased breathing, when they've laid us all under the ground, only one thing will remain. The Lord. Heaven and Earth will pass away, but the Lord will always remain."

I held my breath.

"When time is no more, Jesus will yet live. That's the only eter-nity we have. Back when we thought they might flood our land, I learned that once more and for good. Even as much as I love it, it's not the land that matters, never was. We all forgot that for a while, me included. The Lord is the only thing that matters."

My eyes teared. Granny Abby touched my cheek. Her voice softened.

"Lisa, don't you worry none about my passing. It's the way of the Almighty, a final reminder not to put our trust in anything but Jesus."

"You've been here all my life," I said. "Even when I didn't come see you, I always knew you were here."

"That's a pretty good way of speaking of the Lord," she said. "Even when you can't see Him, the Lord is here."

"I don't want to let you go," I said, openly sobbing now.

"I've lived my time," said Granny, and she closed her eyes once more. "Ready to move on, I reckon. Time to go see Thaddeus again."

Silence moved into the room. The sun burned through the win-dow, its light falling on Granny Abby's face. I brushed her hair back and thought of my pa, Porter. I never knew him. If Granny Abby saw Thaddeus, she would see Porter too, along with her brothers, Daniel, Laban and Luke. And her aunt Francis, who had raised her, and her ma and pa, Solomon and Rose. I thought of what a wonderful day that would be, the day Granny Abby finally got to meet the ma who had died bringing her into the world. Did that truly happen? Did glad reunions like that really take place?

I wiped my eyes. I wanted badly to meet my pa. I lived in Washington and had visited the Vietnam Memorial many times and touched the name *Porter Waterbury* cut into the black stone. Yet I still felt empty inside when I thought of him. Like Granny, I had missed knowing a parent, one of the two whose blood coursed through my veins. Would Granny Abby see my pa? Would she tell him about me? Or would he already know?

I sighed, wearied by all my questions. Granny Abby opened her eyes and smiled at me.

"It's all at my house," she said.

"What?" I asked.

"The letter my mama wrote me the day she died. My sewing basket, the cane my pa carved, the one Daniel carried for so long. The title to our land too. Although all of us own some of it, I got the title. The note your pa sent from prison—that's there as well. I've kept all those things. I want you to have them now."

"But I don't deserve any of it," I protested. "Surely somebody else in the family—"

"It's not about who deserves it," Granny said. "It's a matter of favor, like the Lord gives to us. Solomon gave the cane to Daniel instead of Luke, then Ed gave it back to me instead of to one of his children. Maybe because he knew I'd stay on the land, in the highlands. I don't know exactly why, but you're the one the Lord wants me to give it all to, I know that for sure."

Still feeling unworthy but not wanting to argue, I swallowed and accepted her decision. I kissed her forehead and said thank you.

"Go on now," she said. "Let me take some rest."

"I'll see you again in the morning."

She smiled and said, "The Lord be with you, give you peace."

"See you in the morning."

———

I never saw Granny Abby alive again. She died about two the next morning, her breath slowly oozing out into eternity. Rose sat beside her as she died. "She went out peacefully," she told us over and over again. "Like a baby drifting off to sleep."

We buried Abby three days later in the family plot on the ridge behind her house, her spot beside Thaddeus under a stand of tall trees. As at her birthday reunion just a few days earlier, all the family gathered for the burial, a whole slew of aunts, uncles and cousins.

The day turned out bright and sunny, and a light breeze played through the trees. All the women dressed in black, myself included. Strangely I didn't feel as sad as I had expected. Granny Abby had made her peace with dying, and that gave me some comfort.

While the preacher from Jesus Holiness, a young man with thick hair and wire-rimmed glasses named Bruce Silver, said his words over Abby, I stood to the side and leaned against a tree. I thought about Granny Abby's family—her ma and pa, her brothers, her aunt and uncles—all of them and others buried a few acres away in mountain soil on ridges like this one, under trees like these. How peaceful these highlands, how beautiful a spot to rest for eternity.

Preacher Silver read from the Scriptures, and the words sounded familiar to me, in spite of my not having attended a church in a very long time. Yet they sounded different this time too, alive somehow, almost as if something had injected an energy into them that made them leap like darts into my soul.

"The Lord gives us life," said Silver. "Life right here on this earth when we're born and then, if we're faithful to Jesus, life when we die and go on from this world to the next."

My heart thumped harder as the preacher kept going. Granny had tried to tell me this, had tried to get me to believe it. But could I? At the age of thirty-one? After all my years of neglecting it, of doing nothing worthwhile with myself?

"We don't deserve any of this!" the preacher shouted. "None of us do. Not even this special woman." He pointed to Granny Abby's coffin. "As good as she was, her goodness didn't earn her God's favor, didn't earn her the joy she's now experiencing in heaven with the Lord."

I glanced toward my great-uncle Steve. He wore black sunglasses, a well-cut gray suit. His wife, Claire, held to his elbow, their boys, Frank and Robert, and their wives beside them. Steve had tried to earn approval all his life, from his ma and Jim and everybody else, including God. But he'd finally concluded he couldn't do it. In that instant, God had come to him and offered him what he couldn't find by himself.

"It flows out of the Lord's grace," continued Silver. "All we have, all we are, all we hope to become. By the blood of the Lamb the grace flows, freely bestowed on all who believe. Granny Abby knew this as the truth, lived by it all her days. Yes, she's gone from us now, but she's in the arms of the Lord, reunited with all those she loved, all those who went before her."

I closed my eyes. My knees felt unsteady, my mind jumbled.

"You know what she would say to you all?" Silver said. "She'd say you all need to trust this grace; you all need to come to the Lord Jesus. Come to Jesus and find the life He wants to give you, just as Granny Abby did so long ago."

I stared at Granny's coffin. *Did you tell him to do this?* I wondered. *Did you tell him to preach this message?*

Silver concluded his words and stepped forward to the coffin. After lifting a handful of dirt off the ground, he nodded to Jim. I watched my grandpa as he eased over to the preacher, took the dirt and dropped it onto the coffin. Rebecca followed him, then Steve and Claire. The rest of the family lined up behind them, each one taking a handful of dirt and dropping it on the coffin as they passed.

I joined the line, my hands shaky as I picked up dirt and stepped toward the coffin. Taking a deep breath, I stood for a second over Granny Abby's body. "I'm trying to understand," I whispered. "But it's just not true for me." I let go of the dirt and filed past.

When everyone else had finished, the crowd gradually moved away from the graveside and began to talk quietly to one another. I walked away, my heart still heavy. Wandering up the ridge, I eventually reached the top of the mountain. A few lazy clouds drifted by. I watched them for a while. So slow, so calm. I stared out over the valley. I bent to the ground and scooped up a handful of mountain soil. Granny Abby had loved this land. In the end, though, she'd decided it didn't make that much difference in the long run. No matter how long a person lived, he never really owned anything.

I opened my fingers and the dirt fell away. Stepping to the edge of the ridge, I looked over the side. At one time Will Stowe had figured to flood this land. That effort had failed. But what if it hadn't? Would it have made any difference to Granny Abby in terms of her faith? Surely not. Even if she had lost the land, her faith would have stayed just as strong.

I gazed down at the spot where Granny Abby had been born. I thought of the last time I talked with her. She'd said that nothing lasted. Not a house, not a garden, not a valley, not a mountain, not a person's life. Nothing remained forever. So where did that leave me? I wouldn't last either.

I knelt down again, rubbed my hands in the mountain dirt. When I passed from this life, did another world await me? Not if I didn't know the Lord, Granny Abby would say. But I didn't deserve to know the Lord, had never done a thing to merit that privilege.

I knew what Granny Abby would tell me. One word—*grace*. But was it all that easy?

I looked over the valley again. One way or the other, I had to decide. I sat down and stared at the sky. A breeze touched my face.

"I want to believe," I whispered. "I really do. But, I don't know, it sounds too simple."

The wind stirred. I brushed back my hair. The time for making a choice had come. Grace sounded easy, yet I knew it called for a full commitment. As Granny Abby had often said, "Grace is free but not cheap." Not for God and not for those who received it. Grace called for a person to follow Jesus no matter what. No matter whether life blessed them or hurt them, no matter if a loved one died or a child was born. Grace called for a person to receive what God gave and accept what God took away.

Granny Abby had trusted that grace and lived by it. It had not prevented bad times from coming her way. It had, however, given her peace in the midst of the bad times. I had seen that with my own eyes. Regardless of the weight that bore down on her, Granny Abby stayed true to the Lord.

I stood and wiped off the back of my dress. Then I turned my palms to the sky and closed my eyes. "I am here," I said, "ready to receive whatever you want to give."

The wind picked up even more, and my hair blew into my face, but I didn't move. My hands lifted higher. Tears edged into my eyes.

"I ask you to come to me," I whispered. "I give you my life."

The wind suddenly settled and everything became quiet.

"I accept your grace. Here on this mountain where so many of my family lived and died."

The tears kept coming. I sensed a presence, a touch of life not my own. I opened my eyes but saw no one. Something sounded in my spirit, a voice but not a voice, something speaking but not so audibly that I could hear it.

You're home, the voice said.

"Blue Springs Mountain?" I whispered.

Not the mountain, the voice sighed. *Home.*

I smiled as I understood the meaning. I had come home to God's presence, God's arms. On the day Blue Springs Mountain disappeared under the wear and tear of time, my spot would remain. By the grace of God I had found my place.

A Grand Series of Faith and History!

Epic in scope, Gilbert Morris's HOUSE OF WINSLOW series is nothing less than the compelling story of the forces and people that shaped American history. Each book has a plot that sweeps you away with characters whose lives are examples of heroism, courage, faith, and love.

The Leader in Christian Fiction!

BETHANY HOUSE

11400 Hampshire Ave. S., Minneapolis, MN 55438 • www.bethanyhouse.com